The Spark

Titles available in The White Gates tetralogy (in reading order):
The Kicking Tree
Ultimate Justice
Winds and Wonders
The Spark

Available to download free:

Cutting Edge
(A bonus White Gates adventure that occurs between
Winds and Wonders and The Spark. See page 177.)
http://trevorstubbs.com

THE
SPARK

Trevor Stubbs

Matador
9 Priory Business Park,
Wistow Road, Kibworth Beauchamp,
Leicestershire, LE8 0RX
Tel: 0116 279 2299
Email: books@troubador.co.uk
Web: www.troubador.co.uk/matador
Twitter: @matadorbooks

ISBN 978 1788035 835

British Library Cataloguing in Publication Data.
A catalogue record for this book is available from the British Library.

Printed and bound by CPI Group (UK) Ltd, Croydon, CR0 4YY
Typeset in 12pt Aldine401 BT by Troubador Publishing Ltd, Leicester, UK

Matador is an imprint of Troubador Publishing Ltd

This book is dedicated to the people who live in the darkness of poverty, war, oppression, hunger and fear – wherever they live in the world. Against all expectation, many of them shine as beacons of hope when all around them is destruction. Although subject to hatred and exploitation, they continue to share the reality of love and forgiveness. May we all be inspired by such as these.

I could run into the shadows if I choose.

"Yes, let's hide," I say. "Awesome. We could do anything we wanted if no-one were looking. And all that is bad in me would remain secret... if no-one really cared..."

But it is not like that; they do care... and so do you. Even on a starless night you are there, watching over me, a spark in the dark. Even if I elect to dwell in the emptiness of death, you are there; there is no place you cannot be.

Yet you do not pursue me against my will, you do not deprive me of my choice to tell you to be gone – I can banish you, reject your light. I, and I alone.

But why should I flee from you when all you want to do is keep me safe, make sure I am who I am – free to be me?

With you, it's good to be me.

So, Lord of the light, Lord of the darkness, Lord of everything there is, let my heart be set on fire with your indestructible spark; all that is bad in me burnt away.

Give me courage to hide no more; I am me – I have no need to hide.

1

It was the screaming that convinced them they had to leave. Over the past twelve hours they had become used to the crunch of heavy weapons and the crack of small-arms fire; but because they had been attending to the immediate needs of the patients, they had learned to ignore it. Then, suddenly, it was upon them. Out in the street people were shouting in languages they knew not. Retreating soldiers in government uniforms ran past the hospital and melted into the maze of streets and alleyways beyond. The doctor yelled at his assistants to keep their heads down. Military vehicles turned the corner and began trundling down the main street of the town, spewing bullets as they went. The rebels were intent upon looting and killing. This is what they had come for. They had already entered the market and were ransacking every building – plundering goods and lives without mercy.

"Surely we'd be safe in the hospital. We have no weapons here!" shouted Kakko over the din.

"No! Nowhere is safe. They will kill all... steal... burn. You run," instructed a young nurse.

"But what about the patients?" demanded Dah.

"Leave them. Now come... You want to be killed?!"

Before they could protest further, John, Tam and Shaun dragged the two girls out through the double doors at the end of the long ward. They had to jump over the many patients who lined the walls of the corridor, and they followed the hospital staff, and as many patients as could move themselves, out through the rear doors.

Dat-dat-dat-dat-dat!

The crack of gunfire reverberated around the hospital grounds. The five aliens, led by Tam and Kakko from Planet Joh, ran like everyone else with their heads low. As they crossed the road they heard the screams of the women and babies who had come to the hospital as some sort of sanctuary, somewhere safe away from the war which had already driven them from their homes in the villages. Kakko turned to see one woman jump from a window and then fall under a hail of bullets.

To his surprise, from the gardens at the rear of the hospital, Shaun found himself shouting obscenities he didn't know he knew. They cleared a low hedge and ran. Dah was a picture of terror. One of the nurses tripped and fell full-length on the ground; Shaun lifted her to her feet – her hands, elbows and knees red with blood – and propelled her forward into a patch of scrub that surrounded a wall on the far side of the street. An iron gate beckoned. The group streamed through it and behind a wall out of sight of the hospital. They hugged the rough bricks and listened while they took stock of where to go next. They were joined by a dog who decided to tag along with them. A dog who did not want to be alone. The rebel army was occupied with sacking the hospital. The air was filled with smoke from burning buildings somewhere beyond it.

"The church," said a nurse; "maybe they will not attack the place of God. We go to the church."

They crossed the garden to a deserted house. The dog followed. Shaun tried to dissuade it but it was not going to go away. It was quiet enough. Like all the dogs here, it was thin but athletic and wanted company.

The house was well appointed; it clearly belonged to a

well-off family. They had probably taken their car and left at the first signs of trouble. Unlike the hospital staff and those in the church, they had felt vulnerable and exposed – certain targets of any army, however disciplined.

Beyond the house, the half-dozen hospital staff, together with their five foreign volunteers, jogged along the road that led towards the church. As they came within sight of it, however, a truck bearing rebel soldiers came from a road that joined from the left and they ducked down. The truck rammed the gate to the church compound. Soldiers charged through the gap. Shaun signalled for the group to creep back the way they had come. As they retreated, they heard the same sort of screaming as they had heard at the hospital – the spine-chilling screams of victims of unthinkable horror. The rebels were attacking the women church workers and the children they had taken in to protect. Later, they were to learn that all had been killed. This so-called army was no more than a bunch of psychopathic criminals bent on violating anything that moved, wherever they were, no matter how weak and unable to defend themselves. Men emotionally damaged as children from the years of civil war had been given guns and heavy weapons and they were wreaking their revenge on the world that had let them down. If they had arrived just minutes earlier, Shaun, Kakko, Tam, Dah and John, together with the rest of the fugitives, would have been among those who'd died in the church.

★ ★ ★

Mercifully, within half an hour, the sun had set and the moon had not yet risen. Although it was dark, the nurses knew the way to the river well enough to find it by starlight.

Shaun looked up at the stars and thought of home. He had

arrived in this awful place via a new special otherworldly white gate in the hedge of their peaceful cottage garden on Planet Joh. Only the day before, they had been joined there by their friend Da'yelni Lugos – Dah for short – and her boyfriend, John. These two, despite hailing from different planets light years apart, had become inseparable over the past two years. John had decided to say goodbye to the United States on Planet Earth One and move to Atiota, Dah's planet, so that they could live together. They had thought about staying in Connecticut, but to live in the USA was fraught with too many obstacles – not least the laws pertaining to immigration. Dah had no acceptable papers – and never could have. On Atiota, however, papers did not matter – all the police were interested in was where a person lived and, as Dah had an address, so did John.

Four days ago, however, in the yard of their lodgings in Gulaga, their city on Atiota, they were presented with an unmistakable white gate. It was shiny and new, smooth to the touch and waist high with a gentle curve in the top bar. All these special white gates had the same appearance – and each one was an invitation to those who saw it to step through into another world – a world in which the Creator had a task for them. No-one seeing a white gate, though, felt compelled beyond choice to open it – but the Creator is not someone to resist. Once you have encountered Her, you can never really say no. You knew She would not have invited you if She didn't feel you could cope and contribute to someone else's need. Shaun had grown up with the understanding that life was not just about pleasing oneself, but making the planet – or in their case, the universe – a better place for someone else. This often entailed danger, but the Smith family had long since learned to go with the flow and trust the Creator.

So, as long as John and Dah could stay together, neither

of them gave stepping through this gate a second thought. And they had been overjoyed at finding themselves on Planet Joh in the very cottage garden they had heard so much about. There were four siblings in the Smith family: Kakko at twenty-one was the oldest, followed by Shaun and Bandi, two and four years her junior. Despite being only three, the youngest, Mahsnyeka – Yeka as she was always called – had already been on a white gate adventure but, mercifully, this present horror was not for her. Kakko was engaged to Tam, whom she had known since first school. Her mother, Jalli, her father, Jack, and Matilda, her father's mother whom they called Nan, were very pleased to meet these two friends their children had often talked about. When John and Dah arrived they had spent a wonderful evening catching up and telling stories.

But then, a day later, another white gate had appeared in the hedge of White Gates Cottage. This led them straight into the grounds of the hospital on the edge of a war zone. The five friends had immediately got down to helping where they could. The one doctor and several nurses there were impossibly stretched and were extremely grateful for their help. It was not every day that five fit and energetic foreign aid workers just walked in. Those who went through the Creator's gates were used to finding themselves in difficult places. They had survived being bombed, falling down cliffs and being kidnapped, among other things. They could never be absolutely sure they would survive in this life – but one thing they *were* sure of was that the Creator was with them. All the security She offered was that She loved them. And that was all that really mattered. Shaun's great-grandmother, Momori, had died in the faith that God would take her into a new world, where she would be reunited with all her loved ones who had gone before her. Shaun had watched as Momori had placed herself into the Creator's hands.

Shaun was not frightened of dying – but, now, the thought of his sister and friends being treated violently by vile evil maniacs terrified him. His mother had been attacked by a dissolute monster on her home planet, Raika, and it had taken Jalli years to come to terms with it. His father, Jack, had been blinded in the same incident. Why had the Creator brought them to this dreadful place? God always seemed to lead them into difficult situations, and here they were again.

Kakko was not the sort of person to go anywhere quietly and Shaun heard her calling God names under her breath. He began to think of this planet as *God-forsaken*. Could it be that even God had been driven out of this awful place? In the face of so much evil, you couldn't blame Her for giving up on it. But if *they* were here through a white gate at the Creator's bidding, then clearly She had not forsaken these people. What amazed him was that the terrified nurses never doubted the presence of God – they trusted She knew all about it, and cared. They never ceased calling on Her. Kakko learned that they and the doctor could have fled days before but they had felt it was too soon to run; they did not want to abandon their patients. And now at least one of the nurses had failed to escape with them. They had lost her in the panic. Shaun found himself hoping that she had died instantly, hit by one of the bullets that had whizzed around them. But the thought that this caring nurse was lying somewhere in pain with nobody to care for her was horrible. And to what end? Despite all this nurse had done for her patients, armed psychopaths had come and killed them.

Kakko had experienced the deliberate killing of women and children before. On that occasion she had managed to rescue a little girl from a bomb dropped from a plane. That family, too, had fled. But this time the evil had not come from the air but from the land.

The group retreated beyond the wall, slid down a steeply shelving bank and hid in the scrub that lined the river. This place was not without its dangers as many-toothed predators up to three metres long lived here.

As the night progressed, all was still. Rebel soldiers could be heard drinking and singing somewhere in the town. The fugitives were too thirsty and shocked to talk; they were silent. As the forces of evil drank stolen beer and altar wine, all the five friends craved was a drop of water. Shaun's stomach felt taut and hollow – no doubt so did everyone else's. But the hunger and thirst were as nothing compared to the fear that the haunting scenes they had seen instilled in them.

The moon rose and they explored the riverbank looking for a boat. They found none. Then the nurse in the lead spotted the outline of a canoe drawn up on the dark bank. She turned and smiled. "Boat," she whispered. But then, suddenly, the boat sprang into life. The nurse let out a blood-curdling screech. The dog, who had up to now been their faithful silent companion, began growling and yapping defiantly. From the former silence of the night, the air was now filled with the cries of people, the barking of the dog and the wild hissing of the enormous scaly creature. Shaun stood still, too stunned to move. They were trapped. Should they retreat? Were they being heard in the town behind them?

Then the creature lunged, grabbed the dog in its huge tooth-lined jaws and swung backwards into the water with a great splash. One moment the dog was there, barking, and the next it and the creature had vanished; and the water flowed on as if it had never been disturbed. The party were stunned. No-one uttered a sound. After what felt like an age, but what was in reality perhaps less than a minute, someone began to sob in the darkness. Then Kakko spotted something. At first, she thought it was another of the creatures, and was about to sound the alarm, but, in a shaft of light from the moon now rising above the waters, she made it out more clearly; this time it was a long, narrow fishing canoe.

"A boat." She pointed. "There."

"Ah-eeh," said one of the nurses. They crashed their way towards it. It would be safer on the river than the bank. Shaun spotted a second canoe and found a couple of paddles with it. Their luck was in. Eleven people boarded two canoes.

They pushed off and the current quickly took them downstream, but the nurses knew the river. Shaun and Tam paddled hard at their directing until they were in the lee of an island. The nurses took them round the other side of it. Then they found themselves in calmer water, and straight in front of them was a little landing. They pulled in alongside and disembarked.

Five round mud huts with thatched roofs stood a little way back from the water's edge. They called but all was quiet. No-one. Hidden among the houses they saw a stump with a handle – a pump! Shaun did not want to raise their hopes but he strode over to the well and pumped the handle until he felt the satisfying resistance of water. Three strokes more and it was splashing out of the pipe.

As he drank the cool, clear water, Shaun felt that it was among the greatest gifts he had ever been given.

Refreshed a little, the group of eleven sat together in the moonlight, their clothes torn and dirty. The rebels would not cross the river that night. They were safe for now – apart from the mosquitoes that attacked in droves. After all the din of the battle, the silence was palpable. Some of them wept. Some moaned. Dah clutched her John. Tam and Kakko sat opposite each other with both hands interlocked. Shaun sat alone and reflected on how unjust he thought life had been when he had received a yellow card on the football pitch and the coach had substituted him. On that occasion, he had thought life was so unfair – but he had had no idea what fairness really meant. These people that day had been forced not just off a football pitch but out of their homes, out of their town, leaving behind those they were tending to be killed. He smelt the smoke as it drifted across the river from the burning buildings glowing against the gathering clouds. How could people behave like this? What could have got into them to fill them with so much evil? It seemed that the Creator, if She still cared, was on the back foot.

2

"Mummy. Can I go and talk to Jay and Kay?"

"Of course you can, Yeka. But finish your breakfast first," said Jalli.

"But it's just stopped raining. Jay and Kay will go away when Daan comes up too high." She pointed to where the Johian sun would top the trees.

"Oh, alright. But just say hi, and then come back."

"Thanks, Mummy."

Yeka didn't have a pet dog like some of her friends in Woodglade. Jalli was a working mum, and her dad, Jack, found he had enough to do without looking after an animal. Being blind, things took longer and, to tell the truth, he wasn't really interested. He had never had a live-in pet as a child. And now with the white gates being active, no-one – not even his mother, Matilda – could guarantee to be around all the time. Yeka, however, had not been short of creatures to talk to. She had made friends with all the wildlife in the garden and had called them all by name. Jay and Kay were amphibians who lived by the pond beside the greenhouse. Somehow, although they were wild, they did not object to being prodded and stroked by a three-year-old. To give her her due, Yeka was very gentle and talked to them in a calm voice. She told them stories that included all the creatures in the garden, from the vivid orange flame-birds that were never quiet, to the tiny willy-beetles that crawled silently up and over the grass and stones.

For some reason Jay and Kay had gone from the pond that morning. Perhaps the rain had encouraged them to forage further afield. Yeka sighed. The flame-birds hadn't visited for days either. Yeka felt abandoned. She missed them all, but especially Shaun and Kakko. For some reason, and Yeka made no secret of it, Shaun was her favourite. It may have been because Kakko had been hands-on since she was born and shared the mothering with Jalli. And Bandi was mostly away on Planet Earth with his girlfriend, Abby, where they were both studying at a sixth–form college. But Shaun didn't get involved with the practical things. He was a playmate who played with her, making the dolls jump and talk, always ready to read to her and join in her tales to the wild creatures. Shaun did have friends, but not like Kakko with Tam, and Bandi with Abby – Yeka claimed him for her own.

There had been a girl in Shaun's life for a few weeks around his eighteenth birthday – Wennai – but it hadn't lasted. Apart from his family, the one big interest in Shaun's life was football where he had made a name for himself as a skilful midfield player.

Yeka returned to finish her breakfast.

"When's Shaun coming back?" she moaned.

"It has been a long time this time," sighed Jalli. She spoke lightly, but secretly she worried. Mothers always do. But it was not Shaun she worried about so much as Kakko because Kakko had so often returned from her white gates adventures worse for wear as Matilda put it. She had had a broken arm on one occasion and a lump of shrapnel in her leg on another.

"Everybody gone," mumbled Yeka.

"Not everyone. You have your mummy and daddy and nan. I only had Grandma when I was your age… and I didn't have brothers or sisters either."

Yeka couldn't imagine that. So she thought of what she hadn't got.

"Kammy has a baby. A *real* baby. I haven't got one. Will we be getting one soon?"

"No, I don't think so, Yeka. You already have a sister and brothers. It's just that they are older than you."

"But I want a baby, too."

"I think," smiled Jalli, "that our little cottage is full up. No room for any more babies."

Yeka sighed. Far from being full up, the house seemed to be empty. None of her older siblings were around.

"Baby can share my room."

"That's very nice of you but babies grow up."

"Like Kakko. She was the first baby."

"Yes. That was twenty-one years ago. It doesn't seem possible… Now, it's time to drink up and get ready for kindy. You will have lots of friends to play with there."

★ ★ ★

A week after crossing the river, the eleven refugees trudged into the outskirts of the city and were stopped at a makeshift barrier across the road. Seeing the foreigners with paler skin, the police asked for papers.

"We have nothing," protested Shaun.

A quick examination revealed they had indeed nothing but the rags in which they stood.

"Westerner?" demanded one of the policemen.

"No," replied Shaun truthfully. "Planet Joh."

The policeman didn't want to show his ignorance and looked across at his mate.

"You work where?"

"In a hospital."

"Missionary…? God…? Church?"

"Yes," answered Shaun decisively. "We were at the hospital because God sent us."

The policemen were satisfied. Missionaries never had any money. They were a peculiar breed, and there was clearly little to be gained by detaining them; they allowed them to proceed.

Some sort of normal life was visible in the streets of this place. Shops were open, and people at wooden stalls with corrugated metal roofs were selling fresh produce. For the past week, the party had existed on what they could find in the bush that lined the road and the kindness of others in the same situation. The alien volunteers had nothing with which to buy food for themselves. A little further along the street the refugees were being herded into a turning that led to a tented compound beyond a wire fence. Soldiers with clean, smart uniforms ushered them into a reception area. Here, the five aliens were taken aside without having a chance to say goodbye to their colleagues.

They were treated with kindness. It was soon clear they were not expected to remain at the camp. They had no papers – clearly anyone fleeing as they had done was unlikely to carry any form of identification – but their appearance and foreign intonations, despite the special translation the Creator provided, marked them out. To their amazement, they were driven off in a comfortable, air-conditioned vehicle to a hotel where they were greeted by a smiling uniformed official. He did not share the appearance of a local man.

"You will not be permitted to leave until your organisation claims you," he explained. "And we will also require full statements from you. In the meantime, you will find clean clothes to choose from in your rooms."

He ushered them to a reception desk where they were asked to sign their names. The forms were totally unreadable but, despite his instinct never to put his name to anything he didn't understand, Shaun didn't resist. Kakko had already signed – she always got to doing things first.

They were led along air-conditioned corridors and into lifts that took them to two rooms somewhere high above the street below. It was like stepping out of one world and into another, just like a white gate. It reminded Kakko that they did not belong to this place, even if they were away from the violence.

"I don't know how we are going to get back home," she reasoned. "But I am going to take advantage of that shower right now!"

"Will we need to get back to the hospital grounds to find our white gate?" asked John.

"No idea," said Shaun. "Better go with the flow for now. Not that we seem to have much choice." Tam was already searching through the pile of clean used clothes that had been put on the table. Kakko rummaged with him.

Two hours later, reasonably presentable in fairly nondescript clothing that fitted where it touched, the party were summoned to a meal. They had been without proper food for so long they had forgotten to be hungry, and the rich fare they were offered turned their stomachs. They munched the bread, slowly.

"We need to eat the greens," insisted Kakko. "We need the vitamins."

Once they had started, eating came easier.

"How long do you think they are going to keep us here?" wondered Dah.

"I shouldn't think it will be for long," answered Shaun. "Someone's got to pay for this."

He was right. That evening an official came to ascertain their nationality and status. They were truthful – they were not from anywhere on the planet.

Kakko, who was always good at turning the conversation to what she wanted to talk about, managed to discover that the town they had had to flee from had now been retaken by government forces. It had taken another bloody battle but the criminal rebels had left. How much the government forces could be trusted was another question – still, it meant that the possibility of returning to the hospital grounds and the white gate was open.

"We do not belong here," stated Kakko firmly. "Will you take us back to the hospital?"

The morning came incredibly quickly; all of them had slept like babies. An army sergeant arrived as they were consuming more of the breakfast than they had of the previous evening meal. She told them they were to be returned to the town from which they had fled, and she had transport waiting for them. She issued them papers in a language that meant nothing.

"Pack your bags," she ordered; "we leave in half an hour."

That won't be difficult, thought Shaun. They begged a plastic bag and filled it with additional clothes from the pile, and toiletries. Life was improving – they had more than they stood up in.

This time the transport was not an air-conditioned upholstered vehicle but an army truck which they shared with soldiers and sacks of foodstuffs – some kind of grain, Shaun guessed. They travelled between two other vehicles through the streets of the city and across the bridge that spanned the river – it was the same river they had first encountered but narrower here than it was downstream.

Then they were out in the country, bumping along the open road. Shaun was aware he had lost weight from his bottom – the bones of his pelvis felt just under his skin as he sat, or tried to sit, on the hard bench he had been allocated. He winced as he looked at his sister opposite him.

"What's wrong with you, Shaun?" shouted Kakko over the roar of the engine. "I thought you were a tough football player."

"OK. It's just that my hips are not as wide as yours."

Kakko looked daggers at him.

"I mean proportionally," he continued. "Girls have wider pelvises... and I'm heavier than you," he added to try and sweeten the atmosphere.

But Kakko knew that in fact that was only marginally true, well, when they last got weighed at home on Planet Joh... Planet Joh; that felt light years away. It was. Kakko shivered, despite the heat, the dust and the hot fumes from the truck.

"How far is it?" asked John. "It took us a week to walk."

"It'll depend on the road," said Tam. "If it stays like this, it could be a few hours. If it worsens it could take all day."

"They have given us provisions and water for a day," said Dah. "The sergeant said so." She gestured to the box containing some kind of rations and a dozen bottles of water. "The road is not that comfortable but I'm glad I'm not walking it – I couldn't do that again."

"Sing us a song, Dah," asked John. Back on Atiota, Dah had become a popular folk singer. She struck up with something and soon they were all singing, their spirits lifted. Compared to the previous few days, things were looking up. They were not going to die of exhaustion or starvation and these army personnel seemed to be well trained.

They were still singing when the air was split with the loudest bang Shaun had ever heard and the floor of the truck swung up and smashed into them. Then they were airborne amid a jumble of people, sacks of grain, metal tools and anything else that was not tied down. The whole world tipped over and kept tipping over for what seemed an eternity. Shaun's foot caught on something and pain shot through his ankle as it twisted. Then everything stopped with an almighty jolt. Shaun gasped as the side of the truck thudded into his back, and Kakko's flying body landed with a heavy thump on top of him. He felt his leg crunch and he yelled in pain but he had saved his sister from colliding with metal. She rolled off him in one piece and Shaun tried to call out again but all the air had been driven from his lungs. Then the roar of the engine and din of the crash ceased.

"You OK?" It was Tam. At least Tam had survived.

"Yeah," said Dah, "I don't think anything is broken. John?"

John moaned, "What the hell happened?"

"I'm OK," said Kakko. "Shaun, sorry I landed on you… I'm sorry… Shaun?"

"W… winded," gasped Shaun. Then, "My leg… My ankle…"

"Oh, Shaun, what have I done?"

"I'll live… I think…" muttered Shaun. "You OK?"

"Yeah. Soft landing with you underneath… We seem to be on our side. I don't know how many times the vehicle rolled. Like being in a washing machine."

Tat-tat-tat-tat. Small-arms fire sounded from somewhere.

"Keep down!" ordered Tam.

They were quickly surrounded by the sound of machine gun fire on all sides. A volley of bullets tore through the tipped-up roof of the vehicle just above their heads. Bits of the floor flew around them as the rounds bit into it. Through the rear of the truck they could see the open vehicle behind them containing soldiers attempt to make a U-turn. Bullets were puncturing it but it completed the manoeuvre and began driving away. Then it was hit by some kind of rocket-propelled grenade. The five were never to forget that sight. The vehicle exploded and then lay dead – a ball of flame.

The shooting stopped. The firefight seemed to be over. More silence.

"Better get out of here," said Tam softly. "We could catch fire."

All but Shaun pushed themselves to the back of the truck. John put his hands under Shaun's armpits and pulled. Shaun shouted, "Be careful!"

"Sorry, mate. Got to get you out of here."

Tam came and helped take some of Shaun's weight. Kakko lifted his legs.

"Ow!" uttered Shaun. They slid out of the vehicle which lay on its side in a ditch. A motley-looking boy, who could not have been more than twelve, strolled up to them and poked a semi-automatic rifle into Tam's chest. He sneered, and called to his comrades. One of them walked up to the cab of the truck, looked in and then raised his gun and sprayed it with bullets. Their driver and the sergeant, if they hadn't been up till then, were now clearly dead. Dah uttered a cry of horror. Tam hoped the men would finish them all off quickly and not torture them. He could not bear the thought of what they might do to the girls.

An older man barked an order from behind them. He seemed to be in charge. Turning to the group still clustered around Shaun, he ordered, "You, on your feet!" He motioned to a rough-looking soldier to search them. Apparently they were not to be killed... well, not immediately. Shaun wondered whether the gang had begun to see their trade value. Foreign nationals from better-off places could be ransomed – rich relatives, even governments, would produce handsome sums to ensure their safe return.

"You walk!" bawled the leader.

"I… I…" stammered Shaun.

"Can't you see he's injured?" rounded Kakko, aggressively. "His leg—"

The commander thrust his rifle into Kakko's face. "You shut your mouth. You will not speak!" But it was obvious, even to him, that Shaun was not able to go anywhere. "You leave him!"

"No!" Kakko's anger blazed, despite the gun. Tam winced. The man methodically lowered his gun and put his face right up to hers until their noses touched. His breath stank of rotten food or perhaps some kind of chewing drug. He spat on her face. "Last warning. Women are nothing. You hear?"

Tam put his arm round his girl and pulled her back. He did not have to say: *Not now, Kakko. You'll get your chance.* She knew him too well. Tam was right. Reluctantly, Kakko subsided and bowed her head. The commander rejoiced in his apparent victory, pleased with his ability to cow upstart foreign women. Later he would take her for himself. "Good," he said. "Now leave him and walk."

The four walking wounded were forced at gunpoint across the road and into the trees. Shaun remained standing on one foot, leaning against the upturned truck. Were they going to carry him? The commander turned to the soldier who had fired into the cab. "Kill him," he ordered.

The ragged assassin grinned. It would be a pleasure. He strode across, his weapon on his shoulder. Perhaps he could make Shaun scream before he finished him off.

"No!" shrieked Kakko.

"Don't mess. Just do it!" bellowed the bossman.

The assassin raised his gun, savouring the moment.

Tat-tat-tat. The soldier swung round as a bullet struck his shoulder. His mouth opened in shock and the gun fell from his grip. Then another volley tore into him, spattering bits of him across Shaun's body.

Tam yanked Kakko down into the ditch on the far side of the road. The first volley had drawn her attention to the road behind them and she had looked away from her brother. John and Dah dived after them; the man holding them fled into the bush. The rest of their captors hit the road, firing wildly in the direction from which they thought the shots had come. Then one tried to make for the ditch, too, but was felled instantly. Bullets ricocheted off the hard road in clouds of dust. One of the gang raised two arms high and shouted something that was tantamount to a surrender. The leader, however, attempted to get off the road by rolling towards Tam and Kakko but a new volley ripped into the road beside him and he too surrendered, wounded. A vehicle sped forward and the rest of the gang, flat on the road, held up their hands.

It was the soldiers of the lead vehicle in the convoy. They had escaped the ambush and had returned – just in the nick of time to save Shaun. It was impossible to say who was the most dazed: Shaun who had at that moment reconciled himself to being shot, Kakko who hated being out of control and terrified as she saw her brother about to die, or John who was shaking violently, being comforted by Dah. John had signed up for a peaceful life with a lovely singer, not a war on an unknown planet where everyone was killing each other.

In the silence that seemed to follow the noise of gunshot and screams, Kakko was the first to get to her feet. She didn't hear the orders of the soldiers as they attended to their captives. The hot still air, charged with gun smoke, dry dust and the stench of torn flesh assaulted her lungs as she struggled to breathe again. She leapt to her brother's side across the blood-soaked road.

"Shaun!"

"My leg. It hurts," he mumbled.

Tam joined them.

"We'd better get you a splint, mate," he said in as calm a voice as he could muster.

★ ★ ★

Six hours later they were back at the hospital where they had started. The place was a mess. The bodies had been removed but nothing else had been done to put it to rights. Smashed furniture lay everywhere. The drugs cupboard had been pulled from the wall and was lying open; glass was scattered around it. Bullet holes could be seen in almost everything. In a wistful moment, Kakko had thought that the hospital might be able to do something about Shaun's leg which was clearly broken above the ankle. She had tied him together with a rudimentary splint made from a baton they had found lying on the road but he needed something for the pain and especially to prevent any infection. But the hospital was no different from any other building in the town – even the church had been completely wrecked. All but two of the two dozen people killed there had been women. They had been the social glue of the town, keeping families cared for, tending the newly born, comforting the bereaved – working for God in a place that had known so much violence over so many years. Now they had died a horrendous death.

Tam wondered whether the five of them were called to begin again as volunteers. But Dah told him wisely that they were too traumatised – they all needed time to recover. And, without proper medication, not only Shaun, but their minor wounds too, could become infected, and that was life-threatening.

Yet there was no white gate in the compound.

We need to pray... together," croaked Tam.

"Agreed," said Dah. "Let's join hands and talk to God."

Linked like this, they prayed. It was amazing just how close the Creator appeared to be at that moment. "Lord, what do you want us to do?" asked Kakko. She heard a gentle breath behind her. She looked up. They were not alone. One by one, local people began to enter the ward where they sat. Then one of them began to sing – her voice rhythmic, soft yet powerful. Others joined the strain. Dah began to hum as she learned the tune.

Then the song got louder and the rhythm more insistent. The key developed into a major one and, in amid all the wreckage and misery of war, people began to sing a song of praise. *Amazing*, thought Kakko. *Utterly amazing.*

The people seemed overjoyed to see them. They had returned.

Kakko wanted to say that they had come back to look for a way out – but she hadn't the heart. She was actually glad that they were there because they were no longer alone in their trauma. They had all been through the terror.

From somewhere people arrived with native herbs and remedies. Cuts were all bathed in some kind of juice that, even if no substitute for proper medicine, would serve to clean and protect torn skin. A better splint was found for Shaun but it was clear the break was not a simple one. Kakko prayed that they could get him home soon.

Food and water also materialised from nowhere. Kakko began to protest, saying they needed the food more, but then she remembered that, on a previous occasion, people not unlike these had taken delight in giving her all they had. They felt they needed to give. Kakko recognised one of the women.

"I weighed your baby," she said. "Is he alright?"

"He fine," smiled the woman. "You made him better."

"Good," said Kakko relieved. At least one child had survived.

"You good people. God send you to us."

"In these horrible things, why does God seem so near?" Kakko asked.

"He always close. God hurts when his people hurt," answered the woman.

"Don't you ask him to stop these violent people?"

"Mend their hearts? Yes, we ask Him to mend their hearts. But bad in them is so big…"

"I mean, stop them – prevent them killing."

"How? God does not fight with guns. God is with us."

"I understand," said John. "God is bigger than all of this."

The woman smiled. "God made sun, stars, river. Guns, bombs cannot stop Him. We belong among the stars."

Tam began to clear a space for them to sleep, and Dah managed to find some cushions on which to lay Shaun.

"I don't know about you but I must sleep," said John. Dah sat beside her boyfriend and hummed a soft lullaby.

The sun rose and a cool morning breeze swept through the broken walls and windows. Shaun was not a good colour.

Tam pulled himself up from beside Kakko and offered him a bottle of water. Shaun tried to sit up. Tam helped him. If they didn't get out that day, it could be very serious indeed for the nineteen-year-old.

John stirred too and went out to find the toilet. He came bounding back.

"Gate! White gate!" he exclaimed. Kakko ran out to see and then came back.

"Let's get Shaun out of here," she bellowed.

Their excitement raised the locals.

"It is time for us to leave," explained Tam. "Our brother will die if we stay," he added. He hoped the people would understand.

"You can go? How?"

"It's complicated," said Tam. "We just need to get Shaun outside by that tree."

Many hands lifted Shaun to where Kakko indicated.

"OK. We can take him from here. We will leave you here but not before we have prayed with you. Dah, will you sing?"

Dah sang a gentle song of hope. "God with you," she finished.

"God is good..." said the woman who now stood with the baby Kakko had weighed.

"... all the time," they responded. "It is His nature."

"We go and leave you with our prayers," said Tam. He took Shaun's shoulders while Kakko and John linked arms beneath his bottom, and Dah very carefully put her arms under his knees. The gate opened as Tam pushed against it and they carried Shaun onto the lawn of White Gates Cottage. Kakko glanced back to see, just before the gate faded, a knot of local people standing with a look of amazement. The woman with the child was saying, "The Lord has taken them. Praise the Lord..."

"Such good people," said Kakko. "They have nothing but they have everything."

They looked up to see Yeka running across the grass squealing with delight.

"You've come home! Mummy, they've come home!"

Jalli did not hesitate. She immediately sent for an ambulance.

3

"Best leave him here on the grass," said Tam. "The ambulance will not be long." Matilda had already appeared with a blanket. Shaun did not look good. He was beginning to mutter but what he said made no sense. Jalli felt his forehead.

"He's burning up," she declared. "What about the rest of you? What happened?"

Kakko decided that the story was too long to tell right then. "The place is in a huge mess. We were in the back of a truck that came off the road. I landed on top of Shaun. He was only joking about my weight a bit before."

"I think you're all very lucky by the sound of things," said Jalli.

"Indeed," said Tam. "Kakko could have done herself some real damage if Shaun hadn't been beneath her when she landed."

"You all look as if you've been through a lot. You look half-starved… and filthy," said Matilda. "I've got the kettle on."

"Brilliant," said Kakko. "Just what we all need."

John was sitting on the grass with Dah beside him. He said nothing.

"Shock," said Matilda. "I've seen it before. Bring him into the kitchen."

Dah persuaded him to his feet.

That girl is acting strong, thought Matilda, *but I doubt it will last. She's being strong for the boy.* She knew Kakko and Tam to be quite resilient. But even they looked rough.

Yeka stood on one leg holding onto Kakko's hand. She just looked at Shaun, confused. She had never seen him look like that before. He wasn't the Shaun she knew. Kakko held her hand tight and Yeka cuddled up to her leg.

"You smell funny," she said.

"I expect I do," answered Kakko. "It wasn't nice where we have been."

"What did you do there?"

"We helped in a hospital."

"Like the one downtown?"

"A bit like that but not so big and not so nice."

Jalli had rung Jack. He arrived about the same time as the ambulance.

The ambulance crew wouldn't allow anyone to ride with Shaun. The concern they showed confirmed their fears. The paramedics ran their eyes over the others and ordered them all to attend A&E but not to rush. It would be unlikely that they would be able to see Shaun for some time.

"They'll want to take him for tests," they said. "Come when you're ready… Is he allergic to antibiotics?"

"No," said Jack.

As soon as Shaun was safely inside and the paramedics had connected him to a drip, the ambulance raced away, disappearing from sight in the direction of Joh City. Jalli shuddered. Jack held her. Yeka was crying silently. Kakko became aware. She bent down and picked her up. "Let's get that tea," she said.

★ ★ ★

Two hours later Kakko, Tam, John and Dah had been injected,

disinfected, bathed, and their scrapes covered in an antiseptic liquid that made them wince. Shaun was in theatre having his leg dealt with.

"You only just managed to get your son here in time," explained the consultant to Jalli. "He is suffering from a blood infection but fortunately he appears to be responding well to the antibiotics. He's very dehydrated too – in fact they all are… We've done a scan and his right tibia and fibia are both fractured in two places. There is also some damage to the veins and surrounding muscles, but his arteries and nerves seem intact… He's a lucky young man. It could have been worse…

"The other young people have suffered some quite considerable bruising. Your daughter Kakko has suffered a significant blow to the side of her head – I have ordered a CAT scan. The young man – John – has sustained significant whiplash and, although he says he did not pass out, I suspect some mild concussion… Tell me about this road accident – it would appear to have been serious. I haven't heard of such an accident locally."

"It didn't happen here," explained Jalli. "They were on another planet in the midst of a war of some kind. The truck wasn't travelling fast. They think it was blown up by some kind of mine… They say they were ambushed."

"Another planet…? Ah, of course, your family is the one that travels through portals – white gates or something."

"Exactly."

"Your daughter's boyfriend, Tam – his parents are here. They don't sound best pleased but seem reconciled to his association with you."

"I wouldn't blame them for being doubtful about their son's commitment to Kakko. She isn't the safest girl to have as a partner… I'd better go and talk to them."

"Ah, yes. Kakko. According to her records, she has been

treated for a broken arm and had metal removed from her upper thigh – both injuries sustained on other worlds. This time it is her brother who has suffered the most severely. I recommend that you dissuade them from travelling like this."

"Sometimes, I wish I could, but they are all over eighteen – just. At their age I never turned down a white gate. In fact, I never have…"

"What about the relatives of the other two." He checked his clipboard. "John and Da'yelni?"

"Both on different planets. John is from Earth One and Dah from a planet called Atiota. That's where they live… They can't return without a white gate."

"Ah, I see…" But the doctor didn't seem to have really understood.

★ ★ ★

As soon as it was available, Jalli obtained a copy of the local newspaper, the *Daily Messenger*. She anticipated a report. This was the sort of story the readers enjoyed. She read Jack an article on page three. There was a picture of Shaun posing in his red and yellow City United football strip with a football under his boot – his right one. It read:

> *Footballer Injured on Alien Planet*
> *Shaun Smith (19) of City United, and training for youth and community work at the City Academy, sustained a broken leg and other complications in a road accident that was reported to have taken place on another planet.*
> *Smith's parents, who have been living on Joh for the past quarter of a century, have a cottage in Woodglade that has been occupied by other travellers before them. Jack (48), who is blind, works as a teacher in the Woodglade School for the*

Blind. His wife, Jallaxanya (47), has been an entomologist at the Institute of Agriculture since their arrival on Joh.

The name and location of the planet on which the accident happened is unknown to them. "We never know where we will end up," explained Jallaxanya. "We are called there for a purpose... to help the people – but it is always a challenging place and is often in trouble. This particular planet seems to have been engaged in a gruesome war."

Shaun was born in Joh City Hospital where he is now being cared for. "Shaun is poorly but we expect him to make a good recovery," said Mr Crant, his consultant, in a statement. Asked about his future as a footballer, Mr Crant said that it was far too early to speculate. "Whatever happens he will take many months to recover from this injury," he added.

Shaun's sister, Kakko (21), was also in the crash, as was her partner, Tam Klempt (21), also of Woodglade.

They were accompanied by two other friends reported to hail from different planets: John Richards (20) from Earth One, and Da'yelni Lugos (18) from Atiota. All were severely dehydrated and suffering from minor injuries. They were treated but not detained, and have now returned home to Woodglade.

"That sounds fair enough," remarked Jack. "It's factual. They've done more sensational pieces in the past."

"I know... But I wish we weren't bringing so much attention to ourselves," sighed Jalli.

Jack laughed. "The truth is that they don't know the half of it. The white gates take us to places most people cannot even imagine. Even if you told them, they wouldn't understand it."

"What worries me this time is that I don't think *we* know the half of it... I've never known Kakko to be so unforthcoming."

"She's growing up and seeing deeper into things. She's not bouncing off the surface so much these days. This latest experience has been really traumatic for all of them. I have come to believe – not that I have been told in so many words – that they feared Shaun was going to be killed – and not just from the road accident."

"Oh, Jack. All of this scares me… No-one on this planet has any idea of what it's like being our children's mother and father."

"Except for Tam's parents."

"Yes, of course… The doctor said that they seemed *reconciled* to the fact that their son wanted to belong to Kakko."

"That's progress, Jalli. You can't expect them to be enthusiastic. Anyway, he, of all of them, came back the least traumatised this time. Very much together – more confident."

"Yes. You're right. We're lucky with him, Jack. He's really good for Kakko."

"Whatever happens, Jalli, we've got more now than either of us, or my mother, or your grandma, had when we were their age."

"Yes. That's so true. And the more we have, the more we have to worry about; I can't imagine having no-one, like some people."

★ ★ ★

Two days after his op, Shaun demanded of his doctor, with a note of impatience, "When will I be able to walk?"

"So we're feeling better, it seems," smiled the doctor. "Ready to get mobile. That's a good sign. You've got quite a bit of metal in that leg but we'll see about a lighter cast in a couple of days and then you'll be begging us to ease off on the physio. I want to see you build up a bit of muscle, too. You appear to have been quite malnourished over the last week or so."

"Yeah. We got past the point of feeling hungry… But now I'm ravenous."

"Good. Get stronger." The doctor glanced toward movement in the doorway. "Oh, you seem quite popular." Shaun looked up to see his friend Aril with his sister, Wennai, and Gollip, the City United leading goal scorer, hesitating at the entrance of the ward. "You can come and talk to your friend now… I've quite finished." The consultant moved on to another patient.

"Hi," said Aril.

"Hi," answered Shaun.

"Just thought we should check you out, mate," said Aril.

"Sorry, Gollip," said Shaun. "It looks like I shall be out for some time."

"We missed you," said Gollip. "Lost the match… Got the message from your mum to say you had been summoned away. Couldn't believe it; just before that important cup match."

"Sorry," said Shaun again. "I didn't plan on being away so long." The atmosphere was tense. The teenagers weren't used to hospital visiting and they certainly weren't used to seeing Shaun lying on his back in bed. The presence of Wennai didn't help. She and Shaun had dated for a month around the time of his eighteenth birthday and, although it was just over a year ago that they had agreed to part, it had been pretty serious between them at one point. Since then, Wennai had started dating Gollip, which made things a bit awkward.

The conversation was mostly about football. They didn't ask much about what had landed Shaun in such a state. After twenty minutes, Gollip suggested it was time to leave. He and Wennai were going to a venue that evening. Shaun thanked them for coming.

"Come again, you guys. It gets a bit lonely in here sometimes."

"Sure, mate," said Aril. "We'll come after the match on Saturday and tell you all about it."

As they left, Shaun thought to himself, *Yeah, you will. Gollip won't, though. He'll be out celebrating or commiserating with the rest of the team. And Wennai will probably be with him now they are an acknowledged item.*

Shaun's leg began to hurt him and he lay back. His family wouldn't be visiting until later. He closed his eyes and began to nod but then he was back there on the dusty road and he saw the man's expression of ecstasy anticipating pulling the trigger, only to—

Then he was wide awake, staring at the ceiling.

★ ★ ★

To Shaun's surprise, the next day, in the afternoon, Wennai returned. This time alone.

"I wanted to come," she reflected. "I didn't manage to get to say much with the two boys."

"Nah," agreed Shaun. "Your brother always has lots to say."

"I didn't want to talk about football. It must be cruel for you not being able to walk, let alone play."

"Pretty much of a mess at the moment, I'm afraid… They hope to get me up for a few minutes tomorrow when I have a new pot on."

Wennai looked at their artwork from the previous day on his existing cast. "Pretty naff. You'll be glad to get that off."

"Yeah, not just for Aril's doubtful cartoons… although they have caused some amusement among the nurses." Shaun laughed. It wasn't difficult talking to Wennai.

"I expect what happened to you was a bit scary."

"You could say that." And then more softly, "… I didn't think I was going to get through it, if I'm honest… Actually—"
Then, sob after sob rose from somewhere deep down inside.

Wennai reached to hold his hand. When Shaun managed to gain control again, he apologised. "Sorry… that was stupid."

"No it wasn't. It has to come out. You can't bottle it up. You were saying: Actually…"

Shaun reached for the tissue box. Wennai took it from the bedside table and handed it to him.

"Actually – you won't tell my mum and dad this, or anyone else. Kakko, Tam, Dah and John know – they were there. We're not telling anybody just yet. We couldn't cope with all the fuss. Nan will hit the ceiling when she finds out… and… and I've got to have the strength to deal with that before saying anything." He smiled. Then became serious. "A soldier was pointing his gun at my head and would have fired if someone else hadn't shot him first. I definitely thought I was going to die."

"Oh, God," said Wennai. Her eyes filled with tears; mascara streaked her cheeks. A look of dread showed on her face.

"You OK? Sorry…" asked Shaun.

"You silly boy. Don't you dare apologise again… I want you to tell me."

Shaun described the time from when the truck left the road. "That's how my leg got broken. If I hadn't been underneath her, Kakko could have smashed her head on the side or broken a lot more bones than me."

"So this leg is kind of, like, a good trade-off."

"Definitely. Kakko is pretty shocked still, though. She's doing her best not to show it… Then the truck behind us just blew up – with all the men still in it… It was horrible… I still see that every time I close my eyes… And then there was this boy, no more than twelve, with a gun that looked far too big for him, pretending to be grown up."

Shaun told Wennai the whole story. He ended with them carrying him through the white gate.

The pile of tissues mounted between them.

"Thanks for coming, Wennai... I don't know why I told you all this. You won't say anything until I tell you?"

"No, of course not..."

"You're a good listener."

"Thanks."

"How'd it go last night... with your date with Gollip?"

Wennai shrugged her shoulders. "OK. He's OK. He's very attentive."

"Good. I hope he makes you happy. He's a fun kid."

Kid, thought Wennai, *exactly.* She had hoped Shaun would show a bit of jealousy. They were silent for a minute, eyes cast down. Then Shaun spoke gently.

"Wennai, despite all that happened out there, I still believe in God. Even more. She was really there, in the middle of it all..."

"I know. I know you believe that. And I don't want you to change your mind."

"What? Not to change my mind about God?"

"No. She's not just important to you, She's the canvas on which your picture is painted."

"Wow, Wennai. That's poetic."

"It's not me. It was in a book I read."

"You were reading a book about God?"

"Not about God exactly. It was just what one of the characters said."

"You believe in God now?"

"No. But you do. I can see that nothing is going to alter that. Not even a..." Wennai didn't complete her sentence. She couldn't say the words.

"A gun at my head," supplied Shaun.

Wennai nodded.

"But *you're* still angry with Her because of your mum?"

"I can't accept that if God existed and cared, He... She

34

would have allowed my mum to die... But I know what you would say."

"What?"

"That She was always there – even as she died."

Shaun reached for another tissue. "Yep."

"And I don't want you to stop believing that, Shaun – even if I can't."

"Thanks, Wennai."

They saw a nurse, hovering.

"She wants to give me my medicine," smiled Shaun.

"I'd better get along... Don't tell Aril or Gollip I've been to see you."

"Mum's the word. So many secrets. I understand."

Wennai lent over and kissed him on the cheek. He felt her soft fair hair on his neck.

"Bye," she said lightly.

"Bye," he smiled.

Wennai nodded to the nurse as she passed her. At the door of the ward, she turned and waved before she disappeared.

"You're a lucky young man," said the nurse.

"Oh. She's not my girlfriend," said Shaun firmly.

"Oh, really? You could have fooled me."

Late that same afternoon John and Dah discovered a white gate for them. Peering through it, they saw their little place on Atiota. They took their leave and went home, gratefully. They had no doubt they would meet up with the Smiths again but, they hoped, on a gentler adventure.

★ ★ ★

Jalli bought the morning newspaper at the little shop in Woodglade. They hadn't used to get it but these days so much of the news involved people they knew. The article about Shaun inspired her to buy it on the way to work, rather than at lunchtime.

At work she leafed through it. She was about to push it aside, when she caught sight of the heading of a letter in the correspondence column: *Aliens misusing the health service?*

Dear Editor,

Yesterday we read of the latest so-called adventures of the Smith family and their friends to another world. Apparently this ability to flit between planets, exclusive to them, occurs through ethereal white gates that only they can see. This is not the first time this behaviour has resulted in hospitalisation at the cost of the Johian Health Service. This time, apart from the injuries happening off-planet, your paper reports that at least two people alien to Joh received treatment at the hospital. We do not know the details but are we to believe that people who have no residence here have received treatment at Johian expense?

What are the authorities doing to look further into this phenomenon that is having an effect on the security of our planet? What assurances do we have that these are not the beginnings of a serious threat to our future? Or are we to turn a blind eye to this? One of the Smith family is already working in the space centre, where, we are told, they are liaising with an alien race called the Thenits. Am I the only one to believe we have grounds for a thorough investigation?

Name and address supplied.

Jalli stood rigid, leaning on her desk for support. She and Jack had been living on Joh for the past thirty years. All of their children had been born on the planet. They had paid their taxes and health insurance from the beginning. And, compared with many less fortunate families, they had not been heavy users of the hospital. The authorities knew all about the white gates. They weren't the first alien residents of White Gates Cottage – and historians believed that all Johians descended from immigrants who had arrived through portals more than a thousand years ago. The accepted opinion of the expert historians was that they had originated as a species on Earth One – the question was whether they had come direct or through some other colony. Whatever their point of departure, they had arrived as a relatively primitive community with little or no technology beyond stone tools, and did not write. But they had soon developed in Joh's peaceful and comfortable environment. The white gate phenomenon was not under-investigated. But it was not the injustice of the claims in the letter that disturbed Jalli. She was afraid. This name and address supplied seemed to have it in for them. She was frightened for her children.

Jalli was still standing deep in thought when the principal, Mrs Trenz, came in.

"Problem, Jalli?"

Jalli pushed the paper across her desk to her. The principal read the letter.

"For what it's worth," she said, "I think this is not only outrageous, it's preposterous."

"Thanks."

"And I should think that 99.9% of the population agree with me."

"There was a demonstration when Kakko returned from the spacetruck rescue two months ago... outside the space centre."

"I heard about that. It seemed to die down very quickly though."

"There are some people bent on causing trouble," said Jalli. "We get snide remarks occasionally – and sideways looks."

"I think you should make sure the police hear about all of these incidents – no matter how small… I hope they look into this letter writer's past, too… Are you going to respond to it?"

"No. We don't have to justify ourselves. It'll only get him – or her – to come back with more nasty stuff. The papers like a tit-for-tat."

"Very wise."

But Jalli and Jack did not need to put up any defence. The following day there were letters from the hospital administrator pointing out that Jack had paid a bill for John and Dah in the same way as any Johian who had opted out of the state insurance scheme; and the Professor of Interplanetary Relations at the university commented at length on the portal phenomenon, explaining that it had been carefully studied for many years. He referred the letter writer to his book: *Portals and Planets: the Benefits to Human Progress*.

Over the next three days cards and letters poured in both to White Gates Cottage and the hospital. The orderly who brought up Shaun's post needed a special bag. It took Shaun half the morning to get through it. Most of the cards came from fans and people connected to City United but there were others from friends and erstwhile schoolmates whom he hadn't seen for ages, and a great big joint card from the worship centre. The controversial nature of the correspondence had only served to stir up more support. Some people were outraged, and said so.

Letters in defence of the Smith family were posted by the director of the space centre, the principals of the Institute of Agriculture and the School for the Blind. The paper printed glowing praise for Shaun from the manager of City United which was signed by all the players in the squad. "No-one," he wrote, "made any protest about Shaun Smith's background when he led the team to victory last season. Shaun is not just a wonderfully gifted footballer but a thoroughly likeable lad who provides quiet leadership on and off the pitch – something we are missing at the moment."

During the rest of his three-day stay at the hospital, Shaun received dozens of visitors. Wennai did not manage to visit alone again but she spoke with her eyes as her brother talked non-stop about the things Shaun was missing.

The physiotherapy was good. But Shaun quickly learned that it would be many, many months before he would be able to run again, let alone play in midfield which would require him to cover much of the pitch for ninety minutes. Midfielders were expected to both defend and attack, even score goals, which meant always being in the right place at the right time. The one thing Kakko talked about more than anything regarding the truck accident was that, from her point of view, he had been in exactly the right place to save her. The thought cheered him. And, somehow, the Creator was using the one person who denied Her existence to help him get better.

4

Light years from Joh, Shaun's younger brother, Bandi, looked up as his girlfriend, Abby, stomped into her parents' sitting room on Earth One.

"How'd today's exam go?" Bandi asked.

Abby was in the midst of lower-sixth exams in Longmead Sixth Form College.

"OK," she said in a non-committal voice as she threw her bag down onto the sofa on her way to the kitchen where she fished a Coke out of the fridge.

"Want one?" she called over her shoulder.

"No thanks, I've got tea... One more to go," added Bandi brightly as Abby plonked herself down beside him, "and then you'll have completed all your lower-sixth exams."

"Yep... I wish I had your brains, though."

"So you're dense, right?"

"I feel like that right now. Like... I dunno..."

"It always feels like that after you've sat an exam – especially when it's something like history. You can always think afterwards of things you didn't put."

"Or different ways of saying it. Like, there was this question about the abolition of slavery in the nineteenth century. It wasn't just straightforward, like: 'Explain or describe the progress of the anti-slavery movement in Britain or America in the early nineteenth century'. Nothing so easy. It went: 'Compare and contrast the attitudes to slavery in Britain and its former colonies in the United States. Did the actions of the British reformers have any impact on the political opinions in Washington DC? Give examples to illustrate your answer'. I mean, you need a lot more background stuff to answer that."

"Which you didn't know."

"Obviously."

"So what did you do?"

"Guessed. Made it up. Blagged it."

"Did they?"

"Did they what?"

"Did the British reformers have an impact on Washington DC?"

"I said they did – a bit. Both countries passed a law abolishing the transatlantic trade in the same year, 1807. But we didn't get on very well – the British and the Americans we still hadn't got over the war of independence in 1776. In 1812 we were at war again, and in 1814 a British contingent occupied Washington DC and set fire to the White House and the Capitol, so the Americans weren't predisposed to think much of us. After all that, I guess the slavery question in America was more of an internal affair than international—"

"Woah… So, right. You know a lot more than you're letting on. Look it up – check it out."

"I will… History's so hard. It's much easier for those doing maths. They always know whether they have got it right or not."

"Well, I don't… not even at GCSE level. And, as for English, it's, like, a steep learning curve."

"You had no English at all two years ago. I think it's brilliant that you're sitting GCSE English next year – you're better than most of us natives."

"Hardly."

"I mean it. And all that Old English is not easy."

"I know, but you like Shakespeare and I want to learn him too."

Abby laughed. She was feeling better. Bandi was always so good at cheering her up. Always ready with a Shakespearian quote that seemed to fit, she declaimed, *"'Here let us breathe and haply institute a course of learning and ingenious studies.' The Taming of the Shrew*, Act One, Scene 1."

Bandi was ready for her. "Aye, let us so commit ourselves, 'ere the year is fled."

"Wow! I don't know that one. Where's that from?"

"The Comedy of Bandi, Act One, Scene Two." Bandi laughed, amazed that he had so easily taken his girlfriend in.

Abby pushed herself away. "But you can't make them up in a proper essay or exam." Abby was annoyed with herself that she had fallen for it.

"I know… I just wanted to make you laugh – cheer you up," continued Bandi. Abby relaxed. She didn't really mind that Bandi was clever.

"I am so glad I met you, Abby – and your dad. Being here is really good. I couldn't have done any of this on Joh."

"I never thought boring old Persham was that special – but you have helped me see it with fresh eyes. I'm glad I met you, too. I'm starving."

"Your mum said she'll be late and not to wait for her… No idea when your dad will be in."

"He's taken a group of teenagers to the swimming pool. I guess he will eat with them in the centre before he goes on to his meeting with his school governors. He won't be home until later."

"It's mad having a priest as a father. You never know when you'll see him."

"It's much better now he's a diocesan youth chaplain than when he was in a parish," said Abby firmly. "At least we get the house to ourselves. And he gets proper time off when he's away from the YAC."

"And we get to do stuff there all the time… It's going to be a great summer," said Bandi. "How many kids are lucky enough to have their parents working at a youth activities centre?"

"Four in Persham – me and Dad's assistant Mark's three. Five if we count you… and I'm starving. I'm going to see what's in the fridge."

"And I'm going to get back to this statistics stuff. The exam's next week… Tell me when you're ready to eat."

"Yes, master."

"Shut up."

"You really are learning English, aren't you. That's—"

"You find food and let me study."

Unlike the rest of the family, Bandi and Abby didn't have to wait for a white gate to appear – one stood permanently in the garden of the house the Church of England had purchased for Abby's dad, Dave, ever since they had left the rectory at St Chad's and he took up the job as director at the YAC. This house was more convenient for Longmead Sixth Form College, and the whole family were definitely happier since the move. Abby and her mum, Lynn, together with Bandi, mostly went to help Dave when he was leading worship at the centre on a Sunday. Now the summer weather had begun, it was very busy with groups coming from far and wide for weekends and the spring bank holidays. Primary schools used the centre during the week when Dave took the children for walks in the woods on nature rambles. Abby and Bandi sometimes joined them as a break between studies.

★ ★ ★

Two weeks passed and the atmosphere in the house changed from one of nervous tension to summer joy. Bandi bounced through the door.

"Finished!" he yelled. "That's the last exam and I've got a hundred per cent."

"How're you so sure?" asked Abby.

"I'm not. I won't have all of one hundred per cent but there's nothing wrong with positive thinking. *'Merrily, Merrily shall I live now, Under the blossom that hangs on the bough.'* I haven't made that one up. I quoted it."

"*The Tempest*," said Abby.

"*The Tempest*?!"

"Yeah."

"Oh… And I've just put it down for *Midsummer Night's Dream*." They both laughed. "Ninety-nine per cent, then."

"I guess you will want to get back to see your family, now that you're free," said Abby thoughtfully after they had stopped giggling.

"Yeah. We haven't been for days, with the exams and everything. They will be expecting me… You know, it doesn't seem so far away with the gate… but when you can't just call them…"

"I know. But you can just, like, drop in."

"Yeah – but that takes time. It's not as easy as texting. Tomorrow. Let's go tomorrow."

"Yes. After breakfast."

★ ★ ★

"Wow, what happened here?" said Bandi open-mouthed at all the get-well cards around the White Gates Cottage living room.

"You should have seen it here last week," said Matilda, dryly. "It was like a flower shop."

"What's with the pot, Shaun? Bad tackle?"

Jalli summarised the events since Shaun's return. Shaun appeared to be doing well, she said. He seemed fine in himself, getting better each day. But Kakko was taking more time to get back to being her confident self. Kakko gave her mother a withering look.

Shaun took up the tale. He dug his sister in the side with his crutch. "It was me who gave my loving but weighty sister a soft landing... I saved her."

"If it makes you feel better, I'll admit you probably did," said Kakko quietly. "But less of the 'weighty', thank you."

"Wow, sis. It was serious, then?" said Bandi more quietly.

"Yep... and then when we got back here, someone had a go at us for being aliens," added Kakko. "Said we didn't deserve free hospital treatment."

"Oh, not that again," said Bandi irritated. "They're just jealous."

"Said we're abusing the health service getting injured on other planets."

"That wasn't nice," said Abby. "This is your home and, anyway, I thought you paid some kind of state insurance?"

"We have been since the moment they were born," answered Jack. "We've paid in more than we've had back, that's for sure."

"They accused us of getting John and Dah treated for free. But we didn't. Dad paid a bill straightaway," continued Kakko.

"So," smiled Shaun, "because of the fuss, everyone knew about us and hundreds of people have sent cards and presents."

"Hundreds?" said Bandi. "You mean literally."

"Two hundred and fifty-eight cards, twenty-two letters and fifteen bunches of flowers... oh, and ten boxes of sweets and biscuits, and counting. We're trying to reply to them all."

"Wow!" said Bandi, still amazed.

"There are things from people we don't even know because they are disgusted at the whingers," explained Jalli.

"And Shaun has lots of football fans, too," said Jack. "So all in all…

"He had to come home because the hospital couldn't put up with it," said Kakko.

"What about Wennai?" asked Bandi.

"What about her? She came to the hospital with her brother Aril and Gollip," said Shaun, casually.

"One of the first – before the hospital stopped people just rocking up," said Kakko.

"Gollip? Oh, the centre forward… Wasn't he dating Wennai?"

"Yeah. Why's it so important?" asked Shaun, as casually as he could.

"You know why," said Kakko, crossly.

"You really like her, don't you?" Bandi gave him a knowing smile. "She's good for you."

"Is she? She's a friend, that's all."

"So tell us about what *you've* been getting up to, Bandi," asked Jalli, changing the subject.

"Oh, nothing… just revision and exams… and the occasional visit to the YAC."

"Have you passed the exams?" asked Matilda.

"Don't know yet. We have six weeks to wait for Abby and seven for me."

"But they went OK?" asked Matilda.

"Tell you when we get the results."

"You're all the same," sighed their grandmother. "No-one wants to tell anyone what's in their hearts these days."

"I understand," said Jack. "It's not right to ask them to speculate... When I was sitting exams I didn't want to talk about them. I was dreading the results."

"You were positively rude," said his mother. "I had to nag just to get you to admit you actually sat them... You did well, though."

"I *did*... amazingly... but I don't think these people want to talk about exams."

"No," agreed Abby. "We'll know soon enough... I just can't get over everything you've been through here."

"And Shaun, Kakko and Tam haven't told us all about that last adventure, either," complained Matilda.

"Some things are best not gone over," said Jalli cheerfully. "But we're all together now. Cheerful subjects only allowed... and it's time for tea."

"Hurray!" shouted Yeka, who had been playing quietly in the corner with her dolls. Bandi had been gone so long that she was not going to forgive him for deserting her that easily. But now she sidled over to him and put her arms around his knees, before climbing onto his lap.

Bandi kissed her. "I'm sure you've grown since I last saw you."

"Yes," she said.

Tea was Bandi's favourite beans. Then it was Yeka's bath and bedtime which involved about half a dozen people. Everyone had to say goodnight and Bandi and Abby had to go to the bedroom and read stories.

5

The following day, Kakko arrived at the spacedrome to find it abuzz with excitement. A tiny, unknown space vehicle was approaching the planet at some speed. What was it? Where was it from? And, more to the point, was it on a collision course with Joh? Assessments indicated that even if it was, and even if it contained fissionable material, it would not prove a hazard to the populace. But it would be disastrous for the craft, as it would almost certainly burn up in the atmosphere.

The JOT – the Joh Optical Telescope – showed it to be no bigger than a small bus with extending solar panels correctly orientated towards Daan. It clearly possessed functional positioning engines.

The whole staff at the spacedrome were gathered around their monitors which displayed the optical images plus a data stream. The tower was busy with communicating course suggestions to the craft and trying to get reciprocal contact. But there was no response.

"If they don't do something quickly," said Kakko's boss, Prof Rob, almost under his breath, "this is not going to be pretty."

"Could it be hostile?" asked Kakko.

"We can't be sure but I can't see what anyone would gain by sending an isolated tiny vehicle straight at us."

"Plague?" suggested Kakko.

"You've been reading too much sci-fi," smiled Rob. "You tell me a virus of any description that can survive 2,000 degrees centigrade which is what they'll encounter even if they hit us at a glance— Ah, it's changing course... Look."

As they watched, the craft veered... two... then three degrees to starboard. The read-out indicated that at the new course it should miss the planet.

"Are they attempting a slingshot, I wonder?" muttered Prof Rob, thinking aloud. "Ah, no. There is a forward burn. They're slowing down. Now they will take the atmosphere at the correct angle and speed... Clever."

"So, not 2,000 degrees – a virus would survive."

"We have to be prepared – but let's not be too hasty to assume we're all doomed," said Rob, half to himself.

"The tower still hasn't made contact," observed Kakko. "They are not acknowledging our signals on a wide radio spectrum... They must be aware by now that the planet is populated."

"You're making two assumptions," replied the scientist. "The first is that it is equipped with the right kind of 'eyes' and 'ears' to detect us and the second is that they recognise a need to reply. They might simply not be interested in us."

"That's pretty rude of them," said Kakko with a hint of sarcasm.

"Now you're assuming the craft contains sentient beings with a moral compass like the one you were brought up with..."

"Sorry," said Kakko, "it wasn't meant to be serious." Once again her mouth had preceded her brain. She tried again. "Their 'eyes' and 'ears' might not be based on electromagnetic waves of *any* frequency. They could be using some advanced technology – quantum transparency, for example, that we are only just experimenting with."

"Now you're talking. But I think the probability is that a craft as small as this is merely a probe that is not equipped or programmed to respond to incoming— Ah! There. There we go. A signal."

"On an extremely long frequency," observed Kakko. "Those waves could travel great distances but we're well within standard radio wave communication distance."

The signal turned out to be an echo of one that they had dispatched when the craft was first detected a week before. "There's your answer," said the professor. "They are simply transmitting data from us back to us. It's a probe. We are probably capturing what are meant to be transmissions back to its home planet."

Ten minutes later the atmosphere in the room changed again. The craft was now in interior spectral-scanning distance, and the read-outs were reporting hydrogen, carbon and oxygen consistent with carbon-based life.

The probe manoeuvred into a high but slowly decaying orbit. The spacedrome computers calculated that it would take four orbits of the planet before it was in a position to enter the atmosphere, and land right outside! So it had been reading the beams all along.

Sirens sounded in the suburbs bordering the spacedrome and a speedy evacuation was underway. This was the standard practice for the arrival of an unknown ship which they couldn't guarantee would lock safely onto the automatic landing beam. It was standard practice but had never been actually employed before. The news was all over the news screens in every home. The excitement across the city, and indeed the whole planet, was high.

"What do you think it wants here?" asked Kakko, echoing what was in the minds and on the lips of all the residents of Joh.

"A craft of that size, at the speed it is travelling, could have been in outer space for decades," suggested Prof Rob. "It is far too small to possess a drive of any description. No, that craft was travelling at the velocity it last left its own system... I think they are simply coming here for a spot of R&R."

"How could a carbon-based life form live long enough to complete such a voyage?" wondered Kakko.

"That is what we are about to find out."

The team watched patiently for a further five hours, then the craft retracted its solar panels neatly into casings on each side, turned its back on the planet and safely entered the atmosphere, heat shield first. As the entry burn ceased, it extended a pair of flight wings, banked and lined up with the spacedrome runway. The craft had automatically activated the EMLS, the electromagnetic landing system, and was now in the beam. A second siren in the centre sounded a warning that everyone was to abandon the centre buildings and congregate in several predetermined places beyond the perimeter. Kakko and Prof Rob and the people from their department hadn't even got as far as the perimeter gate before they were recalled. It was going to land using magnets of alternating poles that served both to arrest and suspend the craft above the tarmac until it came to rest.

"That makes the craft one of a recent spec," commented Kakko. "The full EMLS was only installed last year."

"And, up to now, used only once," added her boss.

"How do they know we have the system?"

"They may not necessarily," said Rob. "It could just be artificially intelligent enough to decipher our signals and respond. It may be that this craft has come here by mistake."

Its descent was now being controlled entirely from the computer in the tower. All breathed again. Kakko, Prof Rob and their team stood and watched from outside as the craft appeared in the west and descended at the correct speed to make a perfect landing.

That was the beginning of the adventure. Kakko later reported that the next stage felt like getting a wrapped present that you could not guess the nature of. She had been to some surprising places through the white gates – but this was different; this adventure had come to *them*. On this occasion, they were the recipients in their own world; they were the visited. What could this mean?

The craft, measuring no more than ten metres by four, sat silently three-quarters of the way down the runway. The ground crew sent three vehicles to surround the visitors and a fourth immigration team zoomed out with an inflatable immigration bubble that was big enough for a shuttle twice the size – they didn't possess anything smaller. The bubble was quickly deployed and the immigration team, wearing BIGs – biological isolation garments – entered it and began to examine the outside of the craft. A hatch was discovered above the starboard solar panel retraction pod. It was locked shut; there did not appear to be any conscious life within.

Kakko and her team were now back inside the building and following the proceedings from their monitors. Etched into the heatproof glass of the hatch window, the immigration team noticed some emergency opening diagrams. The spacedrome commander eventually issued the order to attempt to open the hatch. However, it was decided to drill through the hatch to minimise the impact of anything undesirable inside. It took what seemed like an hour but was probably only a quarter of that time. Trans-metal scanners detected a mixture of oxygen and nitrogen. Eventually the hatch was breached – with a slight hiss as air leaked into the craft. The internal gases had been under a pressure just slightly below that on the surface of Planet Joh. The leading immigration officer peered inside with a chemi-camera probe. The readings indicating the chemical composition of the interior atmospheric suspensions were transmitted directly to the lab. Kakko's screen revealed pictures of what looked like two chests with glass or transparent plastic covers.

"It's pretty humid," commented the professor. "This at least 'smells' biological."

"There isn't anything moving," observed Kakko. "Not that I can see."

"Those chests are probably cryogenic chambers," said Rob.

"Deep freezers to keep people in a state of hibernation for long-distance space travel?"

"Correct."

"So there might be someone still alive in there?"

"Maybe. But that craft has been travelling a longer time than any known successful cryogenic suspension. The longest we've ever come across is ten years – and even then the results were pretty negative."

"Yeah. If I remember rightly they died just weeks after they woke up and they were in constant pain all the time they were conscious."

"Which was mercifully short. We know of no-one who has yet mastered the technique for long-term success. The makers of this craft, however, may have known how to do it. Let's wait and watch… We shall soon see what the chambers contain, if anything…"

The immigration crew were now inside and lifting the lids of the caskets. First one, then the other. One contained an all-in-one suit for a four-limbed being; the other was empty.

★ ★ ★

"It knew to come here," observed Kakko to her family gathered that evening. Speculation on Joh was rife. There was unrest in one part of the city where the rumour was circulating that the craft had been sent to infect them all with some kind of virus in advance of an invasion. "But the craft contains no DNA. There is no risk to anyone. You heard the director on the news," remonstrated Kakko.

"There's always someone suspecting a cover-up," said Jalli. "You can be as transparent as you possibly can be but some people are naturally distrusting and suspicious–"

"And some just want to make trouble," broke in Kakko.

"This used to be a very open society," sighed Jack. "I am disappointed by the apparently increasing intolerance."

"They're scared of immigration from elsewhere," said Shaun. "Joh has been isolated for centuries – but recent improvements in space travel, and the interplanetary co-operation in the development of the fourth generation of the intrahelical drive – not to mention our white gates – have made them feel it is only a matter of time before the whole universe gets here."

"That's silly," said Kakko. "If anyone comes, it will be in very small numbers. At least in our generation."

"Agreed," said Shaun, "but when the Sponrons came with the prospect of a permanent Sponron population with those young refugees, it was quite a wake-up call for some."

"But they didn't stay!" said Kakko. "We took them back – through a white gate."

"But all that proves is that the old barrier of distance no longer exists," sighed Jalli. "The moat of outer space no longer works. I've definitely noticed a change in attitudes since the gates became active again, with all of us coming and going so often… and bringing others in."

"Who? You mean Abby?!" Kakko threw her arms in the air. "Abby hardly represents an invasion! Why do people have to be so thick?"

"It's only a few," said Shaun. "Anyway, some people, like Pastor Ruk, think that the planet needs some immigration – new blood, new ideas… He'd love the opportunity to meet people from other parts of the universe. He believes he's a 'citizen of heaven', in temporary residence on this planet, and that all self-aware beings, wherever in the universe they live, are citizens of heaven – and are his brothers and sisters."

"I agree with him," came in Bandi, who up to this time had just been listening quietly. "Those Sponrons were definitely 'citizens of heaven'."

"I'd like to think so but how do you know that?" asked Kakko. "How can you be sure?"

"Because they knew love. There are three things that are above all constructs of sentient beings—"

"Constructs?"

"Yes. Things like culture and other human 'baggage' – language, conventions – human stuff that we, or any sentient life form, invent."

"I get it. Like 'red' means 'stop' and 'green' means 'go', and which side of the road we drive on."

"Right," said Bandi. "And the words we use, too. Those things change from place to place depending on the local conventions."

"But some things are not invented, like two plus two equals four."

"Exactly. There are three things that are common everywhere in the universe: mathematics, the laws of nature, and love."

"And love is from heaven. God is love," Kakko stated emphatically.

"If you have faith."

Kakko looked at him. She was confused. Where did the 'if' come in?

Bandi had got into his philosophical stride. "Love exists. That is a *fact*. Then it is *faith* that tells us that it comes straight from God. God is love."

"So faith is a human construct?"

"In one way, yes. In another, no."

"Explain," said Kakko with a sigh. She was struggling with this.

"OK. You can't *prove* the existence of God. God could be just a figment of our imagination. But wherever you go, people seem to share the same idea about a Creator who cares about us…"

"But God doesn't wait for us to invent Her," protested Kakko. "She lets you know She's there! I don't make her up."

"That's the point. That's what I was going to say. Everyone that believes, claims that the Creator makes Herself, or Himself, known to them – reveals Herself. And it is the same wherever you go in the universe. When believers of different faiths talk together, some of them quickly realise that they have all encountered the same divine Person, whatever Name they call Her or Him by."

"So the Sponrons are one with God, even though they don't keep to the Johian Scriptures?"

"Of course. They have their own faith. You remember Abby had a run-in with the churches in Persham?"

"Yes," said Jack. "How could we forget? It makes me ashamed to be from Persham. It's not the kind of impression I got when I was there when I was young."

"They were there then, Dad. You were just lucky you didn't meet them…" said Bandi. "Anyway, she came out of that believing firmly that God includes everyone in His Kingdom as long as they call upon Him, by whatever Name they know, according to their own lights, Scriptures or traditions."

"She and Ruk are of the same mind," said Jalli. "We'll have to see they get a proper opportunity to talk together sometime."

6

Various teams worked around the clock on analysing all the data from the alien space vehicle. It was quickly ascertained that it was of no known type among the local planets in Joh's group and that there was no biological hazard. The vehicle had indeed once contained at least one living being – all the constituent elements were present in the right proportions for carbon-based life - but there was nothing left beyond the simplest of molecules. The beings had completely decomposed.

"Nothing but carbon dust, water molecules and traces of heavier elements," explained Kakko to her brothers. "We know a lot about them from the non-organic suit we found – size, body mass… they were a bit like us - as well as the technology in the craft."

"How did it know to come here?" asked Bandi.

"It was programmed to go into hibernation until it came within range of a star, when it would deploy its solar panels and 'wake up'. Then it simply scanned the system, found a habitable planet and homed in on it – automatically."

"But the crew had woken up too early?"

"Prof Rob knows something about cryogenics. He says, using current science, it can only work well for a few years. After that it gets risky. The temperature inside the craft would not have been more than a few degrees above absolute zero for much of their journey… Prof Rob thinks they were dead before that, otherwise the bodies would have frozen without decomposition…"

"Do we know where it came from?"

"This is the most interesting bit. Prof Unt from the maths end of things is going to be interviewed on TV tonight. Basically, they have extrapolated from the data of the craft's course and speed, when we first picked it up, that it must have come from somewhere very far away indeed. There is no known habitable planet within fifty light years in the region of space from which it came. The most likely possibility is Gax sigma, a yellow star not unlike Daan, fifty-five light years away. The star has just one exoplanet in the Goldilocks zone. But looking at the carbon isotopes that help with dating, there appears to be hardly any carbon fourteen at all – which means many, many thousands of years. The craft could be hundreds of thousands of years old and come from anywhere in that part of the sky."

"Outside of the galaxy?"

"Maybe."

"So it could be from Mum's planet," observed Bandi.

"No-o. You're kidding me? This craft comes from somewhere tens, perhaps hundreds, of thousands of years ago. The Raikans haven't even developed space travel yet. And anyway, Andromeda is not in that part of the sky."

"So what you're saying," said Shaun, "is that this craft represents the work of people who lived many years before us but possessed the ability to fly in space…"

"And have even learned to respond to a state-of-the-art electromagnetic landing system," smiled Kakko. "Technologically they were more advanced than us in their development of artificial intelligence. Their computer has continued to learn all the time it took to get to us – although it has had to be shut down most of the time."

★ ★ ★

59

Like the rest of the planet, the Rarga-Smith family were clustered around their TV sets as Prof Unt and a couple of other scientists were being interviewed.

"So, you have concluded that the craft is no threat to us," said the interviewer towards the end of the broadcast.

"Definitely not. As I have said," reiterated the professor, "we can say with certainty, from the condition of the craft and its possible occupants, that it left its home planet at least 50,000 years ago. The carbon fourteen would register anything less. We know its speed – it would have been constant as it has no independent drive. It only possesses attitude engines and a forward-arresting motor with sufficient fuel for landing. Looking back along the path it must have taken, and that the nearest possible star is fifty-five light years away, I would estimate that this craft has been in space for a minimum of a million years."

There was a moment's silence as the interviewer took in this piece of information. "So this, then, is definitely the oldest man-made object we know about?"

"Not *man*-made. This craft was made by a biological intelligent being with four limbs and the size of a human being, but they weren't human. The craft began its journey when the precursors of human beings were still simple life forms living in the seas of Planet Earth One."

"Amazing... What will happen to this craft? What do we propose to do with it?"

"This is still yet to be decided," said one of the other scientists, "but, in my opinion, it should be preserved in a transparent walled vacuum chamber as it is, in its own building where all can come and see it for the next million years."

"A special museum?"

"Precisely..."

"Wow, the oldest known intelligent beings," said Bandi.

"Pity they didn't perfect the cryogenic chamber – I would love to have met them."

"I'm not so sure. I reckon they would be quite unhappy waking up a million years in the future having missed the place they were heading for and finding themselves in a relatively backward world," said Kakko, with as philosophical an air as she could muster.

"If they are citizens of heaven," said Shaun, "one day, Bandi, you may get to ask them."

"You never know. It'll be pretty crowded there… in heaven," replied Bandi.

"But I reckon you'll get to meet anyone you want to," put in Jalli wisely. "Otherwise it would be a limited place and heaven is by definition not limited, any more than the depth of love is."

"Amen to that!" said Kakko.

★ ★ ★

The conversation concerning the long-term home of the craft hadn't got very far before a second craft was seen coming from the same direction. The mood among the populace was now definitely one of alarm. Was this the beginning of an invasion? Were they all going to be as innocuous as the first craft appeared to be? Already there were completely unjustified claims of biological pollution, of the first craft calling others in in some kind of way, and other bizarre ideas. An impromptu demonstration formed outside the president's offices demanding this second craft be met with force. They were calling on the government to institute a defence capability and arm the space vessels they possessed. One of their most vociferous spokespersons was Kris Salma, the man who had made Jalli's life a misery the previous year at her agricultural college – the man who had got himself dismissed for his racist comments. He paraded a banner: No Aliens on Joh.

The government sought to reassure the people. The craft that had already landed was not armed in any way. It had been carefully screened for any alien biological elements and contained no chemical substances not already abundant on Joh.

They were also adamant that no weapons would be manufactured; history of other worlds indicated that in every place where weapons had been made, they were always used – used against people of the same planet. Joh had so far been spared any internecine violence – but the existence of arms would be tempting fate.

"The greatest danger that these craft pose," said Prof Rob, "is that which sets us against ourselves."

As the craft drew nearer, it was identified as identical to the first. It made the same manoeuvres as its sister, moving into orbit ready to land.

But then things seemed to go wrong. It appeared to lose confidence in the automatic system and pulled out, then readjusted to resume a semblance of the correct course. The engineers in the Joh control room strove to regain control but the signals from the craft's computers were confusing.

"What's it playing at?" demanded the senior engineer. "Get that control back or we'll burn up."

But the craft continued its descent under its own command. A last-minute correction on its part avoided annihilation and then it was within a single degree from bouncing off the atmosphere and out of orbit altogether. Eventually it got it right.

"It's coming in… It'll make it!" declared a technician, with relief.

"But where?" asked Rob. "It might survive the atmosphere but the ground is pretty hard."

"It's on track for our runway... but it's on its own. It is not locked into the EMLS. It's going to take a hell of a pilot to land that thing accurately."

"Do you think it's under pilot control?" asked Prof Rob.

"It's not being landed by computer – I'm sure of it."

"How long to touchdown?" called the station commander who was standing peering over the shoulders of her technicians in the control room.

"One hour, twenty minutes."

"Sound the alarm. I want everyone living around this place at least a mile away – and not up or down the flight path!" she barked into a headphone. "That includes all but level five in this office, too. Your job is done."

People rose from their stations and moved toward the door. Kakko hesitated. The commander eyed her. "Are you level five, Kakko?"

"No, ma'am."

"Then out... now."

"Yes, ma'am." She rose and headed for the door but not before she received a wink from the commander.

Kakko, Prof Rob and the drome staff who were not needed at this stage watched and prayed as the craft approached. It was making a good fist of things but, as the technician had guessed, it looked as if someone was trying really hard to control the craft in an unusual environment. Unlike its predecessor, this craft deployed its wings rather later and had, yet again, to readjust its approach. In the end it was the speed that did for it. The touchdown was on the runway but without the EMLS there was no magnetic arresting and the craft hurtled on beyond its sister ship off the end of the tarmac, through the perimeter fence, across a ploughed field and into a ditch and its associated hedge a hundred metres beyond the buildings.

Fire engines followed the line across the field as best they could but the mangled craft didn't seem inclined to burn.

Eventually the biological isolation tent was deployed with some difficulty. Water was being pumped out of the ditch for fear of pollution. Red hazard lights were flashing in all directions.

This time the reception crew knew how to get inside the craft. They inserted their probe and found two creatures in flexible suits strapped onto a kind of plate and humped over a console. They were not human but they did appear to have four limbs and a torso with a head end. No neck. They showed no signs of life. But if they were dead, they had died very recently.

It was quickly ascertained that they were not dead. The impact, however, would have taken its toll on any variety of flesh and blood – if that was the way their bodies worked.

A makeshift tent was set up in the field and the bodies carefully brought out and laid out on trolleys. Like humans, they were kept rigid by some kind of internal skeleton. Doctors were sent for but as soon as they saw their patients they recommended the attendance of a veterinary surgeon. They found one in Jalli's agricultural college. The staff and students had all been outside watching the craft land. Jalli had her hand to her mouth – after all of Kakko's traumatic scrapes it would be just like her to get killed right there on Planet Joh. But as Kakko was vacating the scene she had rung her mother. And then again afterwards to say she was safe. Jalli was grateful that her girl was at last thinking about what it feels like to be an anxious parent. If nothing else, her experience with Tam's people had taught her that.

Jalli and the staff learned that the vet was required to advise on the treatment of the occupants of the craft long before it became public knowledge that there had been any. They were asked not to talk about it. In fact, Jalli knew before Kakko! A fact that did not go down too well when Kakko found out later.

Samples from swabs from the creatures' skin and from inside orifices at the head end were analysed at the scene but they failed to show any kind of bacteria at all. A doctor made the observation that in his opinion the creatures were far more at risk from the environment on Planet Joh, than Planet Joh was at risk from them. But the damage had already been done. The integrity of the craft had been breached by the impact before the hatch had been opened. The question was how and if they could restore the creatures to consciousness.

When Jalli and her family were reunited in White Gates Cottage that evening, Kakko was filling everyone in on the bits that were not on the news and correcting the bits that were that were not true. She was not privy to anything not in the public domain. Five hundred metres away from the spacedrome and a kilometre away from the crash, she had not seen the monitors in the control room or what was happening at the site. But she knew there was nothing to panic about. Rumours of a cover-up of facts circulated. People were talking about invasion, weapons, deadly microbes, poisonous gases; and accusations of a conspiracy were growing. Apparently there was a plot in which these aliens had been invited to Joh. Some expressed a theory that working on spacecraft and their engines was only part of what the professors at the spacedrome were up to – it was all a big cover-up for sinister goings-on.

"I don't know where people get all this rubbish from," said Kakko.

"People are frightened of things they don't understand," said Jack. "People have always been worried about what others might be getting up to. Sadly, on Earth, many people were quite right to be distrusting of their leaders. The further away you are from the action, the more suspicious you are… You're fortunate to be on the inside to some extent, Kakko."

"Yeah. That's true."

"And people are suspicious of anything to do with people from outside, including us," muttered Shaun. He was feeling despondent because he was going to have to visit outpatients the following day for a check on his leg, and the hospital was not his favourite place on the planet.

Kakko was trying to think of something to cheer him up when there was a knock on the door.

"I wonder who that can be," said Jalli.

"The thought police," suggested Shaun.

Jalli went to the door and came back with Dzeffanda Pinda from Wanulka.

"Look who it is!" exclaimed Jalli. "Come on in, Dzeffi. What brings you here?"

"A white gate, of course. I was so pleased when I saw it. I was on my way out to Parmanda Park."

Everyone stood and welcomed her.

"Tell us your news," enthused Jalli. "How did the project go?"

"Ah. Brilliant. Yeah… I did a project about some little beetles and I learned so much – mainly from watching them. I know exactly what they get up to. Now I go to the park and places and watch nature all the time – especially the little things that people mostly overlook."

"So a great success, then?"

"Yeah. I got a C+ which is good for me… I know you got As but I'm not so good with words. There was this other girl who studied some variety of songbird. She did loads of research in books and didn't do half as much as I did outside.

She got an A, though, because she's clever with words, and she can draw, too. You should have seen her project. The teacher said her presentation was perfect… He said nice things to me, too, but he said that I needed to 'organise my research better' and 'use proper sentences'… He went on about sentences having to have, like, a verb in them. He said a verb is a 'doing word' – but these beetles aren't doing stuff a lot of the time. Mostly they're sitting in the sun and waiting for other bugs to come by."

"Isn't that doing something?" wondered Kakko. "I mean 'waiting' is doing something."

Remarkable, thought Jalli *Kakko thinks waiting is doing something! That's worth remembering.*

"Yeah. I thought so. But the teacher said that 'waiting' is not a verb but a party something."

"A participle."

"Yeah. That was it. So my sentences were all wrong."

"But in real life that doesn't matter much," suggested Jack.

"Yeah. Right. So I've left school now and I'm going to work."

"Great," said Kakko. "What doing?"

"Sis, I have to tell you that that's not a sentence," said Shaun.

"You shush," snapped Kakko throwing a cushion at him.

"Ow!" said Shaun. "Don't throw things at me… I'm injured My sister broke my leg…" he teased.

"Yeah? What happened?" asked Dzeffi concerned.

Shaun and Kakko shared a moment of silence.

Shaun shrugged. "An accident – we were in the back of a truck and my dainty sister fell on me and I don't let her forget it."

"Siblings!" broke in Jalli quickly. "Do you have a brother or sister, Dzeffi?"

"No. Well, yes. A half-brother, but he is twelve years older than me and he doesn't live with us."

"Definitely not the same thing… So you are going out to work. What sort of job?"

"A care worker with old people… that is, when I get qualified. I have to have two references from people who I'm not related to whose old people I did things for to say they think it is worth me training."

"That seems harsh," said Kakko brusquely. "What if you don't know anyone? It's, like, you need experience to get a job but can't get the experience until you get a job."

"Yeah. Well, loads of people have done the training but it turned out they didn't like old people when they had done it, and it was a waste of time and money. They need to know that old people who don't belong to you aren't going to get up your nose."

"That makes sense," said Jalli. "Do you think you will like old people?"

"Yeah. Doing things for them is much better than working with children. You can talk to them and they don't make loads of noise."

"I like kids," said Kakko. "Better than old people. Old people go too slowly for me."

"I like the slowness," said Dzeffi. "They seem to like me, too."

"That's because you like them," said Jalli. "Just like Kakko likes children, and Bandi likes books. I think you may have found what you're good at. Old people don't mind if you can write or not and most of them are not interested in parts of speech. They want someone who watches over them and listens to them – like you do the beetles. I know what you mean about the 'doing words' not seeming to fit. You like the 'being words'."

"Yeah. That's right. Old folk don't *do* much but they are good at the *'being'* things."

Matilda looked up from her sewing and said, "If you can stay until tomorrow, me and Ada are going into a care home to see Sadie. I'm sure they will let you talk to a few people, and write you a letter of commendation."

"A commendation from another planet! That will work. You definitely won't be related to them," said Kakko with enthusiasm.

"No. But they'll probably think I've made it up."

"Maybe," said Jalli, "but I will give you a Wanulkan translation."

"But my mum will worry if I don't get back tonight."

"Of course, you must go back. Then tomorrow look and see if the white gate is still there for you. If it is, then you will know the Creator wants you to come back here."

"Yeah. Thanks. I must wait and see," she answered.

Kakko picked up the Wanulkan word for 'wait'. "*Spoolk! Spoolk*. I hate that word."

"It's a verb, Kakko. You said it yourself."

"I know. That doesn't mean I don't hate it. It reminds me of when Tam got— But let's not talk about that."

"Looking after old folk is not going to be your thing, Kakko," affirmed Matilda. "You carry on doing the hair-raising stuff. Leave the tender care to Dzeffi."

"You got it!" said Kakko with a high five that surprised Matilda so much that she pulled her needle off the end of the thread and dropped it.

★ ★ ★

It quickly became evident that the alien creatures were alive and breathing in some kind of way. When they removed some of the clothing, a small mouth that had been covered with a breathing mask was revealed. An air supply from tanks to the rear of the shuttle had been restricted in the crash but with their mouths uncovered the creatures began gulping in the fresh Johian air. To the doctors' and the vet's relief the basic signs were being restored. He ordered them to be cut out of the rest of their clothing and washed down with an antiseptic solution – although their skin did not appear to be damaged. The vet took close note of the anatomy he could see and feel from the outside. He spoke to a dictaphone as he went. He was pleased to see that the creatures appeared to be recovering and that the second gradually responded more and more as the examination proceeded.

"I believe these creatures are viable in our atmosphere," he declared. "And I don't think that they are severely injured. I suspect that they lost consciousness through partial asphyxiation but they appear to be responding." He called for thermal blankets and recommended they be moved into a permanent building as soon as possible.

Within an hour, the aliens were in a special isolation ward in the hospital, and within two hours they showed signs of regaining consciousness. The first to wake up was shocked to find himself outside of the craft he and his companion had lived in for many years, but was quick to ascertain they were being cared for. He turned towards his companion and studied her. He seemed satisfied that she, like him, was not seriously damaged. He tried to speak. The sounds were strange and guttural and not understandable. His sign language was not much clearer.

Then one of the doctors thought of Shaun. He had just come from the outpatients' department where he had been examining the progress of Shaun's broken leg, and he remembered the Smith family's ability to understand the

Sponrons, the previous alien species to pay a visit. He asked an orderly to see if Shaun was still in the hospital. She found him with Wennai in the refectory.

When the orderly returned with Shaun and Wennai, they were immediately detained by a severe-looking security officer.

"I've come because I've been sent for," explained Shaun. The orderly repeated the request she had received from the doctor. They were made to wait while the officer got clearance for them. A senior uniformed man appeared and began questioning Shaun and Wennai.

"It's his ability with languages," explained the orderly.

The important-looking officer snorted. "And what makes you so sure you will be able to understand our visitors?"

"I'm not. I suppose I was sent for because I can pick up a translation in my head when different languages from other planets are spoken… sometimes."

"And how often have you had contact with aliens from other planets?"

"Quite often. Through the white gates our family get given… We make no secret of it."

Shaun detected a personal disapproval. The man turned to Wennai in an officious manner. She confessed she had never been anywhere off the surface of Joh.

"I will authorise you." The officer almost spat the words. He didn't like people sending for people without his permission. These doctors thought they knew everything; but they didn't know anything about security. "The girl must remain here."

"Fine," said Shaun. "Thanks for coming to the hospital with me, Wennai. I'll text you later."

"She stays here until you return," stated the officer. "Then we will decide what is to be done with you both."

"You're *detaining* her?" said Shaun, getting cross.

"You will go with my officer. Do your translating... if you can. No more questions." A security guard led Shaun away into the isolation ward. Wennai was made to sit on a chair in the corridor. Shaun was angry but now was not the time to make a scene.

Inside the ward, the first thing he noticed was an odd smell. Then he was shown into the room where the two alien creatures were now fully conscious. They were conversing in low guttural sounds from a mouth at the top of an oval torso from which sprouted four even-lengthed limbs. For the most part they were bluish-green – but they didn't look particularly unhealthy. Shaun thought that a line of slits below the speaking mouth might be some kind of eyes.

"Hello," he tried. "I'm Shaun."

The couple instantly looked at him. He must be sounding intelligible.

"They have asked me if I can speak to you because you might be able to understand me."

"We can," said the creature on the left of his colleague. "You know our language?"

"No. It is complicated to explain but I have the ability to hear and speak in ways the Creator translates."

"Ah. You are His prophet?"

"No. Not exactly. Let me explain as best I can. Then you must let me tell these people where you're from and why you're here."

7

After a few minutes, during which the security officer grew increasingly impatient, Shaun was able to make some sense of things.

"They're telling me they come from a planet they call Zath, or something like that. They want to know where they are and how they came to be here."

"Tell them this is Planet Joh," said a scientist from the spacedrome before the uniformed man who had assumed command could answer. "Tell them they arrived on a small craft no bigger than a shuttle – you saw it. Tell them there was another that landed before them – but it bore no life…"

The uniform raised his hand but Shaun ignored it.

"You are on a planet called Joh. Do you understand me?" The Zathians grunted an affirmative. "You arrived – crash landed – in a small ship no bigger than a shuttle." The mouths and eyes showed expressions that Shaun began to interpret. They were not surprised to hear the description of their craft and clearly moved by the news of the other craft that bore no life.

"Our planet is in crisis," explained the male Zathian. "We know our sun is coming to the end of its life. It will soon explode into a red giant. Whatever happens to us, we know Zath will be utterly destroyed. Our forebears decided to try and preserve our race by building space vehicles to take some of us into outer space. They also developed a way to suspend life at super-cold temperatures while we were in hibernation. Over several years it has been tested and works well – but we have no idea how long the state can be endured."

"You've been frozen a long time?" asked Shaun.

"We have no idea – we have no point of reference. The idea was that when the sensors came within range of a solar system with a habitable planet, it would deploy the solar panels and reactivate the computers and defrost all biological life. It appears we have drifted until our computers detected your system and we were brought back to consciousness. You say there was a similar craft to ours that also landed?"

"Yes; your craft contained this." The scientist withdrew a metal plate from a clear polythene bag. "It is titanium. It seems to have markings on it of some kind. Does this mean anything to you?" Shaun translated.

The Zathians took the plate and held it so that the light revealed what appeared to be several squares of scratches. The female placed a digit that protruded from her left upper body on the plate and said, "It is a message. It has been put on metal to prevent it degenerating. It reads:

'I am writing this in the hope you will one day awake on a new planet. Your craft and five others have been equipped and dispatched with the programmes necessary for you to survive and revive as planned. We shall continue to equip and dispatch craft as planned until C-day.'

C-Day is Critical Day – the day when our world comes to a final end."

The Zathian continued to read.

'As you know there are twelve prepared people in the six craft in your batch. We are well aware that twelve is not sufficient

to provide a viable breeding colony. We have no expectations of preserving our race through you. It is the best we can do. Our hope is that you can make contact with other races and instruct them in the history and culture we treasure, then that which belongs to Zath will be passed on through them. Your computers contain digital facsimiles of the major treasures of our history. You have been selected for your understanding and appreciation for these treasures, including the priceless Divine Testament.

Brave adventurers, we wish you well and thank you for providing the only hope we have. May God bless you. Brill Peek, President of the Supreme Executive of the United Council. Anno 24790."

"Just twelve of us," sighed the male Zathian. "You say that there is another craft here. What of the people aboard?"

"It landed intact… but was empty of life, I'm afraid," answered the scientist with concern in his voice. "It contained the elements and compounds for life but they were completely without structure. We have analysed the carbon and can say that life came to an end at least 50,000 years ago… A standard year is 300 days here on Joh. It was probably more than that. It could be millions of years. We identified a star which we call Gax sigma but it is a yellow star. If your star has become a red giant, we have not identified one in the area of sky you came from; neither is there any record of a supernova occurring in that vicinity in the recent past."

Shaun repeated this so that his explanation could be translated.

The Zathians spent a moment in silence as they did some mental calculations. "That is when life ended on that craft?" asked the male.

"Yes, at least."

"But we do not know how long they were in cryogenic

suspension before the decomposition... That could have been even more millions of your standard years."

"Clearly," agreed the scientist. "You have been travelling a very, very long time."

"Travelling and travelling until we came into contact with another inhabited system..." reflected the female. "C-Day will have been so long ago that maybe many more civilisations will have come and gone around the galaxy in that time."

"Almost certainly," agreed the scientist. "We can trace our own species back to Planet Earth in the Sun system but that only makes us a few tens of thousands of years old... Your cryogenic suspension technology is incredible."

The female nodded slowly. "It seems so. We—"

Shaun was interrupted in his translation by the arrival of Prof Rob. He was carrying a metal plate similar to that in the hands of the Zathians from their wreckage.

He greeted Shaun, then acknowledged the Zathians and introduced himself. "I heard you had regained consciousness and were conversing through Shaun Smith... We have found this stowed in the intact vessel that landed before yours and thought you might like to see it... I see you already have a similar piece. From your own craft?"

His scientific colleague concurred. He went on to explain that they had learned it bore a letter from their president. "This looks like an exact copy."

The female took the plate from the first craft and turned it over in her digits. Unlike their own, the reverse contained scratchings too. These were light but distinct – lines and curves in square boxes.

"It recalls how our friends died," she said. "They were revived far from any visible system. They had provisions for only a short time. They spent that time trying to ascertain why the computer activated their revival in a hopeless place.

Shortly before their end they detected a faint trace of a large dark object that was travelling like them in outer space… But it was a long way off. They conclude by saying their computers had recorded no change of course which would inevitably have been the case if they came within the influence of such a body. They can offer no plausible reason why the system had revived them early. The last square indicates that, before their computers exhausted all power reserves, they were going to reset the system to bring down the craft when it reached a habitable planet. The craft would then be in suspension and they would die. They finish by saying that they rejoice in their confidence that they would be taken into the divine realms beyond all spacial dimensions, and wish any who encounter their craft in the future much joy."

As Shaun translated, the female caressed the engraving.

"What about the other craft?" asked the male. "The president seems to say that twelve of us were on the same course."

"We have not detected any more craft," said Rob. "Over so many years just the slightest thousandths of a degree of difference could mean other craft would miss our system entirely. The miracle is that two of you made a similar landfall."

"Can we find something for these people to wear?" asked Shaun. "Like us, I don't think they are comfortable naked."

"We don't have clothes for their shape," said the military officer, in a nonchalant tone.

"I have their measurements," smiled the scientist. "I'm sure something can be made."

"Thank you," said the Zathians. Shaun had begun to understand more than just language. "We are grateful."

"Thank you," said Shaun. The officer intervened. The chatting had gone on long enough. His instinct told him Shaun was not to be trusted, and was about to have him and

Wennai transported to his headquarters for questioning, when Prof Rob asked for his authorisation to do so.

"You are here to protect these aliens, not to arrest those whom we use to help us help them," he complained.

Reluctantly, the officer allowed Shaun to leave the room, collect Wennai and exit the hospital.

Outside in the street, Shaun was shaking. Wennai looked at him concerned.

"What's wrong, Shaun. Are these aliens frightening?"

"Frightening? Oh, no. They're lovely. Friendly... No, it's the security man who has disturbed me. I hate bossy men in uniforms. They think because they have official uniforms on, they can rule the universe." *Soldiers again...*

★ ★ ★

After a few weeks, the Zathians began to look increasingly well. Their blues and pinks were brighter and their eyes shone. Whatever the scientists had found to feed them on, it was good stuff for them.

Translation was not left to Shaun alone. It was soon discovered that Kakko had the same gift. Jalli too. Kakko was released from her duties in the spacedrome for a time each day to translate and teach the aliens the Johian language. They were remarkably adept at picking it up – especially the written script. Kakko asked about the squares with the lines and curves of the Zathian but she could not begin to fathom how it worked, and quickly abandoned it. This was much to Bandi's disappointment – he would have loved to have had a go but, being on Earth for much of the time, he didn't volunteer himself. Kakko's failure to grasp Zathian script gave her a lot of patience with them. She really respected them.

The question of what should happen to two complete

strangers with intellects as great as the most intelligent beings within contemporary Johian society was one that exercised the Johian authorities for a while. It was solved, however, by the Zathians themselves who understood the problem. It was one they had anticipated in their training in preparation for their cryogenic suspension. They wished to be housed in a place of learning where they could share their race's accumulated knowledge with a science team. Their computers contained a large amount of data which they were able to extract and present to the Johian Faculty of Science and Technology. Johian computer science was to benefit enormously, as was Kakko's space development department.

The Zathian knowledge extended far beyond that of science, however. Their understanding of Zathian personal interaction and culture was not one that could be readily translated into Johian everyday life but on some points there was a very close correlation. Pastor Ruk was keen to ask them about spiritual matters. After several days in their company, he recorded what they described as the indestructible spark of the divine in the created universe. It is revealed through pure love – the complete self-giving of an individual to his or her fellows out of the deepest respect and honour, a respect that arises with the detection of the signature of the Creator within them. In this love, there is no vestige of self-interest. This is only possible because of their profound trust in the divine love and the promise of amazing realms that lay beyond all physical order or created dimensions.

Sadly, however, in some parts of Johian society, the prevailing mood was one of fear rather than love. Opportunists who relished the opportunity to become leaders played on this. They were not willing to contemplate relinquishing any control or personal power, and preached a message of exclusion and hate. Pastor Ruk got a brick through his window after he preached a sermon on love as taught by the Zathians. "How can they do that?" despaired Kakko. "He talks of love and they hate him!"

"That kind of love is far bigger than their small world," explained Jack to his daughter. "They do not understand it. The other day at the school, I spoke to someone who is really scared of anything outside his immediate space. He was scared of going out at night."

"That was probably because he was blind," volunteered Kakko.

"No. He isn't blind. He might feel safer if he were. This man is scared to go out at night because of the stars; looking into space scares him. It is a vast unknown. He doesn't allow his family to go to space movies or read books with space in them. He only feels safe at night inside with his door shut."

"What about the loads of stuff you can't see because they're too small? I mean, he's shutting himself in with millions of microbes that are potentially far more hazardous than outer space."

"I know. I haven't dared to tell him that, though."

"And don't you go telling him that either, Kakko," intervened Jalli. "He'll blame us, the Sponrons and now the Zathians for introducing them."

"But that's ridiculous. Microbes are everywhere in the universe."

"That's correct. But he won't believe you."

"Your mother's right, Kakko. We are going to have to work very hard to overcome this climate of fear."

"Where will it all end?" sighed Kakko.

"Those who believe in love and inclusion are growing stronger, too," said Jalli. "A lot of people have responded and have written letters of support for Pastor Ruk. Some have asked him to organise the Zathians to teach their children."

"They're right, aren't they?" said Kakko. "About the indestructible spark, I mean."

"I have no doubt about it," said Jack, "if my experience and that of your mother is anything to go by."

"And Grandma; she knew she was going to God's realms. She knew she was going to meet your grandfather and your dad."

"She did," said Jalli firmly. "And so shall we all in due time. For now, all we have to do is keep loving."

"No matter what."

"No matter what."

8

It was July in Persham. Compared to other mothers she knew, Abby's mum, Lynn, was aware that she was more than lucky. The young man her daughter had brought into their house was both sensible and a gentleman. She was pleased they had both signed up to go with a group led by her husband to Taizé in France – they would enjoy it and she would enjoy the space for a few days.

Taizé, halfway between Paris and the Mediterranean, was in the middle of the French countryside. It was a community of religious brothers and sisters from a variety of Christian traditions that had begun being popular as a place of pilgrimage for young people in the 1960s. In the summer months, the community made large fields available for young people to camp in. They came from all over the planet.

Bandi was looking forward to travelling around a bit. He may have crossed interplanetary frontiers but he had seen very little of Planet Earth, even though he lived there. Kakko was the one who had been to three of its continents, and she told of places very different from Persham. The prospect of travelling down to Kent and then taking a boat to France was intriguing. On the strength of having a British father, Bandi had managed to obtain British citizenship, so getting a passport did not present a problem.

"You probably won't need it to get into France," explained

Dave, "but they generally like to see them when we get back…
I wouldn't want to see you stranded…"

"How's the transport working out?" asked Lynn.

"That's settled," said Dave. "I've procured the diocesan minibus."

"I'm glad after all that you went through to get licensed to drive it."

"It gets heavily booked in the summer but I got a cancellation. It means we don't have to hire anything. We've got just fourteen people signed up, so the list's closed."

★ ★ ★

Three weeks later, Bandi, Abby and a dozen others with Dave were on the ferry to France. They had arranged to stay overnight in a church hall in Normandy.

They pulled up to the place in the late afternoon and were greeted by an enthusiastic group of French young people who, with their parents, had laid on a sumptuous feast – something the French do so well.

"*Bienvenue en Normandie!*" they chanted.

"It's so good of you all to welcome us like this," said Dave, amazed. "We were just looking for an easy place to put up. We didn't expect a feast. Thank you so much."

"*De rien,*" replied the lady in charge. "No problem. Today you are our guests. In France we want to greet you well."

"You have indeed."

The young people were quickly getting to know one another. The French were quite excited to welcome a bunch of English strangers to their village.

"*Notre village,* it is very dull. We do not make the holidays until next week. You are all so beautiful," said a bonny French teenager in her best English but with a heavy French accent that Bandi was slowly getting used to.

"That is very kind of you to say so," he replied. "This is my first time in your country."

"*Il est ton copain? Si beau*," said the girl to Abby. "Your boyfriend? He is beautiful."

"Yes... *oui*," answered Abby hastily. "*Il est... mon copain*." She saw she was going to have to keep a watch on Bandi. He was clearly enjoying the attention.

The girl smiled and led them to a table.

"*Asseyez-vous*... You sit down."

When everyone was seated – the English all mixed up among their French hosts – the lady leader called on an elderly French priest to pray. He did so in a fashion difficult to follow but Abby picked up *nos amis anglais* – our English friends – and gathered he was praying for them as well as giving thanks for the food.

There were five courses, and wine too – watered for the children.

When the feast was over, Abby had a bit of a headache and was very tired. Whether it was down to the wine or trying to communicate in French, she couldn't decide. She had done very well in French at school but this was the first time she had had an opportunity to use it in France. There were so many words she didn't know, and remembering the grammar was hard when you weren't writing it. She heard herself make many mistakes – there must have been many more she didn't recognise. She was embarrassed. But Bandi was impressed.

"I made so many mistakes... and got stuck all the time."

"I was amazed at just how well you did. Did you notice that they gave up trying to talk in English to you? They spoke in English to me but French to you. They knew you understood them..."

"I suppose so…"

"You were brilliant. Just imagine how good you'll be after a week."

★ ★ ★

They all slept well and after a huge continental breakfast, they were back on the motorway. Nearing Paris, they pulled into a service station. Despite the croissants and *pains-au-chocolat* they had consumed in Normandy, they all piled enthusiastically into the burger place. They emerged three-quarters of an hour later happy and full.

"This is OK for a treat," Abby told Bandi. "You mustn't eat it all the time though – it'll give you a heart attack."

"I don't doubt it," agreed Bandi. "Where's the van?"

The group had all headed in what they thought was the right direction but there was no van.

"It was definitely here," said Bandi. Dave was looking perplexed.

"Someone's nicked it!" said Sharon without hesitation.

"Sharon, reluctantly I think I have to agree with you," said Dave sadly.

"What are we goin' a do?" lamented Sharon's friend Dawn. "They've got all our stuff!"

"Not all of it," said Dave. "That's why I told you all to bring your passports and valuables with you everywhere you go."

Abby nodded. "Yeah. At least we've got our purses and wallets. Are we going to report this to the—"

"I ain't got mine," burst in Sharon.

"You ain't… you *haven't* got your what?" asked Dave calmly.

"My passport. I left it in the bus."

"Sharon. After all I said—"

"You never said anything about passports – you said *valuables*."

"And that includes passports, Sharon. When you are abroad your passport is one of the most valuable things you own."

"You're going to have to stay in France for *ever!*" contributed Dawn helpfully.

"Shut up!" retaliated Sharon.

"OK, you two, let's be constructive," said Dave. "Let's take stock." They all checked on what they had got and what was left in the minibus. Apart from Sharon's passport, there was nothing that couldn't be replaced – the most valuable was the camping gear, and one of Sharon's best party dresses that she said cost a hundred quid, until Dawn pointed out that it had come from the Heart Foundation charity shop, which Sharon forcefully refuted.

The police responded remarkably quickly – they already had a presence at the service station. They took the details of the minibus and the names of the passengers.

"Does this happen often?" asked Dave.

"*Pas tous les jours, mais la plupart* – not every day, but most," said the officer.

"What's the chance of getting the bus back?" The officer raised his shoulders, opened his hands and extended his lip. Dave didn't feel reassured. He rang the insurance company in England who were very helpful. They arranged for them to be collected from the service station and taken to a van hire company in the nearby town. They wouldn't be able to take the replacement bus onto the ferry but at least it would get them to the port. They were to phone the insurance company again when they had docked.

"It's a good job the diocese has a decent insurance policy," said Dave on his mobile to Lynn. "We'll overnight here and drive directly to the port tomorrow. We'll get rooms in a motel…"

The group gathered round him, "Sorry, guys, it looks like we're not going to be able to get to Taizé after all."

★ ★ ★

The motel was strange but fun. There was no reception – you just got a ticket from a machine; a total contrast to the welcome that they had received in Normandy. It was a block of rooms with no internal corridor. Access to all the rooms was by external walkways which were exposed to a pretty strong wind.

"In a proper gale this could be positively dangerous," yelled Abby, battling along on the top floor. "It's like climbing to the top of a roller coaster, only on foot and without being tied down."

"Just hang on to the rail!" shouted Bandi. "On the corner it *could* become a gale." He was right. Two further doors, and at last they tumbled safely into their rooms. They could hear Sharon and Dawn bellowing to each other on the floor below them.

"What an adventure," laughed Abby. But their adventure had only just begun.

★ ★ ★

The next morning they did see a human being in the breakfast room on the ground floor. She didn't say much, though – just took their room numbers.

By half past seven they were on the road.

Getting through the town was tedious but Dave

eventually got them back onto the motorway and they were off. This bus had more power than their own; it was a pleasure to drive. They were in an outside lane making good progress when Sharon declared, "Ain't that our bus?"

They were passing a minibus that could well have been theirs. It was plain, though; there was no lettering on the side.

Dave throttled back and pulled in behind it. It had a German number plate and there was no cover on the spare wheel. But then Sharon, who seemed to be up on these things, pronounced that it was definitely theirs; she recognised a scrape on the bumper and a dent in the rear door.

"You might just be right," said Bandi. "It's exactly the same colour blue, and the roof rack's identical... and it's right-hand drive."

Dave pulled out to take a look at the side – the letters were missing but they could still make out the outline. It was their bus! He fell in behind again and asked Abby to phone the police. To be safe he allowed another vehicle between them; he was worried they might have drawn too much attention to themselves already.

They followed the bus for a further two junctions and when it left the motorway he decided to keep it in view. This wasn't easy through a town. Roundabouts and traffic lights intervened but, eventually, as they left the town, they spotted it turn down a narrow country lane. The lane was no more than a narrow track that wended its way through some fields. They saw the bus round a bend and disappear behind a copse. They couldn't follow it without being seen and Dave did not want to put the young people in danger, so he decided to park up, call the police and head back into the town.

"What're you waiting for?" yelled Sharon. "They're getting away."

"And when we catch them, what do you propose we do, Sharon? I do not fancy coming face to face with thieves. That's a job to leave to the police."

Sharon let out an audible sigh of disappointment. Some of the others felt let down too.

"This is boring," groaned Dawn.

"I feel sick!" announced Sharon all of a sudden. "Let me out!"

Before Dave could do anything, the girl was out of the back of the minibus and heading for some trees that lined the road. Others followed her – Dawn to look after Sharon and a boy called Wayne because he needed to.

It was then that the stolen bus reappeared – in a yard across a field on the other side of the hedge beyond the trees. The track had doubled back.

"There it is!" shouted Sharon, all traces of sickness leaving her. "It's in that yard… There's loads of other stuff there too. Do you reckon it's all pinched?"

"Sharon," ordered Dave, "come away from there. If you can see them, they can see you."

"Where? Show me," demanded Dawn, taking no heed of Dave's call.

Abby pushed herself through the undergrowth to take hold of the girls and force them back onto the road. But by this time teenagers were all over the place and keeping a low profile was an impossibility. Dave was so busy trying to regain control of the teenagers that he hadn't got round to ringing the police.

Eventually order was restored. Dave explained that, unfortunately, despite what happens in the films, thieves are not romantic characters. They were people who needed to be caught by surprise – by the *police* – and if they wanted their bus (and visit to Taizé) restored, they should all get back into the bus and wait. He took out his mobile to phone.

"*Donne-le-moi!*" a gruff voice spoke from behind Dave.

Dave turned to see a very rough-looking man with a shotgun, backed by four others armed with a collection of clubs and metal bars.

"S… Sorry," uttered Dave, pretending to wonder what all this was about. "What—"

"*Donne-le-moi… Le portable!*"

"Excuse me—" began Dave, but the man raised his shotgun and extended his hand. "*Portable!*"

"Give it to him, Dad," urged Abby.

Dave handed him the phone.

"*Et le reste.*" He gestured to his henchmen to collect all the phones from the party. Wayne's friend Darren pretended he didn't have one. But that was futile. No-one hears of a teenager without a mobile phone, no matter how ancient. The man manhandled him, feeling his pockets and extracted it. He looked at it, spat, dropped it on the ground and crunched it under his boot. As he did so, he said something in French that Abby couldn't understand – but the sense of the words was clear.

"*Qu'as tu vu?*" the man with the gun demanded of Sharon. "*Dis moi tout, pimbêche. Avoue.*"

"What? I ain't done nothing. What's he on about?" panicked Sharon, looking at Abby for support.

"I think he reckons you've seen something. He wants to know what you've seen."

"Me? I ain't seen nothing."

The man looked at Abby.

"*Elle dit qu'elle n'a rien vu,*" said Abby.

"*Des bobards! Ils ont trop vu,*" said the man who had destroyed Wayne's phone.

The leader nodded. "*Je pense qu'il est temps qu'ils disparaissent tous…*"

"*Où?*" asked the phone destroyer.

"*La cave. Enferme-les. Verrouille la porte…*"

"What are they talking about?" whispered Bandi.

"I think they are saying they want to shut us in a cellar," answered Abby.

"*Tais-toi!*" commanded the leader. "*Allons-y. Suivez mon ami.*" He addressed the young people with a snarl, brandishing his weapon. "*Vite.*"

Abby and Bandi took the lead behind the brigand. They were flanked by the rough-looking men, Dave drawing up the rear, followed by the man with the gun.

"*Les clés!*" he ordered, gesturing to the vehicle. "*Le minibus.*" Dave handed over the keys, and the leader tossed them to one of his colleagues. "*Amène-les à la ferme.*"

"What do we do?" Bandi asked Abby as they walked.

"It's better to do what we're told. We can't fight them. That thing's aimed at my dad." She nodded towards the man with the shotgun.

"Agreed. We'll wait for an opportunity… Never seen Sharon and Dawn acting so quiet…"

"*Boucle-la!*" barked one of the men, prodding Bandi with his metal bar.

They followed a footpath that led to the farmyard in which their minibus was parked. Dave hoped they could pass it without showing signs that they knew it but that wasn't possible with Sharon and Dawn in the party. Sharon couldn't help looking through a window to see if her bag with her passport was still under her seat. A man pulled her violently away.

"*Là bas, petite chipie.*" Sharon was clearly not popular. At that moment she wasn't popular with Dave either. He didn't know what a *chipie* was but it was clearly not meant to be polite.

They were ushered into a barn and down some steps, at the bottom of which was a heavy wooden door that opened into a cellar. The air smelt of some kind of fruity liquor – cider, perhaps old wine.

As soon as Dave was inside, the door was slammed shut. It was pitch black, except for a dim light coming from under the door. There didn't appear to be windows of any kind. Dawn began to cry.

"I hate the dark," she snivelled.

"Please be quiet," hissed Dave. "I want to listen."

Dawn's snivelling quietened. They listened as the last of the men reached the top of the stairs, then left the barn. They heard nothing more.

"Have they gone?" whispered Abby.

"I think so," said Dave. "Sorry, Dawn. I didn't mean to be cruel but we just had to make sure of our situation."

As their eyes became more accustomed to the dark, they could see a bit by the light that came under the door. There was a generous clearance. Sharon was cuddling Dawn. Dave checked around his group.

"All OK?"

"What about Wayne?" asked Darren, nonchalantly.

"What *about* Wayne?" replied Dave quizzically.

"Well, he's still out there, ain't he?"

In the drama of the situation, Dave hadn't missed him.

"Goodness… Where'd he go?"

"Into the bushes behind them trees. He went to—you know what… and he must have hidden behind the bushes."

"I think he sounds very wise to remain out of sight," said Bandi.

"Or shit scared," remarked Darren.

"Let's not use bad language, Darren – even if we're in a bad fix."

"Sorry… but I bet he is. On his own out there with them men with guns everywhere."

★ ★ ★

Wayne had indeed been both petrified and wise. He had gone a long way into the undergrowth from the group. He was keen to avoid the stares of the girls who were as keen to tease him about being seen, so he had kept going until he couldn't see anyone. When the men appeared and started to bark their orders, he had crept nearer so he could see what was happening without being seen himself. Spotting the gun, he was so scared he kept possibly the stillest he had been at any time in his life. He watched terrified as the group were marched off along the footpath. He winced when he saw Bandi jabbed by the man's bar; he thought he was about to hit him. Then one of the men got into the hired minibus and started it up. He reversed it, turned into the lane and drove away. Then all was still. After a few seconds, nature stirred again and the birds recommenced their singing. A single crow cawed and, apart from a robin protesting his proximity to her nest, he was alone. The air smelled sweet and clean.

Wayne felt a mixture of relief that he had avoided capture and panic at being on his own somewhere he didn't know – he had no idea where he was, other than in France. His first thought was to ring his parents. He pulled out his phone but his battery was flat. There had been only one plug for everyone in his room the previous evening and they hadn't all got round to charging their batteries.

Wayne crept to the edge of the undergrowth to watch the group as they entered the farmyard. He saw them pass their own minibus and then enter the barn. A minute or two later the captors reappeared. Some hung around the yard, most of them lit up cigarettes or, by the way they were smoking them, they could be spliffs. Wayne watched as they began arguing among themselves – some gesturing so wildly that Wayne thought they might start fighting. It was too far away to hear anything.

What Wayne needed more than anything was another person to whom he could explain what was happening. He returned to the road, which was quiet. He hadn't heard anything come along it since the minibus had been driven away. He tried to remember whether they had passed any houses as they'd approached the turning. The French countryside seemed to be sparsely populated – this bit at least. But he remembered the town through which they had passed several kilometres back. He would go that way.

It took him forty minutes before he came to a house. He approached it diffidently. There was a wide gate beside a letterbox. On the gate were the words *Chien méchant.* He thought this must be the name of the house... but there was a picture of a dog too, and somewhere Darren had come across the word *chien* and he remembered it meant dog. He could see another group of cottages further on, so decided to head for those instead. He didn't like the idea of a dog.

These next cottages had very short front gardens and looked more friendly. He found a knocker and rapped on the door of the first. It was opened by a short stocky woman.

"*Oui?*"

Wayne stood transfixed. He had tried to put together in his mind something in French, but spoken French had never been his forte. It was difficult enough understanding the French teacher – but actually saying stuff in French he found just impossible. He couldn't imagine how people like Abby did it. All he could think of at first was: "*Je voudrais une glace, s'il vous plaît,*" and "*Chez nous, il y a deux portes et huit fenêtres.*"

Desiring an ice cream and giving a vague description of his home in England would hardly get him anywhere. He could tell them his name and nationality. That might be useful.

"*Excusez moi…*" he began hesitantly.

"*Oui?… J'suis pressée,*" the woman hurried him.

Wayne began. "*Je m'appelle Wayne. J'habite en Angleterre.*"

The woman's expression softened.

"Yes. What is it that you do here, in France?"

Wayne breathed a sigh of relief. English!

"My group," he spluttered gesturing up the road. "A man with a gun has taken them away."

"A man with a 'gun'?"

"Yeah." Wayne mimed holding a gun.

"*Entre. Jean-Paul, il y a un garçon qui parle d'un homme avec une arme à feu…*" Turning back to Wayne she asked. "*Tu es seule?* You are alone?"

"No. I mean yes. Only me here. The rest…" Wayne gestured up the road.

"Your group… how many?"

"Fifteen… We're in… We *were* in a minibus… The men didn't see me."

Jean-Paul arrived. He was perhaps sixty – the same age as the woman and of the same deportment. All Wayne could think was that he looked French, with an open-necked shirt and loose trousers held up with braces. His English was not as good as his wife's.

They showed Wayne into a dark front room with heavy wooden furniture and brass ornaments. Wayne told his story as best he could, describing the place. The woman nodded.

"I know it. *Deux kilomètres* à *gauche – La ferme, Contraille…* The buildings were bought last year by a man *inconnu. Ils ne sont pas sociables.*"

It didn't take them long to contact the local gendarmerie. While they waited they plied Wayne with cake, an apple and Coke (*"Nous l'avons ici pour les petits-enfants* – we have for the grandchildren," she explained).

Meanwhile, in the cellar, Wayne's friends were not faring so well.

9

We have to have a plan," said Bandi quietly, after things went silent beyond the door. They could hear the men talking outside the building but their voices were indistinct. "We need to find a way of getting out of here."

"You're right," said Dave. They had come to terms with the initial shock. Even Dawn was more cheerful – cheerful enough to complain in turns that she was hungry and needed the loo.

"Wayne'll get us out," said Darren. "He'll go to the police."

"Let's hope so," said Dave. He couldn't imagine what Wayne was thinking right now. Pretty scared, he guessed.

At first they could hear the men arguing in the yard. Abby tried to listen to what they were saying but couldn't follow it. It wasn't easy to hear and the French was fast and colloquial. After about half an hour they heard the hired minibus start up. Then it went completely quiet. At least some of the men had gone somewhere in their new bus.

Bandi felt around the edges of the door, while Abby pushed her way around the walls of the cellar. There was no opening anywhere. She was just contemplating asking her dad to lift her high enough to explore the ceiling, when Bandi called her over to the door.

"I think we might get this open…"

The door had been bolted from the outside but was very loose. As he forced it, it moved a little. He backed up and kicked it beside where he could see the bolt through a gap between the door and the door jamb. Soon he and Dave were co-ordinating their kicks and on the fifth strike the hasp broke and the door flung open. Sharon went to cheer but Abby put her hand over her mouth and stifled it. Sharon fought her for a second but Abby held on.

"We all have to be like mice now," whispered Dave. "We've made enough noise as it is."

They tiptoed up the stairs into the barn and Dave made them hide behind the open door. The group ducked down – they were catching on.

"I'll do a recce," said Abby. She peeked out of the door. No-one. The new minibus had gone but their own was still there. She rounded the corner and looked across at the rest of the buildings. There was a house that appeared semi-boarded up and another low farm building. She sidled her way towards it. A hum emanated from the inside but otherwise all was quiet. She returned to the barn.

They decided the best thing would be to leave the barn and hide somewhere else. The big shed was a better bet than the house – there might be someone in there.

"There could be people in the shed too," said Bandi.

"Yes. We must go in carefully," said Abby. "But I didn't see any sign of anyone. It seems to be full of plants. If we duck down we can hide among them. It'll be safer than staying here."

It was bright and warm inside the shed. Dave checked for people. There were none. The plants, which seemed to be all the same, gave off a distinctive pungent smell. Apart from the hum that came from an electricity box just inside the door, all was quiet inside. Dave ushered them in and warned them to duck down and stay quiet. Sharon was learning fast.

"I think I know what this stuff is," whispered Abby. "It

smells like this round the back of the sports hall at Renny after the weedy gang has been there – cannabis."

"I believe you're right," answered her father. "I never knew there was a problem at Renny – I mean Renson Park High…"

"Dad, I keep telling you. You live on another planet. Loads of kids at Renny smoke it. The real problem is that it gets traded there. Silent Sam hasn't a clue – or refuses to believe what he's told."

"Maybe he's in denial. Doesn't want the notoriety of the fuss it would cause. What about Longmead?"

"Of course. Weed is everywhere. The police are only really interested if there are class A drugs going around… But the biggest problem is spice – it's legal, same as tobacco…"

"Hey," broke in Bandi, "can we talk about this another time! I mean, this stuff is worth a huge amount of money. If we're caught here, who knows what they might do to keep us quiet!"

"You're right, Bandi. I don't think this is a safe place to hide anyway. There are no dark corners. Look, I've been thinking. We need to raise the alarm. I want you, Abby, and Bandi, to go and find someone. You can speak French. Meanwhile we'll get the rest out of here into the fields."

"There's not much to hide in. It's all grass… I mean the sort cows eat," corrected Sharon, who was quite aware that the stuff growing in the shed was pot.

"I know. We'll make for the copse Let's hope we can make it before they return. We *cannot* be found *here*."

"Agreed. Come on, Abby," said Bandi. "Let's go. We've got to get to the road and find someone."

They left the shed cautiously. There didn't appear to be anyone in the house. They ran across to where the minibus was parked and found the footpath along which they had come. Dave watched them go.

He was about to call the group together and explain the plan when, through the slightly open door, he caught sight of a movement beside the house. There was someone there. Had they seen Bandi and Abby? They didn't appear to have done. Two men sauntered across to the barn.

Uh-o, thought Dave, *they're going to find us gone.* He wanted to escape from the shed but only one of the men went into the barn. Dave carefully pulled the shed door closed.

"Hide," urged Dave, in a low voice, "keep your heads down and, if you can, stop breathing!"

There was a cry and an expletive from inside the barn. Their absence was discovered.

"*L'hangar,*" Dave heard one of them announce. They were coming towards the shed.

The men entered. "*Où êtes-vous, fripouilles? Je sais que vous êtes ici. Sortez… Montrez-vous!* "

No-one breathed.

"*Non. Pas ici,*" said the second man.

Then Dave heard the minibus return and heated shouting in the yard. The gang was back. The two men left the shed, leaving the door slightly ajar.

Dave watched them through the slit of the open door and, to his dismay, saw that they had caught Abby and Bandi. They hadn't got far. On the road they had been too exposed. The teenagers began to stir.

"No," Dave whispered, urgently. "Remain exactly where you are!"

There was more arguing and the gunman was screaming at the two who had been left in charge. They made pitiful noises. They were clearly frightened of him.

"*Où sont les autres?* Where are the others?" he demanded of Abby.

"Escaped – in all directions."

"*Menteuse!* You lie!" and he went to strike her with the butt of his shotgun.

"She's telling the truth!" Bandi intervened. "We split up."

The man spat his disgust but he still stood tall and scanned the fields in every direction. The land was flat. They couldn't have got all the way to the trees.

"*Non. Ils sont dans l'hangar,*" he barked pointing to the plant shed.

Dave saw Abby and Bandi being held roughly with their arms behind their backs, and the bossman ordering them to be tied up and taken back to the cellar. Gun raised, he then led the rest of the men to the shed.

All was stillness as the gang entered. Dave was proud of his group but also terrified for them. It might be better to give themselves up.

"*Vide,*" declared one of the men who had just checked. "*Ils ne sont pas là.*"

"*Non. Ils se cachent,*" said the leader. He was not going to be so easily convinced. He ordered his men to search down the rows.

The situation was desperate. Dave resolved on making a diversion. He ran to the open door.

"*Là!*" shouted the gunman. He lifted his weapon and fired. Dave threw himself to the floor feeling shot catch the back of his shirt and graze his skin. Above him the power box on the wall exploded and the shed was thrown into complete darkness. Pieces of the box, plaster, brick and lead shot fell onto Dave.

"*Merde,*" swore the gunman.

Dave pulled himself beneath the nearest bench. The man heard him and blasted a second barrel into the dark but again mercifully too high. Pots shattered. Plant debris was flung into the air. One of the gang cried out. He had been hit. He began to simper.

"*Merde!*" said the boss again. "*Trouvez une lampe.*" One of the men nearest the door felt his way forward.

"*J'y vais. Ne tire pas,*" he shouted as he gratefully fled from the building ostensibly in search of a torch but instead making for the hired minibus to desert the scene as quickly as he could. He had sensed the game was up and he was not going to be an accessory to murder.

He didn't get far. The two who had taken Bandi and Abby back to the cellar had come out to the sound of the shots.

"*Où vas-tu?*"

"*Moi. Je m'en vais. Le boss est devenu fou…*"

But he was interrupted by the sight of the gendarmerie coming down the lane in force. Wayne's report had been taken seriously. The three men stood with their hands held high.

As the half-dozen vehicles poured into the yard, they heard another blast in the plant shed.

"*Il est devenu fou,*" declared the same man.

Inside the shed, Dave had heard the gunman reload. He threw a piece of debris towards the door. The man turned towards it and fired. Dave saw the man silhouetted against the flash and propelled himself onto the man's back. As they both fell, Dave found the man's right arm beneath him and felt for the shotgun. He grabbed it as the man heaved himself up and began fighting for control of the weapon, his finger on the second trigger. Dave desperately directed the barrel upwards. The gun went off, blasting a hole in the roof. Daylight streamed in. Then the rest of the gang ran from the building… to be confronted with a phalanx of blue-uniformed gendarmes. Like their colleagues they thrust their hands aloft.

"*Ils se battrent…*" they declared.

The gendarmes did not hesitate. Within seconds they had entered the shed and had both the bossman and Dave out into the open.

It took a few minutes longer for the gendarmes to coax the teenagers from their hiding places.

The gang had quickly reported the whereabouts of Bandi and Abby, and they, too, were freed.

★ ★ ★

Reunited a few hours later in the canteen at the gendarmes' barracks, Dave's group were in high spirits. Wayne was basking in the praise he was receiving from the others, especially Sharon and Dawn, who couldn't get over the size of the force sent to rescue them. Darren was talking about the stink of the plants – especially when they got blown up. He couldn't imagine why anyone would want to smoke that stuff.

"You remember that," said Dave in a serious tone. Despite everything, he had still not quite come to terms with the thought that Renson Park High was part of a chain for cannabis distribution.

"Course," said Wayne.

Dave's status had soared in the eyes of all in his group. He wasn't just a vicar, he was an intrepid action hero – a wounded action hero, even. He had had iodine applied to his back where the bullets had hit him. (Or, to be more accurate, where a couple of pieces of shot had grazed him.) The wonderful thing in Sharon's eyes was the holes in his shirt. She had forgotten how scared she had been at the time – so scared she pretended to be the quietest mouse in the world.

But Dave had not felt brave then and certainly not now. All he felt was an immense relief.

Abby, however, who had always looked up to her father, had an even deeper impression of his worth but would never forget the fear she had experienced hearing the gun going off.

★ ★ ★

The gendarmes took them to a hotel for the night. The second unplanned hotel stay – only this one was quite luxurious. The deep baths, the rich lather of the soaps supplied and the soft voluminous towels made them feel like film stars. And in the sumptuously decorated dining room, the food seemed to go on forever!

After a well-earned sleep in the softest beds they could ever remember, their own minibus was returned to them. Their camping gear was intact but there was no sign of Sharon's passport.

"Well, guys, what shall we do?" asked Dave. "We can either go back home now or we can carry on to Taizé as planned."

They all elected to continue. They had had their phones restored to them and Dave had spoken to each and every distraught parent. But the young people did not want to go home so soon. They had become a close-knit group and they did not want to break the sense of camaraderie and face endless questions from worried relatives. They felt they were grown up enough and persuaded their parents that they were safe together under Dave's heroic leadership.

Back home in Persham, parents were gathering together and forming their own support group.

★ ★ ★

Their time in Taizé went really fast. They assembled for worship three times a day. The worship was simple but quite deep and, immersed in it, the group managed to forget the farm some of the time.

The community imposed few rules. The main one was that everyone was expected to help look after the place –

cleaning, washing up and other essential tasks. That might sound dull, but the wonderful thing was meeting people from so many other countries. Young people came from all over the world. Abby spoke lots in French – much nicer French than she had heard from the drug gang – and she used her German, too. The Germans all spoke excellent English, as did most of the other nationalities, so the rest of the group were never isolated.

"All the world speaks our language," remarked Sharon. "I don't see why we have to bother with anyone else's – and besides, there are so many of them."

"It makes them happy if you try and speak someone's language," smiled Abby. "We're not really the centre of the world in Britain."

Sharon was forced to agree. Even she managed to see that it wasn't fair to expect other people to do all the hard work at communicating. Taizé was helping her to understand that the world was a big place – a really big place – and Britain was just one small, if significant, part of it.

"And Bandi doesn't even come from Planet Earth," reminded Abby. All the party were learning to expand their horizons.

"When you are here you can't think, like, Persham is at the centre of the universe," commented Darren. You could almost see blinkers falling from his eyes.

★ ★ ★

After nine days there, they were all sad to leave.

As they pulled onto the A6 in the direction of Paris, Sharon said, "All that really happens at Taizé is three church services a day and washing up and jobs… But I *wanted* to go to the worship. It *sounds* boring but it isn't… Somehow it's just as exciting in its own way as being…" She tailed off because she did not want another drama like the last one that had begun on a French motorway. This time she felt she wanted to get back home. They all did. She remembered her passport and broke out into a cold sweat. Would they let her back into Britain? What did they do to kids who had lost their passports? Dave assured her that they wouldn't abandon her to a permanent stay in the port customs shed, although it might take a bit of time extricating her.

Abby was still thinking about the worship. She had experienced a few styles but not one quite like at Taizé. "The worship is unpretentious," she remarked. "No-one stands at the front. I like that. You have no idea which brother is leading the singing or reading. They let the worship speak for itself… So different to those places where someone is trying to be important." She recalled the fellowship she had had a brush with the previous year, and shivered a little.

"Absolutely," agreed her father. "What you get there is God. It was at Taizé that I first felt Him calling me to be ordained… On that occasion, I was not interrupted on my way there."

At that moment, Wayne dropped his sweets. They rolled all over the floor of the minibus. His hero status, although not entirely forgotten, had not made him less clumsy. He was still the same Wayne.

"Wayne, we can't take you anywhere," scolded Dawn.

Wayne retrieved what he could from around him and, as he did so, his hand felt something shoved down between the seats.

"What's this?" he asked, pulling out Sharon's passport.

"My passport!" exclaimed Sharon. "Wow! Thanks, Wayne. Now I can go home properly."

"That's a relief," said Dave. "Thanks, Wayne."

"No problem," smiled Wayne, reputation restored. Being the hero was getting to be a habit.

10

The months passed in Persham and the days grew shorter. Bandi was struck by the gloom of a string of cloudy and rain-soaked days and bleak starless nights. It was dark when he got up and dark again soon after he got back from the college. But, among the children, there was a thrill of bright anticipation. Bandi was soon to become part of the excitement, too – the dark days were signalling the impending arrival of Christmas.

On Advent Sunday, four Sundays before 25th December, Abby's parents unveiled an Advent calendar with a pocket for each of the days of Advent. The season of preparation for the big day had begun. Each pocket contained two items: one for Abby and one for Bandi. Bandi was treated the same in every respect. Dave and Lynn had always wanted two children but it had not happened – not until now, that is, when this year they would have two young people in their house for Christmas. Lynn delighted in making the special calendar. The pockets had sweets in them but also an object, picture or reading about the Christmas story or a Yuletide tradition of some kind.

On Joh, Matilda had always insisted on keeping Christmas. She said she couldn't think of life without it. The trouble was that no-one else in the Johian community apart from Jack had ever experienced it, so it lacked the collective hype the season had on Earth. But in Persham, surrounded by fairy lights and seasonal music, Bandi soon caught the Christmas fever with a vengeance.

In the Johian Scriptures there was no baby Jesus, of course. The Johians celebrated the powerful presence of God with his creation but it was a spiritual presence. God came, they believed, but only in the hearts of people – the Creator had taken no human form on Joh. But nevertheless, the Johians enjoyed their festivals.

This included a traditional annual celebration of light. Few took the rising of Daan for granted – it symbolised the great blessings of the Creator. The gift of light was an essential ingredient of the gift of life, and life was the dwelling place and the supreme workshop of the Creator. It seemed to Matilda that this would be the appropriate time for her Christmas celebrations so, in addition to all the Johian traditions, she insisted on a Christmas tree in the cottage and told her family the story of the babe in a manger.

Listening to Matilda, Pastor Ruk had been so taken with the story of Christmas that the previous year, when the Festival of Light came around, he had preached about the coming of God to his creation in human form. It did not matter, he concluded, that this had happened on another planet. The truth remained that God had been born in human flesh, and that was a visitation to all human beings wherever they lived in the universe – in fact it had been the deepest involvement of the Creator, not just in things human, but in the whole of creation. This was not a matter of intellectual interest; it was the most powerful and significant thing the Creator had done since the beginning of creation itself. Ruk had read Matilda's translation of the Christmas story in Luke's Gospel to the congregation and added that his fervent prayer was that one day he would be privileged, like the Smith family, to visit Planet Earth One, and if that was granted he hoped it would be at Christmastime.

After the service, Jack joked that Ruk wanted jam on it.

"I don't think the Creator will blame me for asking," the pastor replied with a twinkle in his eye.

"Certainly not... But, if you do get to visit Planet Earth at Christmas, I'm afraid you will be disappointed. It is not always the best time of the year for everyone on Earth."

"Why? Don't they recognise the significance of a Saviour's birth and rejoice?"

"No. Not everyone. Many find it hard to believe in God at all... I know that sounds, well, odd – given all the creation that surrounds them and the miracle of life itself – but some people are only aware of what they *haven't* got, and they miss seeing the wonder of it. They are too busy grumbling to count their blessings. And on Earth we have become good at destroying and spreading hate, and God gets the blame for that," said Jack, ruefully.

"But *you* don't blame God for the bad things... I mean what happened to you and Jalli when you were so young. The celebration of light for you and your blind friends is probably a bit... well, a bit of a disappointment..."

"No. Light is more than what you see with eyes if you have them," Jack said. "You do not need eyes to see God's presence – in fact, sometimes seeing things with your eyes can distract you; when I was a child the teachers always taught us to close our eyes when we said our prayers. And, no, I don't blame God for it. Don't get me wrong, I did for a few months before I realised He lives in the darkness too... There's lots on Earth that is far from perfect but the vast majority of it is down to the behaviour of human beings. And I don't believe that's God's fault. It's God that has given us each other and the power to give and receive love. Because of that, I am rich.

"But, the truth is, I didn't feel like that when I was a child," added Jack, thoughtfully. "To be honest, I didn't think Christmas was for real."

"Not for real? How do you mean?"

"I mean, in my experience it was all–" Jack sighed. "So many things about it were make-believe. Father Christmas, I knew, was made up – well, I did when I got to seven if not earlier. The presents – I got presents from Mum, but not like some of the others who had big families and got really cool stuff. I resented them. And then there was all the alcohol. Thinking about it, I guess some of the excessive drinking is people trying to drown out the disillusionment they feel around Christmas. The hype doesn't deliver.

"I knew my dad had left because of drink and sometimes I was glad he wasn't there like some of the kids' parents who got drunk and spoiled everything. This boy in our class – he told us how his father and his grandfather used to drink all Christmas afternoon and end up in an argument... every year!

"So, the bit about Jesus and God just got lost for most of us. A baby was born in a stable – so what? Angels and wise men – they were just all made-up stories."

"But you worshipped with your mother at the religious festival?"

"Worshipped? Nuh. We never went to church. That only started when Jalli came along."

"I didn't know that."

"Like the angels at Christmas, she came from the stars. She and her grandma showed us how much we are loved... And so we have Christmas here with all the light and hope and none of the drink or the arguments. When I came to know God, I realised that the 'Jesus bit' is about the only bit of Christmas that is truly real. The only bit that is real throughout the universe and forever..."

Bandi was delighted the family Christmas tree on Joh was associated with the Festival of Light because it meant that he and Abby were going to get two Christmases. And Yeka was especially excited about the tree this year because her brother and his girlfriend had brought some baubles and lights from Persham. She couldn't wait to see them on the tree. Up until then they had had only homemade ones. According to Kakko, these Earth jewels were just awesome.

★ ★ ★

Shaun was now out of plaster and wearing a plastic boot that he could take off to bathe and sleep. It was great having his leg back, which was getting stronger every day. He still needed the crutches to get around with but he could swing along faster on them than other people could walk. They had to run to keep up with him. Once he met Wennai while she was out jogging and swung along with her. It became something of a regular occurrence but he never talked about meeting her. Whenever anyone mentioned it, he would tell them they were just friends.

"I don't know why she puts up with you," said Kakko two weeks before the Festival of Light. "I mean it's quite obvious she really likes you and you keeping saying you're just friends."

"She's a fan, that's all," answered Shaun, dismissively.

"Really? A football fan? You haven't played for weeks and it could be months before you get back in the team… Anyway, I heard that Gollip was on good form."

"He is. He's scored in each of the last three matches. She's his girlfriend now."

"Oh, Shaun! What's wrong with you? You know she likes *you*."

"There's nothing wrong with me, absolutely nothing. She's dating Gollip. That's fine with me."

"Is it?"

"Look, Kakko, stop saying that…! OK?" Shaun's anger was rising. His sister could be *so* annoying.

"OK… OK." Kakko backed off, her hands raised in submission.

"Just… Just change the subject."

"OK… You sleeping well?"

"Now why do you ask that?" retorted Shaun crossly. Kakko could be impossible. First Wennai and now his sleeping habits.

"Because… because sometimes you shout in the night. And you come down to the kitchen and eat stuff. I can hear you – my room's near to the kitchen."

"It's nothing. My leg hurts."

"It's more than that, Shaun. You're cross and sullen most of the time and you never used to be… and just before you tell me to back off again, don't forget you and I go all the way back to when I was two, and I know when something's up… And burying it doesn't work. If you want to yell at me, yell at me – I don't care; but I want my brother back, not some boy who clams up on me as if I were a stranger," said Kakko, more forcefully than she had intended.

Kakko retreated to her room leaving Shaun with his head in his hands. Had she said too much? *No,* she told herself. *What you see is what you get with me. He's got to sort himself out – or let someone else help him. And, besides, it's not fair on Wennai – even if she is too coy to stand up for herself.* Kakko didn't go much on the girlie stuff that Wennai chose – dresses and shoes and make-up – but that was not the point. She might have been different, annoyingly different sometimes, but she was who she was. Wennai was not trying to pretend to be anyone other than her true self. And, in any case, for whatever reason, Shaun liked her and it was unfair of him not to admit that to her or himself.

Shaun withdrew upstairs. Kakko could be cruel sometimes.

She had no sensitivity. But, as always – well, mostly – she was right. Both about Wennai and about his sleeping. The problem with Wennai was that she didn't believe there was a God, and that mattered to Shaun – or at least it used to. He was finding that praying was getting increasingly difficult. He didn't blame God for this, he was just so... so mixed up and tired. He couldn't forget that gun in his face and the mocking words of the man behind it as he prepared to blast him into oblivion. And then the shock of seeing the soldier die instead – right there in front of him. But, he told himself, he was going to conquer this – it was just a matter of time. He didn't need all this female help, not from his sister, or his mother, or his nan, and certainly not Wennai whose solution to losing her own mother had been to deny God altogether.

The following morning, Shaun woke refreshed. He hadn't dreamed of the roadside terror and the sounds of guns for once. *See*, he told himself, *I'm getting better.* It would soon be the Festival of Light and Christmas in the cottage. *That will drive away any lingering demons*, he thought.

The next thing he was aware of was that a white gate had been spotted. If his name was on it, he was ready for the first time ever to face up to God and turn Him down. He couldn't cope with another challenging adventure. But it wasn't for him, or Kakko. It was for his parents and little Yeka.

★ ★ ★

"This place is dark. I mean darker than nighttime," said Jalli, shivering. She, Jack and Yeka had stepped through a white gate wearing a set of nondescript grey clothes that the Creator had provided. In the garden of White Gates Cottage, it had been a delicious bright morning. Daan had been sending beams of light that made the dew on the grass sparkle like little diamonds, and a morning chorus of birdsong had filled the air. Yeka had found a grey bag containing colourful jelly beans – every colour of the rainbow – alongside her grey clothes. The bag was large but not too large for her to insist on carrying it herself.

"For me!" She pounced.

"For you to take through the gate. Don't eat any now," said Jalli softly.

"Aw." Yeka pouted.

This side of the gate they were stopped by a smothering wall of darkness; it was like walking into a place of deep nothingness that permeated even the brain.

Jack had lived in a sightless world for more than half his life but he too felt the oppressiveness of this place.

"It's more than the absence of light," he said. "It's... heavy."

"I don't like it!" whined Yeka clutching her bag of jelly beans. "I want to go home!"

But the white gate behind them had faded and there was no retreat.

"God, are you in this place?" prayed Jalli with her mouth and heart.

In her heart she knew His presence but her spoken word seemed to be stifled – out there, everything seemed dead.

"This is a nowhere place," mewed Yeka. "I want to go home!"

"It's not a nowhere place if Mummy and Daddy are here, Yeka. Give your mummy a cuddle. And the Creator is inside you – always. She'll never ever let you go." She lifted Yeka into her arms and Jack embraced them both.

They felt their way forward towards a place where the black admitted a streak of grey. There didn't seem to be much else to do. There must be something in the direction of the slightest sign of light. After a while the greyness grew light enough to see people walking about. They were in a street in mid-winter – but it was unlike anywhere on Planet Earth they had heard about.

"It's like the darkest time of the year when the clouds are really heavy," suggested Jalli.

"Like Christmastime when the sun doesn't shine," said Jack.

"Yes. Only, here there are no artificial lights to break the dullness. There is absolutely nothing bright in this place at all. Even the people are all dressed in grey."

"Like us," observed Yeka.

"Yes, exactly like us," agreed her mother.

They walked along and joined the groups of grey-clad people. After a while some of the people looked at them, but said nothing. They occasionally talked to each other, but in subdued tones. Soon even Yeka felt that if she spoke she must do it in a whisper.

"This place is horrible. It's yuk. Where is God? Why won't She let us back into our garden?"

"Not for the moment, Yeka. Look, I think you can have a sweet now."

Yeka opened the bag. The colourful jelly beans positively glowed in this place.

"Um, I think I will have… I will have…" she mused as she decided which colour to try first.

Jalli saw some of the people were staring at them. She grew embarrassed.

"Yeka, just take one and close the bag."

Yeka chose a yellow one and licked it. But it was too late; some children had already seen what Yeka had in her bag and one of the braver little boys strode across, followed by some of his friends. He looked at the bag and then at Yeka. Yeka held out the bag and whispered, "Would you like one?"

The lad gazed at her cautiously.

"It's OK," she said instinctively, "they're really nice." And she smiled as she chewed.

The lad took a red one and, looking around furtively, popped it into his mouth. Then four others came over and did the same. Jalli thought she detected a flicker of a sparkle in their eyes and a doubtful smile on their faces. Up to this point the children had looked as dull and serious as their grown-ups.

The children, grouped together, attracted the attention of one of the adults who came across to see what was going on. As soon as she saw the colourful sweets, she grabbed her child out of the group.

"Do you want to get us all in trouble?" she demanded angrily under her breath. Then, looking up at Jack and Jalli, she said tersely, "If you don't care about your own child, you have no right getting us all arrested." Then she swept her son away.

Soon, children were scattering in every direction and melting into the passing traffic, leaving Yeka and her mother and father exposed in the centre of the street, but an elderly couple came up to them and whispered, "Better put your food away, little girl. It's not safe here... You her parents?"

"Yes," answered Jalli firmly. "She is only sharing her sweets."

"You don't come from around here, do you?"

"No."

"Come with me. Better get off the street in case someone has reported you. The authorities have their spies everywhere."

Jack had been listening carefully, taking in the situation.

"Jalli, I think we should accept this kind lady's offer."

"Yes. Thank you," said Jalli.

The old couple led them down a number of side streets and alleys and eventually into a small house.

"It isn't much, but they won't think about looking for you here. We weren't followed were we, Hann?"

"No, I don't think so, Jodwa. We would have noticed them when we doubled back and went down Narrow Place."

"Good. Now then, sit down and make yourselves comfortable. Would you like something to drink? What about the little lady?"

Yeka looked up at her mother. Jalli nodded.

"Thank you. We don't wish to impose—"

"Nonsense." She gave Yeka a grey mug containing a murky liquid. Yeka looked at it doubtfully.

"It's my special cordial. It's fine. Ignore the colour. Watch." Jodwa poured some into a mug for herself, sipped it and smiled broadly.

Yeka smelled and tasted. "Nice!" she declared.

"Good. Now, tell us. Where do you come from? And how did you manage to find those lovely sweets?"

Jack and Jalli explained about the white gates in the way they had become accustomed to whenever they arrived somewhere different.

"So you see, we were given these sweets for a purpose. We don't know what that is, but Yeka is by nature generous. It just seemed right to her to share them."

"Good," smiled Jodwa. "Hann, they have no idea about us and our situation. We'd better start from the beginning."

Hann had been checking through the window. No-one had come near the house. "Yes," he began; "do you know about the anti-colour laws?"

"Is that a racial thing?" asked Jack.

"The colour of our skin? Like you are pale and your wife is dark? No. You can't change that. They do not legislate concerning skin colour."

"They would if you had bright blue or pink or vibrant yellow skin," said his wife.

"But no-one has, have they? No. It is about the using of colourful things. Everyone must wear a shade of grey – and the duller the grey, the better. For the last fifty years, colour reproduction has been banned. All photography and art has to be monochrome. All homes must be painted grey – pure white or black is permitted in only small quantities. No enhanced colouring can be added to food. Music cannot be colourful – nothing that leads to dancing... So you can appreciate the impact your colourful sweets made."

"As you may have gathered, I am blind – totally blind," said Jack solemnly, "but even I can detect the colourlessness of your world. Why these laws?"

"Seventy years ago," began Jodwa, "our culture was brimming with colour. I can remember it. It was so vibrant. But many people were selfish and pleasure seeking. They exploited the planet without regard for its beauty or its sanctity. They were ignoring its Creator and abusing His gifts. They were using colour and music for their own ill-conceived self-gratification. People were suffering from corruption and there was a spreading poverty. The poor were rebellious and when a group of religious people came into focus calling people back to God, promising universal equality and freedom under Him, they responded and rose up against the establishment. There were riots in which the rich people with their colourful stuff were thrown out. Soon the religious purists were in power and they ordered the big houses to be broken up into apartments. They banned all the dancing and the light-hearted partying that the rich people had enjoyed. It took twenty years, until eventually, fifty years ago, the colour laws were passed. Since then, no colour has been permitted under pain of imprisonment. There is a special police force that is deployed to enforce them – and they do."

"From one excess to another," said Jalli.

"That's the way of it. You'll have to be careful," said Hann firmly. "I don't know what your creator is playing at but it's dangerous to do what you have done."

"What about religious festivals?" wondered Jack. "Is colour and music allowed there?"

"There are no festivals anymore."

"What? None at all? Don't you even celebrate your birthdays?"

"Shh!" Hann continued in a hushed voice. "We keep our voices down. You never know who is listening. We *used to* but now birthday celebrations are forbidden. Every day, we are taught, is as special as any other – and celebrating birthdays leads to inequality."

"What about God? We celebrate Christmas when—"

"Twistmas!" bounced Yeka. "I want my Twistmas twee… Can't we go home now?" She dragged at her mother's arm, pulling her toward the door.

"Yeka, don't be rude," commanded Jalli.

Hann bent down, smiled at Yeka and said quietly, "Tell me about this Twistmas… Only, around here it has to be a secret, so whisper it."

Yeka stopped tugging. "Twistmas is when…" she looked up at her mother, "baby Jesus?"

"Yes, Yeka, that's right," said Jalli.

"On Planet Earth where Bandi is, and Abby, and where Daddy came from, God borned baby Jesus. So we have a big tree – inside the house – and put lights on it and shiny bright balls – I like the pink ones best – and things, and sweets… and then we have presents. Abby has brought mine from Planet Earth and it's all wrapped up in paper with a big man in a red coat drawn all over it. And she brought tinz… tinz… sparkly stuff like long spaghetti with soft shiny yellow feathers… And—"

"It sounds like a very exciting thing, this Twistmas," whispered Hann. Yeka was getting more and more animated and louder as she went.

"Yes, and—" began Yeka again.

"Christmas is a wonderful time for children," said Jack softly. "And my little daughter here can see the contrast between your world and hers. I can understand where your government is coming from, though. There are a lot of people who miss out on things on Earth who find Christmas painful."

"By making life painful and dull for everyone?" said Jalli. "That is no solution. I saw the longing in those children's eyes. You cannot pretend that light and colour don't exist—"

But Jalli never got to finish her sentence. She was interrupted by a sharp rap on the door.

"Police! Open up!"

"The sweets – hide them!" commanded Hann in a whisper. Jodwa took the bag from Yeka and dropped it in among a pile of logs beside the hearth.

There was a second rap.

"I'm coming!" shouted Hann.

He opened the door and three policemen in dark-grey uniforms stood looking stern.

"What can I do for you?" said Hann with a feigned look of surprise.

"You have been reported as harbouring a child with coloured candy." He strode over the threshold without being invited.

"I'm sorry, officer, there is only this small child here – and as you can see, she has no candy other than what we make here… Besides, where would she come by that sort of thing? We could not colour candy even if we wanted to."

"Would you want to?" barked the officer.

"Why? Sweet stuff is made to eat. As the government says, colour would distract you when you ate it," answered Jodwa, politely.

"You all live here?" continued the leading policeman, picking up a colourless glass vase and examining it.

Jack was not going to let these generous people get into trouble for being kind to them. He answered promptly before Hann or Jodwa could speak.

"No, officer. My wife, child and I are visiting."

"From where?"

"Our friends come from White Gates… beyond the mountains," cut in Hann. "Our friendship extends over time."

The officer kicked around a bit as he made up his mind whether or not to order his men to conduct a search. Colour is pretty easy to spot in a grey-scale world. Besides, there was no evidence beyond that of one person's reports. If sweets had been coloured, they were probably all eaten in any case. He decided to terminate his enquiries – the raid had served its purpose of reminding people that they were being watched and must adhere strictly to the law. It was a known fact that some people would be tempted to change things if given a chance – and the government could not risk that.

"You are aware that even though you may come from beyond the mountains, you are subject to the law," he addressed Jack brusquely. Then he looked him in the eyes. "Are you blind?"

"Yes," answered Jack matter-of-factly.

"How do you know if your family are complying with the colour laws?"

"The use of colour changes more than appearance. I would be aware of the behavioural differences that would cause."

"Good. It is behaviour that matters…" He stared at Yeka who shrunk into her mother's skirts. Then he looked up with a false smile. "I think we can leave these people to their fellowshipping," he said brightly. "Come, men, we have work to do." And he left the house without another word.

Hann invited his guests to sit again.

"Sorry about that," he said quietly. "That was too close for comfort."

"What would they have done if—"

"If they found any coloured candy?" said Jodwa. "Arrested us all. Many people have been known to have been taken to the Off-white House never to be seen again."

"Just taken away?" asked Jalli in whisper. "Where do they take them?"

"No-one knows. They just disappear. We expect they are executed."

"For having something coloured?"

"For inciting rebellion. Tomorrow you must return 'beyond the mountains'."

"Our white gate was no longer visible when we left the street…" said Jalli slowly. "I am not sure if we have achieved anything here yet."

"What do you intend to do? Stir up the people? We are not powerful enough to overthrow the government. It would just make the authorities more oppressive than ever. They know only one way to keep us in our places. A chink of light, a blast of colour and we gain strength and hope."

Yeka was now curled up on her father's lap and sliding off to the land of dreams.

"I think the little lady has had a busy day. We can offer you one large bed in the guest room for the night. Tomorrow you can search for your white gate."

"Thank you," said Jalli. "That is very kind of you."

"We are honoured. You have brought more hope than we have had in a decade. The sweets are just a sign that all is not drab in the rest of the universe."

"Far from it," smiled Jack. "I know what colour does to children. It excites them. I spoke truthfully. It is not difficult to be aware of the joy my children express when they encounter their Christmas tree."

"Twistmas," said Yeka sleepily. "Twistmas tree. I want to go home."

"Tomorrow," soothed her mother. "Tonight we have to bring joy into this house. Would you like to share a big bed with Mummy and Daddy?"

"Yes." Yeka was aware of this being a very big treat.

"Come on then, little lady, we'll go to bed together."

"We are honoured to have you, our friends across time. I will show you to the guest room… I'm afraid the decoration is rather dull."

"I'll use my imagination," whispered Jack, "and festoon it with the brightest colours I can remember."

11

Several hours had passed when Jack and Jalli were awoken by Yeka thrashing in a dream.

"Leave!" she grunted then woke up with a start.

"It's alright, Yeka." Jalli cuddled her to her. "It's a dream. It's only a dream."

Yeka was cold and wet with sweat. It had been a nasty dream.

"Where are the sweets, Mummy?"

"They are safe. They are here under the bed."

"Let me look!"

"It's OK, Yeka. No-one's been in here."

"I want to see!"

"Alright. I'll get up and find them…" said Jalli, a little peeved. It was not yet time to wake up. She lowered herself from the bed and felt beneath it to where she had hidden the bag containing the sweets. "Here. They are just as we left them in the same bag under the bed. No-one has touched them."

"I want to take them and plant them."

"They aren't seeds," said Jack, sleepily. "Sweets don't grow into trees."

"These do."

"Explain," said Jalli laying a finger on Jack's lips.

"In my dream, we were chased by horrible men – like that man who came in and shouted at us. They wanted the sweets.

We ran and ran up a little lane and into a field where a farmer had dug it to put his seeds in."

"A ploughed field. Bare soil. No grass."

"Yes, like that. It was all brown and bare. I fell over and the man nearly catched me and the sweets came out of the bag all over the bare field. They were like treasure – all sparkly and bright."

"What did the man do?"

"He tried to pick up the sweets but they got stuck and then started to grow. Big and sparkly trees came up. He got an axe thing and chopped down a red one, then a blue one but I shouted at him telling him to stop but he didn't... We have to put the sweets down in the ground... properly, before he finds them. We have to take them *now*."

"Yeka, it's the middle of the night. We can't plant anything until it is light. And we don't know where this field is."

"I do! I know!"

"Yes, but you don't know how to get there. We have to wait until morning. These nasty men say everyone should stay inside at night. If you go out now you will get these nice people who are looking after us into trouble."

Yeka calmed down. She didn't really understand. She wanted to go to the field and plant her sweets but when Mummy said something, she knew she was not going to change her mind. She looked momentarily at her daddy but an appeal to him would never work – he always backed her mummy up. She'd seen it too often.

Jalli began to sing and, before Yeka realised it, she had fallen asleep. The next thing she knew she was waking again and it was light. She climbed over her daddy and went looking for her bag. The sweets were all there.

"Daddy," she pleaded, pulling at him to sit up. "Now. We have to plant them now!"

Jalli touched Jack's arm. "We do need to leave these people, Jack. We are a danger to them."

"I agree," he said, getting to his feet. "We'll set out in the direction of the mountains. That would look right."

Jack and Jalli dressed quickly and got Yeka ready to go. She was extremely compliant. She knew what she wanted and where she was going.

Jalli called their hosts.

"Jodwa, Hann. We must go. We must leave you."

Hann opened their bedroom door. "It is early. The weather is not good. I think it will rain."

"But it is light and we do not want to be here should your police return. You have risked too much for us already."

Hann saw that they were dressed and ready for the road. He grunted. "But you must eat before you go. Jodwa."

Jodwa and Hann put bread and a grey/brown-coloured jam before them. Yeka took two mouthfuls and was on her feet. Jack and Jalli finished their meal but they were soon taking their leave.

Outside, they encountered an oppressive mist that didn't allow them to see very far. Yeka, however, immediately appeared to know which way she wanted to go. Jalli thought it best not to argue with her. And anyway, at this stage, any way was good. They couldn't see to the end of the street, let alone the direction of any mountains.

They passed along some quiet streets but all the while gained height. Eventually, they emerged from the mist and were able to see that the town was in a broad valley, and in the distance against a sky laden with slate-coloured clouds, Jalli made out the jagged shapes of snow-topped mountains.

"Beautiful," she whispered. "Jack, I see the mountains. Out here on this hillside it is not so dull."

"The field is up this way!" urged Yeka. Jalli and Jack had never known her quite so determined. She was beginning to show some of her sister's impatience.

They continued up a lane that had now become a rough track as the houses became less and less frequent. Soon they were in the open countryside. The mist was lifting from the valley but the dark clouds now obscured the mountains. It began to rain.

Jack stopped. "Children," he said. "I hear children."

"Where?" asked Jalli. "Oh, yes. Behind us." She looked back the way they had come and saw a group of children approaching along the lane. Then she spotted a red sweet on the path.

"Yeka, you have dropped a sweet." She went to pick it up and then saw another – there was a trail of them every twenty metres or so the way they had come. The children had found them and were following them.

"Mahsnyeka, what have you done?!" Jalli used the crossest voice she could without shouting.

"What is it?" asked Jack, concerned.

"Our daughter has laid a trail of sweets and the children are following us – and soon, I guess, half the population of the town!"

"Yeka, that's naughty!" exclaimed Jack, crossly.

"I have to do the dream…" Yeka sobbed.

"No. You don't," answered Jalli. "Jack, we'd better hide. But there's nowhere to go apart from over the fence in among bushes. And I don't know how I'm going to get you over quickly enough."

"Not much point, Jalli. They'll just look for us where the sweet trail ends… And I guess they're nearly here. Let's just keep going. It's all we can do."

They strode out as fast as Jalli dared with Jack on her arm on a rough road – which wasn't very fast.

"Yeka, give me that bag," commanded Jalli, as the little girl struggled over the stones. But Yeka clung on to it, forcing Jalli to stop. "I don't know what has got into you, young lady. But this will have to end here if you ever want to go through a white gate again. This is a dangerous situation and you have no idea, have you?"

"No. She hasn't," said Jack. "Getting cross won't help. She's inherited the Smith streak of defiance from her father... We can't outrun these kids anyway. Maybe we should just let them catch up and give them the whole bag."

"No. It's mine! We have to plant them... in that field." Yeka pointed out a field some thirty metres in front to the left of the track. As Jalli let go of her to look, Yeka took off and covered the distance to a gate which she squeezed under before Jalli could do anything to stop her.

"Jack, I don't know what's got into her. I've never known her like this."

"There's definitely something bugging her here," said Jack. "She knows exactly what she wants to do. It's not really in character... Maybe we should just go with the flow."

"No choice. She's scattering the sweets across a harrowed field like farmers did before they had tractors."

"When she's finished, she'll be different. We can carry on. At least the children will stop in the field to harvest the sweets."

As he said this, the first of the children came running up. He spotted Yeka in the field and dived under the gate like she had done. As soon as Yeka saw him, she shouted at him to leave the sweets where they were.

"No, leave them!" she called.

Other children arrived and she repeated her command. "Leave! Let them grow."

"That is when she woke up from her dream," said Jalli. "She won't know what comes next."

Yeka had begun running around screaming and pushing the children off the sweets. While Jalli stood wondering what to do, the first of the adults in pursuit of their children arrived. He came puffing up the lane and stood alongside Jalli and Jack while he too watched the children scrabbling for Yeka's plantings.

"Goks," he commanded. "Come here! Now!"

Goks gave his father a pout but stopped hunting for sweets and quietly came back towards the gate.

"And you, too, Mags… All of you!"

He clearly had some authority. The children knew the game was up. Jack called to Yeka.

"Yeka, enough. Come back to Daddy."

Yeka, seeing the last of the children leaving the field, obeyed without question. Her sweets were safe, her task completed.

Within minutes, a dozen adults had arrived to retrieve their children. They were soon followed by the same group of colour police that had accosted the family the previous evening.

Jack and Jalli stood together with Yeka in hand. Seeing the police, the adults began accusing the Smiths of leading their children astray. They had to make sure that none of the blame rested on them or their children.

"What is all this?" barked the officer in charge. "What is going on here?"

"This child has been scattering candy, officer," said a mother, hastily. She lowered her head and added in a whisper, "*Coloured* candy."

The officer looked across the field. He could see no sweets. To Jalli's surprise and delight, they had all melted into the soil.

"I'm sorry, officer. My little girl has quite a vivid imagination… Somehow, she has managed to persuade these children she had some sweets," said Jalli, with a charming smile.

"They—" began a child in protest. But his father immediately intervened. "Our children, officer, are not used to lies. I'm sorry; they must have believed this naughty girl from across the mountains."

Some of the children were getting restless. "May we take our children home, officer?" said a mother in a trembly voice. "They have never behaved like this before… We need to teach them not to follow and listen to strangers in future."

The officer ignored her and turned to the Smiths.

"So, if you are going home to your place beyond the mountains, why are you on *this* track? You are on the wrong side of the valley."

"Are we?" said Jack. "I'm afraid I can't see and my wife and daughter cannot read the directions."

"Sorry," said Jalli. "I just thought that if we came up here I could see which way to go. It was foggy in the town. Everything looked the same."

As she spoke a shaft of sunlight came through the clouds and, at the same moment, the mountains reappeared from behind the dark-grey clouds. A rainbow appeared, growing brighter and brighter as they watched.

"Look," said Yeka. "Wainbow! Red and orange and yellow and green and blue and indigo and violet!"

"So, she knows her colours," declared the officer in an accusatory tone.

Jalli felt emboldened. They had run far enough. The rainbow reminded her of the presence of a loving Creator who had infinitely more power than these policemen. She also remembered that they were in this place because of Him. And the sweets had never belonged to Yeka – they had been a gift from Him at the white gate they had used. The sweets were His.

"Yes, my daughter knows her colours," answered Jalli. "She also knows who created them. You see, officer, you can demand that people live in a grey town but you can't paint the whole universe grey. It is vibrant with colour." She turned and looked at the field in which Yeka had scattered the sweets. In the sunlight it was now full of wild flowers – yellow, red, pink and blue.

"Mummy, Mummy! They growed... I said they would."

"Yes, Yeka. You were right." On some of the trees beyond the field there was pink and white blossom, and the leaves were many shades of green. "The Creator rejoices in colour," she added defiantly.

"I may no longer see them," concurred Jack, "but I hear and sense them. A coloured world is a free world. If I may say so, you are living in a false world. You may be able to control people but you cannot control nature."

"Look, Mummy. Bee!" Yeka had spotted a bright yellow bee buzzing from flower to flower. "Mummy likes bees," she told the policeman. "Bees make flowers happy."

"They do indeed," agreed her father. "So, officer, are you going to arrest us for admiring the God-given wonders of nature?"

"I could arrest you for conspiring to cause a disturbance."

"But, officer," protested Jalli, gently, "we have done nothing but attempt to leave. The rainbow, the flowers, the bees and the trees are not of our making."

"... and the mountains and the sunshine," enthused Yeka, "and..." she was going to add, "the sweets" but they had quite vanished. "And... and..." she played for time, not wishing to finish without a proper ending. Then she spotted something, then another. Iridescent blue butterflies had flown in from the edge of a red, brown and green wood. "But... but-flies!" she added, triumphantly.

The officer looked where she was pointing. Then something happened to him. He stood transfixed as he watched the brilliant blue insects flit from flower to flower. His men followed his gaze, then the adults and finally the children.

"What is it?" said the little boy called Goks.

"A butterfly," said his father.

"They're so pretty," said the little girl, Mags.

"God makes them," declared Yeka, decisively. "She makes everything. She makes things nice."

Jack gave her a squeeze.

The officer pulled himself together.

"Well, since you are leaving, I think we shall take no further action."

Jack became aware of a sensation in his brain that he knew well. "I think you will find there is a white gate up this way a little," he said to Jalli, raising his arm.

"Yes," said Jalli. "In the lane about thirty metres ahead of us… It has just appeared."

"White gate?" mused the officer. "What miracle have you now?"

"You will not see it," said Jack, "unless you are called to come with us."

"There tis!" said Yeka. "Twistmas! Twistmas tree!" She began to pull at her parents' arms.

"Thank you, officer," said Jack. "I hope we have not caused too much unwanted disturbance… We have not brought unwanted colour to your world; it has been here a long time. You have a beautiful place; I can hear it sing… We shall be on our way."

"Oh, yes," said the officer, distractedly. One of his men had just seen another butterfly settle on a bush right in front of him and had bent down to examine it. "You are free to go." He dismissed them and turned his attention to the field which was now a sea of colour.

"Thank you," said Jalli. "Goodbye, everyone." She waved. "Wave to the people, Yeka." Yeka waved and they stumbled off up the track towards the gate. When they reached it, Jalli looked back but the people were not watching them. They were engrossed in other colourful wonders they had just become aware of. Yeka bounced through the gate and Jalli held it for her husband. They were back in the garden of White Gates Cottage and by the time Jack had gathered his thoughts, Yeka was already telling Shaun all about their adventures.

"I was going to have a talk with her when we got here," said Jalli. "She was very defiant this morning. I don't like that."

"I agree. She was quite naughty, but she was so sure of what she needed to do. So determined. It may not happen again but if it does, I think we must tell her she must try and explain to us the reason she feels she wants to do her own thing."

"You don't think we should say anything now?"

"Not unless she appears proud of her defiance in her telling of the story. I don't think she was aware of being naughty. Let her delight in her triumph. I think the Creator used her today."

"That's true," said Jalli with a sigh, allowing her concern to evaporate. "I am so glad I don't have to live in that world."

"It is a beautiful world and I think a few more of the people who live there have discovered that, due to Yeka. You never know, if we get to go again, things might have changed – it could be full of Twistmas trees!"

Jalli smiled. "It may just be."

★ ★ ★

Christmas was certainly catching on on Joh. Pastor Ruk was introduced to the Christmas tree in White Gates Cottage by Yeka. She had insisted he call round to see it.

"Do you have these in your places of worship on Planet Earth?" he asked Matilda.

"We certainly do, inside and out. Back in Persham, some Christmases they have Christmas tree festivals. St Augustine's was packed with fifty trees one year – all decorated by local organisations. The church looked beautiful and hundreds of people came to see them."

Ruk listened intently. He could see many benefits from doing something that brought people together.

"Perhaps we could do something similar here?" he said.

"It's a lot of hard work, mind you," said Matilda, aware of the amount of time some people put into it all.

"But it would be beautiful. And it will bring people together," said Ruk. "Perhaps next year. I will need you to help, though."

"Yes. I guessed you might say that," smiled Matilda. "Should have kept my mouth shut. But I think that if I were still in Persham I would be involved, so I'll do it. Perhaps, if she is around, Abby could help, too. The best thing would be if the Rev Dave could come."

"I would love to meet him," enthused Ruk. "I am praying that he and I can make contact some day."

12

"What's that smell?" demanded Bandi. "Yuk! What're you cooking, Mum? Is there something in the oven?"

It was evening and Yeka had been in bed for a couple of hours. She had not been in a good humour – the Christmas tree had been taken down the previous day and no amount of telling her that they would get another next year would console her. She had gone upstairs reluctantly and had taken some persuading to put her head on the pillow.

Kakko looked up from her paper on the latest specs concerning the intricate components of the recycle buffer of the thrust system of the 4G intrahelical engine she was working on. Jack was marking some of the work the children had done on their blind script machines; Shaun was studying Abby's latest speech that she was due to give at the Longmead debating society in the new term; and Jalli was reading an article about integrating solar panelling with pollinator hives. Matilda had taken herself off to her room to read herself to sleep.

"No," answered Jalli. "It could be next door. Perhaps Hatta and Callan are having a barbecue."

"It doesn't smell like that," said Bandi. The smell grew stronger and he got up to see where it was coming from. When he opened the door, he was struck by the stink of acrid fumes.

"Something's on fire!" he yelled. "The place is full of smoke!"

"Yeka!" screamed Jalli. But Kakko was already out of the room and running up the stairs three at a time. Bandi followed. On the landing the smoke was so thick they couldn't breathe.

"Down! Down on the floor," urged Bandi. "Crawl."

Kakko managed to get to Yeka's door. They could now feel heat from above – the fire must be in the thatch. She pushed the door open. Shaun coughed. "I'll get Nan," he croaked and crawled on to the next door.

Inside Yeka's room Kakko couldn't see anything. She felt for the bed and found her sister wrapped in the bedclothes. She tried to wake her but couldn't, so she rolled her off onto the floor and then began crawling and dragging the bundle to the door. It seemed a long, long way to the top of the stairs. Kakko had no idea whether her sister was alive or dead – she appeared to be unconscious. At last Kakko reached the landing and slid and stumbled down the stairs with Yeka in her arms. Jalli was there to catch them. She swept up her youngest and rushed her into the garden where Jack was waiting with Shaun standing on his crutches. Kakko turned and climbed back up the stairs and found Bandi. He was attempting to pull Matilda's lifeless body along the landing. With Kakko's help they soon had her down the stairs. The outside air was rushing in through the front door and it was easier to breathe but the heat and the terrifying noise from above intensified. Kakko pulled herself up and then helped Bandi carry their nan into the fresh night.

The roof was now well alight – especially above Jack and Jalli's bedroom. If Yeka and Matilda had been at that end of the house, they probably wouldn't have stood a chance of getting them out.

Bandi was coughing and struggling; Kakko tried to turn her attention to Matilda but couldn't summon the strength. Jack was with her and was intent on giving her CPR, and

Jalli, to her relief, had managed to stir some life into Yeka. Then they heard sirens and, before they knew it, firefighters in protective gear were storming through the gate. "Anyone in the house?" one yelled.

"No, no," replied Jalli. "We're all here."

Then another woman with a heavy bag came hurrying into the garden. "Paramedic," she shouted, and put her hand to Matilda's neck. "We've got a pulse. Well done! Let's get her into the ambulance." A second medic was already conducting Jalli carrying Yeka out of the gate.

Soon, inside the vehicle, both Yeka and Matilda were on oxygen. Then a second ambulance drove up, blue lights flashing, and they took care of a coughing Kakko and Bandi and put masks on them, too. The pure, fresh oxygen flowed into Kakko's lungs and she felt herself recover almost instantly. She nodded she was OK. Bandi gasped, "Yeka? Nan?"

"The little girl and the old lady?" asked a man in a paramedic uniform. Bandi nodded.

"They're in the other ambulance. You brought them out?" Bandi nodded again and pointed to Kakko.

"You did well. A fire in the roof of a thatched cottage takes hold very quickly."

"How? How…?" stammered Kakko.

Then Jalli was inside the vehicle. "You OK?"

"Yeah. Yeka? Nan?"

"Alive. Both of them. Thanks to you and your dad's CPR. I'll never tell you not to act without thinking again!"

"How?" said Kakko. "How…?"

"No idea," said Jalli.

"Lady," interrupted a paramedic, "we need to treat you and your husband for shock. Your family is in good hands."

Abby walked with Shaun as he swung his crutches away from the sparks that were now blowing almost as far as the road. It was then that she realised that he was in a severe state of shock, too. His former dismissive positiveness had evaporated and he was now almost incoherent – it was clear that he was a very fragile young man. A paramedic took him in hand and forced him to lie on a stretcher and covered him with a foil blanket. Then he took Abby's arm.

"Best get you both to the hospital, too," he said.

As the ambulances drove off, Jalli saw at least three fire appliances. Water was being sprayed onto the roof which was now belching black smoke. Other brave firefighters were up ladders dragging off thatch. Then it hit her. Whatever happened, even though they might all survive, the cottage would never be the same again. Tears began streaming down her face. She didn't see Wennai running as fast as she could towards the scene.

"The people… The family… " shouted Wennai. "Anyone inside?"

The firefighters didn't hear her across the noise of their appliances and the general hubbub. Wennai found some other bystanders.

"Anyone still in there?" she asked as a firefighter came towards them to push them back and deploy barrier tape.

"Can't say. I was in the third appliance. The first thing we saw was a raging inferno." He ushered her back. "Sorry, we need you all to move further back."

"Did you see who was in the ambulances?"

"There was Jack," said another who knew the family. "I recognised him because of his being blind and that. I think Jalli got out, too. There was someone on a stretcher. Can't say I recognised anyone else."

"What about Shaun?"

"Don't know. Was he in there?"

"I think so. I was coming up to see him. I phoned him but he didn't pick up." Then the firefighters were called to manhandle a ladder and the police took over with the tape.

"Will everyone stand further back. Please allow the firefighters to do their job... Now," he barked at Wennai.

Wennai called Shaun's number. All she got was his voicemail. She texted him, telling him to contact her and let her know how he was. Then she watched as the firefighters poured streams of water into the cottage. There was nothing more she could do. She tried to stay calm, tried to pray even but it came out in a moan. Despite the heat and the fervour of the situation, she began to feel cold on the inside. She swung her arms to keep warm and then tried ringing Shaun again. Nothing, except an infernal woman's voice inviting her to leave a voicemail. Why didn't they let it ring longer? She swore at the woman – even though she knew she was only a computer.

The smoke and flames were beginning to subside to be replaced by clouds of steam.

At last the noise lessened.

"Is everyone out?" shouted Wennai again as a policeman came within earshot.

"Are you a relative?"

"N... No. Just a friend."

"Look, lady, you'll have to ask through the proper channels. All I can tell you is some people were taken by ambulance to the hospital... Sorry, I can't tell you any more. Your best bet is to contact the hospital. I don't think you should hang about here..." Wennai swayed. "You OK?"

"Ye... Yes." Wennai's head was becoming light. She had to put in all her effort to stay on her feet. Her head swam, but she couldn't pass out! Not now... Then she lost the battle; her world faded and she slumped forward. The policeman caught her. Looking up for help, he called to his chief. "This young woman's out for the count," he said as he gently laid her down onto the grass.

"Was she inside?"

"No. She was just asking about the family – said she was a friend and then fainted. Looks like shock to me…" Wennai began to come round and tried to sit up.

"I think you should get attention, miss," said the police chief.

"No, I'll be alright…"

But she clearly wasn't.

"Excuse me." Hatta Giroonan came forward. "I'm a neighbour. This girl is a friend of one of the young men who live here." She bent down to Wennai. "Would you like me to take you to the hospital?"

Wennai nodded. She had to find out if Shaun was safe. Then she started to shiver.

Hatta became worried and took her in charge. She wrapped Wennai in her own coat and led her to her car.

★ ★ ★

Inside the hospital, Jalli was immediately reunited with Yeka. They had cut off her smoke-stained blackened pyjamas and dressed her in a clean cotton hospital gown with pink teddy bears printed on it. The doctor pronounced that he didn't think there would be any long-term damage. They had got her out of the smoke just in time.

The nurse allowed Kakko and Bandi in to see Matilda as soon as they had decided they were well enough to do so. They found her sitting up in the bed, conscious but pale.

"They tell me," she croaked, "you saved my life. All I remember was that I woke up coughing, and realised what was happening. I remember getting out of bed but then I must have fainted."

"You were on the floor behind the door," explained Bandi. "I'm afraid I had to push very hard to get the door open. There was so much smoke and I couldn't stand. I had to drag you. I'm sorry. I pulled you very roughly. I wasn't sure we were going to make it…"

"Which explains why I feel bruises in places I hadn't realised I had got. They tell me, although I shall never see it, that my behind is all black and blue."

"Sorry… " said Bandi again.

"Young man, you had no alternative. I think I can put up with a few bruises… Ehrg…" Matilda found that getting animated was not good for her lungs and she fell silent.

"You'll mend," said Kakko in an off-hand, matter-of-fact kind of voice. Matilda smiled and waved her away. The girl was incorrigible. But she knew Kakko was not really in charge of her feelings. None of them were. The shock had hit them deeply.

Hatta drove Wennai straight to the hospital. When they arrived, Wennai became agitated and started asking more questions but Hatta would not let her talk. Hatta explained to the nurses in A&E that Wennai had collapsed while watching the fire. She was now conscious but rambling.

"I want… Shaun… his family…"

The doctor injected a sedative and she relaxed a bit.

"I'll make enquiries for you," he assured her, "but you must rest here. I don't want you roaming the hospital. Can you give me a surname?"

"Smith," said Hatta. "I don't know how many were inside when the fire started. Quite a number I would have thought."

A nurse was back very soon. "They are all here. All the eight are accounted for and receiving treatment – nothing is life-threatening. Like you, young lady, they are in a state of shock and they have been sedated. I will let them know you came."

"Thanks," said Wennai relieved. "But can I go—?"

"No. Not tonight. They must sleep… and so should you. Where do you live?"

"Not far. In the city."

"I suggest we phone your family and ask them to collect you."

Wennai nodded.

★ ★ ★

The warm sun permeated the blinds as the doctor was saying that he recommended they keep Yeka in just for a few more hours for observation, then they could take her home. It was then that it occurred to Jalli that their home was going to be a mess.

"The cot-tage?" she said to Jack. "What are we going to do?"

"We must get back and sort things out," answered Jack. "Let me go see how my mum is getting on and then we'll go home."

"I don't think it'll be habitable," stated Jalli. "You didn't see it. The flames…"

Just then, Hatta and Callan appeared at the entrance to the ward.

"Can we come in?" asked Hatta, gently tapping on the door.

"Of course! Hatta, Callan, so pleased to see you… I'm sorry; we must have disturbed your night. Was it you who sent for the fire brigade?"

"Yes," said Hatta. "Callan saw what happened."

"He saw the flames coming from the roof?"

"Before that. He saw the flaming torch coming from the wood…"

Hatta stopped when she saw the shocked expression on Jalli's face.

"Flaming torch…?" Jalli mouthed.

"They haven't told you?"

"Who?"

"The police. They've been at our house all night."

"We haven't seen them yet. We've only just finished with the doctors… getting over the shock," said Jalli.

"Are you all alright?"

"Yes, thank you. We are. Nobody's severely hurt. Yeka and Nan passed out with the smoke – but they're recovering. The doctors are keeping Matilda in for a few days, and Yeka here is getting better. They just want us to stay in for a few more hours to make sure… So, what did happen? You say a flaming torch?"

"Yes—" began Callan.

Hatta put a hand on her husband's arm. "We thought you had all got out but in all the confusion we couldn't be sure – it was dark, and the flames. We can't say how relieved we are… We brought Wennai into the hospital. She fainted. She didn't know how you all were – how Shaun was. She was in a bit of a state. I took her home after she was treated."

"We'll call her. Where's Shaun?"

"Don't know," said Jack. "I don't know anything. With not seeing. This is about the most frustrated I have been since… since I woke up in that hospital in Wanulka and realised for the first time that I couldn't see… Callan, tell me about this firebrand."

"You know how fascinated I am these days by the stars. Stargazing has grown on me over the years of listening to your tales. Well, last night it was perfect. There were no clouds and the stars were brilliant. I took myself out into the garden and sat in my deckchair to look up at the heavens. Because it was so dark, I didn't see anyone in the wood until he – I say 'he'; it could have been a 'she' – struck a match and lit something. Whatever it was, he must have dowsed it in petrol or something because it flared up fast. Then he threw it onto your roof. I saw it swing through the trees. It landed above where you sleep – on the wood side of the cottage.

"Then he ran away through the undergrowth back into the heart of the wood. I was stunned when I saw your roof catch. It was amazing how quickly it began to burn. I rushed up the lane to warn you. By the time I got to your gates, I saw some of you coming out – I knew you were aware, so I went back home to find my phone and call the emergency services. They got to you pretty quickly because by the time I got back to your gate to see what I could do, I heard sirens and saw the blue lights racing up the lane. Then the police came and prevented us from following. You sure you're all OK?"

"We're fine," said Jack. "Badly shocked of course… but I can't get over what you're saying. You're telling us the fire was started *deliberately*."

"Definitely. I saw somone throw a burning torch."

"Who would want to do that… to us?" Jalli began to shudder. "We could all have died in there. Does someone want to kill us? If we'd all been in bed asleep, we could all have died… It was only the quick thinking of my grown-up children that saved Yeka and Nan." Jalli went cold and began to shake. Jack held her tightly. A nurse came across and felt Jalli's wrist.

"She's still in shock," she pronounced and rang for assistance. They called for a doctor, who ordered another jab.

"She must rest," he said firmly. "I suggest you leave her for now."

"I'm sorry," said Hatta; "we didn't know you hadn't realised how it started." Jack led them out of the cubicle.

"That's OK," said Jack. "We had to find out soon. Better from you than the police. She'll be alright... Tell me, what state is the house in? Is there any chance we can stay there this evening?"

"No way," said Callan. "There's no roof left. It's all blackened down one side and running with water."

"Callan," chided Hatta. "You have no tact at all! But he's right, you can't stay there until it's been repaired. We left the police and the fire brigade still looking for clues."

"I'll make arrangements with a hotel," sighed Jack. "I think the insurance will cover that... But all our documents are in the house, of course. I can't really remember the details of the insurance off the top of my head."

"But you know the insurance company name?"

"Yes, I think so."

"I'll phone them for you if you like."

"Thanks. That would be helpful... Tell them we'll confirm everything as soon as we have access to the files... Jalli's in no state to look for anything at the moment..."

★ ★ ★

Back in Woodglade, the fire service and the police were continuing to investigate. The fire officers declared the fire out but the damage was severe. The lawn was piled up with half-burnt thatching straw, the roof was a criss-cross of blackened and charred timbers, and water was still trickling from a pool that had collected around the greenhouse. Inside, up the stairs, greasy with ash and melted plastic, the forensic team were attempting to verify Callan Giroonan's witness statement. Officers were also over the fence in the wood.

"Inspector," called an officer, "I think I have found something."

The inspector pushed his way carefully over to where his colleague was standing looking at a small, shiny tin lid. "That's not been here long. It's too clean."

With gloved hands, the inspector picked it up carefully by the rim. He smelt it. "That's some sort of accelerant, alright. Should be able to trace this... Call the dog handler. There is a possibility that we can find out which way our suspect went."

The dog was given a sniff of the lid. Then he snuffled at the ground and began moving deeper into the trees. He found the rest of the container and then, urged on, he began tugging his handler over towards the path through the wood that Jalli sometimes took on her way to her college.

"They definitely went or came from this way, sir," he called. They ran after the dog who led them to the gate that led into the krallen field. After the gate, the dog left the path and went diagonally across the field, scattering the krallens who were moving towards the college to be milked.

"Oi!" shouted the stockhandler. "Get that dog out of the field."

"Sorry," said the officer loudly. "Police." He charged through the unhappy animals and continued on towards the far corner by the road. Breathing deeply, the inspector approached the stockhandler.

"Sorry about that. Did you see anything last night? After the fire started in that cottage?"

"No. I wasn't here. I was at home. I don't live here. That's Jalli's place, isn't it? Jalli Smith?"

"I believe so," replied the policeman. "Do you know her?"

"Yes. She works here in the college. Has done for years. What happened?"

"That's what we aim to find out. Can I have your name?"

"Lumg Yulli... I wasn't here, officer."

"So you said."

The dog handler called out. "Must have got into a car or something here. The trail has gone cold."

"Wait for me. Don't trample the area," shouted the inspector. But the dog handler was well aware of the possibility of learning a lot from the site of the suspect's disappearance. The inspector summoned his forensic team.

13

At the hospital, Kakko and Bandi had left Matilda to rest and had returned to their father and mother. Jack was awake with a sleeping Jalli on his shoulder. Abby joined them, too. Yeka was getting fidgety. *A good sign*, thought Kakko. She picked her up.

"Want to go home…" Yeka whimpered.

"I know. But we can't just yet. I know, it's hard to be patient, but we just have to be. Tell you what, let's go down to see if the café is open… Dad, what are we going to do when they let us go?"

"When your mum wakes up we'll arrange a hotel or something. That would solve the problem for a couple of days while we assess the extent of the damage."

Bandi took an empty chair beside Abby and reached for her hand.

"You OK?"

"Yeah. It's all so sad."

"Where's Shaun?"

"Said he was going out for some air. Must have been an hour ago."

"Apparently they brought Wennai here to the hospital. They treated her for shock. She arrived at the house to find it ablaze…"

"I'll go and look for him," said Abby, glad to have something to do.

She found Shaun in a little garden outside the front of the hospital. He was sitting quite still watching the traffic.

"You OK, Shaun?"

Shaun nodded.

"You want to talk?"

"Not really."

"Bandi heard they brought Wennai to the hospital. She came looking for you at the cottage and saw the fire. They reckon Hatta brought her in after she fainted."

"I'll text her." Shaun pulled himself up. His leg was painful but it wasn't just that that was hurting. The horrific events of the night had knocked away some of the fragile props he had been trying to build. He felt somehow even more diminished. Abby instinctively caught hold of his arm to help him up.

"Let me help."

"No. I'll be fine." Shaun shrugged her off.

Abby persisted. "Can I get you anything?"

"I said, I'll be fine," snapped Shaun. "You go back to Mum and Dad." He turned away and limped off.

Back inside, Abby explained that she had found Shaun. "He's not great."

"All this has opened up his wounds – and I don't just mean his leg," said Kakko, thoughtfully.

"I know. Sounds as if he and Wennai need each other."

"They've been special to each other for ages. It's about time they admitted it," said Kakko, frankly.

Half an hour later, Shaun clumped into the room the family were using, with Wennai on his arm. He seemed a little more himself. Jalli was still sitting with her eyes closed.

"How damaged is the house?" Shaun asked. "It looked pretty bad to me when we left. It was still on fire."

"Hatta says it's quite bad. And it's also a crime scene," explained his father.

"A crime scene!"

Jack began to explain but before he had got very far, an imposing-looking man came to the door accompanied by a nurse.

"This is Inspector Dollod," said the nurse. "Mr Smitt, I said it was alright for him to talk to you for a few moments... Inspector, Mrs Smitt is still in shock. Please try not to stress her any further."

"I will do my best," smiled the plain–clothes detective. He described what they had found in the wood. "Have your family any enemies?" he asked. "Has anyone threatened to do this?"

"No. No-one. That's what's so horrifying," said Jack. "We had no idea anyone would want to do this to us... Who would hate us so much they would want to kill us?"

Jalli began to stir. She sat up and rubbed her eyes. Jack introduced her.

"Sorry, Inspector, I must look a sight," apologised Jalli.

"No, I'm sorry. I don't wish to disturb you, but... You know that we believe this was deliberate?" Jalli nodded. "We have followed the suspect to the gate of the agricultural college. He escaped through the wood and across the field. We think he had a vehicle parked up there. We are pretty sure it was a male from the size of the footprints. Have you any idea who this might be?"

"No. N-none at all. I-I can't imagine..." stammered Jalli.

"We have some good leads," assured the detective. "I'll be in touch. Let me know if you leave the hospital."

"We will," said Jack, taking Jalli into his arms.

"Big man!" said Yeka after the policeman had gone. "Mummy, can we go home now?"

"Not yet, Yeka. Sorry."

"Come on, Yeka," said Abby. "Let's go to the café. Get you an ice cream."

Yeka took her hand and pulled. Abby smiled.

"I don't think there is much wrong with you, little lady… Come on, Bandi, come with us."

As they walked along the corridor, Yeka swinging on Abby's arm, Abby told Bandi that she was really worried about Shaun.

"I know he's been through a lot but, the thing is, he's barely said a word to anyone since we got out of the cottage. Everyone's fussed over Yeka and your nan, and Kakko and you for rescuing them. They're treating your mum for shock, but Shaun's been so quiet that everyone's just ignored him. I tried to talk to him but he didn't want a conversation."

Bandi spotted Kakko pursuing them down the corridor. They stopped and waited for her.

"I need an ice cream, too…" Kakko could see they had been in earnest conversation. "Sorry to interrupt… You talking about me?"

"No. Shaun. We're a bit worried about him."

Kakko sighed. "Look, I have to tell you this. Shaun doesn't want anyone to talk about it, but…" she hesitated, then resolved to continue. "What you don't know," said Kakko gently, "is that he, and we all, thought he was going to die on that last adventure. If a man with a gun ready to shoot him hadn't been taken out by someone else the second he was about to pull the trigger, he would have been, and that… that," stammered Kakko, "that takes some coming to terms with… Look, no-one else knows… right. I shouldn't have told you really but I can't not say anything forever. He doesn't want anyone to know – especially Mum and Dad. He was doing kind of fine considering… We all were… But I'm scared that all this has set us back... The thing is, it feels like..." Kakko stopped as she tried to find the right words. "It's as if the floor under you has suddenly become risky to walk on – like you're walking on thin ice that could give way at any time. There is no longer any solid ground. Life, everything is... is so... so fragile... The fact is, we could all lose one another so easily... Poof! And we're going to the next world – or the ones you love are without you, which is worse..." Kakko tailed off.

Abby put her free hand around Kakko as tears streamed down both their faces.

"Sorry, Kakko. I had no idea it was as bad as that."

"Of course not. Look, I'm glad you know. Sometimes it's better to get it out there... But we can't tell Dad and Mum, and especially Nan... not yet and, after this, not for a long time... Come on, Yeka, let's get that ice cream."

"Why are you crying, Kakko?" asked Yeka.

"Oh, I want to go home like you, and we can't... You see, Yeka, there's been a big fire and they've got to mend the house before we can go home... and that will take a long, long time... What sort of ice cream would you like?"

"Strawberry. Shaun likes strawberry... Shaun's very sad, too."

"I know... I know what; after we've finished ours, why don't you take him an ice cream and go and cuddle him while he eats it... Cheer him up."

"Yes. Shaun's my friend."

"We're all your friends, Yeka."

"Yes. But I don't like it when Shaun goes away."

"I know. But with his broken leg he can't go far for the moment... I think you are his special friend, too."

"Only sometimes. He likes Wennai best."

"I don't think Wennai is going to take him away from you, though."

"Can I have some chocolate in my ice cream?"

"Why not? If they have any."

But it was too early for the café. They had a half-hour's wait but Kakko daren't take Yeka back without her ice cream. She proposed a walk.

"Come on, let's explore," she said as enthusiastically as possible.

Yeka pouted but she could see there was no-one to serve them ice cream, so she just folded her arms, lowered her head and said nothing.

"I think," said Abby, "I saw a play area back down that corridor. Let's start exploring there."

Kakko's phone bleeped a text message. It was Tam, who had turned on his phone to find Kakko's midnight message. It simply read: Where r u? U OK? Call me. Tam xxx.

Kakko sat in the play area with Yeka, Bandi and Abby. The toys weren't very exciting but Yeka was making the most of them. Kakko called Tam.

"Hey, Kakko," he replied. "Great to hear you. I've just seen the devastation. You all OK? Where are you?"

"We're all fine. We're at the hospital. Nan's a bit shook up. We had to drag her out. She was unconscious. She's all black and blue but she'll live. They want to keep Yeka a bit longer… We all breathed rather a lot of horrid smoke."

"What happened?"

"The roof caught light. The police say it was deliberate."

"No way?"

"Straight up. Somebody lit something and chucked it onto the roof from the woods."

"Who would do that?"

"Search me."

"Look, I'm coming down to the hospital. I'll get the next bus."

"No, don't do that, Tam. We're OK, honest. There isn't much room and the nurses are getting worked up about all the coming and going anyway. Hatta and Callan came... and the police. The doctor wants Mum to rest. I'll be back in touch. I must stick around for Yeka... She's fine. Just impatient... No, I don't blame her... Yeka, do you want to talk to Tam?" Kakko gave Yeka the phone. She pulled a face but nevertheless said, "Hello, Tam... Yes... No, she's just real dirty and her hair is sticking out. She smells horrid... Oh, no, *I* don't – the nurses washed me after the doctor came... I will, I'll tell her... Tam says you can go to his house for a shower if you like... Wait, no, his mum says, 'make that a bath'..."

"Give me the phone, Yeka. Tam, it's really not that bad..."

"It *is*," shouted Yeka.

"No, I agree," said Kakko down the phone. "I don't think there is anything much wrong with her either." Kakko pulled a face at her little sister. "The café's opening and I promised her something sweet. I'd better go... I'll call when I know more. Bye... Yeka, you didn't have to tell him all those things."

"I did. He asked me what you looked like..."

At least, thought Kakko, *he's not going to get a shock when he sees me... Oh, I better ring Prof Rob and tell him I won't be in...*

★ ★ ★

Inspector Dollod drove into the agricultural college car park. The area around the entrance to the drive, some one hundred metres from the college, was still taped off. Getting out of the car, he asked a student where he might find the principal. He was directed to the reception where he introduced himself, and was taken up to Mrs Trenz's office on the first floor.

"Inspector Dollod," said the principal, "what can I do for you?"

The inspector explained he had come in relation to the fire at White Gates Cottage. "Have you any idea who might have done such a thing to your neighbours?" he asked.

"This is a shocking thing," said Mrs Trenz. "Jalli has been working here ever since they moved into the cottage."

"How long ago was that?"

"Well over twenty years – nearer thirty, I think. Do you want me to look it up?"

"No. Not just now. Perhaps later. Where did they move from?"

"Oh. Another planet. Or planets. You know about the portals?"

Inspector Dollod obviously didn't, so Mrs Trenz went on to explain about the white gates to the astonished inspector.

"That's why it's called White Gates Cottage, when all you can see is one gate."

"I had no idea that people settled here from other parts of the universe through portals."

"They don't go round advertising it, Inspector – but neither do they keep it a secret."

Inspector Dollod made a note in his book, then returned to his next question.

"We know that the perpetrator escaped through the wood and then crossed the field, diagonally, to the field gate beside your entrance drive. This is an unusual thing to do in the middle of a very dark night, wouldn't you think? I believe you have a krallen bull in the field."

"Are you suggesting that it was one of my staff, Inspector? I would be most surprised – very surprised indeed – if this fire was started by any employee here. Apart from the fact that it is not something I think any of them would ever contemplate, Jalli Smith is a very popular colleague."

"The perpetrator stood around for a bit – probably

watching the fire from the top of the field – just before he got to the corner and climbed over the barbed wire fence next to the post. We think he was familiar with the layout. I would like to interview all members of the college staff and, of course, I would have to include you in that."

"Inspector Dollod, you don't mean to imply—?"

"I'm not implying anything, Mrs Trenz, just looking for clues and eliminating possibilities."

"I want to see who did this caught as much as you do, Inspector. You have my permission."

★ ★ ★

A team of detectives set up in the principal's outer office and the adjoining staff rooms. The staff were called in in turn and asked about their whereabouts the previous evening. They were each asked to provide alibis. When they got to Lumg Yulli, Inspector Dollod was aware the man had a police record. He also knew the man looked after the stock in the field and would be completely familiar with the lay of the land.

"This morning, Mr Yulli, you said you were not here when the fire started. Where were you?"

"I was at home."

"Who else was there?"

"Last night? No-one. My wife and daughter had gone to see my mother-in-law. They won't be back until this afternoon."

"Who can verify you were at home, Mr Yulli?"

"I don't know. We live in the country. Mr Ted at the end of the lane might have seen me drive up. His van was gone this morning, though. He starts early."

"Not a very good alibi, Mr Yulli."

"I tell you, I was at home. You can't think I would do that to

Jalli Smith? I owe my job to her. She stuck up for me... said I should be given a second chance. Apparently that man, Salma, said some horrible things to her – but she stood up for me."

"Tell me more," said the inspector.

Lumg Yulli explained that Salma had left the college shortly before he came but others had told him how Jalli had won the day. He didn't know all the details.

"One thing more, Mr Yulli... If I were crossing a field of krallens in the middle of a dark night, how would they behave?"

"These? Oh, these are pretty docile. They wouldn't hurt you unless they felt threatened. The bull was in there last night, though. He wouldn't have stood for any nonsense. If it had been someone, like yourself, who was not known to them, they might have been spooked – unless you know your way around krallens."

"But if that person was familiar to them?"

"Oh, no problem. They know the people who come and go through the field. If you weren't a stranger they wouldn't even get up unless they thought you had come with food... or the vet. And that's not usual at night."

"So a familiar person could walk through without being bothered?"

"Yes. But it wasn't *me*, Inspector."

"Thank you, Mr Yulli. Stick around."

"I'm not going anywhere. I haven't anything to hide."

"Good." Inspector Dollod's mind was working – he had finally identified someone who may have had a grudge against a gentle, but principled, woman. Here was another lead worth investigating.

14

Kakko texted her boss, Prof Rob: Fire at cottage last night. Can't come in today. Sorry. Kakko :(

She had barely got the message to say he had received the text when her phone rang. It was Prof Rob.

"A fire!" he said. "Are you all OK?"

"Yeah. Just. We're at the hospital – they're keeping Nan here under observation. Smoke inhalation. But she'll be fine."

"Goodness. Not a small fire, then?"

"The roof. Apparently the damage is pretty severe. I haven't seen it yet."

"How are *you*?"

"I'm OK. It was pretty bad but we all got out. Nan's the worst; she passed out with the smoke. Bandi had to drag her out. Yeka was affected, too, but I got her outside quickly enough. She's OK this morning."

"Look, I'm coming to the hospital. I live just round the corner. I won't be long."

"But Prof Rob," protested Kakko, "it's—"

But Prof Rob had hung up.

★ ★ ★

Yeka had eaten her ice cream and now sat behind the biggest piece of cake ever. It seemed to Kakko it was half as big as her head. It was amazing the speed children could bounce back after a shock. She, herself, didn't feel much like eating; she had bought herself a large, hot tea.

Kakko saw her boss enter the front doors and go towards the reception desk. She called out to him from the café area.

"Prof."

He was out of breath. He must have run.

"Why do they put hospitals on the tops of hills?" he asked.

"Because the rich people have already built their houses at the bottom of them," suggested Kakko.

"Yep... you're right... Gosh. You've had a rough night."

"Do I look that bad? I told you not to come in. Yeka says I smell."

"Suffice it to say that I don't have to guess that you were inside when it started."

Kakko told him the story.

"So where are you going to stay now?"

"Dad says we should go to a hotel. As soon as Yeka is alright to leave we'll go somewhere we can get cleaned up."

"Come to us... All of you."

"But... we can't—"

"There is just me and my wife these days. It's plenty big enough. A large house at the bottom of the hill where the 'rich people' live – you know it?"

"Yeah. But—"

"No buts."

"Thanks. But it isn't my decision. You'll have to work that out with Dad and Mum."

"Can I see them? I mean, are they receiving visitors?"

"I think the wards are supposed to be closed to visitors in the mornings. They let in our neighbours, Hatta and Callan Giroonan, because they arrived in the middle of the night, I guess... and the police got in... Well, they are the police.

Although the nurse was pretty bossy even with them. Mum's supposed to be resting."

"That's fine. That makes sense... Police? Why did they need to come in so early?"

"Suspicious circumstances. Callan says it was started deliberately. He saw it."

"Gosh!" Rob said again. "Look, will you pass on my invitation to your parents? You can just turn up. I won't go into work today, so we'll be ready whenever."

"I'll tell them," promised Kakko. "But I don't think they would want—"

"Tell them my wife and I insist."

"OK. If you think—"

"I do."

Yeka was getting impatient again. Her large piece of cake had vanished.

"Stop pulling, Yeka... I'd better go now... but thanks. Thanks for coming round... If we *did* come, Mum would need to rest... and Shaun's leg's not great... And there are seven of us – eight with Nan."

"Understood. No problem. Absolutely no problem."

Yeka was tugging at Kakko's arm with both hands.

"OK, madam. Don't be rude. Excuse us, Prof..."

"Bye for now. God bless you."

"Thanks," said Kakko, again.

As she found her way back to the ward, Kakko reflected on the wonderful generosity of a man whom she only really knew as her employer. He did not have to offer them anything other than to understand Kakko's need to be off work for a few days, but he and his wife had recognised their plight and were willing to open their home to a large family worse for wear

"Dad," said Kakko when they got back to the ward, "Prof Rob came round. I saw him downstairs just now. He says when we leave here, we can all go round there for lunch… or whatever. And he is offering us his bathroom."

"That's kind of him," murmured Jalli, still half-asleep.

"Yes. But he wouldn't expect us to take him up on it," said Jack. "We wouldn't presume—"

"Dad! He meant it," said Kakko a little forcefully. "He said to tell you he insists."

"I know he *meant* it but—"

"He did *actually* mean it. He wasn't just saying it. He really wants us to go to his place. He said it was only just down the hill. He got here in five minutes after I texted him to say I wasn't coming in today."

"But he couldn't have asked his wife—"

"He has. She said I could have a bath."

"Kakko, you haven't… What did you say to him?"

Kakko explained the course of the conversation, concluding: "I thanked him for his invitation and, when he insisted, I said the decision was yours… yours and Mum's." She felt tired. They were all tired. Exhausted. Jack knew, too. He felt a bit annoyed. It was irrational, he knew. Kakko realised she had to back off. Her mum was asleep again. But Yeka was bouncing – revived by her breakfast.

The nurse popped her head in to check on them. "Yeka needs something to do," said Kakko. "She's getting very restless."

"I'll get the doctor to see her, and if he says it's OK you could take her out for a bit if you want."

Fifteen long minutes later the doctor came. Jalli was sound asleep and Kakko had been struggling to protect her from Yeka.

"Now, young lady, how are you?" asked the doctor. Seeing that something different was happening, Yeka paid attention.

"Let's listen to what your chest is doing," he said. He put his stethoscope into his ears and lifted Yeka's top. She stood still for him.

"Now the back... Mmm. That's fine. I dare say you would like some breakfast?"

"No," stated Yeka, firmly. "Lunch."

"Are you sure you don't want any breakfast? Why not?"

"Already had it!" she stated, decidedly. Kakko explained.

"I see. So you're now ready for your lunch."

"But it isn't lunchtime yet," said Kakko. Yeka pouted.

"I don't think we need to concern ourselves about you, young lady. You kept that food down alright, it seems."

"Sorry, wasn't I supposed to feed her?" asked Kakko.

"No problem. I think we can discharge her... What about your mother?" Jalli was fast asleep and Jack was now nodding beside her. "I think we can leave these people to nature's healing properties. Are *you* alright?" he asked Kakko, Bandi and Abby.

"Fine," said Kakko lightly. "We're a bit worried about Shaun, though. He got out quickly enough but... Where is he?"

"Bathroom, I think," answered Bandi.

Just then, Shaun appeared at the door. He looked a bit brighter. He had received a text from Wennai.

The doctor looked towards Shaun. "How's the leg?"

"I just need to lie down properly," said Shaun. "It's just a little achy."

"We could probably find you a bed."

"No!" Shaun almost shouted. "Sorry, I've spent too long as an inpatient here already."

The doctor smiled. "Understood. You're not on my list anyway... I think it would be a good idea if you all got some rest in a proper bed. I think I can let you all go." He looked down at Yeka with a smile. "What do you say to that, young lady?"

"I want to go home!" Yeka stated emphatically. Jack was now all attention and Jalli was coming round.

"That won't be possible, I'm afraid," Jack explained to her gently. "The house got spoiled in the fire."

"I think we should take up Prof Rob's offer... At least for now," said Kakko. "Then we can make some proper arrangements with a hotel and the insurance... We need to get Yeka out of here. And we'll only be five minutes from Nan."

"OK," agreed her father reluctantly as he held Jalli's hand. He needed to get her somewhere comfortable. "That does make sense. We can make it up to them later. How should we let them know?"

"I'll text," said Kakko. "Anyway, he said he wouldn't be going into work – just to rock up."

Jalli became aware of the way the conversation was going.

"You can't just appear on someone's doorstep with seven people in our state," she protested. "Give me your phone and let me talk to Mrs... I don't even know her name!"

"It's Tlasa. Rob and Tlasa... OK. I'll get the number and give you to them."

Kakko rang. Prof Rob answered. "Hi," said Kakko. "I think we would like to take you up on your offer..."

Jalli looked daggers at her daughter as she reached for the phone.

"Mum wants to talk to you..." Kakko handed her mother the phone.

"Professor Rob, I'm so sorry about this," she began; "we shouldn't be bothering you like this. Kakko can be rather—"

She broke off as Prof Rob insisted they would be delighted to take them in. He would be up to the main doors with his car in ten minutes. Would that give them enough time?

"Thank you very much, Professor. You are too kind…" She looked at her husband, "He says he'll come with a car." Jack shrugged his shoulders – he couldn't think of a better solution. He knew his mother would have resisted vigorously because she would see it as an imposition, something they could never repay. But he was less of that mind. Community would never work unless people looked after each other – and that meant receiving at times as well as giving.

"OK," he said. "Until we can sort something out with the insurance company."

"Alright. We are most grateful. While we get ourselves sorted out with the insurance company," said Jalli. "But give us a bit longer, would you? We'll be ready in twenty minutes."

Outside the front door, the traffic was in full flow. Life had started up in earnest as people were going about their morning business – some arriving for work, others coming back after dropping off their kids for school and making their way to the shops that had begun putting out A-boards to entice people inside. Kakko spotted a place for fast food and began to realise she was now hungry. She took Yeka to a bench beside a flowerbed near the roadside and the rest of the family followed.

In less than three minutes, a black car had driven up and Prof Rob's wife, Tlasa, got out and came over to them. "Kakko? Yeka?" she asked. "Hi. I'm Tlasa, Rob's wife. He's in the car waiting for us. Oh, you do need to get cleaned up. Poor you."

"Hi… This is my family: Dad, Mum, Shaun, Bandi and his girlfriend, Abby… I told Rob we were seven… Are you sure you can cope with so many of us?"

Tlasa shook everyone's hand in turn. "Of course. We have a big house."

"We are so grateful—" began Jalli.

"Nonsense. You need somewhere and we have this great big house… Come on. The pleasure is all ours… Kakko, you know how to find our house?"

Kakko nodded.

"Well, can I suggest that you take Bandi and Abby… You are all OK to walk?"

"Sure," said Kakko.

"And the rest of you come in the car."

Taking Yeka's hand, Kakko followed Tlasa to the car and tried to hand her over to her mother. Yeka decided she didn't want to leave her sister and protested. "She can walk with us," said Kakko. "The walk will do her good."

★ ★ ★

When they had all entered the large old city-centre house, Kakko could not remember being fussed about so much since the time Tam had been kidnapped by the Wanulkans in the Medlam system. Tlasa led her and Yeka to the bathroom and showed them how to turn on the water. She gathered all sorts of soaps, oils and perfumes and urged Kakko to make use of them. "Pamper yourself," she ordered. "When you are ready, I will see what we can find for you in the wardrobe."

Yeka was already finding things to throw into the water and began stripping off. She was no more of a retiring child than Kakko had been when she was three.

Soon they were both in the water and Yeka was delighting in pouring water over Kakko's head. Kakko let her.

Jalli and Abby were taken upstairs to Rob and Tlasa's *en suite* bathroom.

Meanwhile, downstairs, Prof Rob was explaining to Jack

and Shaun that he and Tlasa had already agreed they could use their beach house until the cottage was repaired.

Tlasa joined them.

"Your young men can use the bathroom as soon as the girls are finished," she smiled. "I hope you don't mind waiting."

"Not at all," said Shaun. "Kakko has always got places before me – even when I didn't have a broken leg to contend with…"

"And in a strange place, I need Jalli to help me," said Jack. "I'm in no hurry."

"I was just explaining," said Rob to his wife, "that we can make our beach house available to them…"

"Nonsense," interjected Tlasa. "There are eight of them over three generations; how do you expect them to squeeze into that place?"

"They haven't anywhere else. You agreed they could have it… Kakko was talking about a hotel."

"I hadn't quite realised how many they were then. No, they can stay *here*. They can take over *this* place and *we* can go to the beach house," said Tlasa in a determined voice.

"Well, I suppose that would work. It'll be weeks before they get back into their house, by all accounts," said Prof Rob.

"That settles it, then. They can't live in our beach house for weeks. Even renting a furnished place large enough would be difficult, let alone expensive."

"We have insurance—" began Jack.

"You are a family. It's not just about rooms…" said Prof Rob decisively. "Tlasa has spoken. This house is yours. We'll move out this afternoon. It's about time we used the beach house anyway. I like it there. And it's only fifteen minutes further from the space centre."

Neither Rob nor Tlasa would brook any dissent. The decision had been made before Jalli returned. No amount of

Jalli protesting, "We couldn't possibly…" made any difference. The house was theirs – Rob and Tlasa were going on holiday.

⋆ ⋆ ⋆

Kakko dressed herself in some of Tlasa's things. They looked entirely wrong on her – and not just because they were grossly over-sized. She joined them at the table and helped herself to heaps of stuff that Tlasa had conjured up. Yeka was hungry too, despite the big cake and ice cream. Rob and Tlasa were revelling in the opportunity to help such appreciative refugees. Just to see them both eating heartily was a joy. Kakko's phone buzzed. It had been buzzing with messages ever since she'd left the hospital and she had ignored them. This one was, however, from Tam. Where was she? Could he come to her? Kakko told him her whereabouts. He replied he was on his way.

After the meal, Hatta rang to say she couldn't get into White Gates Cottage to look for the insurance documents. She had gone round but a policeman wouldn't let her inside the house. They said it was too dangerous. It was surrounded by red and white tape.

⋆ ⋆ ⋆

Just minutes later, Tam was greeted without restraint by a clean but oddly dressed and funny smelling girlfriend.

"Oh, Tam. It was horrible."

"I don't doubt it. The place is gutted."

"Gutted?" said Kakko alarmed.

"Well… almost. The roof beams are all charred, and they poured so much water on it… I dare say, though," he added hurriedly, "most of *your* stuff will be wet but OK. Being downstairs and everything. It's all taped off with police no-go tape. No-one is allowed in."

"Oh, Tam… Look, someone's got to get back to the hospital to see Nan and tell her where we are and what we're doing. Mum's not up to it, and Shaun… I'll tell you about him on the way. I must find some clothes. I can't be seen in these," she whispered.

"I'll come with you."

"We'll go to the hospital," chimed in Bandi. He was wearing some of Prof Rob's stuff that didn't look as out of place as Kakko's. "You get off to the shops."

"Oh. My purse. I hadn't thought of that… My cards are still in the house. I had a note stuffed in my jeans but I spent most of that on food for Yeka. "

Tam smiled. "No problem. My treat."

★ ★ ★

That same afternoon, Inspector Dollod, accompanied by a detective constable, decided to call upon Salma. They had obtained his address from Mrs Trenz's secretary. Pulling up across the street, they noticed a car in the drive which was on a slope, giving them a perfect view of the car's rear tyres. "Look familiar?" asked the inspector as they passed it.

"Could be," answered the constable.

They found Salma at home, alone. He had evidently not been up long because he was only partially dressed, and unshaven. He opened the door to the plain–clothes officers.

"Yeah?" he asked, gruffly.

"Mr Salma?"

"Yeah. What d'you want?" He looked annoyed.

"Police. Do you mind if we had a word?"

"Why? What's up?" He was now properly awake.

"There has been an incident at the cottage next to the college in which you worked until last year. We're interviewing all employees of the college."

"Like you said, I don't work there anymore."

"We know. But you might still be able to help us."

"How?"

"Mr Salma, can we come in?" Salma ushered them reluctantly into his front room which was not exactly tidy.

"The wife… She left me… Took most of the furniture, the clock, the TV and other stuff. I don't rightly know what time of day it is."

"Oh. I'm sorry. Recently?"

"Couple of months… Here." Salma cleared two chairs of their piled-up contents – magazines, newspapers, dirty plates and a muddy pair of trousers.

"She didn't take the car?"

"Couldn't. She's not insured to drive it, or she would have."

"It must be hard for you?"

"It is. Losing my job didn't help."

"Have you found anything else?"

"No, I haven't… I didn't leave willingly. Getting the sack doesn't exactly recommend you to another employer," he grumbled.

"I don't suppose it does."

"But you haven't come to offer me a job."

"No. I'm afraid not… Can you tell us where you were at around ten o'clock yesterday evening?"

"Here. At home."

"Alone?"

"Of course."

"Do you know the occupants of White Gates Cottage?"

"Yeah. I know Jalli Smith. She works at the college…

169

Look, you don't think I was responsible for the fire, do you? Was anyone hurt?"

"What can you tell us about the fire?"

"It was on the…" he tailed off.

"But you don't have a TV, Mr Salma."

"No, the… the car radio."

"You were out in it last night. Where did you go?"

"Nowhere. I heard the news this morning. Look, you don't think I have anything to do with this, do you?"

"Mr Salma, at this stage we're interviewing everyone as a routine. Is there any reason why we should be particularly interested in you?"

"No! Of course not. It's just… I wondered why you made a special journey out to see me – seeing as I haven't been near the college for months."

"What do you know of Jallaxanya Smith?"

"She's been working at the college for a long time – in the entomology section. She's obsessed with bees."

"Have you visited her in White Gates Cottage?"

"No, never. I was never invited."

"Why? Did others get invited?"

"Some, perhaps. A lot of people work at the college."

"So you weren't particular friends?"

"Nah. We didn't have much in common. She and her husband just appeared there decades ago. Some say they are aliens from another planet."

"Do you believe that?"

"She has her very decided views on things. Maybe."

"Have you been out today, Mr Salma?"

"No. Why?"

"But you must have listened to the car radio this morning…"

"I never went anywhere, though."

"Are the shoes behind the front door the ones you used yesterday?"

"Yeah. Why?"

"Do you mind if we have a look at them, Mr Salma?"

"Yeah, I do. You have no right."

"Have you a reason why you wouldn't want us to examine the shoes, Mr Salma?"

Salma was trapped. "Nah," he said in a resigned voice. Inspector Dollod nodded to his constable, who went to study them.

"So you've been in all morning, Mr Salma. You asked me if anyone was hurt. If you had picked up the news on the radio this morning, you would know the answer to that question."

The constable stood in the doorway with the shoes in a plastic bag. He nodded to his boss.

"I put it to you, Mr Salma, that you visited the college area last night and you deliberately set fire to White Gates Cottage."

"No way!"

"Mr Salma, I'm arresting you on suspicion of setting fire to White Gates Cottage yesterday evening. You don't have to say anything that will harm your rights, you understand? And I am obtaining permission from the appropriate authorities to search your house... Bag the trousers, too, if you would, Constable."

"But..." spluttered Salma.

"Save it for the interview, Mr Salma." The detective inspector beckoned him through the door. As Salma passed the constable, he pushed him violently, made a grab for the shoes – and ran from the house.

Inspector Dollod was immediately on his radio. "Suspect at large. On foot carrying shoes in a clear plastic bag. He's dressed in a white string vest and blue jeans and running down Rainy Road."

"Sorry, Inspector. He rather caught me by surprise," said the constable, rubbing his neck that had come into contact with a banister rail.

"No harm done. He's not going to get far, is he? He's more stupid than I thought."

15

Jalli was now properly awake; the effects of the drugs had worn off. Jack hadn't been sure about the injections in the first place – but not being able to see it, had not understood enough to intervene. However, the sleeping hadn't done her any harm. Jalli was now returning to being her usual positive self. She told Tlasa how much they appreciated being able to be all together so near to where Matilda was recuperating.

Tam explained that there was certainly no going back to live in the house for many weeks.

"Right," said Tlasa; "this house is yours until your own is repaired. You can stay here as long as it takes. Rob and I will have a holiday in the beach house."

"But that won't be very convenient for you, will it?" said Jalli.

"Taking the bus into town and out again twice a day will not kill me. Many people where we work travel further than that," answered Tlasa firmly.

"Including Kakko when she's in Woodglade," smiled Rob.

"But—" began Jalli, again.

"You're staying!" ordered Tlasa. "And that's final."

"My wife can be quite bossy at times," laughed Prof Rob.

"Only when it matters," she scolded him.

"You haven't seen the cottage… It's going to take weeks if not months," said Tam, gingerly.

"This house is yours if it takes a year," said Rob decisively.

Jack extended his hand to Rob. "From the bottom of our hearts, thank you."

Secretly, Kakko was thinking how cool the place was and was itching to see where her room would be. She had had the same room in the same house all her life; this was an adventure… But then the thought of her room being spoiled filled her with sadness.

"When can we go and see White Gates Cottage?" she asked.

"I think I need a proper night's sleep first," said Jalli. "There is nothing we can do there, I suppose?"

"Except for informing the insurance people, nothing that can't wait till tomorrow," said Jack. "Look, if you want to go with Tam, we won't stop you, Kakko."

"Thanks, Dad. I might go back to Tam's anyway – but I'll be back here to sleep."

"You won't be late, will you?" said her mum, a little more anxiously than she wanted. She couldn't dismiss the knowledge that the fire had been started deliberately.

"No, Mum. I won't."

"Thanks, Kakko."

Bandi and Abby came in from the hospital. Matilda was getting on fine. She couldn't imagine staying at Prof Rob's but they had jollied her into believing it would be alright.

"We met Inspector Dollod," he said. "He has some news for us. I told him where we were and he said he would come and see us later."

★ ★ ★

Just before Tlasa had finished preparing a grand evening meal, Kakko and Tam returned. Then Inspector Dollod appeared at the door.

"We've got him," he said. "He made a run for it but he didn't get very far."

"Who? Who was it?" asked Jack.

"A man called Salma. What can you tell me about him?"

Jalli sighed. She told the inspector the whole story of Salma's insults and slurs that led to his dismissal, adding, "But Mrs Trenz said that what he said to me was only the 'last straw'. His secretary had been complaining for some time but she hadn't had enough evidence on which to act, and then, what really clinched it was the way he behaved towards Mrs Trenz herself."

"Thank you," said the inspector. "I shall need you to make a statement."

"This is awful. I've always tried to be kind to him."

"He's complaining the whole planet's down on him. His wife has left him and his children don't want to know him… He has confessed. I think his lawyer might be making out a case of unsound mind."

"Oh, dear," said Jalli. "Perhaps if I—"

"He could have killed us all, Mum!" protested Kakko. "I'm not surprised his wife and kids don't want to see him. I doubt they feel sorry for him."

"It might be because you were the kindest of everyone, that he picked on you," suggested Tlasa. "In some perverted way you have made more of an impression on him than less sympathetic people. Why not pick on the principal, for example?"

"Or it could be that your cottage was the easiest target," said the inspector. "The question for us is whether or not he intended to do anyone personal harm… whether to charge him with attempted murder."

★ ★ ★

The more the police questioned Salma, the more they were convinced that his counsel's case of acting while his mind was unsound was going to stick. He showed enough remorse that, in the end, he was charged with arson endangering life. At the trial he pleaded guilty and was committed for an indefinite period of psychological care.

His conviction, however, did not entirely remove the jealousy and bigotry of some in the community against people of a different ethnic origin. Sadly, in the minds of a small minority, the Smith family were still aliens exploiting their planet. It didn't occur to them that perhaps the Smiths had contributed more to Johian society than *they* had ever given. This may have been because they, themselves, did not contemplate giving anything to anyone else; they did not understand that those who give most are often the ones who receive the most from others. They resented the Smiths' popularity but they didn't understand that the popularity was because the so-called aliens contributed without seeking anything in return. Rob and Tlasa rejoiced in the opportunity to help Kakko's family, and they weren't alone.

★ ★ ★

Work on the cottage began in earnest within two weeks of the fire. Jack and Jalli were anxious to return Tlasa and Rob's house to them as soon as possible, and Salma's confession gave some kind of closure to the horror.

It turned out that a lot of their possessions were happily not damaged beyond repair. Even most of their clothes were fine. Jalli and Kakko were able to retrieve their whole wardrobe within a month. The insurance company paid a firm that specialised in restoring stuff after fire and water damage, and they did a good job.

The roof of the house had to be completely rebuilt and rethatched but as soon as that was completed, the decorators moved in.

After two and a half months, the Smiths were back at Woodglade.

"I have no idea how we shall ever repay you and Tlasa for your help, Rob," said Jack the day they finally returned their home to them.

"There is nothing to repay… If it weren't for your daughter and her young man on that exercise in our spacetruck not so long ago, I would have disappeared without trace into the gassy wastes of Planet Sparta. How can I repay her for that?"

"I had forgotten that," admitted Jack. "Kakko is always on to the next thing. I don't think she has mentioned that once since we moved into your house."

"She is an unassuming young person. You must be very proud of her."

"Kakko? Oh, yes. She can be trying at times – but she has a heart of pure gold. We love her dearly."

"She has some holiday to take before the end of the month. Has she any plans?"

"Plans? I don't think Kakko has ever *planned* to go anywhere. Adventures come to *her*. I guess she and Tam will just chill out. The novelty of having her room back in the cottage and everything will occupy her for a day or two… I hope."

"Do she and Tam want a place of their own sometime?" asked Rob. "If that isn't being too nosey?" he added.

"No. They're quite open about it. The answer is: one day. They're waiting for Tam to get a permanent job after he finishes his course next year… But even when that happens, I doubt she'll ever relinquish her own room in the cottage."

★ ★ ★

Shaun went out jogging on his crutches with Wennai nearly
every week he was at Prof Rob's. On the first occasion, she
hadn't told Aril and Patia where she was going; she had
dressed in her sports kit and said she was going on a run.
Having almost sprinted the two kilometres from her home,
she turned up at the house flushed and sweating.

Kakko went to the door. This was the first time she had
seen Wennai not made up. She was impressed. Perhaps there
was more to this girl than she had originally thought. She
obviously cared about Shaun and knew where to find him.

Shaun took her into a corner and they chatted for an hour.

"She's what he needs," observed Abby. Kakko agreed.
Her brother connected to this girl – Wennai wasn't the girly
airhead Kakko had decided she was the first time they had
met.

"Wennai went through some tough times as a child," said
Jalli. "Losing her mother like that has made her what she is.
She has time for people in trouble. And somehow, Shaun
appeals to her."

"At first, I reckoned it was a flash in the pan – someone
attracted by his football prowess," said Bandi, "but it goes
much deeper than that."

"He's going to be out of the game for ages," sighed Kakko.
"It must be very frustrating for him."

"There is a strong possibility that he will not ever play for
City United again," said Jack. "Not with all that metal in his
leg."

"Oh, don't say that so loudly," protested Kakko; "he might
hear you."

"Oh, he knows the score," said her father. "It was him
who told me what the doctor said."

"I know but—"

"Well," smiled Jalli, "one thing is for certain. We can be sure Wennai is not all about football. Look at them." Shaun and Wennai were so engrossed that they had no idea the rest of the family were talking about them.

After that, Wennai's running took her past the house every other day and Shaun went out swinging along beside her. But he consistently assured his family they were just friends. "No. She's not my girlfriend. We just like each other's company."

★ ★ ★

After a week, Kakko took Shaun aside. "You've told Wennai, haven't you?"

"Told her? Told her what?"

"About what happened after I broke your leg."

"Yes… And you didn't break my leg – I broke your fall."

"And she understands?"

"As much as anybody. The thing is… The thing is, she got bitter about losing her mum. But now she's realised that she's not the only one horrible things happen to."

"Do you love her?"

"What sort of a question is that?"

"A straightforward one."

"I've told you, I… I don't think of her like that. Not like a girlfriend."

"How *do* you feel about her?"

"She's a very good friend who understands me more than anyone else outside of our family. More than anyone else has ever done. And she can tell me more about how she feels about losing her parents than she can anyone else. She's never had anyone to really talk to."

"She's attractive."

"And that can be a problem. She gets unwanted attention from men who don't want a proper relationship... And when she goes running, she gets these weirdos wanting to run with her."

"And that's where you come in? What about the boy she's been dating? What's his name...? Gollip?"

"Yeah. She doesn't train with him, though."

"So now it's just you to defend her against unwanted attention."

"I can fend them off with my presence."

"I bet she managed OK before you came along... She really *likes* you, Shaun. I mean, I've got to say it. Someone has to."

"I know... I know she *did*. But—"

"I reckon she wants you more than anything."

"She wants her mother back."

"Yes. But she knows that cannot happen. You're the 'here and now'."

"OK. But I'm not ready for it to be more than just friends... for now." Shaun gave his sister a pleading look. He didn't want the conversation to go on. Kakko was satisfied.

"Just look after her," she said. Shaun nodded.

★ ★ ★

After Shaun moved back to the cottage, Wennai could no longer run past where he was living. He had also now completely discarded the crutches – he could walk pretty well but he still couldn't run. Wennai was now fitter than she had ever been and she did not want to give up running so, twice a week, Shaun took the first bus into town to meet her in the park. He wandered about like a coach while she did circuits.

One day, Aril came to the park with his sister. She had soon confessed to her brother and Patia that she was meeting Shaun but Aril had stayed away to give them space. Today, however, he had a message to convey.

"Hi," he said. "Mind if I interrupt?"

"Aril. Great to see you."

"It's OK. I won't gooseberry." He laughed as Wennai sped away to the far side of the clearing. "The team coach asked Gollip how things were with you because he knows you're supposed to be friends…"

"We are."

"Yes. Well, Gollip is a bit embarrassed by things to talk to you."

"Embarrassed?"

"Well, he is supposed to be dating your girl."

"She's not my girl," said Shaun in a matter-of-fact tone.

"Could have fooled me. She's no-one else's… Anyway, I said I'd pass on the message."

Shaun waved his walking stick and shrugged his shoulders. "I can't play football."

"I know. But… well, they miss you in the dressing room. The team coach thought, if you were around… like… just to encourage them, that would make a difference… He asked Gollip to sound you out."

"I miss being there but I don't know what I can do."

"Can I just say you wouldn't mind hearing from the coach?"

Shaun shrugged his shoulders again.

"Great. They need you, Shaun. We're slipping down the table."

Wennai had passed them once and was now at the bottom of

the hill in the far corner of the clearing which abutted a car park and a toilet block. As she passed, an odd-looking man dressed in Lycra emerged from the toilets and began running beside her.

"Oh no, not again," sighed Shaun.

"Have you seen him before?"

"No, not this one… It was OK when I could swing along with her on crutches. They all think she's looking for a date."

Wennai seemed to wave the man away but he persisted. Eventually, she slowed down and kept going in the same direction, away from Shaun and Aril.

"What's she playing at?" said Aril. "Does she know him?"

"I don't think so. I don't," said Shaun.

Eventually Wennai turned and began moving round towards them. The man followed. Wennai increased her speed. So did the man. She upped the pace again. He followed suit. Shaun and Aril could see his face now – it looked as if it was about to burst.

"You have to admire his persistence," said Aril.

Wennai slowed up and the man caught her up but, just as he reached her, she launched into a full sprint up the hill. The man slumped forward, his hands on his knees. Wennai ran up to Shaun and Aril, a wicked grin on her face.

"What were you playing at?" demanded Aril. "Why did you run away from us?"

"That nice man asked if he could run with me," she joked as she got her breath.

"He is not a 'nice man'. You should have come towards us."

"Oh, Aril. I would never have gone out of sight… He's met his match. He won't bother me again."

"Woah," said Shaun. "Look, he's collapsed."

The Lycra man had turned back towards the car park and then fallen full length on the grass. He didn't get up.

"He's probably had a heart attack," said Aril. Wennai lifted her hand to her mouth.

"I hope not."

Aril and Wennai ran over to the prone figure, Shaun following on as quickly as he could down the slope.

"You alright, mate?" asked Aril. To his relief the man looked up.

"No. It's my back," he groaned between clenched teeth. "I think I've done something." He tried to move but winced with pain. Wennai stifled a laugh that came more from relief than amusement. He wasn't going to die. They got him to his feet with some difficulty but he took one step, then yelled as another spasm struck him. He clutched his back and refused to move. It was quite clear that they were not going to make the car park.

"We'd better call an ambulance," said Shaun. The man didn't object. He looked at Wennai as if it was her fault.

"I told you you wouldn't be able to keep up," she said in her defence. "You should have referred yourself to my coach and he would have suggested you start more gently."

"Your coach?"

Wennai nodded towards Shaun.

Shaun smiled. "Wearing the gear is only the beginning," he said.

"I know you; you used to play for City United... So you're coaching now," grunted the man with a gasp as he convulsed with another sudden twinge.

"Only until I get fit again," said Shaun in an official-sounding voice.

Paramedics arrived. "What have you been up to?" they asked.

"I think I've pulled something... in my back."

After they had gone, Aril said, "Well, at least he didn't pull what he intended to. I don't think he'll try that one again in a hurry."

"He seems to be getting on alright with that female paramedic, though," said Wennai. "His outing may not all be bad news for him."

"I'll leave you now, coach," said Aril. "Look, why don't you come round to our house sometime, Shaun? We'd all like to see you."

"I will, Aril. But don't get out your trumpet on my account. It could be my football days are over for good."

"I shall trumpet the coach, then."

"I'll most likely turn out to be quite useless as a coach."

"I reckon you would make a superb one. I'll tell Gollip to say you're interested."

"Yeah. Whatever."

16

S haun thought all evening about what the coach had asked through Gollip and Aril. He went to bed still thinking about it but that night he dreamed he was sitting in the truck again on that fateful journey. He felt it lurch, up and down, sideways and back and forth as it ploughed along the uneven, dusty, potholed road. He felt sick; he knew how it was going to end – all he could see in front of him was the soldier's mocking face and the hole at the end of the barrel of the gun. He screamed inside his head and made a desperate attempt to wake himself up but that only caused the soldier's face to morph into a smirking Gollip with a possessive arm around Wennai saying, "Why don't you just give up any attempt to get back on the pitch, and look after the juniors? Leave the rest to the fit ones. Hand it all over to me."

Shaun became conscious in stages. He awoke seething with anger towards Gollip. Then, as the logical areas of his brain kicked in and he took back some control of his mind, he told himself that he was being unreasonable. He knew Gollip genuinely missed him, both on the pitch and as a friend. He wanted him back in the club and would have been delighted if Shaun could have played again. He also knew that Gollip had every right to date Wennai; Shaun had consistently denied that she was more than a friend. He knew his jealousy and anger were unfair but that didn't stop him still feeling them. It's one thing to know how you ought to feel but it's another to actually do it – especially when your brain is all over the place.

When it was time to get up, Shaun felt tired and dispirited. He almost texted Gollip to say he had changed his mind about the invitation – then thought better of it. He didn't need to do it straightaway. If he still felt that way tomorrow, he could do it then, or when – or if – Gollip or anyone from the club approached him. No particular arrangements had been made – it may come to nothing.

Shaun was grateful that he didn't have to go into college that morning – he didn't feel like talking to anyone. He got a book and thought he might go and chill in the shade. But when he opened the front door he was immediately aware of a new white gate. What Shaun said under his breath cannot be recorded here. His words and thoughts are not ones to be proud of. Suffice it to say, he was not too pleased at the sight of the gate.

"God, you can stick your gate – I just want to be left alone, OK?" he said angrily. He stomped back to his bedroom and locked the door.

When Kakko came in later Shaun expected to hear a whoop as she spotted the gate, but there was nothing. He checked through the window. It was still there. In fact no-one at all mentioned it that evening. Jalli came through the ordinary gate and couldn't have missed it, and his father always got a sense of its presence and it would not have gone unnoticed. So, in the end, he concluded that the gate was just for him. He said nothing.

As he went to bed, he was curious, but he was still adamant that he was staying put. He was relieved he didn't have to argue with his family. This would have been the first time anyone had refused a white gate invitation and he wasn't in the mood for justifying himself.

★ ★ ★

Eight hours later, Daan's rays streamed through the curtains. Again, Shaun had not slept well. He had been especially reluctant to go to sleep and the thought of the gate glowing in the hedge beyond his drawn curtains troubled him further. Shaun was stiff, his head hurt and he had no energy. *If anyone tells me I look off-colour this morning, they'll get a piece of my addled mind,* he thought. But they didn't. Jalli studied him but said nothing. Kakko was putting most of it down to lovesickness, together with his leg, which Shaun claimed was still hurting him. She believed he was suffering from resisting a clear and obvious affection for a girl who was currently kissing another boy.

Shaun decided a walk in the countryside was the best thing he could do on such a sunny day. Jalli approved. It would do him good to get some exercise.

As he left the garden, Shaun resolutely ignored the new gate that still beckoned in the hedge to the left of the ordinary one. When he returned later that morning, he saw that the gate was still there. But as he watched, Bandi and Abby emerged from it. The gate must lead to Persham. Shaun had never been to Persham. He could visit his brother and Abby in their home on Earth! But at that very moment, as Bandi and Abby greeted him, the gate began to fade and vanish. The invitation had expired. To have visited Earth could have been a healing experience – but he had not trusted the Creator. Shaun, himself, had decided what was good for him. He had taken over the reins of his own life. But in his heart – and up until that time, in most of his choices – he had always known that the best things, the right things, happened when you went with God's flow – when you followed the way of the Creator. She knew him. She understood him. She loved him. And She had promised She would never leave him... And Shaun had rejected Her!

"Hey," called Bandi. "How's it all going?" Shaun did not reply. He did not know at that moment what to say.

"You OK, mate?" asked Bandi, concerned.

Abby stepped up to Shaun and took his hand. "There's something wrong. I've never seen you look so poorly since you came out of hospital. Have you got an infection?"

Shaun sank onto the bench. "I... I haven't been sleeping well. I think I need a holiday."

"Yeah. Perhaps you just need to chill. Where are the others?"

"At work. Nan's gone to Ada's."

"I promised Abby I would take her to the beach here. She's never been. How about us all going there this afternoon?"

"I don't want to be a gooseberry..."

"Abby and I see each other every day. We share the same roof. An afternoon with my brother will do us all good."

At the beginning of that day, Shaun would have told them he needed to be alone. Now he wasn't so sure. The beach appealed. "OK. Why not?"

★ ★ ★

Bandi and Abby were a tonic. They brought news of success in their exams. They were well on course for the next stage in their studies. Shaun was impressed, and happy for them. They were clearly enjoying life. Having Dave working at the YAC was a real bonus. They often went there and helped with some of the activities of the younger teenagers. They were bursting to tell the stories of Sharon and Dawn's latest escapades.

The most recent involved a potholing expedition. Dave

had advertised an opportunity for a party of youngsters to go down a pothole in the limestone of the Mendip Hills in Somerset. Sharon and Dawn had booked to go but, despite all the warnings regarding kit, they had still turned up expecting something more akin to a stroll in the park. However, the instructors were ready for this and gave them wellies and overalls – which Sharon and Dawn did not feel suited their street cred.

Abby told the story. Sharon had begun with her belligerent tones.

"I can't be seen dead in this! I ain't going to wear that stuff – it's naff."

"You won't be seen dead in it. Not if you follow my instructions – and that includes wearing suitable clothing," the instructor had said calmly. "There are eight of you. That's a good number. I want you to work as a team. Look out for one another. Do not crowd each other. Leave a sensible distance between you but do keep up. Above all, do not venture away from the party. We stay together."

Abby said that her dad had tried to separate Dawn from Sharon by making Dawn go towards the front, but somehow, despite his best efforts, they had ended up together.

The cave had started off high and wide. They had lamps on their helmets but when they were all safely together inside a big cavern, the instructor had suggested they turn them off so they could see the natural light of the caves. Of course it had been pitch black. Sharon had been shocked. She had never been anywhere so completely black. She had let out a scream that had made everyone think she had been attacked by some kind of cave monster.

At the same moment, Dawn had begun to sob. In an unguarded moment at the planning stage, Dave had told himself that caving would help these young ladies grow up a bit – fat chance! But, hearing Dawn, the leader had turned on his torch and had spoken softly to her. *Caving instructor – what a job,* Dave had thought. He wondered if all the man's groups were like this – they weren't. The instructor had told him so afterwards.

And so the trip into the caves had continued. The next of Sharon's screams was attributed to the time that water ran into her boot – they had been wading through sparkling streams that had formed the tunnels over many years.

The instructor had told them that the next part of the cave was dangerous if it was raining above, but it hadn't rained for a week and the weather was fine, so he had offered to take them deeper into the cave, as far as a beautiful chamber with fantastic stalactites with stalagmites beneath them. It had slender pillars and pools of crystal water only disturbed by the occasional drip from above. "The colours are amazing," he had explained. Then he had asked, "Anyone like singing?" A few had put up their hands. "The acoustics are excellent here. We can try it out."

To get through into this section of the pot, however, required wading deeper through the running water. By this time their boots were well under the surface. Even Sharon had given up thinking of her wet feet. Dawn had been OK so long as the lights were shining. But it was when the water hit her crotch that Sharon had let out the next scream. "Ow! It's ★★★★ing cold!," she had yelled. The words had reverberated around the cave system for what felt like whole minutes – it had seemed that Sharon's bad language just wouldn't go away.

The sound of Sharon's voice going on forever, combined with the cold water hitting her own sensitive areas had set Abby off giggling, and by the time they had reached the inner chamber with all its delights, the party had quite destroyed the atmosphere of wonder and awe the leader had intended to convey. However, Dave had stepped in and suggested that Sharon sing something. He knew she was quite gifted in that direction.

"What?" Sharon had asked in her best cavalier tone. "What do you want me to sing?"

"Oh. How about a refrain from Taizé?"

And so it was that the same mouth that had, a few minutes before, filled the void with a string of expletives, now began singing about the light of God in the darkness. To the whole group's amazement, she remembered the exact words in French: *La ténèbre n'est point ténèbre devant toi: la nuit comme le jour est lumière.*

"It was amazing," concluded Abby. "Wherever you go, Sharon just suddenly surprises you. You can't help admiring her. Dad asked why she chose that particular song. She said it was the one they sang in the dark while they were lighting candles. It seemed to fit inside a dark cave. She's just amazing."

"I wouldn't want to live with her, though," smiled Bandi. "She's non-stop. After that magic moment, she was going on about her gear again."

"Yeah," said Abby. "Dawn asked what would happen if there was a sudden unexpected downpour outside. The instructor said that there wouldn't be because the country was sitting under a high pressure system."

"The high pressure is being together with her and Sharon, I reckon," laughed Bandi.

Abby continued, "But high-pressure Dawn said, 'Just suppose' and the instructor said the worst case scenario was that we would be safe in the cavern but would have to leave by a different route; the way we had come would flood."

"Then Sharon said something about being stuck in the cavern for a million years before anyone found us. She went,

'Imagine being condemned to wear this caving gear for a million years',' said Bandi, trying to imitate Sharon.

"Dad said that after a million years she would be beyond caring. She'd be living in heaven. But then Dawn, very helpfully, said that her mother reckoned that in heaven you stayed the age you died at on Earth. And suggested that, not only that, you were condemned to wear the clothes you died in for all eternity."

"You can imagine what Sharon had to say to that," chuckled Bandi.

"Dad said, 'Heaven, yes, but your age and what you wear are only things that apply to this life. In the next all will be different.' But Sharon was still chuntering when the instructor reiterated there was another way out of the cavern even if the tunnel they had used to get in was blocked. There would be no chance of them not getting out."

"So then," said Bandi, "Sharon decided she wanted to get out that way – she didn't fancy wading through that cold water again."

Abby added, "The instructor explained that the other way was much further and involved some climbing before they reached the surface. After that they would have a long walk back down a busy road."

"That clinched it. Sharon said she couldn't possibly be seen walking down a busy road in a boiler suit and yellow wellies. She'd rather stay in the cavern a million years." Bandi was enjoying reliving the moment.

"Dad got cross then. He said this was silly talk. They would all stay together and any more trouble and he wouldn't take Sharon and Dawn on another outing."

"They were mortified and sulked all the way home. Sharon protested that she didn't like people shouting at her. She wasn't ever going to come to the YAC again."

"But the following Sunday she was there as if nothing had happened," said Abby.

"Wearing this awful tight-fitting shocking-pink top and tatty jeans," teased Bandi. "The sort of thing she wouldn't mind being seen dead in, I guess."

"It sounds as though your Sharon changes the whole atmosphere of the group. Whatever happens, you have got to laugh," said Shaun, smiling.

"Exactly. She's just herself. Sharon is Sharon. It never occurs to her to try and act differently from what she is… I like that," said Abby.

"Authentic," said Shaun, quietly, lying back on the sand.

They were silent for a few minutes listening to the surf. Then Shaun asked, "What's the exact translation of that French song?"

"Oh. Sorry," said Abby. "It translates, 'The darkness is not darkness at all before you; the night, like the day, is light.' It comes from the Bible – the psalms, I think."

"Psalm 139," said Bandi.

"Wow!" exclaimed his girlfriend. "You are on the ball. You're amazing."

"The dark is not dark with You," pondered Shaun. "The dark is not dark with You… and You are always present. How does it go – the tune?"

Abby looked at Bandi and they struck up the song. They sang it a few times. "It just repeats. That's how Taizé music works. Their songs are meditative."

The night, like the day, is full of light, thought Shaun. "Bandi, Abby, will you do something for me?"

"Sure," said Bandi. "If we can."

"Just pray that my nights may not be so dark – so I can sleep."

"No problem. You got it… Anything else?"

"No. That's all… I would like to have met Sharon."

"You might, one day. If the Creator provides you with a gate we will make sure you meet her."

"I doubt that will happen. Just tell her that she cheered me up."

"We will," laughed Abby. "She'll be impressed that what she did in that cave had an impact on someone the other side of the galaxy. I won't tell her you know about the bad language, though. She might decide to keep using it."

"Just the singing," smiled Shaun. "That'll do. But don't stop her being her."

"No worries," said Bandi. "Nothing in all creation can stop Sharon from being Sharon."

That night Shaun gave thanks for Sharon and apologised to the Creator for being such a wuss. Maybe – just maybe – She would forgive him and let him have his gate back.

But it didn't happen like that. He knew he would be forgiven, but when the time came for Bandi and Abby to leave, they passed through the hedge as if the gate wasn't there. The Creator had new plans for Shaun.

17

Once the dust had settled on the move back to the cottage and the family were getting back to something like normality, Kakko began longing for the next white gate. The old folk, as she sometimes referred to her parents as well as her nan, were not looking for any kind of adventure. They just felt they needed a long stretch without incident, but for Kakko, life was growing tedious and predictable – she needed to get out of its stultifying sameness.

You know, God, she prayed, *what I'm really hoping for is an invitation to visit New England.* When they had said goodbye to Zoe, Buck and the others after the adventure on Zilaka, none of them had felt that would be the end of their association. She wondered how it was all going with Dah and John – not that there was any doubt that this was a friendship made in heaven and set to last as long as either of them was sharing the same four dimensions of space-time in the current universe. Kakko was due some holiday, *and now would be a great time to go,* she thought. She set about informing the Creator of her idea – and pressuring Her to deliver. Then, to her delight, one day – a few days after Bandi and Abby had called in – a white gate appeared for her and Tam.

"It's like Clapham Junction," said Matilda with mild exasperation. Things were moving too fast for her these days. They had become aware that Clapham Junction was a place in London where you changed trains. "All the coming and going, I'm getting quite dizzy. You never know who's where anymore."

"You cannot have been there much," said Jack. "I can never remember you going that far when I was a kid."

"Where?"

"Clapham Junction."

"No, of course I haven't been there. It's not a place people go to from Persham… It's just a saying. And if it lives up to its reputation, it's not a place I would ever want to visit."

"I would," said Kakko. "It sounds interesting…"

"Well, then, you never know. This white gate might take you right onto one of the platforms…"

But it didn't. To Kakko's delight it was indeed New London, Connecticut.

"So God does answer prayer. She knew I wanted an adventure here."

"I'm not so sure it works quite like that," said Tam carefully. "You can't tell God what to do."

"Oh. You can!" Then she added, softly, "But, you're right. You're not supposed to *tell* Her exactly. But if you don't *ask*, you won't get. The Creator wants you to put in your polite requests."

"That is true, I suppose. It's just that some of us seem to have more cheek than others."

"It's not cheek, it's just being honest. Anyway, God can always say no, can't She?" Then she added, half to herself, "She often does… Come on, Tam, let's get inside. It's not so warm this time."

"It must be their winter… Shouldn't we knock?"

But Kakko had already pushed open the door and was shouting, "Hi…! Hi… Anyone at home?"

"In the office," came a voice from around the corner. "I'll be with you in a minute…"

Kakko followed the voice. Amy was with a girl who was just getting to her feet.

"Oh, sorry," said Kakko quickly. "I hope we haven't interrupted you…"

"Why, hello! No. Mary was just leaving… That's alright, Mary. It's all booked. Glad you got your place…"

"Thanks," said Mary. And then, "Hi," to Kakko and Tam as she left.

"So. The travellers have reappeared!" smiled Amy Merton. "What adventures have you had lately?"

"Not so very many," said Tam. "Sorry to barge in but—"

"That's fine. Come into the dining room and let me get you both a soda."

They followed Amy through into the dining hall.

"So, nothing painful to report," said Amy as she pulled open the fridge. "Coke?"

"Fine," said Kakko, fascinated by the colourful cans that seemed so commonplace on Planet Earth.

"Thanks… Nothing but exams," sighed Tam. "It's Kakko who has the exciting job. You know she's working on engines for spacecraft."

"No. Tell me about it… Only I don't know the first thing about engines except that they can be found beneath the hood, need gas and go brum-brum."

"No, my sort are not that kind. They're what *you* might call rocket engines… only without all that flame and smoke pouring out of them like the ones you use on Planet Earth."

"I've seen videos of automobiles with engines here which don't need petroleum. Some don't even need drivers," said Tam.

"You're right. I can't imagine having an automobile that I can't control," said Amy, with a troubled look. "It sounds both weird and dangerous. I like the idea of moving away from fossil fuel, though… But I doubt silent cars will catch on – not among men anyhow."

"They will," assured Kakko. "They'll just suddenly become cool... like lots of things."

"We need something to. Something that steers us away from air pollution, noise, piles of old rotting cars, greenhouse gases, and more."

"Planet Earth is in trouble, isn't it? Abby and Bandi have told me all about it. In my opinion you can't get rid of your oil-guzzlers quick enough..."

"I see you haven't changed, Kakko. You've done the British Prime Minister; is it the US President next?"

"If that's what God wants, then I'm up for it. Take me to see him."

"I'll let you know when he next pops by... Talking of meeting people, Zoe's due back this afternoon. Make yourself comfortable. Dinner's on its way... I have one or two things to finish up, then I will join you."

★ ★ ★

After a lunch of soup and salad, in which Kakko tried not to let her exuberance for life overflow too much, Zoe came in and rushed across the room to greet her friends.

"Kakko, Tam! Amy texted me to say you were here. It's so great to see you."

It turned out that John and Dah were in California, which, Zoe explained, "is about as far as you can go and still be on mainland USA". They were doing really well, although Dah missed her people some of the time.

"I guess that goes with the territory if you fall in love with someone from a different planet... A different country is bad enough," she said, wistfully.

"So you haven't got over Dev, then?" said Kakko, wistfully.

"Nah. I was really keen on Dev. I thought at one time he

was interested, too, but then he just cooled. I don't know why."

"You were keen on Dev!" said Tam with some alarm in his tone. "But I thought... you said... You gave us your philosophy of life and said there were people like you who didn't want to settle into a relationship... I remember it clearly..."

"Yeah, I said that. I said it to keep Buck off the scent. He can be a pain with his 'Zo-lo this' and 'Zo-lo that'..."

"I knew you didn't mean it," laughed Kakko. "That was obvious, but I didn't know how serious— Tam, you OK? You've gone all red."

"What the hell did you say it for, if you didn't mean it?"

"It was quite obvious she didn't mean it, Tam," said Kakko. "People say lots of things like that – you just have to read between the lines. You men, you're so slow at times."

"Well, if you say so. So slow that I couldn't see any space between the lines... and neither did Dev."

"How do you mean, 'neither did Dev'? You were talking to him about Zoe?"

"Look, he asked me a straight question and I gave him a straight answer."

"What—?"

"He asked me if I thought Zoe would welcome his advances. And I—"

"... told him to back off?" finished Kakko.

"I told him what I heard. I said that Zoe had explained that she wasn't interested in relationships – any relationships. And not to take it personally."

The girls stared at him.

"What was I supposed to think? He asked me, right? I told him what I'd heard."

"But you didn't have to be so thick to believe it!" Kakko almost shouted.

"Stop it, you two," pleaded Zoe. "Arguing about it ain't worth it." And she started to cry.

"Oh, dear," sighed Kakko. "We've come from the stars just to upset you." She put her arms around her friend and gave Tam a cutting glare.

"No. It ain't you. It's been there, coming out for months… Actually, it's quite nice to think he actually did like me…"

Tam felt awful. He wanted to go into a corner and disappear. Why were girls so complicated? If you couldn't believe what they said, how was he to know? They kind of communicated by some telepathic signals that his mind didn't possess the capacity to pick up… But what his mind did do instinctively was to try and think of a strategy to rectify the situation. Strategic thinking. That's what was needed.

"There might be a way—" he began speaking deliberately.

"Tam, don't you think you have done quite enough interfering?" said Kakko sharply.

"Kakko, he's only trying to help–"

"Like he did last time!"

"Kakko, you're too hard on him… Tam, I don't blame you. My mouth was too full of my 'philosophy of life'. I got what was coming to me… I want to hear about this way you're thinking of."

"Well, he could, kind of, like, find out that I was wrong…"

"How. Texting him? It won't work," sighed Kakko, exasperated.

"We men can say things straight out to each other – we don't have to be over-subtle. But I wasn't thinking of texting, but I could if—"

"What were you thinking, Tam?" interrupted Zoe.

"Well, I mean, you could kind of be passing by and drop in to see him…"

"Tam, he's in India! Which is, like, the other side of the planet to where we are!" blurted Kakko with a rising inflection.

"How is Zoe supposed to be just 'passing'?"

"She could go on a holiday."

"On her own? That's subtle," said Kakko, sarcastically.

"Don't be down on him, Kakko. The lad's trying, right. He's not the sort of person you want to upset. You've got a good one there."

"It's OK, Zoe. Kakko says lots but I've learned not to take it to heart. She's good for me… But we do have to find a way for you and Dev. That could be why the Creator has brought us here."

Just then, the room filled with other YWCA volunteers and their conversation was curtailed. People were excited to meet Kakko and Tam. Some of them had heard of the Europa/Zilaka adventure. Many hadn't believed it but Zoe's account was now ratified by Tam and Kakko – a fact which cheered her immensely.

"The world is full of doubters. Conspiracy theories abound on this planet. But Dah's trumpet had got them all beat," she told them when they were seated at a table.

"What about a guitar? Has she got a new one?"

"Yeah. John's folks took her to choose the best that money could buy. She's a winner all round. And so are we when she plays it. We tried to get her to enter *America's Got Talent* but she wouldn't."

"I think she had her fill of talent shows on her own planet. If she's happy, then that's everything."

"She's not short of audiences, that's for sure," said Zoe.

★ ★ ★

"Where're the Himalayas?" asked Tam as he, Kakko and Zoe were seated over a cup of cocoa before bedtime.

"I dunno. Planet Earth, I guess."

"Yes, but where? Are they near India?"

"Northern India," murmured Zoe. "They are the highest mountains in the world. They form the border with Tibet. Why?"

"This leaflet. It's about trekking in the Himalayas to raise money for charity. You could join it, Zoe. It'll be near Dev."

"How can she go on holiday on her own?" scowled Kakko. "She'd look stupid. It'd look as if she was chasing him. That's, like, so—"

"No. Don't you see? It's *not* a holiday. It's fundraising. Lots of these people would be doing it on their own."

"Let me look at that." Kakko took the leaflet and checked it out. As she read, her expression gradually changed from disapproval to real interest. "Zoe, I think Tam has actually come up with something here… If you went on this, you *could* tell Dev that you are passing through. Then, when you have met up with him, in his own land, if you wanted to, you could kind of show him you fancied him; be a bit bold…"

"Thanks, Tam. But it's too late. His parents were going to find him a bride. They might already have done so. By the time I get there, *if* I were to go, that is, he would most probably be married."

"Yeah. To some complete stranger. That's just gross," exhaled Kakko.

"It's their custom. It's quite normal in India," said Zoe, resigned.

"That doesn't make it right," said Kakko forcibly.

"It's worked for thousands of years," said Zoe. "In the US there are millions of people who are not happily married even though they got to choose… You could argue that the Indian way is better."

"Maybe, but not for Dev," put in Tam. "He's met the girl he wants to date. Anyone else is going to be second best."

"She's almost certainly going to be pretty and definitely sweeter than me," sighed Zoe. "He'll get over it."

"But I guess Dev doesn't want sweet," said Tam. "Some of us go for girls with strong personalities…"

"I get you. You mean loud, opinionated, outspoken…"

Kakko laughed. "Tam would be hopeless with someone delicate and gentle."

"Yeah, I want someone bold," Tam agreed. "And I want a friend – someone I can talk to; not someone I have to look after all the time. I wouldn't want a girl who, like, looks up to me. I guess that's what appeals to Dev, too."

The doors to the lounge where they were sitting exploded as Buck burst into the room.

"I heard you were back. Great! Are we going on another adventure? Which planet this time?"

"Hiya, Buck," said Tam. "So far we're just visiting."

"Hey, Buck. How are you?" Kakko gave him a hug. She was still clutching the trek leaflet.

"I'm fine. Except for the ridiculous amount of stuff they set me to do at school. Each teacher seems to think that their subject is the only one we're studying."

"That's a common experience," smiled Tam. "Same on Planet Joh."

"No. Not everywhere in the world. People in Britain, for example, don't have to do anywhere near as much as we do in the US."

"That's not what Bandi and Abby tell us," said Kakko. "Some days, even though they live in the same house, they hardly get to meet. They text each other from their bedrooms across the landing."

"What's this?" said Buck, spotting the leaflet. "You going to the mountains?"

"We were just—"

Buck yanked the literature out of Kakko's hand. "But this is perfect for you, Zoe. Look, you could have a holiday like everyone says you should. You wouldn't have to find someone to go with. *And* you can raise funds for the YWCA at the same time… Perfect."

Amy Merton appeared through the same doors as Buck but with far less noise.

"Hi, Buck. It's you. I thought something was up…"

"Nah. Just the whirlwind from the Apocalypse," said Zoe with a wink.

"Look, Amy," enthused Buck, "our Zo-lo's going to do a trek to raise funds for the YWCA."

"I ain't—"

"You don't say," smiled Amy. "Well, what a good idea. I've been saying you should get away. The Himalayas would be perfect… And you could call by and see Dev. The trip includes a visit to Delhi and Agra on the way back… It's in six weeks' time. Short notice, but I'm sure we could attract enough sponsors… This could be just what we need. Three thousand dollars will conclude our appeal."

By bedtime, Amy had already secured 1,000 dollars in sponsorship, and Zoe's fate had been sealed.

★ ★ ★

Zoe emailed Dev to say she would be passing through Delhi on her way back from the charity trek. She got an immediate reply to say she must come and visit his family – he had told them so much about New London and her work. Kakko was delighted and Tam was somewhat relieved that perhaps his misunderstanding might not prove fatal.

Kakko forgave him but that night she explained that if she was reading instructions on the way to put intrahelical engines together, she would take every word literally. But in things of the heart, the world was full of nuances and hidden meanings that you had to listen to.

"You have to take into account the tone of voice, the context of what is being said, the people who are being addressed and any others that might be listening and, like, lots of other stuff," explained Kakko. "It's well known – and this is not sexist – that girls are better at reading it than guys, so I don't entirely blame you. The thing to ask yourself is: Is it about someone's life – is this personal? If the answer is yes, then think more deeply."

"Life would be a lot easier if everything were like your engine blueprints."

"Yeah. But it isn't and never will be. When someone is really adamant about something, then usually there is a sort of *emotional* reason for it. When something hurts, we try and put on a brave face – but hope someone will notice and care all the same."

"I guess so. But all that's so hard to remember… Are you certain Zoe will get to see Dev?"

"She's got to. Dev's expecting her now and Amy's lined up sponsors for the trek… She'll enjoy it. Those mountains look ace. I wish I was going."

18

The Himalayas were impressive – even from the plane. Zoe was enthralled by them. She couldn't take her eyes off them as she came in to land at Kathmandu airport.

To her great surprise, Dev was waiting at the hotel as the transfer bus from the airport pulled in.

"Dev! What are you doing here? I thought I would meet you in Delhi after the trek."

"Yes. You are expected at my parents' home. But I thought I would join you on this hike. You see, I love mountains, but I have only been here to Nepal with my mother and father as a child and I have never been in the mountains. Do you mind a walking partner?"

"I would delight in it. I am so pleased to see you. Why didn't you let me know?"

"I didn't know myself until yesterday."

Inside the hotel bar, they chatted like the old friends they were.

"So… you have someone for a wife now, I expect," said Zoe cheerily.

Dev shook his head.

"What about your family? Weren't they finding someone for you?"

"Yes, they were. But I said no. You see, I couldn't say yes, when I still had feelings… elsewhere."

"Oh dear. Weren't they upset?"

"Yes, a bit."

"Do I know the person you still have feelings for?"

Dev looked as embarrassed as he felt. "You do."

"Do I know her well?"

"Better than anyone. Zoe, you must forgive me—"

"Nothing to forgive. Tam and Kakko came again. Tam told me about your conversation. He was wrong. He told you what I said but not how I felt. I had no idea you liked me."

"I am a quiet man."

"Still waters run deep…"

Dev looked puzzled.

"It's a saying," explained Zoe when she saw Dev hadn't understood. "It means quiet people may have secret passionate hearts."

"Ah. That is true. So you like me, too."

"Yes, I do. I'm sorry I didn't say… I didn't know how to."

"I told my parents about you when we heard you were coming to India. They commanded me to come and meet you here and ascertain your feelings…"

"They packed you off to meet me here?"

"I know that that isn't the way it works in America… But I thought… I would… I wanted to meet you, anyway."

"It's a good job I like you, then."

"Yes. We will walk together for a week – I hope at the end of the trek, you will still like me."

"And you me. I ain't the fastest walker in the world."

"Speed is of little importance if you eventually end up where you want to get to."

★ ★ ★

Six days of steep ups and downs, with fantastic views and a warm welcome from the people they passed on the way made the trek one of the best times of Zoe's life. She had amassed an amazing 5,000 dollars for her charity from friends high and low. She didn't know she had so many. Pledges were still arriving. She had letters with them, too. They were from school and work friends, friends of the family, all her relatives and the young and old she had got to know through volunteering at the YWCA. One of the letters was from Mr Williams, formerly from Atlanta and now feeling at home in New London, who had spoken so much encouragement to Dah. Dah and John, themselves, had given her a one hundred dollar note – a lot for them – and a drawing of a smiley face carrying a rucksack.

When it came to it, Zoe and Dev didn't have to carry much themselves. Their bags were all carried by lines of porters, who also bore the tents, tables, food and cooking equipment on their heads and backs. It was an impressive operation.

★ ★ ★

It would be fair to say that Zoe struggled towards the end. She wasn't as fit as she might have been, but Dev was on hand to help her up and down the climbs; he was the perfect gentleman.

On the final night, all the trekkers and porters gathered around a campfire and danced and sang – each in their own style. It reminded Zoe of the Girl Scouts she had once belonged to, and made her realise just how much of an indoor person she had become. She remembered how beautiful Connecticut could be and resolved to get out more often when she got back – but maybe with Dev, she would live in India. She had no idea what that would be like – a lot hotter than Connecticut, and wetter some of the time. But whatever it took, she was with Dev now and that wouldn't change.

★ ★ ★

At the end of the trek, the party was conveyed back to the hotel and they were immersed in a different type of tourist world of shops and restaurants, street sellers and sightseeing. Then very soon they were back at the airport and boarding the plane.

As they emerged from the arrival hall in Indira Gandhi International, they were met by Dev's parents and driven to a very middle class-looking house somewhere to the south east of New Delhi.

Later, when Zoe reported the events to her friends back in the States, they all had the impression of an interview – but it wasn't like that at all. Zoe was taken into the family almost immediately. Dev had made his choice. To Dev's family, the fact that she had accepted their invitation was confirmation that she had accepted their son's advances. Zoe now understood why it was so important for Dev to be on the trek. In India, a girl doesn't just rock up at someone's house in passing! If Zoe was coming to visit, then he had to clarify the situation. Now, all the talk was about inviting Zoe's people out to India – at Dev's family's expense. Zoe was going to have to learn what was expected of her as quickly as she could. Two weeks before, she had been flying to India with the hope that perhaps things might turn out well – now she was deep into the preparations for a lifelong, life-changing marriage. For a brief moment, she felt herself rushed off her feet and hurtling into something she knew not what, in a place that was completely different to anywhere she had ever known. Even with her eyes shut and her fingers in her ears, she could smell the distinct flavour of this wonderful but daunting country. It was scary – but then Dev's smiling face and his loving embrace convinced her that this was what she wanted to do. She was losing control – but she trusted him and his family. She sent up a prayer: *God, this is what I want. Can I trust You to look after me?* The warmth she felt in her heart was sufficient confirmation.

Zoe then thought of her parents. They were going to have a hell of a shock. But, in America, she had long passed the point where she was expected to ask their permission to accept the advances of a man. When Zoe thought about it, she decided that they would quite like to be drawn in as part of the negotiations – so long as it wasn't going to cost them an arm and a leg.

The one thing Zoe would have wished for, but knew it was highly unlikely, was to have her interplanetary friends with her. They had contributed a lot – including putting forward the idea of the trek. The world had been a different place since they had arrived – even though they never stayed more than a few days. Whenever they came, things happened.

★ ★ ★

"I'm going to have to take my holiday, whatever," moaned Kakko. "I prayed that God would open up a gate so we could go on Zoe's trek. No such luck."

"You know it doesn't work that way," said her father. "God has His own ideas. And they are always for the best."

"*I* didn't pray to go on the trek," said Tam. "Zoe didn't need anyone else around."

"Nah. You're right. They certainly could do without you," retorted Kakko. Tam ignored the jibe. "I can't help wondering how it all turned out, though."

"We may find out one day. We could ask Bandi to email Zoe from Persham."

"Yeah. I didn't think of that. A good idea… God, do You

know how hard it is for us having a holiday and being stuck here at home when there's a universe out there to explore?"

"You've been spoiled," said Jack. "You have had more excitement than almost anyone your age."

"I know. Yeah. I'm spoiled. So what...? Oh, a text from Mum... Can I help carry some stuff home from the college? OK. I'm onto it." Kakko texted her mum, OK. On the way. "Come on, Tam – something to do."

As they stepped out of the door, they saw God's answer: a white gate. Tam smiled. God knew just how much energy this girl of his had, and She expected him to keep up.

"Better help your mum, first," Tam said calmly.

Kakko's mood was transformed.

"Brilliant! Thanks. God, is it because I prayed so hard or because You had this in mind all along?"

"Both," considered Tam. But Kakko was already running up the lane to the college so she could attend to the impending adventure.

★ ★ ★

The sights, sounds and smells of India are unmistakable. The colours, the bustle, the cows, the dung, the cooking, the traffic and the shouts of excited children, all mingled to impress on Kakko and Tam a life they had never before encountered.

"Wow! Another new planet!" declared Kakko. "And it's packed with people... and the technology is primitive – or is it? Look, they have mobile phones." A young woman in a sari was using her phone exactly like the people of the USA. "And the engines. Refined-oil driven – they are just like those in the small vehicles in London I saw. *And* in Connecticut. But it can't be Earth."

"It *is* Earth. I recognise this from the leaflet advertising the trek. This is Dev's place. I'm sure of it. It smells like his cooking," said Tam.

"You're right. So we're on the trek after all. But where are the mountains?"

"Beyond these houses, I guess… Look, there appear to be other trekkers with backpacks like the ones we've been given."

"Yeah. They look like tourists."

Kakko and Tam walked along a busy street with market stalls selling all sorts of things, from some kind of fly-covered meat, to bolts of cloth in vivid colours. The air was full of the scents of the joss sticks burning on tables of roadside cafés. They decided to sit at one of the tables and let their brains catch up with their sudden immersion into this strange and busy place. They had a wad of cash that the Creator had kindly given them with the stuff in a shed beside the gate. The tables were all filled, except for one occupied by a lone young man dressed in casual Western garb like themselves.

"Are these seats taken?" Kakko asked.

"No. I'm alone. You're welcome."

"What's that you're drinking?" asked Tam. "We only arrived today and we're still getting used to things."

"Oh. It's only a lemonade. I've never indulged in anything Indian. Not sure what it would do to me."

Kakko nudged her boyfriend – India. Tam was right – that hadn't taken long to establish.

"We'll have the same, I think," smiled Kakko.

As they sat over their drinks, they chatted with the young man.

"Are you on holiday on your own?" asked Kakko boldly. "Do many travel singly?"

The young man laughed. "The answer is yes they do, but

in my case, no. And most people come with someone else, but not all... You new to backpacking?"

"We're not backpacking... exactly," said Tam hesitantly. "Actually we're here to meet someone else."

"They're going trekking... in the mountains – the Himalayas," explained Kakko.

"That's a long way from here, then. Where are you meeting them?"

"I've got Dev's address somewhere," said Kakko. "Zoe gave it to me when she signed up for the trek... She had a suspicion – hoped – that we'd get the chance to follow... Ah. Yes, here it is... Mathura, near Agra."

"Ah. You're in the right place. This is Agra."

"Great—" began Tam.

"What did you mean by saying no?" Kakko was off on a new tack. "You mean you're not on your own. You don't—"

"I came with a girl," said the young man lightly. "Ruth. She went off with other people and left me... but she is due back here to fly back to Australia. We're Australian."

"So you're waiting for her."

"I was. We were due to fly yesterday but she hasn't showed."

"What about your tickets?"

"I have asked if I can delay them. It'll cost, that's for sure. I don't want to rebook until she shows."

"But where is she?" demanded Kakko.

"Sorry," interrupted Tam. "I'm sorry. My girlfriend is Miss Nosey. Kakko, we shouldn't pry into this man's affairs. We've only just met."

"No. That's OK. Actually, it's good to have someone to talk to about it... I've no idea where she is. She just took off with these guys... To tell you the truth, she was never really interested in being with me. I was just the means for her to get here – to India. You see, her parents would never have given her permission to travel on her own. I was sworn to look after her. But two days after we got here, she met up with these mad guys and took off with them. I made her promise to be back here before we were due to fly. But she told me not to be an old fusspot."

"So where'd they go?"

"No idea."

"So if she ups and leaves you without saying where," reasoned Kakko, "then she has taken responsibility for herself. You could be hanging around here a long time. If it were me, I would just have to accept that she doesn't want me, and get on with life."

"Oh, I decided two weeks ago that she doesn't want me. But the thing is, I promised her folks that I would look after her. They wouldn't have let her come without me saying I would. You see, I can't go back without her. Her dad would kill me."

"Have you tried phoning her?" suggested Tam.

"All the time. At first, she texted me to say stop fussing – then she just rejected my calls."

"So, do you think she'll show?"

"I thought so until yesterday. Today, I don't know... I'm just hanging around the places we went to. This is the place we met the guys. The last place I saw her."

"She could be in trouble," said Tam with a creased brow.

"I hope not. But, that's it, I don't know... My sister's looking out for her at home in case she gets home some other way. But that's unlikely. You see, I have her passport... My sister, Mandy, she's the only one who knows the truth... apart from you now. The rest just think we're having such a great time, we're staying on..."

"You need help to find your friend," said Tam decisively.

"Kakko, I don't think we are here just for a holiday. We're down the road from Dev. Let's give him a call and ask him the way to go about finding Ruth. This story worries me. Sorry, we didn't ask your name?"

"Hi, I'm James." James held out his hand.

"Tam, and this is Kakko."

"Can we borrow your phone to call our friend Dev. We don't have phones ourselves."

"Sure." James drew his pass pattern, and handed his phone to Kakko. She looked at it and screwed up her nose. "Give me a clue…"

"Where did you say you came from?" he joked. The world may have 7,000 languages but the way you used a phone was the same everywhere. "Green square with phone symbol. Bottom left. Then just enter the number including the country prefix."

"Got it."

"We'd better explain," said Tam, as Kakko set about keying in Dev's number. He told James about the white gates. James sat with his mouth open. "You see, we're not from Earth ourselves – although we have a lot of connections… Kakko's dad is British. We met Dev and his friend Zoe in America. Our technology is slightly more advanced than yours – Kakko works on engines for interplanetary spacecraft – but we come to help in practical ways. We never know what and where, and we have to learn fast. Often what we do is just encourage in some ways… Although Kakko generally likes to have hands on— "

"Hang on. Did you say 'another planet'?"

"Yes. Sorry, I know it's confusing."

"Where?"

"It's called Planet Joh in the Daan system. It's the same galaxy but many light years away… We are human, though."

Kakko sat up. She had made a connection. "Hey, Dev…

Yeah, it's me, Kakko… In India… Yeah, the Creator got us here. I'm afraid I bent Her ear rather… We're in a place called—" Kakko looked up at James.

"Agra."

"Agra. We're in a busy street—"

"Behind the Hotel Alleviate, near the Ambedkar Bridge," explained James.

"Outside a street café behind the Hotel Alleviate, near the Ambedkar Bridge… You know it…? Great." Kakko continued to listen to Dev intently. Her face was full of expression – so much that even Tam couldn't make out what kind of news she was hearing.

"Wow, Dev. Congratulations…! You'll be with us in less than two hours? That's brilliant. OK, Dev… A guy called James… Just met him… OK, see you outside the hotel in two hours… Look forward to it." Kakko passed the phone back to James who hung up. "So he's with Zoe," said Kakko delighted, "and, guess what, they're getting married!"

"Woah! That was quick," said Tam. "Hey, we haven't had a time warp, have we?"

"No. He met her in the mountains and it seems things have gone really fast…"

"That makes me feel… well… terrifically relieved."

"And so it should."

★ ★ ★

Two and a half hours later they were seated in the opulent surroundings of the Alleviate Hotel. Kakko felt scruffy but the others didn't seem to be fazed by the swish air-conditioned interior. Tam had explained they weren't staying there but Dev had swept them inside nonetheless and ordered soft drinks for all of them.

Kakko was excited to see Zoe, who was just glowing. She had caught the sun in the mountains but that didn't explain a lightness of spirit that Kakko had not seen before.

"Congratulations, Zoe. That didn't take you long."

"They don't stand on ceremony in these parts – meet the family and you're in."

"Are you sure…?"

"Absolutely. I love this man. He's… he's so perfect. So polite, so attentive, so loving, so… everything."

"And he seems set on you."

"Yeah, amazing, ain't it?"

"You deserve him, Zoe."

"Thanks."

Dev was in conversation with James. "So, you say your friend Ruth 'disappeared' almost two weeks ago."

"Yes," said James. "I wasn't exciting enough for her."

"What do you know about these people she went with?"

"Nothing. Neither did she. Three men and a girl in their twenties – from Europe I would guess… Said they were trekking across India and they were going to some amazing places nearby but off the tourist route… We had been to the Taj and the Red Fort… We had planned to move on to New Delhi… She left with them but she didn't come back. I texted her and she told me she was having a great time and not to hang about for her."

"Did she say where they were going?"

"No. That was it. A short text… I texted back and again the next day and she told me not to hound her. It sounded quite strong – even for her. I was upset and a bit scared. I tried to ring her but it wouldn't go through, so I texted again with the flight details and told her not to miss the plane… I haven't had any contact since. I hung around here – I haven't been out of Agra in case she came back."

"We must look for her," said Dev, taking charge. "She isn't safe. There are some bad types who prey on vulnerable people. How old is she?"

"Nineteen."

Kakko shuddered. Dev seemed so sure she was in trouble. All the girl wanted was a bit more excitement.

Zoe looked up at Dev and asked, "Where do we start to look? What do we do?"

"We put her picture on social media – all my local contacts. We get leaflets printed with her picture on. We make T-shirts and give them away…"

"Wow! That sounds a bit over the top," suggested Kakko.

"No. We need to find her. We won't unless we 'pull out all the stops', as you Westerners say."

"What about the police?" asked Zoe.

"We tell them, too… but we don't leave it to them."

"But this is going to cost money," said James "I—"

"No problem. Leave that to my family," stated Dev.

"But your family don't know us… and I… I have only just met your friends."

"If someone is in trouble in India, we don't have to know her. It is our country, so that is down to us," said Dev, speaking with authority. "Ruth needs to be found… We must find her."

"I don't know what to say. I'm so grateful," said James, and he began, to his surprise, to fill up and then sob. "Sorry…"

"You've done well without a friend," said Kakko. "Now you have some good ones."

"Yeah…"

"What about her folks?" asked Zoe.

James explained. Dev was already on his mobile.

"Well, I think you have to tell them," said Zoe. "Tell them everything. Tell them you and Dev's family are looking for her… This is not your fault."

"I promised I would look after her," drawled James, "and I haven't."

"You are – right now. Short of tying her up, you couldn't have done any more than you have," said Kakko, decisively. She knew how this girl might have felt. It was easy for a free spirit to get taken in.

"Thanks."

"OK," said Dev. "We need to report to the police here in Agra and then get back to my parents' place straightaway and put our operation in hand."

★ ★ ★

It was approaching midnight when they arrived at Dev's parents' large middle–class Indian home. Dev busied himself scanning the picture from Ruth's passport and preparing a picture of her from one on James's phone suitable for a poster and a T-shirt. The guests were treated kindly and shown to guest rooms. James shared with Tam, while Kakko doubled up with Zoe in a room that was set out like a room in a palace – including a bowl of fresh fruit on a low table in the centre.

James called his sister. She agreed Ruth's family should be told. To his great relief, she volunteered to talk to the parents. She said it was better to call round rather than talk on the phone and, anyway, it was only five thirty in the morning in Queensland, and James should get some sleep. He didn't argue. She would go round to Ruth's family's place at first light.

19

The morning sun shone on the roofs of the houses and gardens of Mathura and the night-time trill of the cicadas was replaced with birdsong... loud birdsong. Dev was already up when Kakko surfaced. He was ready to go to the local printers.

Two hours later, he reappeared with a box of papers bearing Ruth's picture and the words: Missing. Have you seen this girl? in both English and Hindi.

"The T-shirts will be ready by midday, then we start work," said Dev with authority.

"That's fast. How did you manage it?"

"My father is a businessman. He knows everyone around here. They are already looking." He showed them Ruth's face on his mobile phone. "All our friends are posting this on to all their friends... This will go all over northern India, perhaps further."

"Wow. That's great," said James. He had slept deeply – he had been so tired. Now things were happening, he was hoping it was only a matter of time before someone found Ruth.

"But there are many ordinary people on the streets who will not see her picture on the phones." Dev spoke with urgency. "This is where we must work. We need to hand out these flyers and distribute the T-shirts."

James's phone rang. It was Ruth's father. Mandy had done

a good job. He seemed pleased that James had galvanised so much support and didn't appear to blame James as much as he thought he would.

"I reckon he wasn't surprised that she went off," he said quietly.

"I guess he knows his daughter," offered Tam.

"It happened so... so quickly. It didn't cross my mind at the time that they might have been up to no good, or I would have made a bigger scene."

"The 'if onlys' won't help," said Zoe. "All of us can think of things we would have done differently after the event."

"Too right," said James ruefully. "If I had thought more with my brain than my heart, I would have been more discerning, and I would never have allowed Ruth to persuade me into coming here with her in the first place."

It occurred to Kakko that Tam may have behaved exactly like James if he had been the boy and she the insistent girl – she had always recognised the power she had over him. Kakko thought she knew what it might have been like for Ruth buoyed up by her sense of power over her boyfriend. That would have been the time she was most vulnerable. Con artists preyed on those who weren't suspicious. That didn't mean they were weak or stupid, just innocent or inexperienced. The thought stiffened Kakko's resolve to find this girl – perhaps she had just been a bit too exuberant, too much of a free spirit who had been too confident of her own powers...

Meanwhile, Dev's family were secretly worried that they might be far too late – but for James's sake they didn't show it. They smiled kindly and encouragingly as they ate a delicious lunch based on salad vegetables, naan dips and sweet cakes. Dev's father called two of his workers from the office to assist with the distribution of the leaflets and T-shirts.

By the end of the day, 2,000 flyers and 100 T-shirts had been distributed around the streets and markets of Agra. Now all they could do was wait.

"Tonight is a full moon," said Dev. "This is exactly the right time to see the Taj. Let us take a rickshaw to the gates. It is open tonight on the full moon."

"The Taj? You mean the Taj Mahal? The actual place – the real Taj Mahal?" exclaimed Zoe.

"Yes. The real one, of course."

The Taj Mahal by moonlight is one of Planet Earth's most wonderful sights. It was commissioned by a man, designed by a man and built by many thousands of men, yet it shone in the moonlight like something God might have created.

"What is it? I mean, what was it built for?" asked Kakko.

"It was built by Shah Jahan as a mausoleum for his wife, Mumtaz."

"A tomb. That must be the world's biggest tomb ever," marvelled Zoe.

"He loved her very much. He wanted nothing but the best for her."

"And she is buried underneath it?"

"Yes. Alongside Shah Jahan himself. He had not planned for himself to be buried here – but his sons put him with his wife."

"So, it's a kind of monument to love?" said Kakko.

"That is an excellent way of looking at it," answered Dev.

They walked down the water garden and up the steps. The huge dome sparkled above them.

"It's as if the moon was made especially to shine on these buildings," marvelled Tam.

"I wish Ruth had seen this by moonlight," sighed James. "It might have made her think again… about being with me,

I mean… You know, beautiful as it is, there is a sadness about this place. Shah Jahan built it because he had lost his beloved."

"Yes. It is a gift to the one whom he mourned," agreed Dev. "But *we* are praying that you will find your Ruth in *this* world, not in the next."

They were just hailing a rickshaw to take them back to the station, when Dev's phone rang. It was his father. Dev listened with a concentrated expression.

He looked up and reported what his father was telling him. "A man has rung from the Kinari Bazaar. He says he saw Ruth with three white men and an Indian ten days ago. He remembers her because they brought her to buy a sari. It was unusual to have so many men around and no women. He says they were talking of going to Varanasi."

Dev told his father that they were on their way back to the station. They could call round to see the man. His father gave them the details.

Apparently the man had been measuring someone for a suit when the five people came into the shop. He assumed they wanted the men's section – there being four men. But instead they engaged the female assistant. While she was attending to the girl, he overheard the men discussing plans to move on to Varanasi as soon as they could get a vehicle. They said something about it being easier when the girl was dressed as an Indian. He remembered them specifically saying *the girl* rather than her name, which struck him as odd. The woman assistant remembered them, too.

It wasn't too difficult to find the shop. It was crowded with dummies dressed in saris and suits, with shirts and bolts of cloth and boxes of all colours and sizes lining the walls. Joss sticks burned on counters which also displayed buttons and a plethora of trinkets and accessories that glittered in the bright electric lights. Kakko and Zoe were fascinated and began examining the colourful material as they waited for an assistant to be free. It was amazing how busy this little shop was so late in the evening. A man looked up as a client left, and Dev approached him and introduced himself.

After talking to him, James was sure it had been Ruth the man had seen. But ten days ago. That was an age. "Where's Varanasi?" he asked.

"East. On the Ganges. About 600 kilometres. It's a place of religious pilgrimage… and a tourist mecca."

"Six hundred kilometres!" breathed James, alarmed. "That's almost, like, from Brisbane to Sydney! How do we get there?"

"The easiest way would be to fly. I'll ask my father."

20

The following morning they were in Agra airport in the queue to board for the one-and-a-half-hour flight to Varanasi.

"This is costing your family a mint," protested James.

"When Dad gets into something, he stops at nothing. We have a lead and we should follow it up... Besides, my family is not short of a few rupees."

"I was given the impression that India was a place with much poverty," said Kakko. "But I see attractive shops, magnificent buildings and a modern airport."

"We have our poor people," answered Dev. "India has a massive population. But we are also making progress rapidly. My father owns a business that makes a lot of money but he is a good employer and does not pay poverty wages... Sadly, there are some who do."

"Most people here are not Christians. I thought I heard my brother Bandi saying they are Hin... something."

"Hindus. Yes, that is the chief religion. It is the ancient religion of India."

"Are you Hindu?"

"My parents used to be but they became Christians. My sister and I have been brought up as Christians."

"Is that hard... being a Christian when everyone else is Hindu?"

"Not everyone else. Our church is full; it is not so bad

for Christians. India has many religions. There are Buddhists, Sikhs, Muslims – the Muslims can have a hard time of it… The Taj is a Muslim building."

"I was going to ask that," said Tam. "The inscriptions around it are not in the Indian script I have seen elsewhere. I have seen a lot of that, but the writing on the Taj is different."

"It's Arabic. They are quotations from the Quran."

"Can you read them?"

"No. I cannot read Arabic. But I know what it says above the gate: 'O Soul, thou art at rest. Return to the Lord at peace with Him, and He at peace with you.'"

"That's beautiful. Shah Jahan really loved Mumtaz. Were they married long?" asked Zoe.

"She died giving birth to her fourteenth child." Dev smiled.

"Ah… That's *a lot*…" Zoe was lost for words. She began to wonder what Dev's family expected of *her*. But Dev was just one of three siblings – so that wasn't quite so bad. She wouldn't mind having three children.

They touched down at Varanasi and Dev ordered a taxi to take them straight to the address of a printer who had already been sent the file to print more flyers and T-shirts. The generous printer had everything waiting for them and declined any payment.

"People need to know that we in India do not tolerate this sort of crime," he said firmly.

"What sort of crime?" Kakko asked Zoe.

"I'm not sure. But I think Dev's family are hoping that these men have kept her alive. She has no value to them dead."

"That bad!" Kakko shuddered. She had been denying the truth to herself and had gone along with Dev's family's positive approach. "Yuk. What sort of value?"

"Oh, Kakko. Use your imagination... And drugs will come into it too, probably."

"At least she will be alive..."

"She may not want to be," said Zoe calmly.

"Oh, Zoe..."

The print shop owner had taken them to his reception room and they were all being plied with tea and sweet treats.

"I have asked two of my apprentices to accompany you. I recommend the young ladies stay here... at least until we know more."

"I—" uttered Kakko. But Tam got in first.

"I think they can look after themselves very well. In fact, I know they can... They are *trained*," he added.

"Ah. I see."

"They will stay with us. If... When we find Ruth, we may need them."

"I see your reasoning."

No further objections to the presence of the ladies was made. Tam caught Zoe's eye and squeezed Kakko's hand.

They were soon out and about on the streets of this new city, once again distributing their flyers and T-shirts. The ladies they met took a concerned interest, too, as Kakko and Zoe approached them. There seemed to be a real desire to find Ruth, even from strangers. Kakko felt strangely warmed by the whole experience. James couldn't get over the size of the operation.

After a while they found themselves down by the riverside at the top of the ghats. People thronged the steps, washing themselves and even bathing in the dirty brown Ganges.

Yuk, thought Kakko, *how could anyone wash in that?*

Reading her thoughts – or perhaps her face – Dev explained. "The Ganga is regarded as the sacred river. No matter how polluted it may appear, the water of the Ganga is deemed to purify the soul."

"Look," said Zoe with delight, "they are floating little tealights with rose petals on tiny boats… I just love it." They watched the small clay dishes filled with lamp oil float past them as the huge river flowed gently on towards the sea.

Dev bought a dish with some oil and a *diya* – a small wick – and walked down the steps. Borrowing a light, he lit it with a prayer and let the current take it. "The prayer is for Ruth," he declared.

"You said you are a Christian," said James, gently. "You don't believe in this religion."

"Oh. This river is sacred. I am a Christian but that doesn't stop the Ganga being sacred to India, nor does it mean that it doesn't belong to God. As a Christian, I believe all creation is sacred to God. And Christ is the Living Water to cleanse and revive – He is also the Light of the world. We are all born through water, but also the Spirit. He came to give us life, abundant life."

"Amen," breathed Zoe.

"Ruth is in God's hands – wherever she is," said Dev firmly. "She is already found and is safe in the hands of God. Nothing can separate us from God's love."

They climbed back up the steps and looked back across the river. Kakko no longer saw the pollution – now she had a sense of awe and wonder. The river represented hope and life; it made sense to her that the dead were being cremated on its banks and their ashes scattered in the waters – the waters of life. Whatever the differing beliefs of the religions of India, few of them believed that death was the end – it was the gateway to another life somewhere. Life after life – all permeated with love.

Just then, a woman approached them. She was shy at first. She spoke in Hindi.

Dev translated. "She says she knows someone who has seen Ruth."

"Where?" asked James, excited.

Dev conversed a little more with the woman. She herself did not know, but she knew a man who might – but the information would not be free. This man was not of the generous kind.

Dev took this seriously. "I have told her that I will pay him after I know that the information is reliable." He nodded to the woman and she set off through narrow backstreets.

"Stick close together," urged Dev. This was scary and Kakko felt the skin on her arms tingle and Tam's hand holding hers became tighter. The danger instinct they had gained through their previous experiences put them on their guard.

The woman stopped outside a small door. She commanded them to wait and entered the house. A few seconds later she re-emerged and beckoned them all inside. The room was small and smoky – but the smoke didn't hide the strong smell of human sweat mixed with garlic and spices. Kakko's eyes burned and James coughed.

Opposite the door, a middle-aged but wizened Indian was sitting on the floor. He chewed betel nut with his mouth open – bright red juice oozing between his teeth. The man's eyes opened wide into what was meant to be a grin. The grin spread to his lips as he spat crimson saliva into the fire, which hissed.

"You have information about this girl?" asked Dev curtly in Hindi, holding out a poster.

The man continued to grin and indicated to his guests to sit on the floor. The young woman bustled over with a hand-held broom and swept an area clean. They sat but the man kept silent. Dev met his eyes.

"I need proof that the information is useful," stated Dev.

"The girl was with six men – three of them white. Dealers."

"What did they look like?" asked James when Dev had translated.

They described them as Westerners. It was a well enough description for James to know they were the same men with whom Ruth had left.

"OK." Dev produced a note. The man said he had seen them dealing with drug suppliers ten days ago. "Where can I find them?"

"They tell me the white men are still in the same place – but the girl has disappeared."

"*Gisurgeh?* – Where? Where are the Westerners?" demanded Dev.

The man held out his hand and Dev gave him another note. He took it and then slid his thumb over his index and middle fingers. He wanted more and knew he would get it. Dev didn't argue, held up a second note, but wore the look of a man who was not willing to give more. The man still held back. Dev looked the man in the eye, then shrugged and made to get up. Kakko was positively angry. If this man knew something about a person whose life was in danger he shouldn't be playing games. He shouldn't want money at all. Perhaps her powerful glare and the clear signs she was about to explode convinced him to speak but it was more likely the knowledge that he would get no more from Dev until he did. He gave them an address.

"Write it down," Dev said hopefully. It may be that someone in the room could write. The man nodded to the young woman who took Dev's ballpoint pen to write on the flyer. The man dictated and she scribbled something and gave it to Dev. Dev read it; then changed his expression. Everyone relaxed and the man said, "Chai?"

"No, we can't stay," said Kakko urgently.

"We stay," said Dev. "Making friends is not time wasted."

Tam pulled Kakko back down beside him and smiled at her. Zoe and James had cottoned on earlier. If this man was their ally he would continue to help them. The young woman poured hot water from the fire into a pot.

Kakko didn't enjoy the brew but Tam drank it like a pro. The cups may not have had handles but at least they were clean.

When they were outside, Dev explained that the woman had indicated she would guide them; she had written that beneath the address. They were to wait around the corner for her. When she found them, Dev offered her money but she wouldn't take it.

"No. My father brings us shame. Come."

They followed her through another maze of backstreets and across two noisy bustling main roads. It would have taken hours for them to find the place without a guide. Eventually they arrived at a place with a sign outside bearing the name Loft Hotel in English.

"It is cheap place for young whites," explained the woman. "Travellers with small money."

They pushed their way inside the hotel where they came face to face with two young Westerners with scruffy beards and dirty hair. They were smoking something putrid. James recognised them despite the hair.

"You!" He spoke loudly – too loudly, for all the eyes of other customers in the small bar were turned on him. "Where is Ruth?"

The young men, who were clearly the worse for wear on some substance, started. They were too far gone to face up to James.

"Gone," said one of them with a shrug.

"What do you mean 'gone'?"

"Gone. She left… a week ago."

"Where?"

"Search me," the man drawled.

"Don't you play with me, mate!" shouted James who was doing his best to look strong. Stronger than he felt. James was no rugged drover from the outback, but an English student in first year uni in Sydney.

The young men began to laugh but Kakko had had enough. She lunged forward and grabbed one of the men by his shirt at his neck and twisted it. The man's eyes looked as though they might pop out of his head. The other went to get up to back away but he found himself forced back into his seat by Tam's heavy hand.

Energised by Kakko's vehemence, Zoe's best biting voice repeated James's question, adding, "If you don't want my alien friends here taking you back to their home planet in bits, you'd better answer."

"Like we said," sputtered the one half-strangled, "she left. She took herself off… Let… go… of… me…" Kakko only turned the shirt tighter.

"More!"

"Look, he's telling the truth," said his associate. "We had a party and she did drugs… We all did. We didn't realise it was her first time and she overdid it – had a bad trip. Next day she went…"

"Is that all?" asked Dev calmly. "What else did you do to her?"

"Nothing."

"OK… OK," said the first as Kakko threatened to continue her assault. "OK. We tried. But she was too far gone, unconscious. The next night she refused the drugs… and us. We only wanted to have a good time."

"Which way did she go?" asked Dev again.

"I don't know. She just left."

"Left her backpack and everything," said the first.

"You mean she ran off because she was in danger from you!" snarled Kakko.

"It wasn't me – it was Seb who started it. Yeah, she just fled."

"Where's Seb?"

"Asleep."

They discovered Seb laid out across a bed upstairs. He was in a poor state. James found Ruth's backpack. It still contained some of the items that were clearly of no use to the young men – clothes and a girly hairbrush – but most of her stuff was missing. It was clear these people had no idea where Ruth had gone, or even cared about it.

Downstairs, the owner of the guesthouse was anxious they should leave. Dev was very polite. He said that it would be in his interest to disallow drugs. The owner grew alarmed; had Dev got influence with the police?

"My friends," said Dev quietly to the two men still seated downstairs under his watchful gaze, "they are indeed from another planet. If you want them to leave you alone I suggest you leave my country on the first available plane." The men nodded. It would take some time for the shock mixed with drugs to wear off.

"I doubt these men will be here much longer," said Dev when they were all outside. "But we are – how do you say it in America? – back to square one in finding Ruth. A young woman with no friends and no money... It is bad."

"If I had no friends and no money in India, I would go to the police."

"She had been taking drugs," said Dev. "She would risk being arrested."

"But that's good news – a bit. Isn't it?" said Kakko carefully. "I mean, if she was dead the police would know because they would have a body."

James shuddered but then said with a positive tone, "Kakko is right… The police would know that, wouldn't they?"

"Maybe," agreed Dev, but not with great conviction. There were many places to hide a body in Varanasi.

"OK. So she didn't go to the police. She may not have known where to go. And, anyway, the police are men and I don't think Ruth would have wanted to have anything more to do with men."

"A woman, then," said Zoe.

"A woman not too far from here," said Kakko. "A woman who is her mother's age who looks confident and intelligent."

"Right," said James. "We ask all the women we can see… in the market."

But by now it was quite late and people were all beginning to shut up for the evening. This part of Varanasi closed down earlier than Agra.

"That is a good idea," agreed Dev. "We need to ask around here. We will return tomorrow – first light."

"I'm pooped," murmured Zoe. "Where are we staying, Dev?"

"My father has made reservations for us at the Hotel Varanasi Palace."

"A palace. Sounds great. Is there a jitney that'll get us there?"

"Jitney?" mumbled James. "What's a jitney?"

"Or a taxi if you like. It just seems the kind of hotel that would have a jitney. Can't say I've ever had the money for taxis."

"Can't we stay looking here just a little longer?" James

was tired but they had been so close; he didn't want to give up now. Every minute, he felt, was critical.

Just then Dev's phone rang. It was his father. An Indian man with a Bihar accent had called the number on the flyers. He claimed to know where Ruth was but wouldn't give an address. He offered to meet at a location of their choice in Varanasi. Dev's father was suspicious.

"I understand," Dev was saying. "He must come to the hotel – on his own." He lowered his phone.

"We have a bite. But it may be a hoax – someone trying to get us to pay money for nothing… Come, I will hail a rickshaw."

It may not have been the hotel jitney but they squashed in and they arrived at the hotel quicker than Zoe thought they might. They checked in and were shown to comfortable rooms on the fourth floor. Kakko wondered whether they expected her to share with Tam but Dev had no intention of spending the night with Zoe. It never occurred to him.

"Sorry, guys," Zoe said with a giggle after Dev and James had gone back downstairs. "He's far too much the gentleman."

"He knows what his family expects of him," said Tam. "And he respects that. We're cool with it. I am sure you two can look after yourselves… I'm going to join Dev and James. I think they are meeting this man. I'll leave you to freshen up."

"Thanks," said Zoe. "I need to."

Down in the bar, Dev and James were sitting at a table with a rough-looking Indian. He did not hold himself like an Indian gentleman. He was not dirty or unkempt – he was dressed in a suit – but there was something about him that Tam didn't like. Tam could see Dev was on his guard. Dev looked at him when he came in but made no sign of recognition. Tam got the message – he needed to stay a free agent. He seated himself in earshot.

"I need to know you are genuine," Dev was asking in English.

"Oh. I have proof. We were just waiting for someone to come looking. We are most anxious to reunite this young lady with her family." He pulled out a smartphone and called up a picture. He laid it on the table. "Enough proof?"

Ruth's head was laid on a pillow, her eyes half-shut. She looked very ill.

"What have you done to her?" demanded James alarmed.

"Nothing. We found her – picked her off the streets. She has malaria. We are giving her medicines; they are very expensive."

"She should be in hospital," said Dev with a firm voice.

"Ah, yes. But hospitals cost money. It is the responsibility of the family to pay the bills. That is why we are looking for the family," he mocked.

"Where is she?" demanded James.

"I will see she gets to hospital. You pay."

"How much?" asked Dev.

"I think I will need three million."

"Three million rupees? That is too much. I do not have access to that amount of money."

"She needs hospital treatment. It is expensive."

"One million," said Dev firmly.

"Oh, no. That is nothing. But I will come down a bit – two and a half."

"One and a half. Or I go to the police."

"Very well. One and a half it is," the man sneered. "You drive a hard bargain…" And then his smarmy attitude suddenly changed and he barked, "And no police, or the deal is off." All pretence of politeness had vanished. "The rupees will be collected tomorrow. I will tell you where – and this silly bitch will arrive at the hospital." He stood to leave.

"Don't forget: any police, no deal. She is very sick..." Then he was gone.

Tam attempted to follow him but he got into a taxi which sped off among the traffic.

21

When Tam returned to the bar, Dev was comforting a very distraught James.

"We must wait until tomorrow. I cannot get money tonight and, in any case, we cannot do anything until he calls."

"We can go out and see if we can find her. Someone will know where she is – I mean, not just this man," suggested Tam.

"Exactly," replied James. "We can look all night – as long as it takes. Ruth is alive but she's not OK. I can't go to bed and just wait. What if she dies tonight? We have to do everything we can."

"It will be dangerous. You should not—"

"I don't care, Dev. You saw that photo. Ruth might not survive until tomorrow. That man doesn't care whether she lives or dies – all he wants is his money!"

It occurred to Tam that Ruth might already be dead, but he didn't say anything.

"I'm going back to the place she was last seen. Now."

"You can't go alone," protested Tam.

"Well, come with me, then!" James almost shouted.

Tam didn't argue. "Fine," he said gently. "Let us go and tell the girls what we're doing. Then we can go."

James calmed down. "Sorry," he said. "You have been so good to me. I had no right to speak to you like that."

"No problem," said Tam. "You're right. It's urgent.

I couldn't sleep either. And besides, I've been in far worse danger than this. We have phones now; we can call for help when we need it."

Back in the room, Zoe lay fast asleep. She had showered and then taken herself to bed and was out for the count. Kakko had just finished dressing after showering and felt good. They left Zoe to sleep while Dev explained the situation in the boys' room.

"I'm going back to look," said James, determined.

Dev protested. He knew this was dangerous; his father would not approve. But James wouldn't relent.

"I'll go with him," said Tam. "Watch his back." He knew what was coming.

"Not without me you won't," said Kakko with her usual vehemence. Tam knew he had no choice but he also knew that Kakko could look after herself better than ninety per cent of males her age. Almost certainly better than James.

They hailed a rickshaw and returned to the Loft Hotel. As they stepped down onto the road, they could smell the perfumed smoke that came from inside. Compared to a noisy venue across the street, the Loft Hotel was quiet.

"All off their heads," Tam suggested.

"Let's walk about and see if we can find anybody... You suggested Ruth would look for a woman, Kakko."

"Yeah, but the motherly sort I had in mind are all tucked up in bed by now."

But there were women. They lingered on the corners in twos and threes. It was quite obvious what their trade was.

"Actually, I guess these women are as likely to know as any," said Kakko, thinking it over.

"Well, it's up to you to ask," said Tam. "They're too scary for me."

Kakko laughed. She walked to the nearest group, wondering if they would understand her when she spoke.

"Excuse me," she began, "we're looking for this girl." She pulled at her T-shirt with Ruth's picture on it.

Whether or not they understood her language, the girls certainly understood Kakko's gist. They looked at one another and all shook their heads.

When Kakko turned, she found the boys surrounded by a group of prostitutes brandishing their wares. Tam seemed to be coping with the situation though. "Ruth," he indicated his T-shirt, "have you seen her?" They giggled and shook their heads. "Your girlfriend?" one asked. Tam pointed to James. "She belongs to him."

Kakko, however, had seen that one of the girls had not giggled along with the rest. In fact, she wore a particularly sheepish expression. Kakko approached her. "You know this girl," she stated; it was not a question. The girl lowered her eyes. "She is in danger. She is very ill. She needs hospital – now… Can you take me to her?"

The girl shook her head. *"Mayhi… No… La…"* She looked frightened.

James had cottoned on to what was happening. "We will not hurt you."

"I don't think she is frightened of *us*," said Tam. "You can take us to your house… We can pay…" He flashed a note.

This was easier for the girl. It would have the appearance she had got punters. And she wanted the money.

She led them up a narrow alleyway and through an open door. Inside they were immediately accosted by a madam who looked them over. At first her face displayed alarm but then it softened into a false smile. Her eyes alighted on the matching T-shirts displaying Ruth's picture.

"You like Padma?" she said softly.

"We are looking for our friend," answered Kakko, curtly. "Her name is Ruth and she was last seen near here leaving the Loft Hotel."

"You sit down. I bring you soda… Padma, Ashish *abees rabda*," she addressed Padma. The girl betrayed an expression of doubt. "Now," said the madam in English. The girl left through the door through which they had arrived. A small boy took her place, looked at the madam and departed through an internal door.

Kakko was becoming impatient. "Ruth. She is ill and needs a hospital. Do you know where she is?"

Tam put his hand on her arm as if to calm her but kept his eyes on the woman. "We fear for her safety," he said quietly.

The boy reappeared with three bottles of Coke on a small tray. Tam thanked him. The boy bobbed.

"You wait here. Padma will return."

Kakko sat as patiently as she knew how but couldn't help feeling uncomfortable. She was just about to ask the woman if things could be hurried up, when there was a noise in the doorway and two men entered. James and Tam immediately recognised him as the man they had met in the hotel but he was no longer wearing his suit.

"Hello, my friends," he mocked with a broad but fake smile. "You have come to bring me money."

Quickly suppressing the tingle of panic that had shot down his spine, Tam replied as calmly as he could. "You will have your money tomorrow. But Ruth needs the hospital tonight."

"I don't think so. You believe you are clever to come here but you are mistaken. You are most foolish. Now I have four captives to trade instead of one."

Kakko ignored his words. "If you are holding Ruth, and if you have an ounce of humanity, you will get her to a hospital right now… My friends will pay you tomorrow."

"No police," assured Tam.

"Yes," smirked the man, "you speak the truth – there are no police. So, you see, you have no power but to submit… Raj," he addressed his accomplice.

"Yes, Ashish."

"You take the girl; let her be with her friend. Tomorrow the price will be three times," he mocked James and Tam. "As for you, I think it will be easier if you just disappeared for a while."

Kakko sprang into action but Raj was ready for her. He was clearly trained in some form of martial art because Kakko suddenly found herself face down on the floor with her arms behind her back. She screamed in pain as the man twisted her joints.

Tam went to move but Ashish produced a nasty-looking blade. "Do as I say and no-one gets hurt!"

The madam produced some very glittery but effective handcuffs and a rope – accessories of her trade – and Tam and James were quickly immobilised with their hands behind their backs and ankles bound together.

"If you do not resist, I may allow you to live," smirked Ashish.

Tam spoke softly to Kakko who was still struggling. "Go with this man. Ruth needs you."

Kakko's dignity was affronted. She was not only furious with this man but angry with herself for being overpowered so easily, but Tam's soft voice did the trick. He always spoke so much sense. If she allowed herself to be taken to Ruth, it would mean that she could nurse her. The worst-case scenario was that Dev's family would have to part with a lot more money than they had originally agreed on. The best-case scenario was that the oaf that was good at combat was too thick to relieve her of her mobile phone in the front pocket of her trousers beneath the loose XXL T-shirt bearing Ruth's image.

Kakko allowed herself to be pulled to her feet.

"OK. OK. You win," she said crossly.

Raj shot her a toothy smile – or what would have been a toothy smile if most of them had not been missing – and dragged her to the doorway.

"*Rugieh!*" barked Ashish. "Wait! The shirt. Do not show that face." He raised his hand as if he was about to remove Kakko's top. Whether or not it was the wild look of defiance or her spitting, "Don't you dare!", he thought better of it. Kakko must be transferred from house to house quietly. There had already been too much noise; customers and girls were assembling on the landing above. Instead of touching Kakko, Ashish took Padma's shawl from her shoulders and held it out to Kakko. "Cover yourself!" he commanded.

"Do as he says," said Tam firmly. "Ruth…"

Kakko took the shawl. Some of her dignity – and her phone – were secured at least for the moment. "If your lackey tries anything on, I'm ready for him next time," she said in imperious defiance.

Raj led her to the door. "You want see Ruth, you come quiet."

When they had gone, Ashish resumed his fake gentleness. "She belongs to you? Perhaps we can tame her for you?"

"She does not need taming," said Tam proudly, "she is the servant of the Divine Creator; she knows what is right and what is wrong, what is just and what is unjust. When you can tame the Creator, you will be able to tame her, but not before."

"You Westerners. You think you know God. It is in India that we truly understand the divine."

For the first time since they had arrived at the house James spoke. "So you think the deities would approve of kidnap and abusing women? Which of them? Where is the karma in what you are doing? If you believed in the deities, you would know that you have no merit in their eyes. Kakko is holy – all women are vessels for the holiness of God." He looked up at Padma who was standing in the corner shaking. She cowered with a mixture of fear, shame and the cold without her shawl. She was dressed very skimpily. "This girl meant well. She has a good heart." He looked at the madam. "She needs a shawl."

To James's amazement, she went to the stairway and shouted up. A girl came down with a shawl and led Padma away. There followed a silence that was so intense they could hear music from across the street. Then Ashish shrugged. He looked at the madam. "*Dehikanah,*" he said quietly. "You will be rewarded... If you behave yourself and your friends in the Varanasi Palace pay quietly – and no police – maybe you can go home... Their pockets," he said to the madam. "Keep whatever they have – a gift for you." Obediently, the woman relieved them of their phones and their wallets.

Meanwhile, Raj was leading Kakko through some more back alleys. He tugged her by the arm but something sharp was pressed into her back. She didn't know what it was – but it definitely felt like a weapon. She thought about escaping but then remembered Tam saying: "Let them take you to Ruth." He was right.

Kakko tried to memorise where she was being taken but everywhere looked the same. Then they entered a wider alley with a temple at the end of it. They left by an alley on the right about fifty metres before they got to the temple, and took the second doorway on the right.

Raj called and two men appeared. They looked interested but Raj barked an order and led Kakko up a flight of stairs and turned a key in a door on the first landing and thrust her into a dark room. The door was slammed behind her and the key turned in the lock. Kakko smelt Ruth before she heard her. It was the putrid smell of fever. Her breathing was slow and rasping. Kakko followed the sounds and found the girl lying on a mattress on the floor. As her eyes became accustomed to the dark, Kakko made out the form of an almost naked Ruth. A bowl of water and a cloth lay beside her. Someone had been attempting to wash her. Kakko filled the cloth with the water and dabbed at Ruth's head. She was burning up. Kakko was more frightened than she had been at any time that day. Adrenaline and anger can drown out fear. Here there was no adrenaline in her system – just pure fear that this young woman was going to die and on her watch. All Kakko could do was bathe and pray. Despite the night hours, the room was baking hot. Kakko found the shutters. They were fastened tightly but not locked. She tugged them open and leaned out. It was at least ten metres to the ground and there was no way she could have got Ruth out in her condition in any case. The view was stunning – not. A blank wall stood less than five metres away. But, mercifully, a waft of cooler air blew through Kakko's hair as she leaned out. She discarded the shawl and then rejoiced. How could they have been so stupid? She still had her phone! Raj was indeed the numbskull she had hoped. The fact was that both he and Ashish wanted her to go quietly; he was not going to risk a fight in the street – searching her was not worth it.

Raj returned to the bawdy house with the two other powerful-looking men. He untied Tam and James's feet but left their hands still clasped behind them. If they tried to flee they would not get very far, even if they could escape in the first place. The madam led the way outside and then down steps into a dank, dark cellar.

To the boys' amazement, after a few minutes, Padma re-appeared now wearing a thick shawl and bearing a tray with two bowls of some sort of hot soup. She had a key and released them from the handcuffs.

"I sorry," she said. "Mrs, she is bad woman."

"Don't worry. You tried. Kakko is with Ruth. That is good," said Tam.

What he didn't know was that Kakko was already working out how to call the police and an ambulance.

Kakko told herself off. She had her phone but no useful numbers on it. Why hadn't she entered Dev's at the time? He had given it to her so he could phone her if they got separated. He might still do so but not for a few hours. Time was of the essence – Ruth was in a critical state. *If only I could remember the number they used in New London when we needed the police, it might work here too. This might be a very different part of Earth, but it's still the same planet.* Then she remembered it: 911. She tried it. A woman answered in Hindi – she sounded official.

"Hi. Is that the police?" she tried. The woman replied in a language she could understand. "We've been kidnapped," she stated. "We need an ambulance, too, urgently… My name? Yes, Kakko Smith. Erm… My nationality?" *What is my nationality? I can't tell them I am from Joh – far too complicated…* "Er, yes, British." *That's not a lie – Dad's British.* "I don't know the address but it's near a temple in the—"

The key turned and the door burst open. A man was fleetingly silhouetted against the light from the landing.

"No police," he yelled and hit out in Kakko's direction. She stepped back but was not quick enough to avoid his hand colliding with her phone hand. The phone flew from her grasp and clattered across the floor. The man followed it but it was lost in the shadows. Ruth moaned. The man swore in some Indian language. As he bent to search out the phone, Kakko pushed him from behind – hard. His head hit the wall but not hard enough to knock him senseless. He was not trained like Raj. He swung round and made a lunge for Kakko. She brought her knee up under his chin and as his head came up she gave him a clout across the ear with her two-handed swing. She felt his beard on the back of her hand as he fell sideways to the ground.

Kakko made for the corner to see if she could find her phone but as she did so a second assailant, whom she hadn't seen come in, hit her with something hard. She turned but her legs gave way. A second blow swished over the top of her head but she didn't notice it sweep through her hair as the world sank away from her consciousness. She fell alongside Ruth.

The phone, however, hadn't broken. All this time the operator at the emergency headquarters was listening and the location of the call was being identified. And just then, at five o'clock precisely, an amplified call of the muezzin emanated from a loud speaker located in a minaret attached to the building opposite. The plain wall Kakko had seen was the external wall of a mosque. The police had all they needed: the location of the cell, and near a temple within metres of a mosque. The phone line remained open.

When Ashish returned, soon followed by Raj and his henchmen, there was a noisy row. They all came into the room in which Kakko and Ruth lay unconscious. The first guard had been dragged out into the corridor. He was in a poor way but that didn't stop him from being further beaten by Ashish – all within hearing of the phone which had now been totally forgotten.

Ruth stirred. Ashish's anger abated. The situation was still in hand. And Kakko being unconscious was a bonus. He closed the shutters and they all withdrew from the room and the door was locked again. Ashish left the two big men outside to guard it, just in case this wild woman recovered.

Ashish went to clean himself up. He smiled to himself –
he now had four people to trade.

★ ★ ★

Zoe woke at the call to prayer. It was not from the same
mosque that Kakko would have heard had she been conscious.
She found Dev already dressed.

"Where's Kakko. Where are the others?"

"Gone to look for Ruth. James couldn't rest."

"Sorry, I was just pooped."

"No. I'm glad you slept. They shouldn't have gone. It
was far too dangerous – but you know your intrepid friends.
I hope they're alright." Dev explained about the contact and
the ransom.

"My father and his brother are flying in – any time now.
As soon as we know Ruth is safe, we'll send for the police.
When my father arrives he will take charge. He tells me I'm
too young to conduct this sort of thing."

"You are. You need experience. Older heads are important
sometimes."

Dev's phone rang. It was his father and his uncle. They
were on their way from the airport.

★ ★ ★

Ashish had just finished combing his beard in front of a
bathroom mirror when the police arrived. Before he got to
the door, half a dozen men swarmed up the stairs. Kakko was
just coming to when the door burst open again. This time it
was men dressed in uniform.

An officer who seemed to be in charge demanded Kakko's
name.

"Kakko Smith," she said. "This is Ruth. She needs the hospital... Thank you for coming. How—"

But she didn't finish her sentence. A doctor came into the room, ordered the shutters be opened and that the half-dozen gawping policemen leave. He felt Ruth's brow, looked into her eyes, felt her pulse and listened to her chest through a stethoscope. Then he opened his bag and pulled out a syringe, plunged it into a bottle of clear liquid and injected it into Ruth's neck. Kakko looked away. Injections were not her cup of tea.

"What about you?" asked the doctor. "Let me look at that blow." Kakko tried to protest but was too groggy to resist and found herself the victim of a needle, too, when she didn't know what tetanus was.

Two men in a different uniform came into the room with a stretcher.

Fifteen minutes later, both girls were in emergency bays in a local hospital. A policeman was sitting beside Kakko's bed taking notes.

★ ★ ★

Meanwhile, Dev and Zoe had no idea that Ruth had already been rescued. Dev welcomed his father and uncle when they arrived at the Varanasi Palace.

"Now, my son, you must tell me it very carefully before we meet this man. A young woman's life is at stake."

Dev explained about the other three heading out on their own. Needless to say, Dev's father was angry. Dev protested that he hadn't been able to stop them. "James was desperate," he said, "and you know Kakko – no, sorry, you don't know Kakko..."

"Take it from me," Zoe came to his rescue, "it would take an army of Devs to stop her."

"We must hope they haven't been picked up by this gang," said Dev's uncle.

But just then they were approached by two policemen. They appeared to know all about the case. Zoe, Dev and his father quickly learned that everyone was safe – the only concern now, it seemed, was proving that they were not all involved in the kidnap.

★ ★ ★

What delighted Kakko the most was when the doctor confirmed that Ruth was on the way to a full recovery. "It is a good thing you found her when you did," he said; "she may not have survived much longer." After that, Kakko would not hear any talk of foolhardiness, and defended to the hilt James's decision to go out that night. Tam sighed – he could almost hear Kakko relating everything to her family back in White Gates Cottage.

"Kakko, whatever you tell your parents, please play it down when you talk to mine."

"Course," answered Kakko slightly piqued. "I'm not wacko."

"No. Of course not." Tam chuckled to himself. How he loved this girl. He must be mad. "Thanks."

★ ★ ★

That same day, Ruth's people flew in, too. Far from being held to blame, James was seen as the hero. If anyone was to blame it was them, they said. They should never have been persuaded to let her travel. Kakko wondered what authority parents had over a nineteen-year-old in Australia. "Not much," said Zoe. "Here in India, young people do not do what we do in the

West. They listen and honour – but then, Dev has parents who are worthy of it."

A nurse came with a message from the British consul. He had been made aware of the situation and wondered if Kakko needed assistance. They would like her to phone the consulate.

"Time to make ourselves scarce," said Tam. "Too many questions."

They were on their way to the hotel in a rickshaw to ask Dev how to get back to Agra when Tam spotted the white gate on the boundary of the Machodari Park. He didn't notice it at first – they like their white gates in India – but when she saw it, Kakko knew at once that it was one of theirs.

They took their leave with hugs and kisses all round. Zoe was sad to see them go. Every goodbye seemed so final.

"I shall ask the Creator for a gate for you to come to the wedding," she affirmed. "Anyway, whatever, have a great life… until next time."

The whole city seemed empty to Zoe after Kakko and Tam had gone. "It would be great for them if they are able to come to our wedding." Then she added thoughtfully, "But I wish they could come without bringing a dramatic adventure."

Dev laughed. "We have a lifetime to give thanks for them. If it weren't for them, we wouldn't have got back together."

Zoe sighed. "Yeah. And if it weren't for them, we might have got it together the first time. Poor Tam."

"No. I asked Tam because I needed courage. I doubt I would ever have had the courage."

"The Lord works in mysterious ways."

"Of course. That is the way it is with God."

22

Shaun had dispensed with the crutches; he was now walking with a stick and, without any support for short distances, things were improving for him. While Kakko was away, he found himself free to see Wennai without his sister rushing things. Kakko was, of course, right – he was more than just friends with Wennai. She wasn't his girlfriend – they didn't hold hands and regard themselves as an item – but Wennai 'walked alongside him' in a way that no-one else did; she was naturally patient with him and listened. Somehow, his experiences of war had brought him even closer to her because she understood grief and heartache. Wennai was deep. Her own loss was not one she tried to bury but she couldn't go around bringing it into everyday life with other people. With Shaun it was different – it didn't have to be spoken of but it was understood. As Kakko had said, they were good for each other.

Wennai knew Shaun believed God would heal him – that was where they differed. She would like Shaun's God to heal him but She couldn't – Wennai still believed God's existence to be a figment of Shaun's imagination. She had not changed her mind on that. But Shaun was not trying to persuade her to believe – he never had. All he required of her was that she give him space to relate to his Creator. She had learned to do that. She respected it, and even envied it if she were honest, and on that basis their friendship prospered. She had been aware that his faith had received a knock but she had also learned that it would take more than the psychological trauma he had received to convince him that God was not with him or that She had given up loving him. But Shaun was still not sure how such a fundamental faith difference would allow their relationship to grow into a committed partnership. One night before she got into bed, Wennai had challenged Shaun's God for a sign. "Heal him," she had said, "and I might believe in you." But there had been no sudden miracle.

That day, however, Wennai was to receive a challenge she hadn't asked for. Shaun had told her, and her alone, that he had rejected the Creator's last attempt to persuade him through a white gate. He had said that he had regretted not going through it and had resolved to accept the next invitation whatever he was feeling at the time. That morning the invitation came; his resolve was put to the test.

Shaun turned to Wennai. He texted her that he had seen the dreaded gate. He was on his own in the cottage. His nan was visiting her friend, Ada, and had dropped Yeka off at her nursery on the way. His mother and father were at work, Bandi was on Earth One, and Kakko was still adventuring with Tam somewhere. He needed to tell someone where he was going and Wennai was the only one who knew the full implications of this new challenge. Having her there in person was going to make stepping through the hedge that little bit easier. The gate had appeared as soon as it had got light. If it had been for anyone else they were bound to have come across it because it was right next to the main gate they always used. He had to tell someone and he didn't want to call his parents back. Wennai was the perfect person. She wouldn't fuss him and she would explain things to his parents. Wennai agreed to come; it didn't take her long.

"So you can see one of your white gates. What are you going to do?" asked Wennai.

"I have to trust Her."

"If you say so. Where is it?"

"Over there to the left of the usual gate."

"Oh, Shaun," she breathed a sigh of relief. "*I* can see that one – that new gate there." Wennai pointed directly at it. "That's not one of your special white gates."

"It is. That is no ordinary gate."

Wennai went up to it. It couldn't be a special white gate because she could see it. She laid her hand on the cool, smooth paintwork… and then looked through into a new, beautiful world. Slowly, she turned and faced Shaun, an alarmed look on her face.

"So it's for you, too. I don't know why but I had never expected you to get an invitation to another world."

"Neither did I… What are we going to do, Shaun?"

"We have three choices."

"Go through it, stop here, or… what's the third?"

"Or I go through it and you don't. *You* don't have to say yes to it."

"If you go through it, I will. If you don't, I won't."

"It could turn out… nasty," said Shaun, in a warning tone.

"But not all places are horrible."

"They all have a challenge."

They looked at one another. They both knew Shaun wasn't going to ignore the gate this time. He had regretted his decision on the previous occasion and he felt stronger now.

"What about your family?" asked Shaun.

"I'll text Patia. That'll be fine."

"Are you sure?"

"I'm an independent person. I don't have a parent to say otherwise. And you need me, and I— actually I'm looking forward to an adventure. I like the idea of sharing one of your escapades – I don't get to go anywhere, do I?"

"OK. Let's do it. I'm glad I'm not doing this on my own. The Creator knows what I need."

"Me, it seems."

Shaun rang his mother and Wennai texted her sister. There didn't appear to be a change of clothes necessary. There was nothing beside the gate to equip themselves with. Shaun was wearing his usual T-shirt and jeans, Wennai a loose top with matching shorts and a floppy hat. She had a crocheted shoulder bag containing a small brush, mirror, tissues and other make-up items, and her mobile phone.

Shaun said to turn off their phones. They wouldn't be able to use them anywhere outside Joh and they might as well conserve their batteries.

"You go first," said Wennai, a quiver in her voice.

★ ★ ★

The place beyond the white gate was beautiful. They stood on the edge of a wood overlooking a green and pleasant valley. One glance told them that this was no place on Planet Joh. The sunlight was different. There was a whiteness about it that reminded Wennai of the kind of light you get from an LED bulb. All the plants, from the smallest flower to the largest tree, were unrecognisable. They were trees, but in every detail they were different. The grass they stood on was like grass, yet it looked alien.

"Wow," said Wennai. She was completely taken aback. "And I thought I was good at biology!"

Shaun was already processing the experience. "It's different but these things are bound to use photosynthesis. They're green."

"It's beautiful," said Wennai firmly, "however it works."

"Joh-like oxygen levels, too," added Shaun taking a deep breath of sweet-scented air. "This place smells deliciously fresh."

Just then, they were aware they were not alone. Someone or something was moving over to their left.

"Locals?" wondered Shaun. "Let's make contact... Something is eating this grass; it's cropped. It could be a kind of cattle."

But before they saw any kind of animal, they had reached a hedgerow beyond which was a narrow road. A four–wheeled vehicle approached them. Apart from a low whir it was silent. It didn't appear to have a windscreen, just a shining metallic front shaped to deflect the wind. Shaun looked for the driver or passenger but there was none to be seen. The vehicle slowed to a stop and scanned them from across the hedge with a threatening lens. Shaun was about to call out when the vehicle abruptly drove off.

"Charming," said Wennai.

"Let's follow the road," suggested Shaun.

"Which way?"

"Follow the vehicle down the hill. We're more likely to find someone at the bottom of a hill than at the top – well, that's true on Joh."

After a couple of kilometres they came to what looked like a house. But it was clearly empty – either that or the owners had completely given up on maintaining their garden. Shaun tried to open the gate. It was seized up – bound by the entwining branches of the shrubs that surrounded it. The door to the house had clearly not been used for some time either. Shaun and Wennai moved on. They found house after house equally abandoned. It was quite sad but also alarming. What had happened to these people?

At last they came to a driveway that was in frequent use.

There were tyre tread track marks and also what looked like footprints made by strange rectangular shoes of exactly the same kind. They led to a yard in front of a very large barn with wide low doors that stood open.

Shaun took Wennai's hand. "Let's go and say hello."

The barn was a hive of activity. Figures of several sizes were standing around what looked like a self-operated production line. It reminded Wennai of the construction conveyor she had seen on a school trip to a factory. They saw no human beings or anything that resembled flesh and blood. There were figures but they appeared to be robotic – mobile machines. Shaun and Wennai approached nearer.

Suddenly a barrier fell in front of them. Another step and it would have struck them.

"Woah," squawked Shaun. "That was close!"

"Sor-ry!" shouted Wennai in a disgusted tone. "They should take more care."

A lens emerged from the door post. It scanned them with several clicks and zips. Then it fell silent. Shaun spoke into the lens. Nothing stirred. Wennai called into the factory. Again nothing. The robots seemed intent on their own business.

Then Wennai noticed what they were making: complete replicas of themselves. Every three minutes, completed middle-sized robots emerged from the production line, stood to attention, spent a few moments motionless as if waiting for something to boot up inside their brains, then turned left of their own will and disappeared through a low door to the right of the metal barn wall. From where they were standing, Shaun and Wennai couldn't see where they went after that.

"To enter or not?" wondered Shaun out loud.

"Well, at least there's life in there… of sorts. We're bound to find someone in charge."

Shaun ducked beneath the newly descended barrier and began walking towards the robots. Wennai followed. Almost immediately four medium-sized robots rolled out from the mass of engineering and approached them with what looked like wands... or swords.

Shaun began to speak. "We want... We would like," he corrected as the bots looked rather menacing. He addressed them because there was no-one else around to speak to. They kept advancing, then extended a pair of arms as a stockhandler might to usher cattle or sheep. Shaun stood his ground. One of the bots stepped forward and jabbed him with his wand. "Ouch!" exclaimed Shaun.

Another did the same to Wennai.

"That hurts," she complained. "Shaun, it's time to leave." She stepped smartly back under the barrier. Having been jabbed a second time, Shaun followed. This time the electric shock was stronger than the first. The barrier lifted and the bots moved behind them as Wennai and Shaun fled back onto the road. The bots kept following. Then, as if from nowhere, a vehicle arrived and barred their path. Shaun and Wennai looked back. They were trapped. But one of the pursuing bots opened a gate into a field and stepped back.

"Better do as we're told," said Wennai breathless. This was quite scary.

They obliged and stepped into the field. The bot closed the gate behind them and then he and his mates turned and made off back to the factory while the vehicle turned and retreated.

Apparently safe in the field, the couple took stock.

"They treated us as if we were escaped sheep," complained Wennai.

"Yes. They are robots that have concluded we're flesh and blood that doesn't fit into their world. They probably haven't seen the like of us before and think we are a sort of animal that belongs in a field."

"They are acting as if they own the place," worried Wennai.

"I think they probably do. They are programmed to behave like a farmer would. They would always act logically and probably learn as they go."

"Artificial intelligence?"

"I reckon so. But the question is: How advanced are they? Do they defer to organic beings?"

"But someone must have made them. They would be in charge."

"You would hope so, but artificial intelligence can get out of hand. Kakko was telling me that the Thenits reported on the dangers from their experience, and Bandi has read stuff from Planet Earth written by authors who could see the way things were going on that planet. A guy called Isaac Asimov has come up with three rules in the programming of any artificial intelligence to prevent it taking control over human beings. I heard him and Kakko talking about it recently. It's a real threat. The prototype for these bots was probably made by some kind of people, but they didn't see the dangers. Did you see what they were making?"

"More robots."

"Exactly. My guess is that they no longer need their organic creators."

"That's scary. What will they do to us?"

"I reckon as long as we continue to behave like sheep, we're safe for now."

"Demeaning, but wise."

"The question for us is, what does the Creator want us to do here…? Look, let's head off across this field and check out those woods."

"What do you expect to find? Are you hoping to find people?"

"If the bots don't want them on the roads and in the houses they might get away with living off the beaten track..."

"And out of sight."

Ten minutes later Wennai and Shaun had entered the woods and found a kind of path. Using Shaun's former plan, they followed it downhill. Without warning, a creature leapt from the undergrowth in front of them. He had some sort of weapon but Shaun did not heed that in his surprise.

"Sponron," he uttered, as he took in the large flat face, skinny body, bright eyes...

Wennai threw her hands in the air. "We're unarmed!" she shouted.

The Sponron visibly relaxed and called out. Very quickly the path in front of them filled with the spindly creatures.

"I am from Planet Joh," explained Shaun hurriedly. "We gave shelter to some of your kind a year or so ago." He desperately tried to think of a few Sponron words but they wouldn't come. He had not spent as much time with the young Sponrons as Kakko and Tam had. They were completely new to Wennai – she had not met those who had spent a short time on Joh. She felt self-conscious in the stares of a gathering number of large, bright blue eyes. At least Shaun seemed to know what was going on and who these alien people were, which was enormously reassuring.

"I remember it well," said a smiling face. It was One – the young male Sponron who had linked up with Shaun and Tam and put in motion the release of the slaves aboard the space cruiser, *Tal,* several years before. "It seems that once again you people have come to rescue us."

"Yeah," said Shaun diffidently. "Tell us about it."

"We will. But first we must make you properly welcome," said an older Sponron who seemed to be the leader of the group.

They led Shaun and Wennai into a village of houses made of wooden branches and leaves. Beneath the trees and among the undergrowth, they were so camouflaged that Wennai and Shaun didn't see them until they were almost upon them. Some houses were in the branches of the trees themselves.

"You blend in well," observed Wennai.

"We had to," said One; "the ASI has developed a drone… but there's little point these days as we're pretty sure they have installed infrared sensors in them anyway – it would be amazing if they hadn't."

"The ASI being the robots we met back there?"

"You met them? ASI – Artificial Super-Intelligence. How did they behave to you?"

Shaun and Wennai explained how they had arrived and what had happened in the meantime. They had actually entered an ASI factory.

"You went right in and they didn't apprehend you?" they said, with expressions of amazement.

"They just pushed us out, down the lane and through the gate at the bottom of the field… Like, as if we were farm animals."

"That must be it," said the elder; "they don't see you as intelligent beings. If they had, they would have taken you away… You do *look* rather more like animals than intelligent sentients… compared to us, that is…"

"Erm… if you say so…" said Shaun.

"Taken us away?" queried Wennai, doubtfully. "Where?"

"We don't know. They began with the robotics engineers and computer technicians that were working on the development of machines that could learn from experience, then the scientists and the politicians—"

"Anybody with any influence in our society," added One.

"Basically the people who had the knowhow to stop

them," said the elder. "I am... was... a farmer. The people in the countryside they have left to run away... so far."

"And those of us who just managed to escape," said One. "They didn't chase us. But if you stood and tried to fight... well, you just got stunned and carted off."

"Were they going to kill them?" asked Wennai again.

"We don't know. They might kill them but we think they just dump them somewhere where they can't interfere with what the ASI wants to do. Finding food would be a problem – they could just starve to death. Finding enough to eat is a problem for any of us."

"Machines don't need to eat," reflected Wennai.

"No, only power – electricity. But they have plenty of that from our panels and hydro plants – more than enough for their needs."

"So they know you are here in these woods," summarised Shaun, "but they are leaving you alone because they don't think you are a threat to them."

"So long as we live like our primitive Stone-Age ancestors in bush huts," moaned a young female. "We'll soon be wearing skins and rough stuff like them, too. Our clothes are all wearing out... We can't go on like this..."

This one looks like a teenager, thought Wennai. *She must be a bit younger than me – depending on how quickly these people grow up.*

"Don't cry, Tlap. You can and you will. The Sponron spirit is not so easily broken," said the elder softly.

"But I was doing well in school. I was getting good grades and I liked learning. Now here I have no books and nothing to write with except sharpened sticks in lumps of clay."

"What you do is wonderful," said One.

"Wonderful! Just a few words takes hours of finding and preparing the clay... What used to take ten minutes on a computer now takes me ten days!"

"You exaggerate, Tlap," smiled the elder. "But I was never one for reading, so I can't say. But what I can say is that where I used to plant several fields of crops with machines and live in a house with running water, I now have to do things in small plots by hand… and the young people here have to work hard to get enough water."

"And we live in constant fear," said One. "We have no idea if there are any other Sponrons left anywhere on the planet. We think there must be but if we were to make the slightest move to try and contact anyone beyond this wood and the farmed gardens, the ASI would pounce."

The teenager began to weep. "My brother, Slop. He tried," she sobbed. "We've not heard from him since. The ASI have got him."

"We don't know that. We have no information to say they captured him," said the elder.

"But he was running – the drones were hovering. Like he stood a chance…!" she despaired, her thin long hands, palms open in front of her. "There's nothing we can do…"

"Oh yes there is," smiled One. "I felt hopeless and trapped once. We were slaves on a space cruiser light years away from home. All we could do was pray… and hope…"

"You were lucky," moaned Tlap.

"We were. We just hung in there. There was nothing else we could do. We know En, the all-present Creator and our Sustainer, doesn't intervene in a military way. He doesn't fight with arms and weapons. We had to be patient… for many years. But all the time we knew that He hadn't abandoned us. Even if I could have, I wouldn't have become one of the oppressors. We knew love, they didn't. They abused the girls – it was terrible for them – but the men with the power never knew love like we did."

"And you were rescued in the end… But why did it take En so long?" asked Tlap.

"As you said, we were lucky. En didn't rescue everybody. The Thenits who built the ship all died. One of the girls died, too. But, although we were trapped, it was as if En was trapped inside with us. En may be the Creator of the universes but He cannot go around zapping people. He is love and he has to *act* in love… always, every time. So He becomes a victim, too."

"Some people would think that if He were Love, He would use force to rescue you," said Shaun. "A father would not stand back and let his children be hurt."

"Exactly," said One. "He doesn't stand back. But He doesn't use violence to defeat violence either. On the *Tal* he was always present. We learned that violence breeds violence – it doesn't solve anything. We saw that in our history books. We knew that the oppressors would fail in the end. They would be destroyed by their own greed. They always have been. We had to hang on in there – even if it didn't happen for us in our lifetime, we knew love wins in the end."

"You're quite a thinker," said Shaun.

"I agree," said Wennai. "Two wrongs never make a right. Your En – if there is a God – can only win by loving, not destroying."

"And that renders him always vulnerable," added Shaun. "But that doesn't mean He is weak or has given up or been defeated."

"He's right here," answered the elder promptly. "We've done a lot of praying and loving… Just as I am tempted to think we've lost and En has abandoned us, I witness the hard work and spirit of these young people and know that, even if we have to begin again on this planet, it is all worth it. The spark of love cannot be put out." They fell silent. Shaun knew what he had to say.

"M-maybe… I'm not promising anything," said Shaun,

tentatively. "Maybe He can use Wennai and me to overcome the ASI. I don't know how—"

"But you are only two – young and unarmed. How can you do anything about these monsters?" asked the elder. "Are you advanced in technology? I think it is more likely you are here to encourage us… That is enough."

"Perhaps," said Shaun. "I have no idea how we can overcome them – yet." He looked at Wennai, who shrugged her shoulders.

"Tlap," she said, "will you show me some of your clay writing and tell me how it works?"

Tlap smiled. She was already being encouraged. "If you want." She led Wennai off to a small hut.

"Come," said One, "let me introduce you to my family." He took Shaun to his hut where he introduced him to his wife, Frut.

"You are married. Congratulations," said Shaun.

"Frut was on board the *Tal*. We got to know each other through the broom cupboard. It was hard, but we fell in love."

"And then," said Frut, "you looked after us so well on Joh… And now you have come to save us a second time."

"Don't get your hopes up," said Shaun. "Kakko and Tam – you remember them?"

"Of course. They are well?"

"Yes. But they're on another planet somewhere. This is my friend Wennai's first time away from home. My family are the experienced ones… We helped your people settle on a planet in the Tatanian system with some colonists from Earth Two."

"We heard. Your family will feature very prominently in Sponron history. It may be that that new colony is where our future lies as a race… It could be that here we have gone too far, too fast. What we should do is tell them not to go down the same path as we have but, of course, there is no way to convey that message... Unless... unless *you* can take it for us. Maybe *that* is why you're here – not to rescue us but to get the message back."

It occurred to Shaun that that could very probably be it. Let them find out as much as they could and then leave through the gate with a message for the rest of the worlds.

That night, Shaun and Wennai slept together on the floor of One and Frut's grass hut. Wennai felt grubby – she was unwashed and her hair was matted with something she couldn't see. But they had eaten. They didn't ask what was in the soup they were given – they daren't. The water tasted muddy, too, but they were assured it was clean; at least it wasn't supposed to contain anything that would cause damage – to a Sponron that is. They had no idea what it would do to them. But their stomachs hadn't objected immediately – which was a good sign.

Remarkably, despite everything, they slept well on the hard ground. That is the gift of youth.

23

The day began with heavy rain. Still half asleep, Wennai took in the hard ground beneath her and she began to remember where she was. She had been aware of Shaun's proximity during the night but now he was gone and a cold fear spread through her. She pulled herself up.

"Hi," said Shaun from somewhere across the hut. "Good morning, sleepy head."

Relieved to hear his voice, Wennai sank back and relaxed into the lumpy soil. "What's the time?"

"Couldn't tell you. From what I can ascertain, this planet spins at a rate not a lot different from a standard day. I woke naturally. One and Frut have gone to make breakfast."

"What's that going to look like – more doubtful soup?"

"It won't be your usual, that's for sure. How do you fancy one of the all-day breakfasts that they serve in my college?"

"I think I would prefer the soup... Have we a plan for today? I've been—"

"Yes. I was thinking—"

"That's what I was going to say," said Wennai, slightly peeved that Shaun was about to say something first.

Shaun stopped and waited. "Go on."

Then Wennai sighed and felt bad about being annoyed. Shaun was now letting her go first. "OK. I thought we should spend the morning listening to everything that's happened and is happening. Take notes. And then head off back through the gate in the afternoon to tell the universe…"

"What will you make notes on? We haven't any paper; and it would take hours to prepare a clay tablet, as Tlap says."

"Ah. You forget. We have our phones. We switched them off before we went through the gates like you said. But we can use them to type in a few notes." She drew out her phone and held it up in triumph.

At that moment One came in with two wooden goblets containing steaming liquid. The sight of Wennai brandishing her beloved second-hand phone, which she had got from Patia for her birthday, nearly made him drop the goblets.

"No!" he yelled. "No tech! Turn it off!"

Wennai was startled. "OK. It's OK, it's off… Like, what—?"

"Sorry," One apologised. "I… I shouldn't shout. Sorry… You see? the ASI can detect any electrical activity. They leave us alone because we do not use anything that might threaten them. But the moment they picked up any tech, we would be for it."

"I didn't think," said Wennai remorsefully. "Of course I should have known… But I didn't get round to turning it on, honestly. Look, we want to learn as much as we can before we go back to tell people of your plight and warn other planets. I guess we shall just have to *remember* as much as we can. I'll write some key words in Tlap's clay, if I may."

The hot herb infusion they called tea was wonderful. Wennai's shock was quickly overcome. She was soon wide awake and alert, although she itched all over. Sleeping fully dressed and not washing was something she had just never done before. Frut detected her discomfort. "Why don't you and I go to the stream this morning? The women go in the mornings, the men in the evenings." She produced a wooden comb which Wennai attempted to get through her long blonde hair, without much success.

"You have soup in it," laughed Frut. "It will be better when it is washed."

Breakfast was some kind of green leaf and delicious berries. "The best," said Shaun.

"Of course. The best for you."

"Everybody eats berries for breakfast?" asked Wennai.

Frut looked sheepish. "They are a special treat. They take some collecting."

"Oh, Frut! And you have given them to us! But we didn't bring anything to give you."

"That is where you are wrong," said One. "You have brought us hope. We are not alone in the universe. Even if our situation stays the same or gets worse, we know we are not forgotten. That is very important... More important than you could ever guess."

Frut gathered a few things to help them wash, and led Wennai out of the hut.

"When will you leave us to take news of us?" One asked Shaun.

"Today... later, we thought. We want to learn as much as we can about these ASI... Tell me, were your scientists working on a plan to combat them?"

"Most certainly. They knew it was only a matter of time before they lost control. You see, I worked at one of the labs. I was out when the ASI arrived. They stunned everyone inside and carried them into one of the self-driving trucks."

"Where did they take them? Did they regain consciousness? Are you sure they were only stunned and not killed?"

"I can answer the last question but not the first two. We are sure they were still alive because some people in the street said some of them were making moaning noises. Where they were taken and what condition they are in now, we have no idea."

"You say they were working on something. Do you know what that was?"

"I know what the software engineers thought would work. They were developing some kind of virus that would neutralise the bots. But I am no software engineer; I'm a hardware man myself – and not fully qualified at that… They were working on implanting a chip into one of the units that would transmit new commands like a virus around the rest… Anyway, it's too late to implement their plan. They could have programmed themselves to resist any new software and, in any case, there is no way of getting it into them because as soon as we got near the lab, or attempted any online link-up, they would swoop, and all the people here in this camp would be put into mortal danger."

"So can it be introduced manually? I mean inserted with some hardware?"

"That was what they were planning to do – they had made a prototype of a chip to slot into the motherboard; but, as I said, we cannot do it because even if we could get hold of it, no-one can get near the lab or indeed a robot or any ASI installation without being apprehended. In fact, none of us can leave this wood…"

"Except Wennai and me," smiled Shaun.

★ ★ ★

When Wennai returned with Frut and Tlap, she was bright, happy and polished.

"The water may not be the cleanest – looking in the universe," she declared, "but it's wet and cool. And it's amazing what soft silt can do as a shampoo. Until today, I had not realised what a treat it is to have water so readily available. At home we just take it for granted that it comes out every time we turn the tap. I'll never make a fuss about a poor showerhead again. It's just so wonderful to have any source of water to wash in."

"Yes," said One. "It's not until you don't have it that you realise just how wonderful it is. Water is not a luxury."

"That's why the ancients went on about it so much in the past," said Shaun. "Water is a metaphor for life in many cultures… A planet might be in the Goldilocks zone but if it doesn't have water, it is dead."

"Frut and Tlap have been telling me all they know about the rise of the ASI," said Wennai, invoking her businesslike tone… "Shaun, I think we should set off home before our hosts give us any more of their precious food… Not that I mind being here, of course. I'm not suggesting we should run away. But the sooner we go, the sooner we can report your dilemma and get the message to others."

"You go and do that," replied Shaun. "I have been talking to One and the elders. I am considering a change of plan and staying on. I think there is a possibility that I might be able to effect a real change."

"You mean defeat the ASI?"

"Yes."

"How…? Look, if there are things we can do, I'm staying too!"

"You don't want to miss the fun?" smiled Shaun.

"The thing is, Shaun, you're clever. But right at this moment you need to be confident with it," said Wennai, deliberately.

"And that's where you come in…? You're sounding like my sister."

"That may be because I'm right."

"OK. I give in. It's just that I thought you would prefer—"

"I'm staying. What do we have to do?"

"The first task is to get into One's lab and get this chip he

271

knows about. The second is to capture a robot and open it up to put the chip inside it."

"That's all?!"

"That's it in a nutshell."

"And how can we do it if the Sponrons can't?"

"Two reasons: the ASI may let us pass, whereas they certainly wouldn't let any Sponrons back into the lab. At the moment they think we're some kind of animal, right? We are harmless, dumb beasts. We don't register on their databases as an intelligent threat. The ASI may not figure out that something has just turned up from another part of the unknown universe – that needs imagination. They learn strictly from experience; they can't think that far out of the box."

"But they can learn quickly, right?"

"Lightning fast. Which means we have to be extremely careful that we are not giving them the impression we are behaving with intelligence. As soon as they are suspicious, we've had it."

"Another reason you need me. I am not an A–grade student, I—"

"You're not very clever? Rubbish. We both know you're clever even if you did finish school earlier than me."

"OK. I have some practical intelligence. I'll grant you that."

"Right – the best kind in this scenario. The brilliant but absent-minded sort might get into more trouble."

"Yes," agreed One. "Some software engineers are totally lacking when it comes to common sense. That's why we're in this mess in the first place. Some of them need a lot of looking after – can't even manage to make a cup of tea."

"Not *all* software engineers, then – just most of them," laughed Shaun. "Do I detect the prejudice of a hardware engineer?"

"All scientists need practical people," stated Wennai. "Seriously... And in this scenario you need an actor, and I think I'm the more gifted at acting... You geeks have to come up with a plan... and leave the rest to me. Leave me to get into the lab and get the stuff."

"That... that is logical. I guess... But I can't let you do this. It's dangerous."

"So we go home, then?"

"No. I was just... I don't know. I don't want you to get hurt."

"Look, forget about being protective. You're a liberated male. It makes logical sense for me to go and get this because – frankly – you are still delicate inside – mending, but delicate. There's nothing wrong with that – you're human. The last thing you want is to upset that recovery – or, to put it bluntly, freak out on the job. You work out the plan and I'll execute it."

Shaun nodded. Wennai was right. He had no idea just how good an actor she could be because right then, inside her chest, her heart was doing a double take. As Shaun walked away to join the Sponrons in planning the heist, she said to herself, *Wennai, you're an absolute fool. But I'm beginning to understand how the Smith family ticks. Shaun must have been really hurt to walk away from a white gate challenge. No wonder he can't tell his family. I hope I'm up to this.*

She didn't hear the whisper in the breeze as the Creator said, "You are. Well done. I am with you."

★ ★ ★

Over the next two hours, Shaun, One and the elders sat together to work out how Wennai could get to the chip safely. Stage two – getting a compliant robot – was put off for the moment. Wennai spent her time learning how to read Tlap's clay tablets.

"I need to be able to read your script. Once I begin this task, I may need to read the signs," she explained.

★ ★ ★

It was just before midday that Slop appeared from between the trees. Tlap was the first to spot him.

"Slop," she yelled, "you're back! You escaped!"

Slop stepped forward, breathless as much with embarrassment as with his exertions. Tlap embraced him. She had urged her brother not to go but he was not the type to believe he could live for the rest of his life as a Stone-Age being. Now he had returned with an air of defeat.

"Slop, come here!" sang Tlap and she took him once more into her spindly Sponron arms. "I never thought I would see you again. You know, Slop," she said over his shoulder, "freedom is important but being stuck with those you love isn't so much of a trap. After all, we have roofs and water – and food, of sorts, for now."

"I learnt a lot," he said, pulling out of the embrace and looking his sister in the eye. He was trying to put a positive slant to his failed attempt for freedom.

Wennai and Shaun were introduced. Slop gave them a curious glance, and One reminded him of the adventures on the *Tal* and on Planet Joh.

"Can you get us all out of here through your white gate?" asked Slop.

"I doubt it. It doesn't work that way," answered Shaun.

"Some people can travel the universe while others are trapped in one small wood on one small planet. Some folk have all the luck."

"Don't be unkind," said Tlap. "If it weren't for these humans, One and the rest would still be prisoners on board a space cruiser in the hands of horrible men."

"What happened?" asked One, after they had sat Slop down. Someone brought him a goblet of hot forest tea, and a bowl of the juiciest berries was set before him.

"Thanks. I'm not hungry. There are berries and roots in abundance over the hill – but the hot brew is good. Thanks... After I left here, I got as far as going down to the stream that runs parallel to ours. I had just crossed it when a stupid drone flew over. I kept still but there is no way to avoid them. I'm sure they have infrared, or even something more sophisticated. It stopped and hovered. I decided to keep going. It couldn't land in the forest and, in any case, it couldn't have stopped me. But, of course, it summoned a party of medium bots and a few big ones, too – you know the kind that run on tracks..."

"Like tanks?" put in Wennai.

"Tanks?"

"Military vehicles that can cross rough terrain," explained Shaun.

"They can certainly do that, but they're not that fast through the brush – certainly not as fast as I was. I dodged to the west. They followed me. I headed for the waterfall and leapt across—"

"Slop, that was dangerous," cringed Tlap.

"Nah. I cleared it by a full zilk."

"How far's that?" asked Shaun.

"About this much." One reached out his arms to indicate a short metre. "If you ask me, Slop, that is cutting it a bit too fine."

"One, it was plenty. OK...? Anyway, the stupid bots all lined up on the opposite bank. Intelligent? Stupid! One medium got too near the edge, slipped on the moss and fell in."

"What, down the falls?"

"No, not all the way down. It jammed in among the rocks at the top. It's still there."

"They will have learnt, and you can bet that none of them will do it again," said one of the elders.

"So, anyway, I waved them goodbye and I carried on through the woods, but so did the drone. Whichever way I turned they were waiting for me. There seemed to be hundreds of them. They didn't come into the woods, they just stopped me leaving. I spent two nights waiting to see if they would give up. No luck. The charging truck – you know the one with the generator on board – just kept trundling behind them, keeping their batteries topped up. I went back to the falls to wash and drink. The medium stuck at the top was still there, its batteries flat. It was dead to the world – if you can say a machine can ever really be alive in the first place. In the end there was nothing to do but come back. I'll have another go after a week or so."

"You may not be here next week," said One boldly. "We have a plan… and you may have just provided us with exactly what we need."

He explained that Wennai and Shaun were going to try to reach the lab, find the chip and bring it back. "We can pull up the bot in the stream and fit it with the new motherboard. Then we take it to the edge of the wood so they can reclaim it and charge it up."

"Are you sure they will fall for it?" said Slop.

"They could well do – once," said One. "They learn from their mistakes – but they have to make one first. They will scan the possibilities – but no bot has ever been given an additional chip. All past modifications have been done through software programming once the prototypes were formed. With a huge amount of spare capacity in its programmable ROM, there had been no need to upgrade the hardware. If our friend can get us a motherboard for a 'medium' containing the new ROM, we can simply replace the existing one."

"And then," continued the elder, "when it wakes up it will start communicating with the rest."

"And the new software will enter the hive cloud and every individual bot within seconds."

"What will it do to them?" asked Wennai.

"I'm not sure. All I know is that the hardware team were putting together the necessary motherboards – each for a different class of individual. I knew that the aim was that the ASI would be neutralised if we managed to get just one new motherboard into any ASI machine, anywhere – always assuming they hadn't anticipated it."

"You mean it will wipe them out?"

"Disable them – all of them."

"That sounds a bit like... like genocide," Wennai murmured.

"Technically not," said Shaun. "If they were sentient beings, that would be true. But they're only machines – they don't have feelings."

"Are you sure?"

"What do you say, One?"

"I say that if we don't fight them," said Slop, "then it is *us* who are going to be wiped out... And, as far as we can tell, we could already be all that is left of the Sponron race on the planet."

"Unlikely," said One, "but I agree, we do not know anything about the welfare of any other Sponrons."

"And," continued an elder, "the ASI could render the planet unstable if they continue in their self-centred way."

"Run amok?" said Wennai.

"They have already overcome the checks and balances the

programmers attempted to impose," said One. "The thing is, they may not have a concept of the importance of carbon-based life for the future of the planet. The weather will eventually destroy them but by the time they discover that, the planet could be on the way to being dead…"

"I don't think we should be morally concerned about the bots," mused Shaun, thoughtfully. "They are machines, so they are not alive and therefore cannot die. And could, in time, I suppose, be reprogrammed and brought back online in the future… I think the time has come for Wennai and I to pretend to be beings without intelligence and see what we can do to get the motherboard we require."

"OK. Tell me where and what we're looking for," said Wennai in her best businesslike tone.

One described the motherboard they needed, together with the Sponron markings he thought it had.

"As far as I can recall, it has something like that on it. I'm sure it's marked 'medium' or at least 'M' – all the motherboards have multi-legged, integrated circuits and other components both on top and underneath. They are delicate and need to be put into a padded container for transport." One described where the boards were stored and where to find the correct containers – assuming the bots hadn't removed them. "The boards are kept in a secure cupboard with a five-symbol access code." He described the symbols that needed to be entered on the keypad by drawing them in the dust with a stick.

"Have you got that, Wennai?" asked Shaun.

"No problem," she said. She erased the symbols with her foot, then redrew them.

"Perfect," said an elder, impressed. Slop looked at her quizzically, then slid his long hand through her hair and suddenly closed his fingers and yanked.

"Ow!" yelled Wennai, alarmed. She turned in shock and then defiance.

But Shaun soothed her. He understood. "No," he said reassuringly, "she is not a bot. She is just naturally good at remembering things."

"She learns quickly," said Tlap. "But not like the ASI. Slop, that was unkind."

"Just testing," he said, defensively.

★ ★ ★

Wennai and Shaun moved gingerly back into the field. "We mustn't move with purpose," said Shaun. "We have to wander and get nearer the lane gradually."

Half an hour later they heard a drone approaching. They carried on working the hedgerow for berries and just ignored it. It hovered for a few moments and then vanished. After a further half-hour it flew back over the field and this time just kept going. It had clearly decided that Wennai and Shaun did not trigger the danger response that Slop had done when he left the encampment.

They eventually came to the hedge beside the lane and approached the gate. A vehicle came along the lane and passed by without incident.

"It looks as if we're still OK," stated Shaun. "So far, so good."

"These berries aren't bad, either," smiled Wennai. "But we'd better not overindulge or we could get the runs – or something."

"Good thinking. But keep looking when we get through the gate." They squeezed through the bars and onto the road, and gradually, metre by metre, along the lane in the direction of the town. Another vehicle approached. They glanced up, like an animal might, then let it pass. When a posse of mediums marched by, they knew they were safe.

They reached a junction. "Which way?" asked Shaun.

Wennai read the signboard. "The town is at the bottom of the hill. When we get there, I have memorised the names of the streets and I think I can find my way... Look, Shaun, the berry thing won't work beyond the hedges. I... I think it would be better if we split up. Two people are more obvious than one and I'm worried that you're overdoing it on that leg."

"Wennai, an hour ago you said you were not going to be left behind, and now you're taking over and saying you don't need *me*."

"That's not what I meant," she said rather too crossly. She was upset; in truth she was still fighting her inner doubt. She collected herself – she mustn't be brusque. She had been unkind. Shaun had issues about the events that surrounded his broken leg. "Sorry. That wasn't nice. But, Shaun, don't you see," she said, kissing his cheek, "it could all be part of the random thing... They have registered our presence and they aren't suspicious – yet. But they may be keeping tabs on us. As long as you are still about, they may remain happy and ignore me. You could go down that way and rest a bit, then circle back... A diversion."

"OK," said Shaun quietly. He had to accept that Wennai knew more about him than sometimes he cared to admit even to himself. "That... that does make sense... I agree it will only take one of us in the town – and it is you who knows the way. But..."

Wennai put her arms around him and kissed him in return. "I know you want to be protective but if the bots get suspicious there's really nothing you can do. You protect me best by pretending to be a dumb, country creature." She smiled lightly.

She was a good actress, but inside she was trying to convince herself that she was really capable of pulling this off.

"OK. A farm animal I shall be… But promise me you'll be careful."

"Of course. I don't want to get caught and, besides, the Sponrons are in enough trouble without me making it worse. I will probably get lost, which will only add to the impression." Wennai attempted to laugh. It was not sufficiently convincing for Shaun to be reassured but she had won her case. Logic had prevailed.

★ ★ ★

Wennai continued to explore the hedge towards the town, while Shaun went down the new road. When he heard the drone, he made quite sure he could be seen. He couldn't help Wennai any other way. He was happy to hear the sound of the engines disappear in the opposite direction from the one she had taken.

It took Wennai around ten seconds after Shaun vanished from her view to realise just how terrified she was. Her logic had been so convincing and her acting so good that Shaun had had to concur. Her theory might have been correct but this was the first time in her life that she had been *anywhere* on her own outside of Joh City district, let alone on a strange and distant planet! It would have been scary enough at home. For about ten minutes she rued her foolishness, all the time hoping Shaun would reappear round the corner. Then for the next ten minutes she rather hoped he wouldn't because she hated the idea of appearing a wimp. If he followed her, she would protest. But when it was quite clear he was not going to reappear, she knew she had convinced him, if not herself, that she could do this better on her own. So, now, either she carried on or abandoned the plan and went back herself.

No! she told herself. *I can do this. In fact, it will be safer than if we are together – and this way Shaun is definitely safer.* She realised that when you think about what's best for others, you get braver. *I'm going to do this, even if I die in the process. But it won't come to that. The ASI is thinking I'm a "bear of very little brain" so I can't bundle it if I act like one.* Abby had read them Winnie-the-Pooh stories one evening when she had gone to see Shaun at White Gates Cottage. *Winnie-the-Pooh succeeded in all sorts of things just singing a hum, didn't he? So can I.* So, when she heard a drone, she sang to herself as she pretended to look for berries. It ignored her. As soon as it was out of sight she made for the town at a moderate pace – as fast as she dared. She wondered exactly how much lateral thinking the machine-heads, as she called them, were capable of. *Whatever. One way or another I'm going to find out*, she thought.

When Wennai reached the edge of the town and the hedgerows stopped, she put on a spurt to reach the central streets in which the laboratory was situated. The gardens were replaced by townhouses that came right to the edge of the road in places; their walls echoed the sound of her footsteps even though she trod as softly as she could. It was eerie. The place spoke of crowds, bustle and the noise of people and vehicles – but it was totally deserted. She half-expected to come across a nest of machine-heads but, no, there were none to be seen. *Why should they be here?* she thought. *They have no need of houses – sitting rooms, bedrooms, kitchens or bathrooms.* The thought of the last two rooms reminded her that she had been hungry for hours, despite the berries; and she was desperate for the loo. Could she get inside one of the houses?

Then the noise of a drone reverberated in the narrow

streets with a roar like the take-off of a jet plane. She thought about ducking into a doorway but it was too late, the drone was already overhead. *Ignore it,* she told herself. But the drone hovered, circled and returned. It was watching her. Wennai meandered forward. Was the game up?

Half an hour passed with Wennai making random turns through the narrowest streets she could find but the drone was still there. Wennai resolved to just carry on. What did it matter now if she was observed? It may be all that they wanted to do; the machine-heads might be satisfied just monitoring her. She couldn't be far away from the lab because it was in the old part of the town, One had said. The sun was getting low. She tried to read the names of the streets but couldn't recognise any of them. Then she noticed a large building on a corner that she had seen before – she had gone in a complete circle.

The sun vanished behind the houses; it would soon be set. Already the street names were becoming too difficult to read. But the darkness could be her friend. She could escape the gaze of the drone – unless it was fitted with night vision…
Then the gloom was pierced by the sound of marching metal. Around the corner appeared four medium robots. It would take her a whole year to admit to anyone how terrified she had been at that moment. They were marching right up to her. Was her life about to end there, on her own, out of all reach of any sentient being on a planet that her sister and brother did not even know she had visited? She thought she would faint – she might lose consciousness even before the machine-heads inflicted the final blow.

But two metres from her, the bots suddenly stopped. They lined up abreast and the furthest right circled around and took a small step forwards while the others remained still. Wennai looked to the left. The way was open. She made to move in that direction and the bot to the right inched forward again. *They want me to walk this way,* she thought. *They're herding me.* She decided to be herded.

After about a hundred metres, one of the bots moved in front of her. Wennai stopped. Now she was trapped – was she to be murdered at this point? The bot behind stepped up and opened a gate in the wall that Wennai hadn't seen, and another jabbed her in the side with his wand – but there was no electric charge this time. "Ow!" said Wennai out loud. "No need for that!" The gate was the only option; resistance was not going to get her anywhere – and anyway if these bots wanted to do her in they had had plenty of opportunity. Wennai stepped into a sweet-smelling garden. The gate was shut behind her. She heard the mediums march off. It was now almost dark but she could still make out plots of what she assumed were overgrown vegetables and small bushes laden with berries. Could it be that the machine-heads had simply taken her to a place where she could browse? On one level it was purely logical: they had learned that her kind ate berries, there were no berries in the streets, she was lost, therefore she needed help to find what she was looking for. On another level, it could be interpreted as an act of kindness. Did they care? Had they become sentient beings? *If so,* Wennai thought, *I have become a terrorist bent on infiltrating their world to destroy them, while they are kindly looking after my needs.* As she stood and pondered, she became aware that the drone was moving away. All was still.

The house to which the kitchen garden belonged bordered one side of it. A rear door stood ajar – perhaps the owners hadn't had the time to secure it in their haste to escape; perhaps they had been captured by the ASI without warning. Perhaps they were still inside… dead. Wennai was desperately thirsty. Surely looking for water inside would not make her a looter. The room was dark – finding anything inside was going to be difficult. Water would be kept in a fridge she supposed. Wennai felt round the cupboards that lined the walls between the windows for anything that resembled a fridge. On the far side of what was clearly a kitchen, Wennai found the entrance to a passage that led further into the house, and laid her hand on the wall beside it. Almost immediately she discovered something small and square that gave beneath her touch. A deluge of light engulfed her – so bright she instinctively closed her eyes against it. But getting used to the light took no more than a few moments. She rushed to the windows to close some shutters that were partially open.

So the electricity was still on. *Of course,* she thought, *the ASI needs electricity like we carbon-based mortals need water. Keeping the power plant going stands to reason.* There was no sign of the Sponron inhabitants – living or dead. The kitchen appeared to have been deserted in the middle of preparing a meal – the owners of this house had clearly been taken by surprise. She found a bottle of water standing on the table. She drank.

Her insides were not great; the berries without anything to dilute them were definitely on the move. A second door led to where she needed to go next. It was a simple affair – and easy to cope with.

After these initial gifts of civilisation, Wennai was feeling much, much better. She had even managed to flush using a bucket that stood ready. It was as if someone was looking after her. No matter how hard she had tried, she just couldn't put the idea of God out of her mind. He (or She) seemed to keep forcing His way in. She soon found herself saying a sort of prayer for the people whose house this was. If she ever managed to meet them, she would thank them – and apologise for her intrusion.

Experiencing a brief twinge of a Goldilocks moment, Wennai tasted the contents of a box that lay open on the table.

They were savoury biscuits, not only still edible but delicious. And on the side there was something sweet. Wennai ate. It was enough.

Now it was time to explore the rest of the house. Wennai decided on a single bed at the top of the house with a fully equipped *en suite* bathroom…

Steam filled the air as the tough heroine indulged herself in a bath of hot water complete with some sweet-smelling liquids that stood on a shelf.

★ ★ ★

Earlier that day, Shaun had decided to go for a circular route. *Just keep turning right*, he reasoned – but it took him further than he had intended – and then, when he realised he would re-join the lane metres from the bots' factory, settled on retracing his steps.

He got back to the wood just as it was getting dark. The men and boys had already returned from their turn in the stream. *Never mind*, he told himself, *it's a bit cold to take everything off. I'll have a good soak when all this is over.*

24

A shaft of white sunlight cut across the room in which Wennai still lay naked beneath some clean sheets she had found in a cupboard drawer. After her bath, she had not put her shorts and top back on – she had felt so wonderfully fresh. She praised the Lord (if She existed) that She had sent her on an adventure with hot water on tap. Unlike Shaun, or even Kakko, Wennai decided she needed to be clean to operate effectively. It seemed that her Creator (if She existed) knew this. But now there was nothing for it – she would have to dress herself in the same icky stuff. There was no borrowing from the Sponron this time; their clothes were a completely different shape.

The kitchen cupboard supplied some interesting foodstuffs. Wennai tried some packets that looked as if they contained food that did not need to be cooked. Some clearly did, but she discovered an absolutely delicious bar of what looked like a mixture of cereals and fruit. It was chewy and refreshing. Pulling open the shutters, she beheld the garden in the early morning sun. It showed signs of having once been wonderfully tended but now was becoming overrun with weeds. The berry bushes were laden with lovely-looking fruit – red, green and purple. *These must all be edible,* she thought, *otherwise they wouldn't have planted them.* She resolved to try them all and eat them with some of the savoury biscuits she had discovered the night before.

She pushed open the outside door and the scents of the garden filling the morning air thrilled her. Her heart brightened. She found a dish and was making her way towards the bushes when she heard the drone. Now her heart sank. Her instinct was to hide – but then the drone *expected* her to be in the garden. The best way of being ignored was to act according to their predictions. The drone hovered, seemed to register her beside the berry bushes, and left. All was quiet.

Wennai gathered enough berries and then breakfasted. She made a final use of the facilities, making sure she had left everything as tidy and clean as she could. Then she decided to write a note on the back of some packaging. She had learned to say thank you in Sponron – *biba*. And although she had never seen it written, she wrote it in Sponron characters, phonetically. Then she put her name. Wennai looked strange in Sponron writing – but great.

So, where to go now to find the lab? *I must be methodical,* she said to herself. But she had no need of any method, for immediately across the road from the garden gate she read the sign she was looking for: Department of Robotics, Mulga Research Centre. The machine-heads had led her straight to it!

The building stood open to the world – nothing was secured. It remained exactly as the day the occupants had been surprised at their posts – except that all the contents had been removed. There were supposed to be experimental robots and electronics in construction, as well as hard copies of documents in filing cabinets. All had gone.

Wennai stood and gazed at the emptiness. In room after room there was nothing left. Was she too late? She followed the signs to the room she had been directed to. That, too, was empty – except for some pictures on the wall and a desk with its empty drawers opened. In one of the pictures she spotted a photo stuck in the bottom corner of the frame. She thought she recognised One. After a moment, she was sure. It was hard to distinguish one alien face from another – and the man in this one was smiling. She had seen that smile the first time One had met them entering the wood. She took the photo from the frame and looked for something to wrap it in. There was nothing, so she put it as carefully as she could in her back pocket.

The safe? Was it still there? She couldn't see it. Then she realised that the desk must have been moved. There were marks made by the legs in the centre of the room. She ducked down and, sure enough, in the wall behind the desk she could just make out the safe. The desk was heavy. It took a lot of lifting and dragging. If Shaun had been with her, he would have justified his presence at that moment. It took her a long time but inch by inch it moved. Eventually she was able to get behind it but she had to duck under it to access the lock. She had memorised the combination a whole day before – now she had to remember it again – but she wrote it in the dust and it looked right. The first time it didn't work. She tried it again. Still nothing. She checked her lettering. One letter could have an extra stroke (like you can easily make a P into an R) but otherwise she couldn't see any alternatives. Perhaps if she tried the code with the extra stroke… It still failed.

After a quarter of an hour, Wennai was on the brink of giving up. The whole reason she had been the one chosen to do this part of the job was that she was supposed to be the better person for it. And now all she could boast was a delicious bath and a good night's sleep. She felt rotten about herself.

OK, Wennai, she told herself, *what would Shaun do if he were here? Approach it logically, methodically. What, though, if I have mucked it up with all my false attempts? Think logically… Right, if someone puts the wrong code in, there must be some way of clearing it. That's the first thing I should do. There could be another code to enter first and I haven't the faintest idea what that is. But supposing it is just one letter. There are twenty letters in all, so if it's one letter then I will have to enter it followed by the code no more than twenty times. If that fails, I have to move on to two characters – a maximum of 400 combinations. I will be here all day! So what if I am? I have a whole house to live in...*

Wennai thought about the code. She was sure she had got it right the first time. The symbols were clear. She began with the first letter followed by the code. No success. After sixteen letters she began to lose heart. Twenty letters, and still failure. Now she was on to the double letters. She was thirsty and tired. She must take a break.

Wennai descended the stairs and crossed the road. Back beyond the gate, she heard the drone. It came up to the garden, hovered and returned the way it had come. She had been ticked off its checklist. *Someone is on your side, Wennai. Thanks... Look, you don't happen to know the way to get into this safe, do you? I've got this far...* But Wennai had never heard of anyone being given a code to a safe by an angel – even if they were well intentioned.

Refreshed, Wennai recrossed the road. *All I need is patience*, she told herself. It was then that she saw a box just inside the front door. It was in the wall and bore a lightning sign on it. It shouted out to her that this may be a way of disconnecting the power. If the power were disconnected and then reconnected, the safe lock might automatically reset. The box opened easily and inside there was an obvious master switch. Wennai pulled it down and all the humming stopped. It was amazing just how much electrical humming had filled the empty building; now it was dead quiet. It was as if the place had died. But Wennai pushed the big switch back up again and new life flowed through all the wire arteries and electronic capillaries. A green light came on above her as if to say: "Thanks. I needed that." It had been red before. Wennai scampered up the stairs, got back under the desk and re-entered the code that she had learned and had first used. The safe door sprang open with a joyful plunk – as if it, too, felt the relief mixed with delight that at that moment surged through Wennai's brain.

Of course, reasoned Wennai, *the machine-heads would have tried to get in and, when they couldn't succeed, pushed the desk against the safe.* They *were the ones that mucked it up, not me. So who's the brightest, then? You ASI might be able to think fast but you didn't think of the power!*

Inside the safe all was exactly as One had described it. She found the motherboard marked Medium where One said it would be. There were two others around the same size. She thought she should take all three just to make sure. But there were no carrying boxes as One said to use. How could she carry the boards safely when all she had was what she was wearing? She knotted her top at the waist to make a little pouch and slipped the one marked Medium into it. She would borrow a dry towel to wrap it in when she got back to the house. But she had just got back beside the berry bushes when she heard the sound of a vehicle. It stopped at the gate and two mediums entered the garden. Wennai clutched the board in her top in an effort to conceal it. The bots did not seem to notice her hands; their task, as they made plain with their wands, was to get her to leave the garden. All she could do was comply. Beyond the door, she was ushered aboard a vehicle and restrained by a metal harness. What next?

To her relief the mediums that got in alongside her also placed themselves in the same kind of harness. It was merely a common seat restraint. Wennai continued to clutch the board as if it was part of her. As they raced through the narrow streets,

Wennai tried to remember which way they were going. If she ever got out of this, she would have to find her way back. They very soon got to smaller houses and then were out of the town altogether – and then Wennai recognised it. They were heading up the same road that she had come by. Were they taking her to the factory? But at the gate to the field that she and Shaun had originally been herded into, the vehicle drew to a stop. Her harness was removed and she was ushered off the vehicle, the gate opened, and there she was, inside – still clutching her top containing the precious cargo. The ASI had brought her home!

As the transport disappeared back down the lane, Wennai felt elated. She had succeeded. Just how much was pure luck and how much was down to her own ingenuity, she couldn't assess. Shaun would have given credit to his Creator; Wennai didn't need to believe that God had anything to do with it. She felt a bit stupid saying those prayers but she might tell Shaun that to cheer him up one day. Just maybe. But one thing she was sure about, she would never admit to feeling so scared – the doubt and the loneliness she had experienced weren't something she wanted to remember. She deliberately wandered up the field as if she was just returning from a stroll. A distant sound of an approaching drone reminded her to stop and look for berries – these were not a patch on the cultivated ones. The drone passed and Wennai entered the wood and within minutes was in the arms of a very concerned Shaun. He had been so worried! He tried not to show it – but couldn't hide it. And that totally disarmed Wennai who, careful with her precious cargo, returned his hug as tears streamed down her face.

"You missed me?" asked Shaun

"Of course… sometimes… mostly…" She let out a sigh. "All the time."

"What's wrong with your belly?"

"What do you think? Where's One?" she said as she carefully produced the board.

★ ★ ★

Wennai's adventure would be forever recorded in Sponron history. Who knows, her picture might even appear on a banknote in some century to come, as the legend of the human, Wennai, was told to admiring Sponron children. But that thought, thankfully, did not enter Wennai's head which was already getting rather big as the delighted Sponrons danced around her.

★ ★ ★

The rest of the plan was executed. The ASI fell for it. The sentient beings only had one chance but that was all they needed. The first sign that all was not well with the ASI was a drone that began circling – round and round it went for hours until eventually, probably for lack of power, it crashed. It was decided that Wennai and Shaun should explore further. They got into the lane and spotted two mediums sitting in a ditch – lifeless. Further on was a caterpillar-tracked bot, standing completely still – its head lowered. They reached the factory. Some small bots were still walking around as if in a trance, while mediums were collapsed all over the place. The hum of the power continued but there was no sign of any of the charging trucks. The ASI was dead.

Wennai recalled just how much help the ASI had given her in their mission to destroy it. She couldn't prevent a few tears slipping from her eyes. "They were *not* evil," she said.

"No," agreed Shaun. "They were not evil because they had no feelings at all. Robots cannot be moral beings."

"But they looked after me."

"They didn't want you snooping around the town. Their logic told them you didn't belong there. They didn't care for you because they *couldn't* care – they were not sentient."

"Are you sure?"

"Completely. Anyway, they had to be stopped."

"I suppose so."

"It was not just the Sponrons. They could have destroyed the entire planet in the end because they lacked empathy."

"They couldn't love?"

"Correct. Love is not something that can be expressed through binary code, no matter how complex the programming. Love cannot be analysed scientifically. Some people would say that the whole of creation is based on mathematical formulae, but there is no formula for love – no matter how many dimensions there might be."

"You cannot know that, Shaun. You have not explored all the dimensions."

"I haven't. But one thing I am sure of in my heart is that love will permeate all of them – somehow. Without maths."

"You don't have to be a maths genius to love."

"No. Loving does not demand intelligence of that sort. We can share love from the moment we are born."

"Yes. Babies know when they are not loved with a genuine heart. They sense it…" Wennai paused. Where might this talk of love lead? "So what are we to do now?"

"Report back and leave the rest to the Sponrons."

"Go home?"

"Go home. But first, just give me a little hug…"

"No way. You stink! Have you washed just *once* since we've been here?"

"I never got a chance… never got my togs off. Anyway, I can't imagine how *you've* stayed so clean."

"Just better use of resources," she declared. One day Wennai would tell him – but not now. It was nice being appreciated – and anyway Shaun *could* have done a better job at looking after himself – he needed training. Nevertheless, she was not going to resist any offer of cuddles after they got cleaned up back on Joh.

Joh City, reflected Wennai briefly; *I never thought I would ever think so much of it.*

One approached with news for them. The robotics engineers had made contact. They had been held under close guard next to a flour mill – which was good news as they were able to cook over a fire. They were among the first to notice the virus taking effect – and immediately recognised what must have happened. They did not know whom to thank but guessed it must be One or one of the others who knew the codes to the safe. They rejoiced in their resourcefulness. Runners were sent out in every direction to look for other Sponrons and tell them they could turn their phones and computers back on and go home. The engineers, it appeared, were less than ten kilometres from the wood and neither group knew of the other.

Wennai sought out Tlap and explained how she had used the house across the street from the lab.

"When they get back can you tell them I'm really grateful for their hospitality? You see, I didn't have anything to eat – or anywhere else to wash or sleep. I hope they won't mind."

"I should think they are very grateful for the privilege of helping you help us all to get home. Most of us wondered if we would ever see our homes again – and I'm sure they are no exception."

"I tried writing a note to say thank you. I spelled it like this." Wennai drew in the dust with a stick. Tlap giggled.

"That's how children write it," she teased. "I suppose, if

you think about it, it is the sensible way – but none of our spelling is sensible."

"Like the English Abby tries to teach me," said Wennai ruefully. "But they will understand it?"

"Of course. I expect they will show it off to all and sundry."

"I hope not! Hey, they'll take me for a child."

"Not after what you did, Wennai."

Shaun came over to them. Wennai changed the subject.

"Will they melt down all the robots?" she asked. "They look so sad… and they can't be bad because they are not real… I mean not human… I mean—"

"They will not all be destroyed but they will be reprogrammed somehow. I think the software guys have learned a salutary lesson."

Shaun decided to offer some advice from Planet Earth One, for what it was worth. The Sponrons were more advanced by centuries in some things but primitive cultures can still somehow make useful contributions. He asked One to write on a clay tablet what he had been told by Bandi of Isaac Asimov's three laws of robotics designed to protect human beings.

"Perfect common sense," ventured One. "I hope the softies listen."

"You're prejudiced."

"Of course."

"Tell them it came from outer space – and is inscribed in stone!" One laughed.

It was time for the adventurers to return home. They found the white gate just where they had left it. Had it been there all along? Could they have escaped whenever they chose? They would never know.

"Shaun, how many Sponrons live on the planet?" asked Wennai as they approached the gate.

"No idea. It could be millions."

"And were they all enthralled by the ASI?"

"Don't know. But one thing is for sure, even if they weren't, they would have been soon enough. The ASI would have turned out bots all over the place."

"So I can safely tell Kakko that we've saved an entire planet?"

"You could… but you won't. I've had quite enough of her bragging and I'm not joining in." Shaun spoke firmly.

"Yes, boss."

"Sorry, Wennai. I… I didn't mean to—"

"Shaun, you are right. We don't need to brag about it… I don't mind you being… well, confident about things. I guess I like you taking a bit of control sometimes… I'm not like Kakko."

"Anyway," added Shaun, a bit flustered and not knowing quite how to respond, "no-one can ever really understand what we achieve. You can never assess how important anything actually is. And the moment we tell our tale, Kakko will tell one of hers… and then, after that, she'll be saying that you and I are more than just friends. You watch."

Just friends, Wennai reflected, but she said nothing. She couldn't imagine wanting anyone other than Shaun in her life. The most important thing she wanted from Shaun was his friendship, even a friendship greater than the ordinary; but she knew she wanted more than that. Her body and soul ached for him. If it had indeed been God who had given them both a white gate as a command to Shaun to get it together with her, then Shaun wasn't listening. But deep down, she believed – she knew – Shaun wanted her as much as she wanted him. Her advice to herself was just to hang on in there.

Shaun had guessed exactly how Kakko would react. And when she did, Wennai just kept quiet. Jalli smiled at her, knowingly. "Like a mug of tea, Wennai?"

25

The furore that followed the fire at the Smiths' house sent ripples throughout the whole of Joh. People had been complacent. They had got so used to living peacefully that the idea of a hate crime against anyone was a real shock. Many were outspoken. How could they remain quiet when such a terrible thing had been aimed at a family that had become such an asset to Johian society for over two decades? The outrage was especially intense among, but not confined to, the people they knew personally in the places where they worked, worshipped, studied and, in Shaun and Kakko's case, played football.

One of the most outspoken was Salma's wife. She publicly condemned her husband's actions. His behaviour to her and his family had been poor, but this was worse than she ever thought possible. She was anxious to be cleared of all association with him and called on people not to blame her children. She refused to visit Salma in prison but instead made a point of going to see the Zathians from the shuttle and organising a friendship group. The Zathians were grateful.

After several months, they had reconciled themselves to the fact that it was quite unlikely that any other Zathian shuttle would be seen. The couple lived in the university and engaged in scientific research. They advanced a number of areas of enquiry – especially in medicine, where their knowledge of cryogenics and cell repair provided interesting possibilities for the treatment of the human body. The conservationists were also intrigued by their ideas. With just a few tweaks, they also confirmed the standard model of particle theory in quantum physics – the Johians hadn't got round to building a hadron collider to verify their own theories. But perhaps the Zathians' greatest single contribution was their rich awareness of the spiritual dimensions that can only come through thousands of years of combined consciousness.

The Zathian understanding of Scripture was a dynamic one. Each generation would select a tiny handful of the insights gained by them to add to the body of Scripture that built up over millennia. The debate about what should be included brought many texts into the public arena that enhanced the consciousness of the people. Only that which was truly original and clearly expressed would be added. Long treatises, or ideas that used complex inaccessible language, were rejected. The Zathian computer contained so much accumulated wisdom, that the philosophers and theologians on Joh were almost overwhelmed. The Zathians learned to speak Johian within a few months and were invited to give many a lecture.

But the delight was not all one-way. The Zathians rejoiced in the wonderful beauty of Joh and took a deep interest in its flora and fauna. They said that they would have to make the final Zathian contribution to their Scripture and it would probably be a poem about the wonders of the Creator's work on Joh. After that they would formally hand over the Scripture to a few young Johians who would be responsible for seeing that it continued to develop. There was quite some interest among the university students.

Shaun's leg was now almost healed for ordinary purposes but the doctor still would not let him take the field for a game. Shaun knew in his heart he would never get back up to the level he used to be; those days were gone. All he cared about now was being able to get about, keep fit and do some coaching at the club – and being able to sleep without dreaming.

He discovered that he was good at teaching. He had gained a following of likely boys and girls who showed a lot of promise – and it wasn't just teaching them about football but listening to them when they wanted to talk.

★ ★ ★

Coming home from the worship centre one Sunday lunchtime, Shaun saw a new white gate.

"White gate, Mum," he announced to Jalli, as carelessly as he could.

"Oh, really. I haven't got over your last one."

"It was two months ago."

"But ever since that time you came home with your leg broken—"

"Mum, last time was OK. I came back whole, didn't I? We both did."

"OK. I know how it works. But I'm afraid I'm getting a bit like your nan these days – sometimes life is just too exciting… I don't think this one is for me. I don't see a gate… Jack," she called through the kitchen door, "do you sense a white gate?"

"No," came a distant voice. "Can you see one?"

"No, but Shaun can."

Shaun called Wennai. She came and looked but this time it wasn't for her either. Shaun had been invited to travel alone. Beside the gate, Shaun found a wide-brimmed leather hat and a rucksack containing a couple of pairs of khaki shorts, some shirts, a sleeping bag, a cooking stove with a nest of pans with lids that doubled as dishes, a sleeping roll and a one-man tent.

"Wow," whistled Kakko. "A lone backpacker."

Wennai looked wishful. "Take care," she whispered. But she knew he would. In that regard, he was as different from his sister as chalk from cheese. That didn't stop her being anxious. They all were, but Shaun was determined not to show it. He was going in the right direction and he was determined to conquer this thing. He would have liked a companion, though – even just one person like last time. This time Kakko would have been good but it wasn't to be.

Shaun picked up the rucksack, donned the hat and stepped through the gate. Unsurprisingly, he found himself at the entrance of a caravan and camping park. A big blue sign depicting a single palm tree with the words Oasis Caravan Park in large yellow letters loomed above him. A second sign just along a drive indicated the way to the Oasis Office. He had no idea where he was but although the words were being translated for him, he was sure they were written in English. An oasis was a desert watering hole, only this place had far more than just the one palm tree depicted on the sign. In fact, the tall trees that surrounded the office were not palms at all; they bore long slender blue-green leaves. The grass was a shade of pale green; although it was clearly not a place of great rainfall, it was no desert. The single sun was up but not high in the sky – it felt like morning. There was a fresh smell in the air.

Shaun checked the wallet that came with the pack. It contained some colourful banknotes. Back in the cottage garden the words had been indecipherable – his nan hadn't been around and the rest of his family couldn't help. They were still meaningless to him but, now Shaun had looked at the signs around him, he was pretty sure they were English, too. As he scrutinised the notes, a man emerged from the office.

"Good day, mate. You coming in or not?"

"Oh, hi," said Shaun. "Yeah."

"What you got there? A small tent. Just you?"

"Yeah," answered Shaun.

"Sure? You ain't got a party of guys round the corner or anything?"

"No – no. Should I have?"

"Absolutely not. Single-sex groups are a nightmare."

"Oh. No," said Shaun, "it's just me."

"Come for the rodeo?"

Shaun looked puzzled. "Sorry, I really don't know where I am just yet."

"You a Pom?"

"Pom?"

"Sorry, shouldn't be rude. English?"

English. His dad was English. Persham was in England. "Yeah," Shaun smiled.

"First time in Oz?"

"Yeah… Still working out the money," Shaun added.

"You got ID?"

"Yeah." He fished in his pocket for his Johian ID and handed it over. The man looked at it. Then at Shaun. At least it was his picture.

"This ain't British."

"No. We don't live in England."

The man was happy. He had ID. Shaun had money and he seemed a likely young man. He was the second in two days to arrive on foot. The other was Australian. Single young men were attracted by the rodeo.

"Right. Don't suppose you want electricity?" Shaun shook his head. "Down the main path and keep left. You'll see the tents at the end."

Shaun followed the man's directions until he spotted a small tent like his and a family-size tent close by it. He chose a patch of ground in line with them. Instinctively he looked for somewhere that was on a little rise. The place didn't look as if it flooded but the ground was hard and a sudden storm might cause run-off into the dips. Shaun was a pretty experienced camper. As a teenager he had been involved in many an expedition into the countryside on Joh, including as a leader in several young people's camps as part of his training in youth and community work.

He found a suitable solid red-brown rock to help him get his pegs into the hard ground. When he had done, he studied it. It was like the rocks in the place where he had got caught up in the war. The memory fired within him but he knew how to deal with it. There were some similarities but this country was not the same. It was different – it wasn't so hot for a start. There were plenty of flies here but they didn't bite like the small ones that buzzed in your ears in that awful war zone.

Shaun walked back to the little shop where he chose a few tins with pictures of vegetables on their labels, and one with fish. His eye caught sight of what Matilda looked forward to Bandi bringing her from Persham: English tea. There was no doubt about it; this was definitely Planet Earth One. He put the tea into his basket and paid for it. He got quite a bit of change. His money was going to last a while. He wished he'd learned the numbers in English. He missed his nan and his brother who were competent English readers.

Back at his tent, he sat down in the shade of a scented tree about eight metres tall. Long green pods dangled from the branches.

"You from these parts?" A man from the family tent wandered over, interrupting Shaun's reverie.

"No," answered Shaun.

"Didn't think so… But you're not new to camping – not

like that guy next to you. Took him ages to pitch his tent. He's just kept himself to himself for the past two nights. Just a kid really... So what brings you to Warwick? The rodeo?"

"Just drifting for a few days," answered Shaun. This wasn't the time to go into tales of white gates. The man was only making small talk. So this place was called Warwick.

"You like it here?"

"It's cool. It's comfortable – apart from the flies."

The man laughed. "They are worse in the spring. It's all the stock they keep around here."

"Tell me about the rodeo."

"That's not the place if you want to avoid the flies! It's the best in the world after the Calgary Stampede, so they say."

"Where's that?"

"Calgary? Canada, I think."

"So why's this one so special?" Shaun was fishing as well as he could to get information without showing his complete ignorance.

"Riders come from all parts of the country – the world, even. I wondered if you were one of them. And we have some of the meanest horses and bulls to challenge them. Lasting eight seconds on one of them bulls takes some doing."

Shaun was getting the picture. It was a competition to see who could ride difficult animals the best.

"When does it start? I'll make sure I get there."

"Next weekend – just follow the crowds... Ah, here is you, neighbour." A fresh-faced young man was sauntering towards his tent across the field. "Says he's nineteen. Don't look it... Hey, mate," the man called. "You right?"

"Yeah," shouted the lad. But he didn't say anything else. He put down a few things and picked up a pan and wandered over to a standpipe.

"Looks lonely," said the older man. "Not like you. You

may be on your tod but you don't seem lonely like him."
The man's wife called her husband over. She had two small
children ready and was putting them in their car. "See you
later, mate." He joined his family and they drove off.

Shaun stayed sitting under his tree. Alongside its pods,
it had narrow shiny dark green leaves longer than the
pods. Shaun watched the breeze rustle through it. The
boy returned. Shaun wondered if he could get him into
conversation.

"Hello," he said. "I don't know... can you tell me what
sort of tree this is?"

The boy turned and studied Shaun carefully. It was a
strange question – unless this man was a foreigner. "You don't
know?"

"No. I'm afraid I don't. I haven't been here before."

"You're not Australian?"

"No."

"This is wattle. It's our national flower. It has bright yellow
flowers in the spring – where those pods are."

"Oh. Right. Sounds pretty."

"It is. Look, check it out on my phone." The boy tapped
something into his phone and showed it to Shaun.

"Wow. That's pretty... So now it's summer?"

"Coming on autumn. It's different from your part of the
world?"

"Yeah," answered Shaun. "I'm just backpacking around.
You?"

"Same."

"So where are you from?"

"Rocky... It's up north."

"You're young to be on your own."

"I'm nineteen," said the boy, too defensively. "What about
you?"

"Twenty," answered Shaun. "What do you do when you're not backpacking?"

"Why do you want to know?"

"No reason. Just talking. It doesn't matter." Shaun's suspicions were aroused. This lad was hiding something. "I'm just about to finish college doing a course on youth and community work. But I've got behind because I broke my leg."

"You broke your leg? You can walk on it now?"

"Yeah. It's almost better. But I'm going to have to give up football."

"Footie. You play footie?"

"Did."

"What position?"

"Midfield. Centrehalf."

"Oh. You mean soccer."

"Do I?"

"Yeah. Around here it's rugby league. That's what we call footie. I support the Diehards."

"They from where you're from – Rocky?"

"Nah. You don't know nothing. The Diehards are from Fortitude Valley… in Brisbane."

"Do you play?"

"Yes… No. I mean I did, but not now."

"You played for a team in Rocky?"

"No. At school."

"Sounds OK. You shouldn't give up. Sport is good for you."

"I might get back to it."

"What's Rocky like?"

"Rockhampton? It's by the sea."

"Oh. A big place?"

"Kind of."

"My city is by the sea. It's called Joh City."

"Where's that?"

"Joh."

"Suppose that makes sense."

"I'll miss it, being here."

"The sea?"

"I was thinking of my family… and my… friend."

"A girl?"

"Yeah."

"Girlfriend?"

"No… Well, kind of."

"How do you mean – 'kind of'?"

"Well, she's a good friend but we don't kiss and cuddle. We're not 'together' like that."

"But you're special friends, right?"

"Yeah."

"How long have you known her?"

"Years – since school."

"You fight?"

"Fight?"

"Yeah. Argue, like."

"Oh. No. We don't fight. Wennai is not the sort to fight."

"Wennai. That's a strange name."

"Not in Joh City. My sister's called Kakko. That *is* strange for Joh… My parents aren't from Joh."

"So what's your name?"

"Shaun."

"That's Irish, isn't it?"

"It was my grandfather's name. What do you go by?"

"Dan."

"That English?"

"Er. Yeah."

"Your family English?"

"Nah. Don't know why they called me that…. You like him – your grandfather?"

"Don't know. I don't think so. He died before I was born. My nan says he took to drink – it killed him."

"That's like my dad."

"What's like your dad?"

"Drink."

"I'm sorry. That's pretty awful. Does it make him ill?"

"He's just angry all the time. He never gets really drunk. It's just a glass with every meal – wine, not beer."

"Do lots of people drink wine in these parts?"

"No. It's mostly beer… It'd be better if he was a beer drinker. But my dad was always a bit beaut."

"Bit beaut?"

"Yeah. Stuck up. Too bloody proud of being middle class."

"Sounds as if you don't get on."

"We don't… Look, I don't want to talk about him. I want to forget about him."

"That's sad. But sure, we'll change the subject… You going to the rodeo?"

"Yeah."

"How long's your holiday?"

"Long enough."

"Great… What're you doing for the rest of today?"

"Nothing. I think I'll just chill out here."

"Right. I think I'll go exploring. Which way is the town?"

"Turn right at the entrance. It's a fair walk. Pass a few streets and then turn right again… It's all in square blocks. You can't miss the centre. It's called Palmerin Street… Not much of it."

"Thanks. I'll find it."

"Want some tea before you go?"

"Yeah. Why not?"

26

Shaun didn't know why the white gate had opened up in Warwick. He needed to explore but he wanted some exercise anyway. A few streets didn't seem like far. But the streets were wide and the distance between them a lot – space didn't seem to matter in these parts. There were few paved walkways; the verges to walk on were coarse mown grass and it was tiring to keep lifting his leg. Finally he spotted a statue some blocks away to the right. Statues generally stood in the middle of towns, so he headed towards it. By the time he found the town centre, the sun was past its zenith and sweat was dripping down his face, as well as his back and chest under his shirt. He was glad of the hat – and the shorts.

The statue stood at the junction of Grafton Street and Palmerin Street. Shaun looked up and down and spotted a set of blue umbrellas a hundred metres to his left, beneath which were tables and chairs. Shaun didn't need a second invitation. *Nan would quite like this place,* thought Shaun, as he sipped a mug of tea with milk. At the next table were four teenage girls. They were dressed in tank tops and shorts; their long hair hung loose about their shoulders. Shaun couldn't help noticing they had bare feet. But then he saw what Abby called flip-flops scattered under the table. His brain tried to make out to which foot each belonged. The girls began to giggle. One blew more bubbles into her frothy milkshake through her straw, making a loud noise that sent the other girls into a paroxysm of laughter. Shaun tried to ignore them but it was difficult; the nearest was barely two metres away from him. He became conscious that the cause of all this behaviour was himself. They were kids but that didn't stop them enjoying the sight of an attractive lone young man so close to them. The town was not big enough for a stranger to hide in and strangers of Shaun's type were a fascinating novelty.

Shaun thought about moving on. But he was hot and needed to sit for a while. He sat it out.

After a while the game grew less interesting and the girls began to discuss their week at the local school. Shaun guessed it must be the weekend. If this was the weekend, then maybe they would do some worshipping the following day. He had passed a place of worship near the statue. That could be something to explore next.

After a while the girls got up and started to look for their shoes.

"You seen my thong?" one of them giggled, kicking one of the flip-flops under Shaun's table.

Shaun noticed it and slid it out with his foot for her to pick up.

"Thanks." Another paroxysm of laughter.

At last the girls walked off down the street. As they did so, they looked back at him and began to giggle again. He wondered if there was something about him that was funny. Then he noticed that one of the girls had left a bag on the chair. Oh no. He guessed that was deliberate. This was getting stupid, so he got up and went inside to pay his bill as a girl returned and stared after him into the shop. He turned his back. The shop was not just a café – it also sold trinkets, so Shaun hesitated to study them. He made sure the girl had quite gone before he walked back out into the street.

Then he retraced his steps in the direction of the statue,

reflecting how much easier it was in strange places with Kakko or Wennai by his side. Kakko had no idea how uncomfortable it could be to be a single young man sometimes; girls behaved differently when she was around. At the junction to his left Shaun saw a large church with a tower made from yellow stone. He made his way towards it and saw that the driveway was crowded with well-dressed people pointing cameras at each other – a bride and groom had emerged onto the steps. The bride wore a fine white full-length dress, low cut with little puffy sleeves. Wennai would have been able to describe it in more technical terms and delight in this and that and, despite trying his best, Shaun would have had difficulty appreciating. The groom was dressed in a dark suit and necktie and looked decidedly hot and uncomfortable. *It's definitely easier to be a bride than a groom in this town*, reflected Shaun. *Weddings are made for brides.*

It got him thinking again of Wennai. He knew that nearly every male friend thought he was really lucky having the devotion of such a woman. But the thing that mattered to Shaun more than anything was that they understood each other – sometimes better than they understood themselves. At first, Wennai hadn't believed it was possible for anyone to understand her – no-one else she knew had lost a mother at the age of thirteen. But then she had discovered that the person who had been attacked in a park that Shaun had referred to was none other than his own mother, Jalli, and, from then on, Wennai began to regard the Smith family differently. But one thing Shaun was absolutely sure of: any commitment he made to Wennai inevitably had to be for life. And he wasn't sure he was ready for that.

Shaun watched the happy couple and the family and friends fussing around them. It didn't appeal to him – he couldn't see himself standing where that young man was standing. But then it occurred to him: for him and Wennai it wouldn't be like that. Wennai had no mother to fuss over her, and Jalli wasn't the kind to act like that mother was doing either. Perhaps... maybe... *Have you brought me here to see this?* questioned Shaun of his Creator. But God didn't seem to want to answer that. All he could get was, "Whatever" and that wasn't the kind of reply you got from God... or was it? *Perhaps... All I am sure of, is that I need to be as open as I can be with Wennai,* he vowed. *And to ignore my sister's impatience...*

Shaun studied the noticeboard. It was headed Anglican Church of Australia. Wasn't Abby's Church of England Anglican? He made a note of the times of the services. If today was Saturday, tomorrow would be Sunday. He spotted an older lady walking to a parked car who didn't appear to be part of the wedding party.

"Are these the times for tomorrow?" he asked.

"Yes," she replied. "You coming?"

"Maybe."

"I'll look out for you if you come to the ten o'clock. I'm on duty at the door... You new here?"

"Just passing through," said Shaun.

"You would be most welcome," smiled the woman. "On your own?"

"Yeah." Shaun smiled back.

"Come to the ten o'clock. I'll show you around."

"Thanks."

"Where are you staying?"

"Oasis something," said Shaun, embarrassed that that was all he could remember.

"Oasis Caravan Park?"

"That's it."

"Going back there now?"

"Yeah, I'd better," said Shaun. "It took me ages to walk and I don't want to lose myself in the dark."

"I watched you. You walk with a limp."

"Oh. You noticed. I broke my leg a bit ago. It's getting better but I'm tired now."

"Get in… if you trust an old woman not to run off with you. I'll take you back. You won't get there before nightfall, walking."

"Well…" Shaun thought about it. He wasn't sure if he could find the place in the dark and his leg was already hurting. The lady looked kind and was about two-thirds his height and half his weight. "OK. Thanks."

She drove in what Shaun thought was the wrong direction at first but she turned right at the junction of a major road. Then right again and Shaun knew he was on course for home.

"Thanks."

"You're welcome. Saturday night can be a bit wild, I'm afraid. Best not to be out alone."

"What, in this small town? Everyone seems to know one another."

"We do. And we know we have some problem families among us… Country places are not immune from the evils of society. Drugs are a menace."

"Drugs?" Shaun was aware of the problem on Earth. "My brother lives in a place in England. He says they have drugs in his college. England, that is on this planet, isn't it?"

The woman laughed. "You're right. Sometimes you wouldn't think so. They can do some of the strangest things over there… but, sadly, we Aussies can be as bad… You might wonder how I know I can trust you?"

"I hadn't realised how many people you can't here."

"It's not really that bad… No. It was the way you were watching the wedding. I've seen that look in a young man before. You were trying to notice the details to tell your girlfriend when you get home. She'll want to know about colours and flowers and styles, and you don't want to sound an idiot."

"How'd you know all that?"

"I have sons. Am I right?"

"Yeah," laughed Shaun. "Something like that."

They turned left and the woman drove a couple more blocks to the park entrance.

"Thanks," said Shaun as he got out of the car.

"Maybe see you tomorrow, then. The name's Daisy."

"Shaun."

She reached out her hand and he shook it. He waved as she swung right, back into the town. Shaun was grateful for his lift. He would have really struggled to get back on foot.

27

As Shaun limped across the field, the family man was getting ready to go out; Dan was lying down in front of his tent.

The family man called over to Shaun.

"Had a good day?"

"Yeah. It was interesting."

"I'm going out to get something to eat... Do you want me to bring you something?"

Shaun was quite hungry. "Well... if it's not too much trouble? I've got some tins—"

"I'll bring you some chips. What do you want? Pie or fish?"

"Either," said Shaun. "Whatever they have. How much do you want?" He went to his pocket.

"Ten should do." Shaun fumbled with his wallet. *I really should learn my numbers in this script*, he told himself. *Mathematics is supposed to be the common language of the universe – but the symbols we use aren't.*

"What about you, lad?" called the man to the prone figure.

"You talking to me?"

"No. The man in the moon. We're getting some chips. Interested?"

"Yeah. Thanks."

"Pie or fish?"

"Just chips. Thanks."

"That all for a strapping lad like you?"

"Yeah. Fine… Here's five."

"Thanks. You'll get some change, I expect."

Dan waved a note towards Shaun. Shaun took it from him, and added two more of the same. Two fives – that makes ten. He memorised the symbol for five. The man got in his car and drove off in a cloud of diesel fumes.

"Should get that fixed," said Dan.

"You know about cars?"

"My dad…" The boy stopped.

"Your dad?"

"He knows a bit about cars. I don't… Anyway, it'll need a computer to fix that. It's the timing."

"Oh. Right. Your dad seems to be quite handy—"

"I don't want to talk about him," said Dan strongly.

"Right… Look, you know I don't come from Australia. Can you tell me how this money works?"

"Sure."

Shaun pulled out some of the notes. "This is a five. Right?"

"Yeah. The purple and yellow fellow with the Queen on it. The blue one's a ten. See it says 'ten' on it."

"I see. It's the numbers I don't recognise… So 'one' and 'zero'… We're working in base ten?"

"Base ten? What's that?"

"It means decimal."

"Oh."

"So eleven will be this." Shaun scratched two ones in the dust.

"Right. You really are foreign, ain't you?"

"I'm afraid so. So that would make this yellow one with a 'five' and a 'zero' five times ten."

"Yeah. Fifty."

"And this green one, ten times ten."

"A hundred. You learn fast."

"So now fill me in. How do you write 'two'?"

Within a few minutes, Shaun had learned his symbols. There were only ten of them. Working in base ten wasn't natural for him. On Joh they used base twelve, so he kept having to do mental arithmetic. Joh had twelve symbols, and a Johian one followed by two Johian zeros added up to 144 in Australian.

"Is it the same in England? These numbers?"

"Yeah. The British colonised Australia over 200 years ago. That's why we speak English and use British names."

"Like Dan."

"Yeah. And that's why they call this place Warwick. Only, the first families here were Scots, so why they used the name of an English place I can't imagine."

"And it's the same for the name of the place you come from. Was that, too, named after somewhere in England?"

"Not somewhere, someone. Brisbane was the name of the governor. He was Scottish."

"Brisbane? But I thought you came from somewhere called Rocky? Is that near Brisbane?"

"Oh… er… yeah. No. No. Rockhampton is up north… but it's in Queensland and Brisbane is the state capital."

"Oh. I see. So Rockhampton is a person's name too?"

"Maybe."

Shaun saw the young man colour up. He decided not to continue with this conversation. There was something not quite right. There was no way Dan was nineteen, and he seemed to come from two different cities. He clearly knew far more about Brisbane than Rockhampton.

"Let's put that billy on. I could do with some tea," said Shaun, lightly. "My turn this time."

"Yeah. Tea. Fine."

By the time they had brewed up, the man in the smoky car came bouncing back over the field.

"Here," he shouted. "Steak pie and chips all round." He passed two paper parcels to Shaun. "Nine dollars. Here's your change."

"But—" began Dan.

"But nothing. You can't have just chips. Warwick is a pie city. Eat it. I know you ain't flush."

"I can't—"

"Argue later. Eat it while it's hot!"

"Thanks."

"You're welcome."

Shaun enjoyed his pie and chips. He made a note to talk to Bandi. He wondered whether they had pie and chips in Persham. It was abundantly clear that Dan was indeed hungry. He ate like someone who hadn't had a good meal for a week.

After they had finished, they put the billy back on. Shaun wondered whether to offer a drink to the family but they were engaged in some kind of card game under a lamp – the light was fading. Anyway, his billy wasn't big enough – nor did he have spare mugs. Then he noticed the beer. They wouldn't be interested in his tea.

Dan was also watching them.

"He's a kind man."

"Yeah."

"They seem a happy family."

"They drink too much."

"You drink?"

"Me? Nah. Seen what it does."

Shaun was about to say, "Your dad?" but thought better of it.

The sun sank in the west but it wasn't dark for long. In the east a bright full moon crept above the horizon. At first, it shone through the trees. Shaun watched it, fascinated. It was the same moon as he had seen in the war-torn land but, here, in this peaceful place, it seemed to have a lot more to say.

"It's bright," said Dan nonchalantly.

"Yes. You can listen to it here… The last time I saw it, you couldn't hear it for the guns."

"The moon. You can't hear the moon."

"Not with your ears. But he's saying something. He's telling us that peace will always win. Sometimes he's sad but mostly he talks of love."

"You're a dreamer."

"Yeah. I guess so… My nan likes the moon. She used to tell us a story about him."

"What? About how he's supposed to be made of cheese?"

"No. About how he learned how important he was. You see, he looked at the sun and Planet Earth and thought he didn't count for much, but then he found out different… You want to hear the story?"

"Why'd your nan tell you that story?"

"I don't know. Maybe because when we were small we used to think we were too small to matter. Listen.

"One night, after four and a half billion years, Mr Moon," Shaun gestured to the moon now rising above the trees, "let out a sigh. No-one heard it with their ears because sound can't travel on the moon as it doesn't have any atmosphere. Nevertheless, Mr Moon felt it vibrate through his heart. He gazed again at the sun as he had done every day of his long, long life and said to himself: *Sister Sun up there is hot and bright and shines with so much power. How wonderful she is and so beautiful. All the planets love her. They encircle her so faithfully. They worship her. She is the centre of everything. The beautiful comets with their long tails hurtle in and swing around her – and even as they leave, they face her with their tails pointing away. Every body from Sister Mercury to the outermost belt of minor planets looks to her and obey her.*

"Then he looked down at the Earth below him and said to himself: *And Sister Earth, how fine you are! Look at you – the most delicate shade of blue. Your seas gleam in the sunshine. I envy your stunning continents and swathes of green forests under your magnificent rich layer of air. And, oh yes, you have power and heat all of your own. Deep within you, you reach temperatures that are the envy of any planet – but not so high that on your surface you cannot blossom and bloom with life. Your surface is teeming with it – from simple cells to complex organisms that can even think for themselves.*

"*But just look at me! I am a mere lump of battered rock. I orbit the Earth, never taking my face from her, as we both encircle Sister Sun. I am her slave, trapped by her attraction. I run at over 1,000 kilometres a second but I cannot escape her. I am doomed to encircle her and admire her for as long as we both live. I am her cold, grey companion, a fraction of her size. How sad is that?!*

"But as he thought this, he was suddenly aware of a small object moving towards him from the direction of Sister Earth. It was tiny but solid. At first he thought it was another meteorite and he braced himself for its impact. Then he saw it glint in the sunshine. Meteorites don't usually do that. It was shiny and didn't hit him but swung around him and then headed back to Earth. A month or two later there was a second little object and then a third. This one stayed in orbit around him. In all his life, he had never had anything orbit him quite like this. Then another and another and this time a piece of it broke off – a tiny capsule that swung down to land on his surface. It was the gentlest landing any moon could experience. So gentle he barely felt it – like the brush of a light kiss.

"He became aware that inside this tiny little capsule were two of the intelligent beings that inhabit Earth in such numbers. They seemed to be in very high spirits. Mr Moon listened in as they spoke to one another. They appeared to think that he was special.

"'To think that we are here – on the Moon!' said one.

"'Yeah. When we consider the important influence the moon has had on the development of life on Earth,' responded the second. 'Life might not have appeared at all without the tides. Human beings would certainly not have evolved the way that we have without it.'

"'Scientists are more and more aware of the influence the moon is having on us,' mused the first. 'The forces of the moon make a considerable impact.'

"'Not to mention all the nocturnal creatures that depend on moonlight,' added the second. 'Ah, under the silvery moon… All those years of moon-gazing. Countless romances, stories and stuff.'

"The other laughed and began to sing a song called 'Fly me to the Moon'.

"'That's not bad, Frank Sinatra,' laughed his colleague. 'This is the one I remember.' He sang Edward Leah's *The Owl and the Pussycat* ending with: '… and they danced by the light of the moon!'

"'Hey. You'd better watch it. You may have been selected to be the first person to walk on the moon but, with a voice like that, Mr Moon might not care for it,' joked his friend.

"'I'll tell him that the best singing voices ever have sung for him – that might cheer him up.'

"'Yeah. Mr Moon, if you're listening, my partner here can't sing – but we can tell you that you have been the centre of attention for the most gifted human beings for many, many thousands of years and they are all rejoicing that we have managed to actually get here and land on you. How's that?'

"'Yeah. If he's listening, I guess that would do the trick.'

"The radio crackled. 'Houston here. Hey, guys, time to get some sleep. You have a big day tomorrow.'

"The next day, Earth rose in the moon's black sky, bright and blue and beautiful.

"'Wow, take a look at that!' said the astronaut with the Frank Sinatra voice.

"'I guess we live on a very beautiful planet… OK. Time to go moonwalking.'

"Soon the astronauts were descending the ladder. As the first set foot on the surface of the moon, he said, 'That's one small step for a man, one giant leap for mankind.'

"*A giant leap,* thought Mr Moon. *I mean that much to them?! Thousands of years wanting to reach me… Life on Sister Earth values me – even depends on me… People get moonstruck! I can't believe it. Am I that important? I used to think I was just a cold battered lump of dead rock in the thrall of Earth.*

"And then something happened. It was a kind of thought that seemed to have been put there from outside. It was as if the Creator, Himself, was saying to him, 'So now you know different, Mr Moon. Everything I make has influence, everything and everyone makes a difference. All things count. All things matter.'

"*Wow!* reflected Mr Moon, *to think I have been running myself down all these years.* 'Thank you, my Creator. Thank you for sending me a message via these tiny creatures. I'm sorry I have been bound up in my own thoughts so long, it never occurred to me to wonder what others were thinking.'

"'OK,' said the Creator. 'Now, just remember that you are loved – and everything else will work out just fine – forever.'"

Dan lay still for a moment and then said, "Your nan told you that?"

"Yeah."

"She make it up?"

"I guess so. She didn't attribute it to anyone else... The first people from Earth to land on the moon did it in her lifetime. She was around."

"Makes you think."

"All my family make me think."

"You have a great family."

Shaun told him about his parents – how his dad was blind and his mum loved bees. How Kakko was as straight as they came and brutal with it, and how Bandi was living in England studying philosophy. He told him about Yeka and how she favoured him.

"I'll be in trouble with her for being away," he said with a smile.

"You're the luckiest man on earth. And you have a girl, too... What you doing here on your own?"

Shaun explained about the white gates. He ended, "So you see, I'm not really the luckiest man *on Earth*. And I never thought of myself as lucky like that – but I guess I am... Wennai's mum died when she was thirteen..."

"But now she's got you. And you don't drink."

Suddenly the family man gave a huge burp – the gas from the four X beer. The children had quietened down. His wife scolded him. He just laughed.

"No. I don't drink," said Shaun. "Not like that, anyway."

They were both quite tired so, after a wander across to the facilities to clean their teeth, they said goodnight and turned in. Despite the cicadas, Shaun went straight to sleep.

★ ★ ★

Sunday was another fine day. Shaun awoke to the sounds of snores coming from the family tent. He had made up his mind that he was going to take up the invitation to attend the ten o'clock service but the thought of walking all the way that morning was not appealing. He didn't know what the time was anyway and it occurred to him that he may not have time to walk. He decided to go to the office and ask them if there was a bus or a taxi or some other way of getting a lift. He passed Dan on his way back from the sanitary block. He grunted a "Mornin'" which made him sound more asleep than awake.

In contrast, the man in the office was wide awake, greeting another man in his forties who had just got out of a clean bright-red utility truck.

"Bruce! Great to see ya, mate," he said enthusiastically.

Bruce appeared to be equally animated. "Yeah, you old dodo." He slapped him across the shoulders.

"Enough of that. I might be twenty years your senior but I ain't extinct yet."

"I brought you that straw you asked for."

"Hey. You didn't have to come all that way with just three bails of straw."

"Nah. But I wanted to give my new wagon a run. Only got it last Thursday."

"Smart. Clean. Run OK?"

"Fine. It's got more power than the last one but uses half the fuel. Should have changed it years ago…"

"So how's that lad of yours?"

"Aw, he's fine. Passed all his exams – so he's off. Got a place in UQ to start in January."

"That's good. You must be proud of him."

"We are. But it ain't good news for the farm. I'm making him help me with the top fence before he goes. It's a three-man job. When he's gone it'll only leave Max – and he ain't getting any younger."

"Can you find a young hand to help you? There must

be someone who would snap your hand off to live out there near the rabbit fence – get out of the human drudge and the overcrowded sprawl you get today. Give me the outdoors any day."

"You would think so. But, like my son, they want the crowds. I met my Marge in Inglewood, didn't I? That was a long way when I was young. There was a bevy of girls my age there – at least twenty. Thought I was spoiled for choice. Not these days. My son, he can't wait to get into the city. Won't even look at a local girl. Ryan in Pratten, he's got two fine girls there but my boy hardly even notices them beyond a how-do-ya-do at the church once a month."

"You advertising?"

"What? For a girl for my boy?"

"No!" His mate fell into laughter. "A hand for your farm."

"Oh. No. Not yet. I'll wait 'til after Christmas. College doesn't start before January."

"I wish you luck. You never know."

"Never thought I would be losing both my boys to the city. You know we're the fourth generation on the farm – we go back a hundred years. Our great-grandfather."

"Yeah. There were three times as many people living out there in our grandparents' day. Now there are just you and a few other families. You enough to keep that church of yours going?"

"That's another worry. It's getting hard to pay our way. Population's a fraction of what it was. Congregation ain't getting no bigger and with our second one gone... It'll be Ryan's girls next..."

"I can't understand it."

"It's not just the lure of the city, there ain't the call for as many hands. The machines we have today can do the work of a gang. Take this new postholer – line it up, press the button and you've got a perfect hole in three minutes. Back when I was young it took a whole day for a gang of half a dozen men to do fifty yards of fencing."

"Yards, eh? It *was* yards in those days."

"It still is for me and Marge. That boy of ours – he comes in saying he's 175 centimetres tall and weighs 66 kilos. Makes him sound like some kind of giant…" And so the conversation went on.

Shaun was just wondering if he should interrupt – neither of the men appeared to have noticed him – when a police car drove in through the entrance and pulled up beside the office. The policeman rolled down his window and leaned out to address the site owner.

"Hi, Greg, mind if I use your facilities? Ate some-ut I shouldn't have, I reckon. Having a job to hold on." He produced a wry smile.

"No problem, mate," said the owner. "Just drive on through. You know where to go?"

"Yeah. Thanks."

The policeman continued onto the site and made his way to the toilet block.

Shaun was just asking Greg and his brother about the best way of getting into town, when Dan came running round the corner and jumped into the new ute. Bruce turned but Dan had already started the engine. Greg instinctively held his brother back as Dan swung the vehicle onto the track and then accelerated through the gateway, turning left down the highway.

"Well, damn me. Only had the thing for three days and some young whippersnapper's gone and flogged it from under my nose!" He took his hat off and threw it on the ground in anger.

Instinctively, Shaun ran to the end of the drive but the utility truck had disappeared from view along the smooth, straight highway. He returned to report as the police car reappeared.

"Thought you were supposed to stop crime!" exclaimed Greg. "A young fella has just flogged my brother's new ute – just as we was standing here."

"Calm down, Greg. Explain what's happened."

Greg described the incident as Bruce retrieved his hat and knocked the dust off it on a fence post.

"You'd better get after him," said Bruce sternly.

"Doubt if you'll catch him," put in Shaun meekly. "He was out of sight before I got to the road."

"He's right," said the officer. "I'll radio it in. He won't get far." He picked up his phone and reported the theft to his controller. "The reg is…" he looked up to Bruce who repeated it. "You got that? Yeah. New bright-red Toyota ute with three bails of hay… Yep, shouldn't be a problem." He leaned out of his car. "OK. They'll have it covered in Stanthorpe and Killarney – he'll not get over the border into New South anyway, not with straw aboard. I'm going to take up a position on the other side of the highway, just in case he decides to double back."

"What if he goes back up through the town via Dragon Street or McEvoy? He could get lost in the town."

"I doubt he will stay in town. I'll get them to stake out the Cunningham Highway on the other side. My guess is that he'll try and put distance between us and him – but we'll get him. He won't get far." The policeman drove out onto the highway.

"You, son, you met this lad. What do you reckon he's playing at?"

Shaun started to tell them what he could.

"Come inside, out of the sun," said Greg. "I'll make us a mug of tea."

Inside the office, Shaun explained his suspicions. "Dan said he was nineteen but I don't think he's as old as that."

"Dan?! He's registered as Mark... Mark Wheeton. At least that was what it said on the ID he showed me."

Shaun explained that Dan/Mark had told him he came from a place he called Rocky.

"Rocky? Rockhampton? Doubt it. He's a city boy – Brisbane. The address on the ID said Indooroopilly."

"That'll explain why he knows so much about Brisbane and all he could tell me about Rocky was that it was on the coast. He supports a football team called the Diehards which he says is a Brisbane club."

"Yeah. Used to be the Valleys."

"He has a problem with his family. He doesn't get on with his father," said Shaun. "Something about him being a wine drinker and always in a foul temper but never quite drunk. And he hates school. He's not the academic type."

"School? At nineteen?"

"That's what I thought," concurred Shaun. "I would be surprised if he were nineteen... I think his father has impossible ambitions for him. Something about higher education... And he hasn't been camping before but he's picking it up fast. Says he likes the wide open spaces – seeing the stars at night and everything. He's not worried by your flies. Dan... Mark... is... was... travelling very light. And he hasn't got much money either."

"Sounds like he's a runaway."

"That's what I thought," agreed Shaun. "That's probably why he stole your vehicle. He could have been spooked by the police car – thought they were after him."

"That's probably it... and I doubt he's called Mark either," said Bruce. "You've never been particular on ID, Greg."

"You can't be. Lose too much trade if I was."

"Your trade? I've lost my ute…"

"Come on, Bruce, he won't get far. Look, here comes the law."

The police car drove back up to the office. The policeman got out and strode across. "They got him… Killarney."

"Killarney! Already. He must have been going some lick," said Greg.

"Apparently he drove into the town like he was being pursued by a pack of dingos. Wasn't difficult to spot… They stopped him at the border. Your truck's safe. No damage. It's in the Killarney police station yard."

"And the young man?"

"In custody there. He's not talking to them. Look, Greg, would you be able to get down there and talk to the Killarney police?"

"Yeah. Sure. This young man knows more about him than I do." He indicated Shaun. "You OK to come along?"

"Yeah, fine. If I can help."

"I reckon you'll be able to pick up your ute. Check it over and file for damages," said the officer.

"I'll want life imprisonment if he's done anything to it. I only got it last Thursday."

The three of them set off for Killarney in Greg's battered old Holden.

28

As they pulled into Killarney police station yard, Bruce was delighted to see his beautiful red Toyota looking a little dusty but otherwise unscathed. He walked round it – no scratches. It was locked.

Inside the station he was reunited with his keys but the police officers plied him with questions. What did he know about the young man who had taken it? Apparently, Dan/Mark was refusing to talk. He wouldn't say who he was, where he was from or why he had taken the truck. Bruce deferred to Shaun. Shaun told them what he knew.

"So he's talked to you. Perhaps you can get something more out of him," said one of the officers.

"I'll have a go," Shaun agreed. "I can't guarantee it'll be the truth, though... Does it have to be here, in a cell?"

The officer laughed. "You mean the interview room." The officers conferred. "Running away won't get him far here. We'll run you down to the Gorgeous Coffee Lounge."

Inside the coffee shop, Shaun and Dan/Mark sat opposite one another. Dan/Mark didn't want coffee – but he readily agreed to a berry smoothie. The policeman went back outside and sat in his vehicle.

"OK," began Shaun, "I'm not from these parts but one thing I do know that is true anywhere in the universe is that if you don't say anything, you'll get into a pack of trouble. Believe me, this place is a dream compared to some of the

331

places I've been to. Places where the police take you to a café can't be that many. If they're bribing you with stuff, it's because they want to help you. I and they can see you're not a hardened criminal, so what is all this about?"

Dan/Mark sucked hungrily at his smoothie. "If I tell them anything, they will send me back."

"Back to your parents? You're not nineteen, are you?"

The boy stared at him.

"Why don't you want to go back?"

Dan/Mark said nothing but lowered his eyes to his glass.

"Do you want something to eat? You're half-starved, aren't you? Hello," called Shaun to the waitress. "Can we have two breakfasts?"

"The works?" she asked.

Shaun examined his dollars. He had enough. "Yeah. Please... OK. Suppose they don't send you back. If it's that bad, they might not—"

"They will."

"How old are you? Let me guess; fifteen?" Shaun deliberately guessed younger than he really thought.

"Sixteen! Seventeen in October."

"So how old do you have to be before you can have your own place in this country?"

"Don't know. But I don't know anybody my age who lives without adults... You have to be in school until you are at least seventeen."

"So you could leave next October?"

"December. I would have to finish the school year. I could get a job then but my father would never hear of it. He wants me to go on to uni."

"And do you?"

"I ain't got the brains... and I don't want to spend my life cooped up in some office either."

"In the city? You do live in the city, don't you?"

"How'd you guess?"

"The folk around here are different from you. You have city ways about you... but you do like the open spaces."

"You know a lot about me. How'd you know so much?"

"From what you said and from the way you look... Your father drinks too much but likes smart city things. He wants you to be in a well-paid professional job where you have to wear a suit. But you don't mind getting your hands dirty and you like the wide open air. You like the night sky – you haven't been able to see it very well in the city – what do they call it, Brisbane? Your football team comes from there."

"You going to tell the cops all this?"

"I have. But they don't know who you are... or who your parents are. Guys do not run away for no reason either. If you tell them the truth and that you don't want to be returned to your father, they might listen. In any case, that's what will inevitably happen if you don't say anything. The police will be putting two and two together right now – maybe they already have."

The breakfasts arrived. "There you go," said the young waitress. "Enjoy."

"Thanks," said Shaun. "Eat this," he instructed Dan, "and then tell them everything. Tell them you don't want to go back to the city. Tell them about your dad."

"They'll make me finish school."

"It doesn't have to be the same school, though."

"Guess not. I hadn't thought of that."

★ ★ ★

Shaun and full and much happier Dan/Mark sat together in the interview room at the police station. The officer seemed to have already solved the puzzle.

"A sixteen-year-old called Rhys Wethers meeting your description disappeared from Indooroopilly two weeks ago. His father reported him missing two days after he was first missed. Is that you?"

The boy hung his head.

"Right, Dan, Mark, Rhys, what's the deal?"

"Tell them everything," said Shaun.

"Yeah. I'm Rhys... But I'm not going back to Indooroopilly. You don't know what my father is like. He's a bully. He's always drinking."

"He hits you?"

"No. It'd be easier if he did. If he tried that I'd hit him back. He's not bigger than me... But he's devious. I hate it at home. It's the 'family name this' and the 'Wethers have always been that'. And I've tried but I just can't do it. I've never come up to expectations. Whatever I do, it's not good enough... Then last week, the teacher lost it with me. He said it was like banging his head against a brick wall. Told me I was a numbskull... I might not be good with writing and stuff but that don't make me dumb," he said defiantly.

"Next day, I bunked off – all day. I knew what would happen. My dad would be mad... So I stole this bloke's wallet from the counter in a shop while he wasn't looking. I never, like, done anything like that before. I took this membership card so I could pretend to be him – it didn't have a picture. I went back into the shop with the wallet... said I'd found it outside. He thanked me and gave me fifty dollars as a reward. So I hitchhiked to Warwick. I knew about the rodeo and figured they might take me on... But it's not until next week."

"Where's the Dan name come in?" asked Shaun.

"Nowhere. Just made it up."

"We'll have to inform your father," said the officer. "And

there's the business of the ute. Theft and driving without a licence…" He called a second officer. "Is the owner of the red ute still around?"

"Yes. He's hanging on for this Shaun fella."

"Call him in, will ya?"

Bruce and Greg came into the room.

"You want to press charges against this young man? There'll be a bit of paperwork, I'm afraid."

"What did you do it for, son?" he asked Rhys.

The lad didn't reply.

Shaun said, "He has been running away from his oppressive father – thought he was going to be caught."

"Oppressive father? Why, what has he done?"

"I don't want to talk about him," sobbed Rhys. "I'm fed up of it all. Put me in jail. Send me to Norfolk Island if you want but don't make me go back to him. If he don't do my head in first, I'll end up doing him in… You don't know how great it was, like, there on that camping ground – all that space, all that sky – no-one to hound you every five minutes… No wine smell all the time. No-one getting on to you about putting your commas in the right place or telling you to recite poetry that don't mean nothing. Stupid maths with letters instead of numbers. You don't know how great it was to forget the ruddy end-of-year exams… You don't know how lucky you are living out here."

"I wish my son wanted to live out here. All he wants is uni and the city like his brother," said Bruce.

"Well, he can have it. I don't want it. Let him go and live with my old man."

It was then that it occurred to Bruce. "So, maybe you would like living on a farm, then? We got plenty of open spaces, and flies and dust. There's no wine, I'll grant you – just the intoxicating smell of the stock on heat," he chuckled.

"You serious? Are you saying I could come and live on your farm? That'd be cool."

"Look, lad, on our farm you're either eating dust or drowning in mud. You have to mend fences no matter what the weather's doing – the roos don't just knock them down on nice days. Some mornings you have to knock the ice off the tank to get to it to work – and in the summer it can get up to well over forty in the shade – that's assuming there is any. And you can go a week before you see another human being – but we have plenty of snakes and red-backs—"

"Hey, Bruce. Don't go getting poetical. You'll put the lad off." Greg was seeing the funny side of all this. He saw Rhys's face glow at his brother's attempt to tell him the worst. This had turned into quite an adventure now the truck and the lad were safe.

"And we don't have many books beyond bibles and hymn books, for that matter," continued Bruce.

"Are you really saying I could come and work on your property? A proper job on a… station?" said Rhys, his eyes all ablaze.

"Station? It's hardly a station, lad. But it is my property – been in the family for generations."

"Hold on a minute," said the officer. "We're not running an adoption agency here. The boy is only sixteen and has a father who must be told he's been found. And he can't take on any full-time work until he's finished his schooling, anyway."

"Can I make a suggestion?" put in Shaun, gently. "Send for Dan's… Rhys's father. Tell him where he is. Get him to come here and let him talk to Bruce… If he agrees, Rhys could go to school out here… if you're serious about what you said," he added to Bruce.

"I can give him a trial for nothing. If he proves he's up to it, then he has a job with me as long as he wants it."

"OK," said the policeman. "Take him back to Warwick. I'll get onto Indooroopilly... Make sure you don't lose him."

★ ★ ★

A day later, a puzzled police officer drew up at Oasis Caravan Park.

"I don't get this," he said to Greg. "The lad's father has been made aware of where his boy is but doesn't want to drive over and fetch him. Says we should take him home."

"That's not right. If I'd lost my boy and found out where he was, I'd be there like a shot. How long does it take to drive from Indooroopilly anyway? He could have his breakfast and be here for coffee time."

They called Rhys and Shaun.

"He don't care. Probably too pissed to drive anyway. Might think that his car would get dirty," said Rhys as an explanation.

"He must love you."

"Nah. He's never loved anyone but himself... He drove my mum to drink herself to death."

"I'm sorry your mum's dead. I didn't want to ask. When—?" began Shaun.

"Years ago. When I was seven. I've been boarded out most of the time since then."

"If his father wants him, let him come!" said Shaun angrily. "He knows where he is."

"I agree," said the policeman. "That is, if you don't mind keeping him here... Oh and, by the way, Mark Wheeton is pleased to get his golf membership card back, and he wants to forget it. You're lucky. But driving without a licence and insurance is on your record, sonny. So I have to give you an official warning – but that is all. Your provisional licence is revoked for a year. Just don't do it again, right? Or else you'll be for the high jump."

"No, sir. I won't drive. I promise."

"So wait here until your father comes."

"Yes, sir."

After the police car had gone, Greg smiled at Rhys. "He means no driving on the highway. That doesn't apply on Bruce's farm... If your dad isn't here by Thursday, you can go there. It's best you aren't around when the rodeo kicks off."

★ ★ ★

On Tuesday, Shaun suggested they walk into the town. If Rhys's dad turned up, he would have to wait for them to get back.

It didn't seem as far the second time. Maybe because Shaun knew where he was headed: the café to try out their smoothies. They explored some of the shops and wandered across a park beyond which stood the high school. It was lunchtime and young people Rhys's age were spreading across the area.

"There you are. They have a school here."

Rhys shuddered.

"Look, it's only until December. You can manage that. And besides, some of these young people are country sorts – destined for a life on farms – so if you went to school here—"

"Dad wouldn't let me."

"I think you've already stood up for yourself, Rhys. You can't get away with running away from him but you can assert yourself a bit. You might not be old enough to leave school here in Australia but you are old enough to have ideas about where you want to be in your life and where you're going. If you get things worked out a bit, then, when you meet your father you can make a deal."

"Yeah. You're right... When he comes, will you be there – help me say what I want to?"

"Sure. If you want."

"You're so wise. I wish I were like you; you really have got your life together. You know what you want to do and where you're going."

They retraced their steps down Palmerin Street. They passed a newsagent's and bookshop. Shaun was attracted by a colourful book and immediately thought of his nan. A book from Planet Earth would be a treat. He picked it up. It was an illustrated novel with a single word for a title.

"What does this say?" Shaun asked Rhys.

"Emma. It's called Emma. It's a girl's name. It's by a woman called Jane. Jane Aust...en."

"She local?"

"Nah. It's old. I mean it was written a long time ago – in England, I think. Most of them were. I don't know much about it. Don't ask me about books."

"Don't worry, I won't. I reckon my nan would like this." Shaun bought it. Come on, let's have a look at the trinkets in the coffee shop. I'll have to buy something for Yeka if I get something for Nan."

In the café with blue parasols Shaun picked up a child's sun hat with a pretty colourful pattern on it. Perfect. Then Shaun saw a little charm bracelet with a heart, a kangaroo, a koala and an emu. Rhys explained they were native Australian things. Wennai would like that. It wasn't cheap. It took nearly all of the rest of Shaun's money. But then, he thought, he expected to be able to leave the next day. And if there wasn't a white gate, he could always bring it back if he kept the receipt. Looking up Grafton Street, Shaun thought about Daisy. He had kind of promised to be in church at the ten o'clock service and he hadn't made it. Back on Joh, he would have texted if things didn't work out but here he hadn't a phone and, even if he had, he didn't know Daisy's number. She would be unlikely to be in the church that day but he could leave her a note.

Rhys was unwilling to go inside the church. Shaun went in and spotted a woman dusting at the front. He approached and asked her if she knew Daisy. She said she did. He gave her a message to explain that he had been otherwise unexpectedly engaged but if he were ever that way again on a Sunday he wouldn't forget. The lady was both pleased and, sadly, amazed that young a person was so thoughtful, and she said so. That cheered Shaun up.

★ ★ ★

That evening, Rhys's dad showed up. A portly man in a dark suit and tie, he walked across the field trying to avoid the dustier patches.

He strode up to Rhys, ignoring Shaun. "Ruddy hell, Rhys, what the blazes have you been up to? Why'd you just flit off like that?"

"I let you know I was OK."

"That's not the point. I pay good money for you to go to that school. Education is your future."

"I hate it there. They're bullies. All they teach is crap."

"Crap? I'll tell ya that there's money at the end of the line. Your crap is other people's gold dust, mate. That's why I've invested so much in you. Without that you're doomed in the world."

"Excuse me," said Shaun as politely as he could, "your son has shown quite a bit of initiative, actually."

"What, in running off? That's not—"

"He was exploring the world to find a way ahead that suits him. He's pretty good in the countryside. Learns fast."

"What's it got to do with you?"

"He's been telling me things about himself and discovering a side to himself that he didn't know he had."

"Complaining about his old man, I suppose."

"He mentioned you but he didn't want to talk about you. He's discovered the wide open countryside and feels at home in it. Pretty cool for a city boy."

"Yeah, Dad. This is where I want to be."

"What kind of work is there around here?"

"I think they're pretty keen on recruiting suitable young people for the country things," said Shaun. "At least, your son has made an impression on one farmer. He offered him a job."

"A job I want to take," said Rhys, boldly.

"What kind of money is in that?"

"Enough. I won't starve on a farm. And anyway, if I'm happy then I'm sorted, ain't I?"

"Never thought my one and only son would turn out to be a flippin' farmer…"

Shaun stood his full height and formally introduced himself. "Hi. The name's Shaun." He held out his hand. "I guess you could say I can act as your son's agent. For free, of course. Shall we send for Bruce, the farmer in question?"

"Where's he hang out?"

"To the west – halfway to Inglewood, near the rabbit fence," said Rhys.

"I can't travel there this evening."

"Of course not," said Shaun in his best businesslike tone. "Let's go and have a word with his brother in the office here. We can make some arrangements… I would offer you a drink, only you're driving." Shaun didn't have any money anyway but he guessed this was the kind of man who would always do business over a drink. By calling himself an agent, he had moved the whole thing onto a business footing – and business was something Rhys's dad seemed to relate to.

It didn't take long to set things up for Rhys's father to return on the Thursday when Bruce would meet up with them and take them out to his place. In the meantime, Rhys would carry on camping at Oasis. Shaun checked his wallet. He had just enough to last until then. But seeing Shaun's wallet, Rhys's father drew out his own wallet and insisted on paying for his son. He paid up until Thursday and gave his son a couple of hundred for expenses. Then, in a cloud of dust, he drove off in his four-by-four.

"What's he need that for in Indooroopilly?" asked Greg.

"He doesn't," said Rhys in a matter-of-fact voice. "But he's got to find something to spend his money on."

That night Shaun and Rhys lay on the grass and studied the stars.

The family next door had turned in inside their large tent and were engaged in playing some kind of game with the children. It involved quite a lot of noise. Shaun reflected on what Rhys had said. According to him, he had got his life together. Had he? He hadn't... yet. But perhaps – just perhaps – it was coming together. He thought again of Wennai. He knew he could be happy as a single man. If he were to live a single life, it would be sufficient. He liked the freedom to lie back and watch the stars. Judging from the sounds coming from the neighbouring tent, a family meant responsibility – hard work and a lot of patience. It was now bedtime and the children were doing everything in their power to delay it. He heard the mother speak a few sharp words. Could he be a family man? It would be nice to be free.

But then, could he have come to that stage of peace without his family; or without Wennai? No. He knew that. And he also knew that Wennai needed *him*. She had no parents. Patia was a great sister, but now she was courting seriously, and Aril wouldn't be around forever. Soon Wennai would be left alone. She had never had a relationship with anyone else except Gollip, and that was never going to work – Gollip couldn't begin to understand her; he didn't work at those depths. Gollip could bury the ball into an opponent's net but he hadn't the mastery of the situation – he needed others to put it at his feet. But Wennai needed Shaun's appreciation of the places most people were not aware of within themselves. No; they needed each other. Kakko was right – annoyingly, she mostly was. They were not only right for each other, they were interdependent – an item. And, although he had tried to deny it to himself, she stirred his ardour. She always had.

Rhys turned in but Shaun continued to lie there under the stars, working out what he was going to do when he got home. The longer he thought about it and the more he prayed, the more he knew he could not put it off. It crossed his mind that perhaps Wennai didn't want any more than the friendship they already had. If he made a move, asked for the relationship to change, what would happen? After all this time would she be too scared to commit herself? But the more he thought, the more he realised that they couldn't just keep going on like they were forever. And he also knew that the solution lay with him; it was he had shown the initial reluctance – he who had called a halt to the relationship after his eighteenth birthday party. That was a long time ago – but the ball was still in his court.

Eventually, Shaun fell asleep, only to be awoken by great splashes on his face. It was raining. The scent of the rain on the dry earth was intoxicating. It smelt fresh and sweet. He couldn't describe it in words. It was nothing like Shaun had ever smelt before. The water of life was soaking into the parched ground, bathing the roots of the rough, brown grass with the liquid they craved. As Shaun pulled himself up and crawled into his tent, he sensed the power of this life force all around him. A cool wind drove against the wall of the little tent and the rain grew heavier. Shaun didn't care that he might get wet.

He must have fallen asleep again because the next thing he knew, it was light and the sun was already shining through the branches of the trees. The birds were singing – making a real din. The children next door were bouncing with new-found energy… and he was desperate for the loo! His body was telling him it was morning, the beginning of a new day. "Morning, Dan," he called as he passed him on the way back from the showers. "I mean Rhys."

"Morning… Call me Dan. I like it. I think I shall be Dan from now on. No-one can spell Rhys."

You're right, there, thought Shaun. *I couldn't.*

29

Thursday came and Dan's father was due. Bruce drove over and they were throwing Dan's meagre belongings into the ute, when his father arrived.

"We're only three hours from Brisbane, if that, mate," Bruce was explaining. "The lad wants a job – and I can give him one."

"He hasn't finished school yet. He's not seventeen," ventured the father. "At least let him finish school."

"I'm aware of that. Finishing at school would be a condition of employment. He can go to school here."

"But he has a place in a good school—"

"Which he doesn't care for. I've learned a bit about this young man. He's a good lad at heart. He may be city-born but he's got dirt in his soul." He took a handful of damp earth and tossed it in the air. "Put him in an office and it'd be like trying to grow a silky oak in a pot – he's the sort that needs root space."

"I'm paying good money for a good education—"

"He'll get it free out here… and I'll give him board and lodging and pay him for the hours he puts in on the farm."

"He's tasted the air," said Shaun, quietly. "He's experienced freedom – and a bit of hardship – and made friends. He'll settle here. He says he's spent a lot of time boarding, so you haven't seen him daily anyway. He'll still be around – visit you sometimes."

"Dad, don't you get it? I ain't going back with you. You'll have to tie me down to do it – and I'm as strong as you."

"'Am not'… The words are 'am not'."

"It ain't, it's 'ain't'. It's anything I want it to be!"

"Look, mate," said Bruce quietly, "let's you and me go for a drink and talk this over."

The father looked about him. He knew he was not going to get Rhys back. Like Shaun said, he was like a bird that had escaped from its cage and seen the wide world. Even if you could catch it, you were not going to persuade it back inside… And he needed a drink.

Later that day, after a trip to the farm, a deal was struck. Rhys agreed to go to school in Warwick and sit his exams. Marge promised to work with him and coach him through. He would learn the work of a farmer at weekends and, if he took to it, he would become a full-time apprentice. In return, Rhys reluctantly agreed to go back to Indooroopilly for Christmas.

★ ★ ★

Shaun reflected on a long mission. It had been much more gentle than his previous ones. There had been no guns, nor had he saved millions like Kakko seemed to do; but that didn't matter. He had been instrumental in opening up a life for a young man at the end of his tether. That made the whole thing more than worthwhile. The Creator of the entire universe knew Rhys, loved him and gave him Shaun from another planet to help him sort out his life. *That, somehow, sums up the love the Creator has for every single one of us*, thought Shaun. He found himself talking to God. "Even if it doesn't work out for everyone like that, you still care; you still love each one of us, don't you? I don't know why but you can't always stop bad things from happening, but even when you can't you help people make the right choices, and when they do, you are there with them. That's why Pastor Ruk is so taken with the Christmas thing – you being born in human flesh. But it doesn't stop there; these Christian churches have got you down as being executed – killed. You didn't stop that; you could have run away but you didn't. You died but not forever. Nothing can put out the spark of your love. Nothing can take you away from us."

30

"Nan, are you sure you'll be alright on your own with Yeka?" said Jalli with an air of concern. A white gate had arrived for them all apart from Matilda and Yeka. "We've no idea how long we'll be. I could ask Hatta—"

"Jalli, I'll be fine. Just take your white gate. I promise that if you are longer than usual, I will draft in the right kind of help."

Yeka seemed more upset about being left out than by her parents and family leaving her.

"Nan has not been invited either, Yeka. Someone has to stay to keep her company. Imagine how lonely it would be with no-one," coached Jalli reassuringly. She kissed her little girl and then hugged Matilda. She didn't want either of them to see her wet face. She, herself, had only been three when she had been left with her grandmother after all her family had disappeared in the flood on Raika. She prayed that her Yeka would not know the same pain. But, when it came to the white gates, you just had to trust.

Soon Jalli, Jack, Kakko, Tam, Shaun and Wennai found themselves on the same beachfront as one of their first adventures. Pero's hotel stood before them.

"Wow, Jack. It's Pero's."

"Yes. I can smell the place – we're under the trees on the edge of the beach. I can hear the surf. Some places don't change."

"There's something up," said Shaun, now well experienced in detecting atmospheres. "It's like the sun isn't shining."

"Which it most definitely is," said Jack.

"Everyone has an expression as if the world's about to end!" joked Kakko. "All so gloomy."

They crossed the road towards the hotel. In the lobby, they watched a TV screen. A serious-faced presenter was speaking whilst they showed a rocket being fired into space.

"The Vaastak rocket that was successfully deployed yesterday," the presenter was explaining, "has hit the asteroid but not precisely where the controllers had hoped. We can go live to the press conference at Stad Mans where the operation chief, Chief Derothis, is answering questions."

"Chief Derothis," a reporter was asking, "what about the explosion that you were hoping to detonate?"

"As you may be aware," replied Derothis, "the idea was to strike the asteroid towards its northern end and detonate a two–megatonne plutonium fission bomb in order to alter its course. We were hoping to deflect it sufficiently to miss our planet… We have deployed on the asteroid but more centrally than we had hoped. We are currently considering whether to detonate."

"Can you send a second rocket?" another reporter stood and asked. "A second go at hitting the target?"

"There is no time. By the time we have readied a second rocket, the asteroid will be too close."

"So we are doomed!" shouted a desperate voice.

"No. We can't say that for certain. If we detonate there are three possibilities."

"Which are?" yelled an impatient man near the front.

"If we detonate, the first, and probably the most likely, scenario is that it will make insufficient difference to the trajectory of the asteroid. The second is that it will shatter the giant rock into several smaller pieces, nearly all of which will land on the planet with destructive force, causing more damage to the long-term health of the planet."

"And the third?" called the impatient man.

"The detonation will deflect the asteroid sufficiently to miss us."

"So why the delay?" shouted another reporter. "If there is any chance, why aren't you going for it?"

"We have to consider the second scenario. If we shatter the asteroid, we may destroy all life on the planet forever."

A young woman stood up and called from the back. "But what is that to us? Surely that is not a consideration if there is any hope at all."

"It depends on the degree of hope. We do have a responsibility to salvage whatever we can, whether or not that will include ourselves."

This was followed by an uproar of noise and the chief raised his hand and waved for quiet. He was just about heard saying he had to go back to his control room. He realised that he and his team could turn out to be the greatest of heroes – but if they decided to sacrifice the current life on the planet for its long-term survival, he knew that they would risk being attacked by an angry mob and not even live to see the final collision when it came.

As they stood and took all this in, the Smiths were buffeted by people who were on the edge of panic, but within minutes reports came in that the operations team had made their decision – there was sufficient hope for the detonation to be attempted. People calmed down. There was still a chance they would survive. Now pictures of the asteroid from a telescope on a high mountain were being broadcast. It seemed so small, so innocuous. It was no wonder that it had only been spotted ten days before.

Some claimed they saw the explosion on their screens. Some didn't. All agreed they didn't see any difference. The asteroid was still in one piece.

The presenter went on to interview a scientist. He seemed distracted. He, like everyone else, was waiting for a report from the control centre. Ten minutes later it came. The asteroid remained intact but there was no detectable deflection. The presenter asked everyone to keep calm; the president was about to make an announcement. It seemed preprepared. The face of a serious-looking balding man appeared on the screen. "All people of the planet," he began, "you have just heard that the only and final hope of deflecting the asteroid, Trum Penta, from a catastrophic collision with our planet has failed. The event that we have been dreading for generations has become a reality. We have to prepare ourselves to perish. Allow me to say straightaway, it has been a privilege to serve you. However, let us not despair," he added hastily. "Many satellites have left the orbit of our planet over the years, bearing the history and achievements of our species. A final rocket with a complete digital library of all we have accumulated through the years will be launched tomorrow. This will preserve our legacy – no matter how long it takes before it comes into contact with intelligent life elsewhere."

He went on to describe some of the highlights of their civilisation – the man-made triumphs to be proud of. It made their civilisation sound like something very special indeed.

He continued, "And now, I urge you not to cause greater suffering by uncontrolled behaviour in these last few days. We want to leave a good account of ourselves should this planet ever be recolonised. Let them find our civilisation intact. We have four days; let that be a time in which we can exercise the highest cultural values of which we are so very proud.

"Attend and tune-in to concerts of the best music, meet

for readings of the richest literature, and let our private art collectors display their prize treasures for all to see alongside the collections of our museums and galleries. May these few days be a culture-fest of enormous proportions.

"Thank you for electing me to be your commander-in-chief at this momentous period in our history. I repeat, it has been an honour to serve."

The people in the hotel bar began to talk heatedly. They had listened patiently to his description of the race but had not been so pleased with the president's talking of his own service. Some wanted to blame the asteroid on him.

However, the president hadn't yet finished. The face on the screen took on a brighter expression. People shushed each other to listen. "You would expect me to tell you that we have contingencies to preserve our species. Indeed we have. One thousand preselected individuals will be taken to an ark in orbit with the intention of resettling the planet when it is habitable again. These people know who they are. I beg you, in the interests of our species, to allow them to proceed without hindrance to the base of which they have been informed. They have been selected to preserve diversity but all have abilities and knowledge that will be necessary for successful recolonisation. One thousand people is as many as we can manage. We are very conscious that this is a very small number in terms of saving a species, so every effort has been put into ensuring the maximum DNA diversity possible – effort that has been contributed by people who have not included themselves in the 1,000.

"I call upon these chosen people to follow their instructions immediately. If you are not one of them, then please listen carefully to the following from a leading professor from our most esteemed institution, Professor Pluck."

The president smiled as his face faded from the screen. *Yuk,* thought Kakko. *He's positively smarmy. I would not put it past him organising an asteroid strike so he can claim the real estate for himself afterwards. I bet he's among the 1,000.*

Professor Pluck came on and began by speaking in a calm voice. He went on to explain that panic was a guaranteed way of having four days of misery. It was in no-one's interest to become violent; the security forces would not tolerate rioting and would maintain order to the end.

People began to make their way out of the hotel and cross towards the beach.

"What do you reckon our role in all of this is?" asked Kakko, the lines on her forehead deepening.

Wennai looked ashen. Shaun was calm and pulled her towards him. Jalli couldn't stop thinking about Yeka and Matilda.

Jack asked, "What about the children we met? Would that centre still be open?"

"Yes," said Kakko, brightening. "That's a great idea. We can go and help them."

They made their way along the esplanade and then into the streets that led to the industrial estate where the Paradise Centre was situated. It was a very strange atmosphere – some people were rushing around in a kind of frenzy, some had slumped onto the pavement with their backs against walls, lost in some kind of reverie, and others were continuing as if nothing had changed. Perhaps they hadn't picked up on what others had, or perhaps they were deliberately ignoring it in some sort of denial.

The Johians found the Paradise Centre in the place behind the harbour where they remembered it. Some of the children and their leaders were sitting all together with the housemother. Most of the rest of the children were away at school.

The greeting was rapturous. The staff and children were

delighted to see them. Could it be that their off-planet friends were angels come to rescue them? As soon as they were seated, they were plied with cake and tea – but the Smiths had little to offer in return other than to remind them that the Creator was with them whatever the emergency.

All Kakko found to say was to ask the children whether they were having fun. Some of those who remembered her and Tam reminded them of the wonderful outing they had had to Lone Island.

"That was the first time," said a girl now in her early teens. "Since then, Mr Zookas has given us the boat to go lots of times. We have lovely picnics – but no-one tells us stories like you."

"Yes, Kakko, tell us a story like the one about the beers," said another.

"The beers?" wondered Kakko, thinking hard.

"Yes," smiled the housemother, "the three beers and the naughty little girl. They love it – but none of us can tell it like you can… Children, let us wait until everyone comes back from school and perhaps Kakko will tell it to us again."

"Ah. Yes, you mean the three *bears*. No problem. Of course I will."

After that, the children were sent back to their chores while the leaders talked.

"The children are not aware of what is happening. They know something is up. Mr Zookas has offered to take us all to the island. We think it might be safer there. We are frightened of a criminal element going berserk. We want the children to end their lives having fun." She wept. "We are trying not to alarm them… It is difficult. But your coming has made it a whole lot easier… I don't know what the Creator is playing at. Why bring you to a planet about to die? You don't have to be here."

"No, we don't," said Jalli. "I would be lying if I were to say that this isn't a scary assignment. But we may be able to leave the same way we came before the asteroid arrives..." She thought of Yeka and Matilda and the resonances of her own life. "But, whatever happens, the Creator will look after us – all of us. I think our coming is to reassure you that the Creator doesn't desert us ever – especially when the worst seems about to happen."

"I know you don't believe death is the end."

"Certainly not. Death cannot extinguish love. I don't know how it happens, or what life is like in the Creator's spirit dimension, but I do believe He has us safe in His hands. I have a lot I want to keep in this universe – I have a three-year-old to mother – but I have a lot to look forward to in eternity, too."

"Thank you," said the housemother, "I needed to hear that... Ah, here is Mr Zookas and Dr Jaffan... Welcome both."

Zookas was delighted to see the Smiths. He was introduced to Wennai.

"You come at a critical time. But I guess you're not staying for the finale."

"Probably not," said Jack taking his hand, "but until then we are here to do what we can."

"Our plan is to get all the children to the island... Dr Jaffan here has a wife and two children – one a new born child... she is only a month old. He wants to come with us and bring them. I have organised our boats and we can get them all in – including you if you want to join us."

Jalli looked at Kakko and Shaun. The island sounded good but their white gate was next to the toilet block on the esplanade.

"When do you hope to leave?" asked Kakko.

"This evening, as soon as the children have returned from school and have eaten. The sooner the better because we do not know how secure things will remain… I am fearful that too many people will decide to raid the liquor shops to drown out their fear."

"A last fling," said Shaun, wryly.

"Precisely."

"We shall be pleased to come with you," said Kakko, emphatically. Tam looked at Jalli, who thought for a moment and then nodded. Her trust in the Creator was getting stretched but she was proud of her daughter nevertheless.

Tam stood by Kakko and said, "Yes, of course. We're here to help… But I don't know if you need all of us on the island. Shaun has been through quite a bit recently. I suggest just Kakko and I go. Maybe the Creator has got something different worked out for the rest of us," he said calmly.

"Maybe," said Shaun, gently.

"Absolutely," said Kakko.

"A cup of tea, Mr Zookas?" said the housemother.

"That would be good. I have one or two phone calls I must make."

Just then Dr Jaffan's phone bleeped. A text. Jalli noticed his expression as he read it.

The others were chatting away, being cheered up by Kakko's positivity. She was saying that the end of the world was not the end of the world. At that moment, she clearly believed it.

Jalli spoke quietly to the doctor. "This is very hard for you," she said, "especially with a newborn."

"Yes," he answered. He looked into her eyes. "You are from the Creator?"

Jalli nodded. "We believe He is the one who provides us with the white gates."

"Can I talk to you without this going outside – out there?" He inclined his head to the door.

"I don't know anyone out there. We only arrived this morning."

"I must tell someone… The thing is, I have been called to be among the 1,000 to leave for orbit… I passed out of medical school as the top-qualifying student of my year and I am the youngest consultant in the hospital here. That has not gone unnoticed among those who have selected the most able to be included in the party aimed at preserving the race… It means I am expected to *rendez-vous* this afternoon at an address near here and be taken to a space shuttle."

"That is wonderful for you. You will survive. You have hope."

"But it's just me. My wife and children are not included… I am supposed to leave in just two hours. I must go home now and explain to them… A big part of me is telling me to stay but…"

"But you want to do your duty as a doctor."

"Correct. It's not about saving my life… truly. I became a doctor because I wanted to use my skills to help people. And this is the best way of doing that now – fulfilling that calling."

"But you are also a husband and a father."

"I am."

"Which calling comes first?"

"It depends on whose point of view you take. Clearly the president believes that I should be part of his race preservation plan… And in four days," he shuddered, "my wife and children will be in the spiritual realms."

"But these four days are so important. Four days in which the need for love is greatest."

"You're right."

"So what are you going to do?"

"I don't know. You tell me."

"I think a policy that divides families is misplaced. You are going to make a new start with bereaved and broken people. They may never get over that."

"You're right. That's what I needed to hear. I cannot follow my calling if I have abandoned those I love. I now have a clear conscience. I shall not go."

Jalli thought a moment. "Look, why don't you just turn up with your family. There might be people like yourself who have decided not to obey the president – people who simply cannot leave their loved ones. It could be that your wife and children can all get a ride, too. If not, you can make your decision then."

"I thought of that. If we did arrive as a family, we would probably not be the only ones. They would almost certainly turn us all away."

"Then the decision will be made for you. You won't know unless you try."

Shaun and Wennai joined them. "This conversation a secret?"

"Not from you," said the doctor. He repeated what he had told Jalli.

"And I said he should turn up with his wife and babies," said Jalli.

"Where do you have to go?" asked Shaun.

"Not a block from here, in fact. There is a truck leaving at half past four from the other side of the industrial estate. It will transport us to the shuttle base. A truck like that will not attract attention."

"So, no hassle. Take them with you… unless you don't want to go at all," said Shaun.

"You don't have to decide now. You don't have to get on the truck," said Wennai confidently. "Can we come with you? If you have to leave your family we'll take care of them. We'll bring them back here and they can go with the children to the island."

"Would you?"

"No problem," said Shaun. "They don't need us here. They're not going anywhere until after school is out. They are not rushing."

An hour later, Shaun and Wennai travelled with Dr Jaffan to meet his family. As soon as he arrived, his wife, Neeka, clung to him. The news was bleak. The official line now was that the asteroid may just miss the planet – but Neeka was sceptical.

"I don't believe it. They are only saying it to keep people calm. The president comes on the media every fifteen minutes, appealing to everyone not to panic. They've got this comedian on, making jokes of how silly some people will look after the asteroid misses…"

"Neeka, I need you to listen to me carefully. Let me introduce some new friends I have just met at the children's centre." He introduced Shaun and Wennai.

Neeka shook hands and smiled. "You are so young. I am sorry—"

"Neeka," insisted her husband, "let's sit down. I need you to listen. There is much to explain."

"But you must," protested Neeka.

"No. I have thought about this. I will not be able to live and be part of any new beginning without you. If the authorities have not taken relationship and emotional needs into consideration in their choice of survivors, then the whole venture will be a failure from the start…"

"But—"

"No. Listen. Jalli here has suggested something that might just work. I will not be the only one of the selected 1,000 feeling this way. There could be any number of people turning down their places. Jalli suggests that I turn up this afternoon with both you and the children. If there are places spare, they may well take you."

"But *lots* of non-chosen people will be trying to get aboard."

"Yes. But they don't all know about turning up at a truck depot. The place is not operating – the workers there have all been sent home."

"What about you?" asked Neeka, addressing Shaun and Wennai.

"We have our own way of leaving this planet," explained Shaun. He explained about the white gate. Neeka found it hard to believe.

"Their parents first came here many years ago," her husband told her. "They brought their children last time – a couple of years ago. Pero told us about them. They are often talked about at the Paradise Centre."

"So someone outside this world knows all about us," said Neeka.

"Someone cares enough to help us now."

"We – my family – believe it is the Creator who provides the white gates," said Shaun, "but whether or not the gates come from God," he gave Wennai a glance, "you can be certain that this planet is not the only one to have human beings on it. We know of six more, and a seventh which has just been colonised. There will be more."

"Somehow that makes this crisis seem less awful," said Neeka ruefully.

"It might be literally world-shattering but it's a local crisis…" said Jaffan.

The president reappeared on the TV with his appeal.

"If we are going, we have to go now. Just pack what we need for a few days. We are allowed two suitcases."

"I must take my favourite novels…" said Neeka.

"No need. Everything that was ever published has

been uploaded onto the spaceship's database. Take the children's picture books – all the family pictures are on the computer—"

"How long have you known about this, Jaffan?"

"I have known I was on a preserve list since I passed out of college. I never thought it would happen but the rules were to back up everything we needed – just in case."

"Brilliant. What else don't I know about my husband?"

"I never thought it was important…"

"You'd better get ready," intervened Shaun. "Can we help?"

"You could tell the kids a story – The Three Beers."

"Fine," smiled Shaun, "only I can't tell it quite like my sister."

Shaun and Wennai, however, made a good team. Soon the three-year-old was engrossed in the fairy stories Shaun had in his repertoire. He had had a lot of practice with Yeka.

I can see why he is Yeka's favourite, thought Wennai to herself; *he's so good with children.* But soon she found herself playing with the baby and trying to get her to smile. She was also aware of the need for a nappy change. She called up to Neeka. Neeka told her where to find things and she soon had her dry and comfortable. Shaun was impressed.

"Where'd you learn to do that?"

"I don't know. Mostly instinct, I suppose. There's nothing highly technical about changing a nappy."

"No. I don't suppose so. But if that had been me, I would not have looked so confident."

"That's because Jalli and Kakko have always got in first. And that's why Yeka likes you so much. You don't have to be so practical. You can look after the inner needs." She held her hand to the three-year-old who was getting impatient because Shaun's attention had been diverted.

"Does that mean that if I ever had any children, I should avoid changing happies and feeding?"

"No. It doesn't," said Wennai decisively.

It occurred to them both where this conversation was going and, feeling embarrassed, Shaun looked away and began to look for a toy to play with, and Wennai cooed to the baby from whom she had extracted a smile – or perhaps it was just wind.

"I do hope they all get aboard," said Shaun, becoming a little agitated. "What about all those others…?"

"Don't think about the 'what ifs'," said Wennai. "You of all people should be the least worried because you believe life is forever."

"You're right. And, whatever happens, this moment is good, now. What has gone, has gone. What is to come, has not happened yet."

Wennai stopped cooing. Yes, now is good. I don't want now to change but it will, and it will not change backwards. The bad things of the past have gone, never to return. And the future… There is always hope."

"And there is always love. That doesn't depend on us."

"You are right. You know, you have taught me something about love… Not like most other boys. Love for you isn't that romantic."

"I know. I'm sorry."

"Don't be. Your kind of love is deeper, beyond words. You're the only person outside of my family who has a clue of what it was like to lose my mother when I was thirteen…"

"Right," grunted Dr Jaffan, as he and Neeka staggered down their stairs with five large suitcases. "All packed and ready to go… I see you have made some new friends, children."

They all bundled into the doctor's car. Shaun sat in the back with Wennai on his lap next to the children in their car seats. It was a bit of a squash but they only had a few hundred metres to go. A few minutes later they had pulled into the car park of the truck depot. A few other cars were there but not that many. This particular departure point was for only seventy of the 1,000, and they still had half an hour to go before the scheduled departure. There were two men in uniform checking identities against a list.

"Dr Jaffan?" He placed a tick against his name on his list. "But there is no mention of anyone else in your party."

"No," said the doctor, "but my wife and children are on the reserve list."

"Reserve list? I haven't heard anything about a reserve list."

"Haven't you? You are not allowed to leave light," he said in an authoritative tone. "If you have spaces at the scheduled time of departure, you are to include reserves."

The officer looked at him suspiciously. "And these others…?"

"… are here to take the children away if there is no room for them."

"Makes sense," said the second officer.

"How come my family is not on the reserve list?" answered the first.

"How come anyone isn't? They can only take 1,000. You and I are the lucky ones. Look, we have the president, his wife and the vice president on our list. As soon as they arrive we are to leave. If we do not have a full complement by then, then the president himself can say whether or not these people come."

"Yeah. That would work. OK, ma'am, you can stay here pending the arrival of the president. You need to sit in your car."

"Thank you, officer," said Dr Jaffan with a satisfied expression.

"The president," said Shaun, as they walked back to the car. "You're honoured."

"Are we?" questioned Jaffan with a rueful smile. "I notice he is bringing *his* wife… who is past child-bearing age."

31

Earlier that afternoon in the president's residence, the president and his wife were preparing to leave. Together with the vice president they were to be taken to the truck depot behind the industrial estate. An hour before, the president had recorded a series of addresses due to be released at regular intervals over the next three days. It would give the impression that he was still alongside his people – even if he was holed up inside his opulent residence. In the morning he had emerged in public to be interviewed at a press conference. That would be the last time his people would see him in the flesh.

As they waited for the allotted time of departure, he sat in his office and looked around him.

"It is not a good thought to think that all of this will end," he said to his vice president. "It seems a shame to leave all that top – quality liquor in the cabinet. Let's see. What can we find? Ah, yes. This rare tipple—"

"You have called on your people not to drink. It is a recipe for a collapse of order," said his wife stridently.

The president turned to her, accusingly. "There is drinking and drinking. Do you think we should ignore this opportunity? I think not." He took out a glass and filled it to the brim and gave it to the vice president. His wife declined and walked from the room. She knew what was going to happen. The two of them would be nigh-on drunk before they set off for the transport. Inside the truck, however, there would be no privacy. The president and vice president would show themselves up for the self-seeking mediocre men they really were – in the presence of the nation's finest and most intelligent young men and women! However, the first lady had other plans.

Sometimes she had wondered why she ever fell for the man who was to become president. She had to admit that she had fallen for his charm and his wit, the same as millions of the electorate in the years that followed. They had had no children but the man had fathered a number with other women. She didn't know about them all but she knew of some that her husband didn't. It was amazing how he got away with it. At least three former lovers were being kept sweet by the luxury bestowed on them. But, despite all this, his wife had stayed by his side – there were many perks in being the first lady. And any rift was bound to affect her reputation more than her husband's. But now, she concluded, the game was up. There was no way her husband should be inflicted on the selected survivors. The vice president was equally corrupt.

She strode purposefully towards the little house in the grounds that belonged to the gardener and his family. She had befriended him years before. The magnificent garden was his work. Over many years he had turned it from a wilderness into an amazing collection of the most beautiful plants to behold and the most delicious products to eat. The president never bothered with him – he was too busy to think about who lay behind the garden he used to impress with. But his wife took a great interest. The garden was her escape, her solace, and she knew that the gardener and his son, who, as a boy, had been learning the trade from his father, would be a huge asset among the 1,000 – far, far more than her husband and the vice president.

Two hours earlier, when the president was signing his final decrees – decrees in readiness for a new administration after the impact – she had secreted a paper which declared that, although he and his deputy were honoured to be chosen among the 1,000 to refound the civilisation, they were not going to take up the opportunity. Those recolonising the planet should choose an appropriate governmental structure as they found fit. Furthermore, she ordered that the gardener and his wife and their son be part of the survival contingent.

The first lady made her way to the cottage to check on the gardener's readiness. The family were nervous but ready to go. She then returned to the kitchen and ordered strong black coffee for herself and her husband and the vice president. She waited for it to be prepared so she could take it into the office in person.

Placing the tray down on a hall table before entering, she laced two cups with strong sleeping powders.

The president was saying far too loudly, "You know, with a bit of luck this building will survive." He was already quite drunk.

"Return to power," drawled his deputy.

"Absolutely. Why not?"

"Your term of office is due to end in eighteen months."

"Ah. I see. So you think it is your turn," shouted the president, aggressively.

"Yeah."

"If you think I'm taking you with me so you can take over from me, you have another think coming!"

"If you want my opinion," slurred the vice president, "I don't think you should be going at all. You should stay here and stand with your people – a captain goes down with his ship," he slurred.

"And leave the future in your hands! I shall have you shot."

"Boys! Boys!" the president's wife interrupted. "You've had far too much to drink… Get this coffee down you. They'll be coming for you in less than fifteen minutes."

"Better do as she says," mocked the president. "Pity I have to take you…"

The vice president laughed, "Whereas I am forced to leave my old crone behind… Take my pick of the lovely young—"

"Get this coffee down you," ordered the first lady.

The two men laughed as they heaped spoonfuls of sugar into their cups and stirred.

Minutes later they had both passed out. The benzodiazepine combined with the alcohol had worked rapidly. The first lady wondered if she'd overdone it, but her husband grunted, indicating he was still breathing. She found the order, stepped out into the hallway and entered the garden, where she summoned the gardener and asked him and his family to follow her back into the residence.

The main door was opened by a security guard and a driver admitted. The first lady handed him the order. He read it. He raised his eyebrows, then nodded. He smiled. "Tell the president his people are proud of him… and of you, too," he added.

"I am to accompany them to the truck depot to ensure there are no hitches," she said, authoritatively.

"Come," he said, "let us go."

★ ★ ★

Shaun and the others in the car didn't have to wait long. People kept arriving, being checked in and taking their places in the back of two articulated trucks. Ten minutes before the deadline, a rather grand-looking car swept in

and drove straight up to the impromptu desk the officers
had set up. They watched as the four occupants stepped
out of it.

"That's the first lady," said Neeka. "But I don't recognise
the others... A man and a woman around forty and a young
man in his late teens."

"I don't know them either," said her husband. "But
the first lady seems to be negotiating their passage." They
continued to watch as one of the officers read a paper given
them by the first lady, looked up at her and then passed it to
his colleague. The two officers exchanged a quick word and
the man, woman and young man were directed to get into
one of the trucks. The first lady took each of them by the
hand in turn as if to wish them goodbye. The officer then
spoke again to her, who nodded. She made every sign that
she wasn't going to board. The two officers began to confer.
Something seemed to be wrong – or at least something that
required an earnest tête-à-tête. One of the officers looked
up and beckoned Dr Jaffan to come over. The doctor and his
family, together with Shaun and Wennai, got out of the car
and walked to the desk.

The officer who had beckoned them spoke.

"Doctor, you know our first lady?"

"Yes, of course. I've seen you on the television but we have
not met. Pleased to meet you. I'm Dr Jaffan and this is my
wife, Neeka, and my child, Kijo, and baby daughter, Jade, and
our new friends Wennai and Shaun." They all greeted one
another with handshakes and hugs for the women.

The officer spoke up. "The president and the first lady and
the vice president were allocated places on the shuttles. They
were to be in our contingent. However, they have declined
the invitation and the president has nominated an experienced
horticulturist and his apprentice son. He is of the opinion

families should be together and so the lad's mother is also included. Except for one no-show whom we believe is sick in hospital, this completes the complement... However..." He paused, his face of authority crumpled.

"My friend and I," put in the second officer, "have decided we are going to follow the example of our president and his wife. We are in the number but we are sure that security officers are not necessary... not as necessary as a wife and two babies to support this doctor."

"We want to return to be alongside our own families... and die with them. That is where our hearts are; that is where we belong. We all have to die sometime and we do not want to spend years without them." The other officer nodded his agreement.

"This way, we travel to the next world together," he said. "I do not believe this world is all there is – there is life in a new dimension. We have learned that God answers prayer. This is His answer to mine right now."

"So, Doctor," said the first, "you can take your wife and children in our place." Then he looked up at Wennai and Shaun with genuine sadness. "I'm sorry but we cannot take you. You are still young but—"

"Oh, no!" said Shaun quickly. "We cannot go with you. We must stay here. We... I... have family here. The Creator will see we are where we need to be."

Wennai was appalled at the idea. The thought of being stuck with just 1,000 people with all her family on a completely different planet was horrific. Even if there had been room, she would not have boarded that truck.

"Come," said the first lady, "let us go and leave these people to depart."

Dr Jaffan and his family got into the truck but not before they gave Wennai and Shaun huge hugs. "You are indeed angels from God; there is no way we can thank you enough."

"Whatever. No problem." Wennai shrugged and lowered her eyes.

"All aboard!" said Shaun forcefully to cover her embarrassment. *An angel... from God!* He wondered if Wennai would ever want to talk about that.

The officers spoke to the drivers, who began to secure their trailers.

Shaun and Wennai waved. "Good luck," called Shaun as the doors closed.

The trucks pulled out and the first lady smiled.

"Well, I think that went off beautifully. Thank you both," she said to the officers. "We are proud to have such caring people on this planet. Allow me to take you to your families on my way back to the presidential residence."

"In the limo?"

"Of course, I have no other vehicle. And you two, also. Where are you going?"

"The Paradise Centre," replied Shaun.

Within minutes they were driving up to the Paradise Centre. The children were wild with excitement to see them get out of the president's limousine. Soon they were telling their story.

"The first lady?" said the housemother. "Not the president himself?"

"No," answered Shaun.

"You can be sure who runs this country. I bet she's got him tied up somewhere." They all laughed.

Back in the president's residence, the president and the vice president were coming round just as the first lady walked back into the office.

"What the hell is happening?" demanded the president, holding his head; it felt more painful than he could ever remember.

"You passed out," his wife replied. "I told you not to drink."

"We have to go. They will be waiting for us."

"You missed the boat, or rather the transport to the shuttles, some time ago."

"What?"

She turned on the TV. Pictures of the shuttles about to take off were on the screen.

"A thousand people carefully selected from a cross-section of training and ability are leaving for orbit. They will be safe, but for the rest of us there is a glimmer of hope. Experts at the asteroid-tracking centres are still reporting that there is a chance – a small one – that Trum Penta may just miss us."

An interview with an elderly scientist was screened. He was asked, "Can we believe this or are we being told this just to keep us all calm?"

He answered that no-one could say for certain that the planet was doomed but he felt that everyone should prepare for the worst. "If it strikes the planet a glancing blow, that could be worse than a direct hit because it could disrupt the planet's rotation and even its course in space. But we simply do not know anything for certain. That is the honest answer."

The presenter then said the president had issued an update.

"Many thought that he would be numbered among the 1,000, but he has made a statement that he is still with them." They played his recorded interview.

Afterwards, a commentator remarked that he had made no comment on the latest news, including a riot that had erupted in the south. "Do we indeed still have our president with us? There is a strong rumour that this interview was prerecorded."

"Get some water down you and get out there," ordered the first lady to both men, who were now coming to terms with what was happening. "They need to see you in person. If you get this right, and if the asteroid misses the planet, you will become the heroes of the nation. If you get it wrong, you'll be forever the wimps. You might as well be as powerful and charming as you can while it lasts."

The president went to argue but his head hurt so badly he thought better of it. The thing was, she was right, she always had been. He drank his water without saying a word as his wife wrote his speech.

Distinguished citizens of our planet. I beg to address you at this critical point in our history. I thank you for sparing me a few moments of your very precious time.

Some have suggested that I and my wife would desert our planet in this its greatest hour of need. But while there is life here, I and my dear wife will remain. We have sent 1,000 people to safety – not just for their sakes but for all of us. They are the future. We have bequeathed to them our great culture and we trust them. Maybe they can begin a new civilisation in which our notorious history of conflict is a thing of the past. We have ensured that, not only ability, but the ultimate values of love and commitment are represented among them. That is why some are travelling as families.

For the millions of us who remain on the surface, our challenge is different but the values are the same. Love is the first and last thing about being human. It is the indestructible spark that can never be extinguished by the dark – even the threat of death. The more the darkness squeezes, the brighter the spark shines.

Brothers and sisters, I believe – I know – there is a future for all of us. It may not be on this planet but in the Creator's eternal spheres. Let us keep calm and put love first.

I will be present at the service of prayer and celebration in the City Cathedral tomorrow morning. I hope that as many of you as can make it will be there and in the square in front of it. I charge the city authorities to organise the televising and relaying of this service throughout the nation. Be there, with me, at noon tomorrow when we will affirm the greatest thing that our race has ever achieved. The willingness to give our lives in the service of love.

32

The children squealed with delight when they were told that they were all going to Lone Island again. Kakko and Shaun had returned. Those who remembered the first time they were there began to infect the others with their enthusiasm.

All this excitement filled the hearts of the Smith family with deep sadness. The children had no idea that the odds were they would never return from the island – indeed, that after just three sleeps, there would not even be a recognisable planet, let alone an island.

As each hour passed, a sense of panic mixed with despair was increasing in the city. Some had decided that the answer was to get to higher ground. If Trum Penta hit the sea, the resulting tsunami would be the greatest danger – they may be safe in the foothills of the mountains. But these were remote and accessed by tiny roads which were already congested almost to the perimeter of the city.

Reports of rioting in some places were emerging. The president again appeared on TV appealing for calm – but those who were causing the disturbances had long since given up listening to him.

It was essential to get the children out onto the island so their last few days could be ones of fun and laughter. The Smiths focused themselves on achieving this. Nothing was going to be gained by thinking about what came next.

Jalli, however, couldn't forget Yeka. The thought of her three-year-old being in exactly the same situation as she had been was now almost unbearable.

Jack knew what she was thinking. "Jalli," he said, "all we can do is trust God. Your grandma didn't lose faith in Him despite everything. We are in His hands now. We are here because He wants us here."

Jalli wept. She clung to her husband. Yes, of course, he was right. "But it's so hard, Jack."

"I know," he said, as Jalli sank into his strong warmth.

But now there was no time for many tears. The housemother was calling the children together. Jalli and Jack were pulled back into the group beside the others from Joh. The housemother looked them all in the eye. She was conscious of the sacrifice they were making.

"You people have done so much. Maybe it is time for you to return. Your portal is not on this island and, the way things are on the streets, if you are going to leave, now might be the right time to head for the esplanade and your white gate."

Shaun was taken aback when Wennai was the first to respond.

"I do not speak for everyone. But there is no way I'm going to leave these children. You will need all the help you can get." That was indeed true. Most of the centre's volunteers were at home with their families.

Shaun heard himself say, "Me too... I'm staying too." At that moment, something within him snapped. Somehow the scars in his mind had freed him up. Later he was to reflect that ever since the time when he thought his life was about to end and it hadn't, he had been living in a different, borrowed kind of place; he had already shifted onto a new plane. It was the same with Wennai. In the midst of her bereavement and the collapse of her world, she too had moved on to that plane. For them, choosing to remain wasn't about bravery – although many might call it that – it was simply the obvious thing to do.

At that moment, for the first time, Shaun properly realised that he and Wennai had been given each other. Even if Wennai didn't believe in Her like he did, the Creator wanted them to be together. If they were to die together four days from now and emerge into the Creator's arms, she would have to concede that he had been right all along. He smiled at the thought.

Wennai looked him. "What's funny?"

"I'm just proud of you. That's all."

"If you think *I'm* running away," Kakko was saying emphatically, "you're living in 'cloud cuckoo land' as Nan would call it!"

Tam put his arm around her shoulders and held her to him. "My parents are right. You are a bad influence. If we ever get back to Joh, don't tell them I had a choice in this."

"You don't," said Kakko stridently. "You'll never leave me. I never ever want you on a planet other than the one I'm on."

"Well," said Jack to the housemother, "you seem to have your answer."

"Angels! All of you. Praise the Lord... OK, children!"

The children were so excited they were too high to listen.

"Children!" She held up her hands.

"Listen! Now," bawled Jack. Working with children for so long had given him the instinct of how to control the unruly. The children were instantly quiet. The shock of a loud voice from a stranger worked wonders.

"Listen," repeated Jack in a whisper. "This is very important. You don't want to get lost. And I can't see, so I have to listen even harder."

The housemother looked at him with gratitude. This exercise was going to work so much better with these people.

Half an hour later they were speeding across the waves towards the island. The boat was stocked up with all the things they would need for four days. Zookas had been collecting everything together over the hours before the children's return. They arrived at the tiny island jetty just as the sun was about to set.

Zookas had sent a giant marquee. It had last been used for his son's wedding in the grounds of his villa. From there, Zookas had watched as his boat sped towards the island. He and his family were behind locked gates. They hoped they would avoid any trouble as they relaxed in the luxury of the terrace awaiting the impending disaster. He had done all he could. He smiled at the thought of the children having a great time in blissful ignorance.

The marquee took a couple of hours to sort out but it was eventually erected. The children had been fed. Kakko told stories as the darkness closed in. None of the children had been on the island in the dark before, so huddling together in the giant tent was quite an adventure in itself.

It would be wrong to say that that night was peaceful. Eventually the last child fell asleep at around half past two in the morning. And all were awake at first light around six o'clock. The Johians had been very tired. Entering a new world was always exhausting in itself as the brain has to get accustomed to the sudden changes – but to enter a world with a death sentence hanging over it is twice as hard. They had slept in fits and starts but now this new day had to be faced. Somehow eighty children had to be entertained for the next fifteen hours!

The breakfast took an age. Getting everybody washed and fed was hard through the non-stop bubbling excitement of the children. Eventually it was decided that a walk around the island was the order of the day for the rest of the morning. They split the children into groups as they became ready. The older ones had got themselves sorted long before the younger ones and needed to be organised. Shaun and Wennai took the first batch, Kakko and Tam the second, Jalli and a volunteer the third. The stragglers were collected up by the housemother and a couple of other adults, leaving Jack, together with the boat's crew, to mind the camp.

The first group hadn't gone too far round the island, however, when they came across a few roughly dressed people who had just disembarked from a boat. They had cans in their hands and were smoking something. Then Shaun and Wennai looked up and saw a veritable flotilla of medium and small craft approaching with unhealthy-looking people leaning dangerously over the sides. As the boats got near the beach, some of the occupants disembarked, splashing into the water. They were mostly drunk and began shouting obscenities towards the children.

Shaun and Wennai gathered their charges and withdrew over the dunes, fearful that they would be pursued. They weren't. But their idea of retreating to the island to keep the children from the disturbances on the mainland had failed. These people couldn't have owned all these boats but they appeared to be the kind who would have little compunction about stealing them.

Running into Kakko and Tam's group, Shaun and Wennai suggested they stay together and steer away from that particular beach.

Fortunately, they weren't bothered by the drunkards for the rest of that day, although they could hear their bawling and brawling as the sun set. After one o'clock in the morning the noise seemed to die down. That second night the children were so tired, they slept better. So did everyone.

★ ★ ★

It was the next morning, in the middle of the football tournament that Kakko and Shaun had arranged on some flat ground some way from the camp, that the trouble started. A loud group of half-naked young men came bounding over the dunes that overlooked the marquee. They swung pieces of driftwood over their heads and looked for all the world like stereotypes of Stone-Age cave – dwellers. They stormed towards Zookas' yacht, probably intending to raid the supplies – or whatever else they could get. They didn't get there. The captain pulled a gun from somewhere in the wheelhouse and fired over their heads. He shouted that if they approached any nearer he wouldn't hesitate to shoot them. The only people who stood in the way of the club-wielding mob were the captain, three crewmen and Jack and Jalli. But the group hesitated. The captain ordered them to go back the way they had come. He let off a second volley and spurts of sand erupted in front of them. The men ran back out of sight.

The captain swore. "That's all we need. We'll have to have two of us keep a constant watch."

But the cavemen did not return. That night – the last night before the asteroid was to strike – their noise was less. The asteroid was now very clearly visible in the night sky. Jalli stared at it. It had a name – Trum Penta. It, too, was coming to an end, like it was on some kind of cosmic suicide mission.

"You know," she said to Jack, "if I didn't think it was going to destroy this place, I would say that it was remarkably beautiful…"

In the morning Jack said that he thought their unwanted island residents must have gone: he could hear nothing. Kakko volunteered herself and Tam to go out and check. She really wanted an excuse to be alone with him. They didn't know where or when – or if – the Creator was going to provide them with a white gate for escape. This could be the last time they could be together alone in this universe.

They mounted the dunes and, hand in hand, sauntered along talking and occasionally cuddling. Praying too. Neither felt far from the Creator and, as the strike came closer, they felt even closer to Her.

Then between the trees they saw the cavemen's camp. The sand was strewn with bodies. Some lay quite still, others were moving but only just. The only sounds that came from them were occasional low groans. There were both men and women, all young and all almost naked. The bodies were red with sunburn which would have been painful if they had been conscious.

Kakko and Tam looked at one another with puzzled expressions.

"Suicide pact?" said Kakko.

"It would have been easier and less painful if they had merely waited for the strike," said Tam.

They walked over to the camp. It was clear that many were dead, but a few remained alive – just.

"What are we going to do?" asked Kakko. "We can't just leave them."

"I don't think this was deliberate," said Tam picking up bottles and packets that contained pills of different colours. "I think they must have raided pharmacies and liquor stores and created lethal cocktails. I don't think they had any idea of what they were doing."

"If some are still alive, they might survive," said Kakko.

"They won't out here in the sun."

"Perhaps we should drag those who are alive to under those trees," said Kakko.

"OK. I'll begin doing that. You run and tell the captain. Even if we can get them into the shade, they'll need hydrating."

Fifteen minutes later the captain and his crew were on the beach. They found just ten with signs of life. The captain ordered them to be taken to one of the small boats that they had arrived in and they sailed it back to the yacht.

The survivors were all taken aboard while the children watched. They had seen a lot in their short lifetimes but they had not seen people in quite this state.

"Remember this," said the housemother. "This is what happens when you do drink and drugs. I want you to promise me that you will never use them."

"We promise," said one, and then a wave of "Promise" spread across the group.

"This is our last day on the island so I want you all to pack your things," said the housemother. "Do it carefully. I want you to account for everything. We need to look for Kali's sock – it has to have got in someone else's stuff."

"And my shirt," shouted a little boy.

"Alright, check everything you have, and if you find anything that's not yours bring it to me. If you have lost anything then come and collect it. I don't want anything left unclaimed."

Packing was quite a game but eventually everything was found that was lost. A few items of underwear remained in the housemother's possession.

"Remarkable," she said. "Someone must be lacking them…" She trailed off, as on the horizon the large shape of the asteroid could now be seen. It was coming closer. No-one had bothered or wanted to try and listen in to the media, not even the yacht crew, although they had access to radio and TV on board. The news was too depressing. They had gathered that the event in the cathedral had gone off alright had but around the corner a group of demonstrators attempted to stop the president's car as he proceeded back to his residence. Apparently, they were what the media had dubbed strike deniers, who accused the president of making it all up in order to rescue his popularity. The police managed to keep them at bay and the president's motorcade got through.

Some of the forces – police and army – had deserted to be with their families but, after that night, their commanders managed to convince them of the need to remain on duty until the strike. It was quite clear that, with a breakdown in law and order, no-one would have any dignity left. A sense of pride had at last kicked in. The president praised them to the utmost. He promised that they would be held in honour for as long as their civilisation persisted. He assured them he was in constant contact with the 1,000 – all the broadcasts and his many communications were being recorded for posterity.

After that, the crew no longer tuned in to the media. There was much to do looking after ten sick young people as well as the children; and their happy faces were such a blessing in these end times. But now the sight of the asteroid rising above the horizon in the east told them that the prediction of ten minutes past three that afternoon had been accurate. Less than three hours to go.

"Lunch," announced the housemother. The children cheered. The crew turned their attention to laying out the food in the marquee for the final time. Zookas had managed to find the best of everything – things that he had set aside for his honoured guests were now shared among the street children. Of course, they didn't appreciate what they were eating. But it was a feast all the same.

The ten sick cave – dwellers knew nothing of this. They were being hydrated by drips that the crew had to hand in the well-stocked first aid locker. With a bit of luck, at ten past three some might just be fully conscious.

At half past two the children were getting ready for a walk.

"We have time to walk around the island for one last time before we go," announced Kakko.

No white gate had appeared. Perhaps a walk would reveal one. Kakko gave her mother a cuddle. She simply said, "See you on the other side," and set off with Tam with a group of children.

Jalli wept. "That girl, she'll face anything down."

"And so will we. We brought her up. She gets it from us."

"Does she?"

"Yes," said Jack. "She does. She knows what she's doing. She knows what she believes."

Shaun and Wennai were being dragged by impatient children. Jalli ran to them. Like Kakko, she said, "See you on the other side."

"You really do believe," said Wennai, as she held Shaun's hand. "I hope you're right."

"I promise I'll say, 'I told you so'."

"I guess I will have to put up with that. If there is no God, I don't get the last word. It's not fair."

"I'll be kind," Shaun said as light-heartedly as he knew how. It helped that he was being dragged by eager children. "Whoa. We'd better go. These kids are so impatient."

★ ★ ★

When ten past three came, the party were down behind some trees and the asteroid was mercifully hidden from view.

It was the light that changed first. The sky suddenly became golden with red streaks like flames.

"Look, the trees are on fire," yelled a boy. They all stood transfixed. But the trees weren't on fire – the glow was behind them. Shaun, Wennai, Kakko and Tam held each other. They said nothing – this was no time for words, not even to God.

No words were capable of expressing the myriad of thoughts that raced through their brains.

"Wow," said a girl. "What's that? I never seen anything like that before."

"Happens sometimes," Kakko heard herself say. "It will pass. Come on, let's climb the hill to get a better view." To get higher seemed to have purpose. It might just be that the tsunami was a smaller one than predicted and the top of the island would be safe.

As they climbed, the wind began to pick up. It became suddenly stronger – gale-force with frightening gusts. Then normal nature stopped and all they could hear was the howling of the wind and its effects; the sounds of the birds and the sea on what, moments before, had been a beautiful afternoon were transformed into one huge cry of pain. The little group clung to each other to stop themselves being blown away. Some of the children were crying out in panic but their shouts were lost amongst the noisy tempest: thrashing trees, rattling stones, and the screams of the air being forced through the crevices of the cliffs below them. Shaun, Wennai, Kakko and Tam clung on to each other and as many children as they could, their faces down into the sweet-smelling grass, waiting for the end.

Then, almost as suddenly as it had started, the wind quietened and the sky became its normal hue. Had they survived?

They instinctively continued to lead the frightened children to higher ground – no-one expected the planet to explode instantly; now the greatest threat was the sea. As they predicted, at around half past three, great waves began breaking on the shoreline. Was this the herald of the huge tsunami that was predicted to follow the strike?

But the waves did not advance beyond the beach and

instead of getting bigger, diminished. Within minutes all was calm again and the seabirds recommenced their wheeling. Nature had coughed and spluttered but was now back to its most docile. Lone Island basked in the warmth of a bright sunny day as if nothing had happened. The emergency appeared to have passed – for the moment.

"What's happening?" demanded Kakko. "Are we in the middle of a temporary lull or what?"

"I reckon it's missed," answered Tam. "By now we would have felt it through the rocks if there had been a strike. We were face down on the grass; we would have detected any seismic shock."

"Wowee! Are you sure?"

"Pretty sure. Something happened but I don't think it was a strike. The asteroid was on our side of the planet; we saw it over there. If it had hit, we'd know. I reckon it just skimmed the atmosphere – that would explain the shockwaves we experienced."

"That close, but gone? I can't believe it. God, I don't want to go through anything like that again. I thought I was a goner... Let's get back to the yacht." She jumped around with a joy.

In contrast to his excited sister, Shaun stood up slowly and looked down at Wennai who remained sitting on the grass. He still had hold her of hand; he had crushed it in his own in an attempt to keep her close. Looking up at the sky, he said quietly, "I'm getting used to this. For some reason this universe is not yet done with me."

Wennai looked up at him. "You're telling me that I am not dead? I was just bracing myself to hear you say, 'I told you so'."

"No. We haven't died. We still have that to come."

"Can I have my hand back?"

"Oh. Yeah. Sorry. I didn't want to let you go."

"Thought you would pull me through, did you?"

"Something like that, I guess."

Tam called on the children to stop racing up the hill. "Time to go back," yelled Kakko. Some of the children were beginning to get a bit naughty. They sensed something momentous had happened. The wind had given them extra energy; they didn't want to go home to the mainland and they were applying all the usual delaying tactics.

When they came in sight of the boat, the captain was waving to them.

"It's over!" he was shouting. "It's over!"

As Kakko, Tam, Shaun and Wennai puffed up to him, he spluttered, "Just point two of a degree to starboard. Skimmed the upper atmosphere, swung round us and hightailed it back to outer space! We're safe."

The housemother was coming over with her party of children, too. Soon they were all reunited and cuddling each other. The children were bemused at this zealous joy.

"What should we do now?" asked the housemother.

"I think... I think we should stay here a bit longer," suggested Jalli. "The celebrations in the city might be a bit extreme for a few hours."

"You're right," said the housemother. "Captain," she called, "are you OK for staying a bit longer?"

"We might be able to do another frugal breakfast," he replied. "But beyond that things will be getting a bit tight. Water will be an issue by tomorrow afternoon. Let me radio Zookas."

They boarded the yacht and listened into the radio station which was transmitting from the streets of the capital. Everyone was going berserk it seemed. But the criminality had evaporated. The captain shut it off before he called Zookas. Zookas answered immediately.

"All present and accounted for," reported the captain. "Plus ten idiots from up the coast recovering from drug overdoses, over... Yeah, I reckon they'll make it. They're very sore, though. They are severely sunburned, over... Yes, until tomorrow midday, over... We'll see you mid-afternoon, then. Out." They were to stay until midday the next day.

The housemother called for attention. No-one heard her, so Jack bawled for silence – and got it.

"I don't know what I would do without your voice," smiled the housemother. "Ting, Kloa, settle down... I'm *not* going to shout... Children, we have just been talking to Mr Zookas and he says we can stay one more night... that is... shush... that is, if you behave yourselves, and if these wonderful angels have got the energy to entertain you until then."

"Who wants to go swimming?" called Shaun.

Kakko, Tam, Shaun, Wennai and the other volunteers managed to keep some semblance of order as the children stripped off and dived into the water.

The captain radioed the coastguard and was surprised to hear someone was manning the station.

"Thought you would be busy," he said.

"I'm here for a bit of peace," said the operator. "If these celebrations keep up, we're going to get busy later."

"Sorry to say this but I have some work for you now. We have a couple of dozen dead bodies on the beach on Lone Island – the results of a drug-fest that didn't see them survive. I have ten who are recovering but they are in a pretty bad way – dehydrated and badly sunburned..."

"That's awful. Who are they?"

"I don't know. Young people in their late teens and twenties mostly. They have been too sick to answer many question and, to be honest, I didn't think there was much point but—"

"We'll send a boat out and get them."

"Thanks. There are ninety-five in our party, including eighty children. All of them well. We plan to return at midday tomorrow."

An hour later the coastguard pulled into the bay. A doctor leapt ashore and examined the cave-dwellers, who were now really feeling the pain. The doctor was reluctant to give them any painkillers because he could not be sure what was still in their systems. They were transferred, grumbling and groaning, to the coastguard vessel. They didn't ask any questions – about the strike or their dead friends. That level of consciousness was still to return.

A small group of children formed a line on the water's edge and watched.

"That's what drugs and drink do to you," Kakko explained.

"I know," said one sombrely. "That killed my mummy… Why do they make them?"

"What, drugs? Sometimes they can make you better – but only if a doctor gives them to you."

"I ain't ever going to drink booze," said a little girl. "My mummy was horrible when she drank it. She said it was telling her to drink it – but I didn't hear it."

"Yes," said Kakko. "You stick to water and fruit juice."

"That's what Mummy said."

"She was right. Good advice. Then you will not ever hear the booze talking to you."

★ ★ ★

When they had got all the children safely back into the centre,

Kakko and Tam ventured out along the esplanade. The celebrations were mostly over and an army of people were out clearing up the debris. Kakko wanted to check to see if there was a white gate next to the toilet block. The gates to the toilets were chained but their white gate stood pristine and bright next to them.

It was hard taking their leave of the Paradise people. When you have been through so much together, even if it was only a few days, the bonds become very strong. But Jalli and Jack were desperate to get back to Yeka, so they joined in with some cake that Zookas brought, and then stood up to leave.

"Children, our holiday is coming to an end and our friends have to go home," smiled the housemother. "Thank you all so much for coming. You have no idea—"

"We'll see you all again, I'm sure," said Jalli. "The Creator keeps connecting us up. Next time, I hope the adventure isn't quite so extreme."

"So do I. So do we all. Safe travels."

"It won't take long," said Jack with a shrug. "Four steps through our gate and we'll be in our garden."

33

Back home in White Gates Cottage, Yeka seemed extraordinarily calm.

"Did you miss us?" said Jalli as the three-year-old continued to play with her dolls. Yeka shrugged. Jalli picked her up and tried to cuddle her. She resisted but not for long.

"Has Nan been good?"

"Don't be silly. Of course she has," said Yeka. She was cross with her family for deserting her.

It wasn't long before they were joined by Bandi and Abby from Earth One. They listened, enthralled by the account of the adventure.

"I'm glad I missed that one," said Bandi with a deep sigh.

"I'm not," said Shaun, gently. "It was what I needed. It kind of helped me get things into perspective. It's difficult to put into words."

Wennai nodded. "He's right. I have been angry for a long time – inside – because my mum died. But going through all that with the children, and the whole planet... It kind of puts things into context. I'm glad I can come with you through the white gates. But words... there just aren't any—"

"Sometimes there might just be," said Abby; "as a matter of fact I was just thinking of some:

'Love alters not with his brief hours and weeks,
But bears it out even to the edge of doom.
If this be error and upon me proved,

I never writ, nor no man ever loved,'" she quoted.

"*Even to the edge of doom* – how very true," said Wennai. "Who wrote that?"

"Shakespeare. Sonnet 116," said Abby.

"Hur-ray!" exclaimed Kakko. "It took you *to the edge of doom* but hey, you have eventually seen what everyone has known, like, forever… And the quicker you two can shack up together, the better. Then we can all get a look in at the bathroom."

"Kakko!" exclaimed Jalli.

"Sorry, Wennai," said Kakko. "Only joking." She put her tongue out at her mother.

"Apologies accepted," said Wennai, quickly. "I take that as a compliment – it means I'm part of the family."

"Precisely," said Kakko. "See, Mum, she understands…"

"But I don't do 'shaking up'," said Wennai.

"Quite right," replied Nan, who was glad to have the house full again.

★ ★ ★

Back in Joh City, Shaun lay beside Wennai on a grassy bank in the park. Looking into the sky, Shaun reflected on the last time they had lain down on the grass of a hillside, expecting to die together. One day they would, but not then and not today. Wennai was breathing heavily after a couple of circuits. Shaun had exercised as well as he could by jogging from one side of the rise to the other. It was getting easier. Walking and swimming on Lone Island had been good for him.

"Thanks, coach. Without you keeping me to it, I would be lazy," breathed Wennai.

"No. The thanks are mine. You get me out and about and you are patient with me."

"No patience needed."

"Wennai… I've been… I thought a lot when I was away on that last mission. About you and I being boy and girlfriend…"

"What's all this about, Shaun?" said Wennai sitting up with a start and looking intently at him. "I thought… I thought we had decided… What is it that you want to say now?"

"I'm saying that I had doubts in the past but that's finished. I'm ready to be all yours now – if you want me."

Wennai understood. It had taken a long time for Shaun and a lot of courage to allow himself to do this.

"Are you telling me there is no going back – ever?"

"Yes. I know that for certain. I've always wanted you but I couldn't see how it could work. I can now – because it's been working all along but I didn't realise it…"

"Well, then. You know what my answer is. Of course I want you. There has never been anyone else, Shaun. And there never can be."

"Gollip?"

"Oh. Gollip. I went out with him to make you jealous. I shouldn't have; it didn't work. You just gave in."

"I *was* jealous. It did make me think. But… I've been so mixed up. I didn't know where or who I was some of the time."

"But you've found yourself now?"

"Finding. Getting there. I now know that I can't be fully myself without you."

"What about God?"

"He's there too. Always will be – that's the wonderful thing about God. Never gives up on anyone…"

"So God's a 'He' now?"

"Whatever. I was thinking of when God came in human form, as Jesus on Earth One. God was a 'He' in him."

"OK. I think I can put up with Him/Her being around.

393

It's who you are, and the one thing you have always done is let me be me... So if I am to be your proper forever girlfriend, are you going to kiss me?"

"Yeah, of course... Wennai, I've always wanted to kiss you. Very much."

"So what are you waiting for?"

"What, here, in the middle of the park?"

"Oh, Shaun, just come here!" Wennai rolled over, put her arms around him and, as their lips met, the world of the park receded. They were only vaguely aware of the scent of the grass, the sounds of the children on the swings, the distant murmur of the traffic and the gradual setting of Daan in the east, as they lost themselves in each other – the years of confusion and doubt ebbing from their souls.

Epilogue

Six years on…

Living on two different planets with two distinct sets of family is a hard thing to do – especially when it comes to a wedding. After graduating with honours degrees, Bandi and Abby were impatient to be married. In Persham they had to get special permission to marry at the YAC but it seemed quite the natural place – they had no real connection to the parish in which Dave and Lynn's house belonged. They had rarely attended that particular church. But what about Planet Joh? There was nothing for it but another ceremony there. All were praying for a white gate for as many to get to both events as possible.

A week before the ceremony on Planet Earth, Bandi had a party and said goodbye to everyone at White Gates Cottage. They wished him well but longed to be there with him and Abby on such a special occasion.

Pastor Ruk was very aware of how the family must be feeling. Despite all the praying, they had seen no white gate. On the eve of the wedding, the pastor called in to pray with the Smiths.

Jack had said that it was all part of letting go. "We only borrow our children – one day we have to wave them goodbye," he said, trying to sound wise. He became what his mother called philosophical. But Ruk knew that no matter how philosophical – accepting – a person was about things, they still grieved, and the Smiths were all grieving.

While he was there and they were sitting quietly together in the sitting room, Kakko got up to put the kettle on. In the kitchen she let out such a whoop that Jalli rushed out of the room wondering what she had done. She found her daughter standing in front of the kitchen window, bouncing up and down with excitement and yelling, "White gate! White gate!"

Jalli followed her gaze and, indeed, there in the back hedge was a white gate. Jack had already joined them. "Me too," he said.

Two minutes later, everyone, including Pastor Ruk, was standing in the garden admiring a brilliant white gate. The pastor wept. Perhaps, after all these years, he might get to the home planet of the human race and meet and talk with Abby's father.

And that is how it happened. Bandi and Abby were astounded and delighted to see nine people from Planet Joh, including Pastor Ruk, walk up the garden path of Abby's house on the night before their wedding.

Dave rang his assistant at the YAC, who swung into action to ensure all the necessary alterations to the arrangements were made.

The wedding was even happier than Abby and Bandi had even dared to hope. And Ruk and Dave had three whole days together, exploring the deepest truths of the universe. God, they concluded, was one and the same wherever you were.

★ ★ ★

Following their honeymoon – a passionate fortnight in the English Lake District – Abby and Bandi went to St Augustine's for a Sunday service to meet some of Abby's old youth group friends. They walked via Renson Park Road. As they passed number sixty-eight, where Jack had lived all his young life, a strong gust of wind blew and a cloud of winged seeds floated down from the tree and lodged in their hair and clothes like confetti. "Look," danced Abby, "the trees are celebrating with us!"

★ ★ ★

After that, Bandi got into serious study at Oxford. They took a small apartment in the city. Although they struggled on next to nothing, they were intensely happy and soon announced that a baby was on the way. How they would manage it all financially didn't seem to bother them.

Jalli remarked that it was interesting that her third-born was providing a grandchild before either of his older siblings.

★ ★ ★

Kakko was so keen on doing all the different things that presented themselves, she could not imagine having the patience she would need to be a mother. Tam had suggested that he work only part-time from home and look after any children they might have – but Kakko reminded him that, for several months at least, it was *she* who was going to have to abandon her adventures in order to bear and give birth to a baby. One day, when she was ready, they would have a family, she declared, but not yet.

★ ★ ★

Everyone knew Shaun and Wennai would be friends for life

but it had taken until Shaun was twenty-four to ask her to marry him. Wennai no longer worried that God was in any way a rival – God didn't work like that. And anyway, she had long concluded that, if God existed, She or He was telling Shaun that he belonged to her.

But if the Creator was no longer a rival, nine-year-old Yeka most certainly was. She made it abundantly clear that Shaun was her favourite brother. She adored him. In her eyes he could do no wrong – until, that is, he had talked about moving away. Shaun had asked Wennai to marry him. She had accepted but Yeka had objected.

One sunny day, when Yeka was watching the bees busy among the blossom in the White Gates Cottage garden, Wennai sat down beside her on the grass.

"Yeka, when I marry Shaun, can I come and live here? That way Shaun can stay."

"Then you would be my sister?"

"Yes."

"Alright, then. You can marry Shaun if you don't take him away… Will you have a baby?"

"Maybe. Someday," laughed Wennai.

"Good. I always wanted a baby."

So that was decided upon. Shaun and Wennai set a date for the following year – it was to be a quiet wedding with just a few friends. But those who knew them realised that that wasn't ever going to happen. Kakko remarked that they were going to have to hire the football stadium.

In fact, they didn't have to book anywhere. City United put on a massive reception in the City Hall.

★ ★ ★

"White gate," announced Jack, as he came in with a cup of tea to the waking Jalli. Jalli drank her tea, then got up to check it out.

"Me too, and there is a shed beside it."

She called the others.

Shaun groaned, as it was still early for him, despite him coming up to his twenty-sixth birthday.

He and Wennai extricated themselves from the bedclothes and pulled back the curtain. Yes, there it was. "And us," Shaun called as he made his way to the bathroom.

Matilda had been up for an hour and was in the kitchen. "Better check, Mum," suggested Jalli.

"It won't be for me. I haven't had a white gate adventure for years," said Matilda firmly. But she went to look all the same and came back into the kitchen wearing a shocked expression. She looked at Jalli and nodded. "What about Yeka if we're all off somewhere?"

Yeka was bounding down the stairs and out into the garden to see if she was included. To her delight, she was. There was the new white gate, all shiny and smooth. She peered through it and saw what looked like a busy street. Then suddenly her view was obscured by a large red bus that passed across the gap in the hedge. She could see it but couldn't hear it.

"Yay. Mum, Dad, I'm going on an adventure, aren't I? I saw a bus – a big red one!"

"Did you?" said her father. "What else is out there?"

"A street... a busy street, with cars, but different from ours."

"Right," stated Jalli, "that means all of us. Breakfast, and then we'll see what's in the shed."

"Wanulka!" exclaimed Jalli. "Look, check out these banknotes."

Yeka was trying to find the right way to put on a straw hat with a pretty pink trailing ribbon.

"Ibon straw," observed Jack as he caught the scent of the hat Jalli had given him to feel. There were two bigger ones – one for Jalli and one for Matilda; both were attractive but lacked the trailing ribbon that so enthralled Yeka.

They opened a cardboard box which contained other clothes. "These are special," said Jalli. "They are smart by Wanulkan standards. You wouldn't wear a suit like that one, Jack, for everyday things – unless you were a lawyer or something."

"What if I were a teacher?"

"You *are* a teacher… and, no, this is for best. A wedding or a special event of some kind."

"What about you?" asked Jack of Shaun.

Shaun divested himself of his dressing gown and put on a very smart outfit.

"Well, I can *definitely* say I have *never* seen you so smart," declared his grandmother. "You should do it more often."

Jack, Jalli, Matilda and Yeka took their clothes inside the cottage. Yeka looked lovely in a navy-blue dress with a pink ribbon around her waist to match the one in her hat. She was particularly taken with the shoes which were also dark blue – open-topped with a strap and a simple silver buckle.

"Look, I'm a princess!" she announced. "I'm going to a party!"

"It certainly looks like it," concurred Jalli, as she smoothed a smart sundress over her slim thighs. She gathered her hair and put on the matching jacket. It made her look young but sophisticated, as befitted her fifty-three years.

Matilda, of course, ever since she had come to Joh, had looked comfortable in more formal clothes, and a maroon suit became her. Jack looked great. Whatever he wore he looked at home in it – he behaved as if his attire was the way he generally dressed. Perhaps his confidence came because he couldn't see himself in the mirror; he relied on Jalli to tell him he was fine and that was far more reliable than any self-assessment. By contrast, Shaun felt rather self-conscious.

Then Wennai emerged from the bathroom and made her way to the shed. She found a most attractive outfit that seemed to yell, 'Wennai'. With its pleats and tucks, and splashes of lace on bodice and sleeves, only Wennai could have carried it off. It was her to a T.

"I just love the way you're allowed to be yourself," she declared, going upstairs to change. When she came down, Shaun put his arm around her and whispered in her ear that she looked beautiful. She felt it. She was.

When they were satisfied they were all ready, they stepped through the gate, Jalli leading Jack, and Shaun holding Yeka's hand. They stood in the busy street. It was indeed Wanulka City as Jalli had anticipated. They had barely adjusted their eyes to the glare of the Raikan suns – Suuf had just risen to join Jallaxa and Shklaia already ascending in the western sky – when Yeka spotted her sister, Kakko. They had left a message on her phone that they were taking a trip through a white gate, but it appeared that Kakko and Tam had already got their own. With them, from Planet Earth One, were Bandi and Abby. Abby was looking very pregnant.

"Kakko! Bandi!" yelled Yeka rushing across the pavement. They were completely unconscious of the scene they were creating in one of the main streets of a planet they had only just arrived in. Passers-by smiled as they walked around them.

After several minutes of greeting, Shaun commented on how they were all 'done up'. "It appears," he said, "that we are here for something special."

"That," replied Matilda, "is clear. But what?"

"Look," said Kakko, "those people over there, they're all dressed up too. They seem to be just standing around."

"No, they're standing at the bus stop," stated Jalli. "They're waiting for a bus."

"The same stop that you used when you emerged from your white gate when we first met?" asked Jack.

"The very one," said Jalli.

"I remember it, too," said Matilda. "It was here I phoned Momori when you, er…"

"Quite," said Jack. "Don't remind me."

Just then a bus drew up. On the side it displayed its destination – Zonga. The Rarga-Smith party joined the queue.

They passed the house that had been home for Jalli for fourteen years of her life. She said nothing. It still sported the garish plaster garden ornaments; it wasn't worth interrupting her family to point it out. They chatted on, catching up on all they had been doing since they had last met. Jack was aware of where they were, of course, and of Jalli's stillness as they passed the house. He squeezed her hand. "Still there?" he asked.

"Same ugly curtains," she replied with a smile.

The bus rounded the last bend on the descent onto the Zongan coastal plain. This time, unlike fifty years before, there was no hold-up, and it continued on down the hill, rounding the corners of the final two yukets towards the bridge that marked the site of the former community of Zonga. The air was full of the scent of ripening ibon. Except for a couple of houses and a modern building bearing the Wanulkan words, 'The Zonga Museum', the village had not been rebuilt. There were, however, a few fishing boats bobbing in the little harbour, and a tractor parked in a gateway into one of the fields.

In the car park in front of the museum a crowd of people in animated mood were gathering. This was the first time Jalli had visited Zonga since the day she had left for the dental appointment in Wanulka Hospital fifty years before. Then it came to her: it was *exactly* fifty years ago that the dam had burst – fifty years to the day since she had lost her mother, her father and her grandfather, as well as aunts, uncles and all her cousins. She and her family, along with all the others, were now gathering to remember.

Jalli explained to the others. The former excitement of meeting together had become slightly tempered when they had realised where they were going – but now they were very subdued as Jack put his arm around his beloved Jalli. Her tears flowed.

They followed the crowd making its way around to the back of the museum building. A small dais had been erected next to the memorial stone put up many years ago in memory of all those who had lost their lives. Jalli led her family to the memorial. She had never seen it before. Momori had been once when she was at school but had expressed no desire to visit again with Jalli, and Jalli had taken it that Grandma would prefer she didn't go, and she had accepted that. They stood, looking up at the pillar, with the names of those who had lost their lives etched in Wanulkan down the four sides – so many of them. Jalli noticed the many Rargas and Butts – her mother's maiden name – and identified her great-grandparents, as well as her grandfather Danga and her own parents – Momori's son, Sol, and her mother, Mahsnyeka. She was about to translate when Yeka, who had learned to spell her name in Wanulkan, spotted it among the others.

"There," she said pointing to the memorial, "there's my name, Mahsnyeka!"

"Yes," smiled Jalli, "well done. Do you know why it's there?"

"Because it is for my grandmother?"

"Yes. Your grandmother, my mother, Mahsnyeka Rarga. And the names above it are your grandfather – my father – Sol Rarga, and your great-grandfather, Danga Rarga."

"So that says 'Rarga'. There are so many of them."

"All my family, Yeka – all your family."

"But Grandma Momori isn't there. I know how to write 'Momori' in Wanulkan too."

"No, she's not. Grandma didn't die here fifty years ago."

"No, she died on Joh… in the hospital… and you put her ashes in the sea. But she was the only one left – the only one of your family who didn't die in the flood."

"The only one, Yeka, apart from me. But now look. Look how many I have now!"

"Yes, nine of us… Only, one isn't born yet."

"Yeah." Jalli smiled at her daughter's including the yet to be born. "So you see, I have lots of people now. I don't remember any of these… except vague memories of my mum. Grandma was my whole life and she was the best grandma anyone could have. Now she has joined all these in heaven."

"Are they having a party?"

"Heaven is one great big party, Yeka, full of the love and the presence of the Creator."

"Does She want us to dress up in party clothes every day?"

"We can't know any of those things until we get there."

"But She gives us the clothes we will need? Just like when we go through the white gate?"

"Exactly. Just leave all the details to God. She has it all worked out."

"I hope I can have a hat like this one."

"You will have a hat far more beautiful than you can possibly imagine."

Heaven, thought Matilda, *I must have a few there I know, too. Mum and Dad did love me in their way – in their rather odd way… but then it was wartime in Europe when they were young and nothing was normal and that's probably why they grew up odd… And my drunken husband, Shaun, he told Jack he still loved me a few days before he died. If God loves him, He will forgive him for the bad bits – not that he was that bad really: it was the drink. Now, God, if people get drunk in heaven, I shall be very disappointed, to say the least…!*

"Penny for your thoughts, Mum," said Jack, aware that his mother had gone quiet.

"Oh, nothing. Just thinking of your father and our ancestors. Reckon they'll get into heaven, too?"

"I'm sure God won't turn anyone away, if they are willing to go through the cleaning up bit."

"Oh, your father would definitely need that!"

"He did quite a bit of it *before* he died, I reckon."

"You were there. I'll take your word for it," said Matilda sceptically.

"Jallaxanya Rarga!" A rather rotund gentleman, accompanied by a well-dressed lady and a bashful eighteen-year-old, was calling through the crowd.

"Mr Bandi," declared Jack, who recognised his voice immediately.

The families pushed their way together and Jalli took Mr Bandi in her arms, then introduced all her family. "And this," she concluded, "must be my namesake, little Jallaxanya – but not *little* anymore."

Jalli Bandi smiled, a little bashfully. She was a demure young lady – not unlike Jalli Rarga had been at the same age. The Jallis embraced.

"We came especially," said Mr Bandi, "to represent you. There are so many of your family up there and you are the only one who is still in this universe. But look now – you and all your family are here!"

"Thanks to the Creator of all, that is," said Jack. "We all got white gates this morning… from three different places."

"You mean your family is scattered around the universe?"

"I'm afraid so. We don't get to meet each other as often as we'd like. So today is quite a big day."

"Jalli," said Pammy Bandi, "we have brought some flowers for the Rarga and Butt families. *You* should lay them." And she handed Jalli two lovely bouquets. Jalli was about to protest but replaced her protestations with thanks. These were for *her* relatives.

"Thank you. I am so grateful to you for coming along today. It was very thoughtful of you. It wasn't until we got here that we knew why we had to come... Yeka, will you lay these flowers for your grandmother, Mahsnyeka?" Jalli handed one of the bunches to her daughter.

"When?"

"There will be two minutes' silence and then they are going to read the names out," explained Mr Bandi. "When you hear them say 'Mahsnyeka Rarga' just go up and put them with the others. Your mum will tell you when."

The ceremony was addressed by none other than the Wanulkan Minister of Local Affairs accompanied by the leader of the rural council that included Zonga. The minister offered his condolences and stated that the government was opposed to any future reconstruction of the dam. Although there had been calls from those concerned with the growing demand for electricity, the demands for any new dam had been mitigated by the introduction of helicate – based power stations. The helicates were brought to them by the new faster space cruisers – two deliveries were due in the next ten years, which guaranteed enough raw material for the production of electricity for the next fifty years. In addition, the discovery of 'multilayered single-crystal padmium' had doubled the efficiency of solar energy, and new padmium panels were due to be installed in the previously flooded valley upstream.

Instead of water, the valley bottom would be covered in solar panels that would produce as much electricity as the dam had once done but at an eighth of the cost. Beneath the panels, commercial egg-laying birds were free to forage in the damp soil protected from the suns, thus replacing the fish that once stocked the dammed lake. He hoped that, one day, people would again inhabit Zonga. Kakko was impressed by how much of this she understood. It wasn't being translated for her.

Then the silence was kept and the names read out. Jalli laid her flowers as they called Danga and Sol Rarga, and Yeka proudly placed her bunch when she heard her grandmother's name. A little buzz of recognition went round when Jalli and Yeka came forward: these must be Momori's daughter's family.

Following the ceremony, other people came up to them and made themselves known – people Jalli didn't recognise but understood where they fitted in after they explained. The few other people who had survived fifty years before had also expanded in number.

To Yeka's delight there *was* a party – inside the museum, which housed exhibits of the village activities before its destruction and an account of the day itself. Tables of food had been laid out, courtesy of the rural council. There were glasses of delicious fruit drink and an urn of bru that Jalli drank with relish. She hadn't grown up with the people who had died and she could not miss them but she did wish Grandma could have been there. It felt odd on Raika without her.

Shaun and Wennai spent quite a long time in conversation with Jalli Bandi over the food. They discovered that she had been accepted into Wanulka University to study entomology, and possibly follow her father and mother into teaching – but that was several years away. She hoped she would see a white gate one day too, like her namesake, Shaun's mum, had done. "What's it like travelling the universe?" she asked.

"It's scary sometimes. You never know where you're going to next. And sad, too, because you meet great people you know you might never see again."

"But how exciting… I mean, like, to have adventures across the entire *universe*! I would *love* to have an adventure. Life here can get so boring at times. I mean, I *know* there are lots of things to discover, like, right here on Planet Raika, but—"

"You sound like my sister," interrupted Shaun. "She was always staring over the horizon and dying to experience white gates adventures. But all that depends on the Creator, of course… Still, if you really pray for it, you never know."

"Don't you pray for adventures?"

"No. They just happen. And, anyway, I have a job I can't just leave."

"Like what?"

"Well, like… being a coach of my football team… and lots of other things."

"That's just it. I don't know *anything* about it – what did you call it?"

"Football. It's a sport. You play it with a ball. You can't use your hands. It sounds simple but it's… well, it's—"

"Yes. What's it like playing football?"

"The buzz is like nothing else. When you score a great goal that turns the game around or when you lift the cup at the end of the season like we did one year when I was playing, it's magic. If you haven't played football, you haven't lived."

"Exactly. I want to live!"

"Right, we both need to get praying, then," he joked.

"What are you discussing so keenly?" asked Matilda, coming across for another cup of bru.

"Football," laughed Wennai.

"Should have guessed. Anyone would think that football was more important than God, Himself."

"Oh, we've been talking about God, too," said Shaun.

"And praying," added Jalli Bandi.

"Good," said Matilda, "it works."

After she had gone, the young people laughed – Shaun smiled at his nan's predictable attitude to football, and Jalli giggled at the way they had told the truth about their mention of God and prayer, without saying why.

You just can't keep God out of anything, smiled Wennai to herself. *God, you butt into everything.*

As they left the museum to take the bus back into Wanulka City, the suns were setting. Jallaxa had already dipped beneath the eastern horizon. The Rarga-Smith family took their leave of the Bandis. "Keep praying," Jalli Bandi reminded Shaun.

Jalli looked up at the memorial for the last time, and, as she did so, felt a gentle breeze graze her cheek. It was as if her grandma was greeting her with the breath of a kiss. She raised her hand to her face.

"What's up, Mum?" enquired Kakko.

"Oh, it's just the wind. I didn't expect it... I was just thinking about Grandma." *Yes,* she thought, *you and Granddad, together with Mum and Dad, are indeed safe and happy. You are remembered in this place but you do not belong here, or anywhere in this universe. None of us do. We belong with you where all love has its source.*

"OK?" Jack extended his hand towards his pensive wife. Jalli took it in hers.

"Yes. Very. I'm glad we came. They aren't here, you know. Their bodies remain in this universe but they are free of them – free of it all. They are happy... and so am I... forever."

As the chill of the evening air struck her, Abby shivered

and her attentive husband took out his coat to lay it over her shoulders. It was the same coat that he had been wearing when they were showered with the spiralling winged seeds from the trees in Renson Park Road when they had walked towards St Augustine's. As he held out the coat, a small seed from the tree outside number sixty-eight fell from the pocket and finished its spinning journey to the ground. It landed in a small crevice in the damp soil a few metres from the memorial stone – a distance equivalent to that of Jack's 'kicking tree' from the front door of the house. As the family left for the bus, Jack stepped on the crack, closing it up and firming in the seed. Unbeknown to Jack, the same foot that had once kicked the parent tree was the one that now ensured a good start for its offspring on another planet in another galaxy in the vast, beautiful universe. It's amazing what the Wind can do!

Afterword

Sadly, this is the last in the series – the tetralogy. And sadly, also, the characters of the White Gates Adventures are fiction. Nevertheless, I have had great fun journeying with them through their highs and lows. I hope you have, too. But, happily, the universe is populated by real people, all wonderful and all unique

The following was written by a very real person, Ruth Eade, who made an impact on the many she met, and many thousands she did not, in Britain and beyond, in her lifelong commitment to education and care.

I include these words here in thanksgiving for her inspirational life that came to its end on Earth in October 2016. Ruth Eade was in no doubt, however, that she had only just begun! New life beyond this dimension beckoned in all its glory.

These words, used at her memorial service, are among the last she wrote. I thank her husband, John, for permission to reproduce them here.

"God rescued us from the domain of darkness and brought us away into the kingdom of his dear Son. There, as children of the Word, let us delight in the joy of the Lord and the playfulness of God—

By living as if peace is breaking out across the cosmos; by learning to say 'hello friend' universally.

By turning round those who fail to face the sun;
by skimming stones on fathomless depths.

By flying kites into glorious sunsets;
by blowing a myriad multicoloured bubbles into time
without end; by skipping to the rainbow's end and
banishing gloom.

In the power of the Spirit let us go into God's world
and do it.

Alleluia! Alleluia!"

Dr Ruth Eade, 2016

Ruth died, aged 74, on 24th October 2016 – United Nations Day.

Acknowledgements

I have many people to thank for their contribution to the White Gates Adventures tetralogy. They extend over many decades and I cannot name them all. Each in their own way has contributed to the adventures, the characters and the themes.

I want to begin by thanking those to whom I owe my education. I was not born into an environment where books played a big part. When I was young it was all about passing the 11+ exam – which, unsurprisingly, I 'failed'. However, the headteacher, Jack Newitt, and the staff of Cherry Orchard Secondary Modern School, Northampton did everything in their power to compensate, and I left school having passed sufficient 'O-levels' to get to the grammar school and eventually King's College London and then, in my fifties, the University of Exeter. When you fail an exam at the tender age of eleven, it can take a lifetime to get over a sense of being 'second rate', and I have never taken for granted the wonderful opportunities in education that have come to me over the years. So, I want to thank those early teachers who went out of their way to believe in us young people of the 1950's and 60's. Another person who did wonderful work in restoring confidence in my abilities, at King's College, was my tutor Professor Gordon Dunstan; but there were others, of course, and I cannot list them all.

I must credit my publishers, Matador, and their editors

and proofreaders for ensuring such a good product. I am grateful for excellent cover designs which have brought universal praise. I also want to thank Lasse Voss for his work on the website. I value the friendship and assistance of the members of the Association of Christian Writers, the Alliance of Independent Authors and Media Associates International. I have gained a great deal from their training days and conferences and thoroughly enjoy meeting fellow authors from around the world. The feedback and reviews I have had from readers young and old have been invaluable – your contributions have been very important in giving me the resolve to conclude the series.

I greet the staff and students of Bishop Gwynne College, where I was based between 2009 and 2011, and Confident Children out of Conflict, both in Juba, South Sudan, and honour them for their inspiring example and encouragement. I am grateful to the people of Keynsham among whom I now live and worship, who give me the time, space and incentive to work. As someone who writes for young adults, it won't surprise you that I love young people and I want to thank them for accepting someone in his later years as a youth volunteer – and, of course, for being just so, like, awesome.

If it weren't for my wife, Tina, I would never have embarked on this project. She has been behind it all at every stage: the initial concept, always there with helpful suggestions, skilled and strict editing, and spending many hours on proofreading. The books wouldn't have come into being without her. Her patience is prodigious.

Finally, I have to thank God who, I believe, empowers all of His/Her creation. God did not create the universe, wind it up and set it going like some great scientific experiment whilst remaining outside of it. He is intimately involved in every part of it, in each moment, at every interface and in all its complexity. He both transcends and indwells it – and that includes each and every human being. I hope those, like Wennai, who do not find God so clearly in the life and loves of the world, will be able to live with my overt language and affirmations and still enjoy the stories.

None of the characters in this series are based on actual people – but, of course, their traits, their foibles and their strengths and witness are all drawn from my experience of working, living and playing with so many people over the years. I love people; they are constantly amazing – especially those who do not seek to be anything other than themselves. We are all 'wonderfully made' and it is great when we can just be that.

Some of my recent experiences come from South Sudan where I was privileged to live for a few years. They live in some of the most challenging places on Earth. We do not have to visit different planets to find different worlds. Unlike the White Gates characters, we are not called to travel the whole universe in search of people who need our help; there is so much we can do in our own world. If these books inspire you to do something, whether it be in your own neighbourhood or overseas, you will find lots of opportunities if you look. Unlike Jack Smith, you no longer have to visit the local library to find them – they are at hand on the Internet. Check them out and see what you can do to make a difference – whether it be for just one person like Shaun in Australia, millions as in Kakko's case or over a cup of tea like Matilda. And, incidentally, you are never too old to start.

Happy adventuring.
Trevor Stubbs

The First Three Volumes of the White Gates Adventures Tetralogy

The Kicking Tree

Two people. Two planets.
One unbreakable bond …

Through a series of "accidents", Jack from Earth and Jalli from Planet Raika are brought together, meeting in a beautiful cottage garden that belongs to neither of their worlds.

Their relationship blossoms through a number of adventures and they appear immune to the evils of the universe, until a terrible tragedy parts them…

Where is their Creator? Has She given up caring for them?

Ultimate Justice

Want to be free to expand you horizons –
even beyond those you can imagine?

We rejoin Jack and Jalli and their family growing up on Planet Joh as they once again travel the universe to new worlds through the white gates the Creator provides for them.

Each character has his or her own role to play in the exploration – outwards to the stars, but also inwards to what makes us who we are and what we can become…

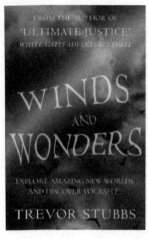

Winds and Wonders

Explore amazing new worlds and discover yourself...

Teenage Abby runs into trouble when she comes up against authoritarian forces in school, as well as the churches she attends. Impatient Kakko still manages to save her millions of people, but goes through the worst pain she can imagine on the way. Shy Shaun makes a great impact on the football field, but how will it turn out in the game of life off the pitch? And parents Jack and Jalli, even Nan Matilda, manage some excitement.